Mark

Thanks for stopping by
chat at BBQ2U

Best wishes
Larry
4/28/2021

THE TURN

a bond that shaped history

More by DL Fowler

Lincoln Raw: a biographical novel

Lincoln Raw: under my father's roof

Ripples: a contemporary novel of suspense

Lincoln's Diary: a contemporary novel of suspense

Bittersweet: Poems & Essays

Transform Your Fiction: Essential Tools

Praise for The Turn

Awards

First Place — Pacific Northwest Writers Association Literary Contest 2020: Historical Fiction

Finalist — Indies Today Book Awards

Reviews

Richly chronicled ... intimate ... poignant ... captivating. One novel I will read again and again. — **Robert Dugoni, NYT, WSJ International Best-Selling and award-winning author** of *The Extraordinary Life of Sam Hell* and *The Tracy Crosswhite Series*

5 STARS! The Turn will surely ignite a flame ... the dynamic writing style makes for a compelling retelling of a tumultuous era ... a gripping and objective look at American history ... DL Fowler fills history's gaps with intelligent deduction and a sharp sense of realism. — **INDIES TODAY**

Much different from the usual Lincoln coverage on many levels ... richer and more complex ... vivid ... a rare ability to delve into the heart and mind of the man. — **D. Donovan, Sr. Reviewer, Midwest Book Reviews**

Intriguing historical elements combined with solid fictionalization. — **The Booklife Prize by Publishers Weekly**

THE TURN

a bond that shaped history

a novel by

DL Fowler

Cover designed by Jennifer Preston Chushcoff

To contact DL Fowler
visit www.DLFowler.com

First Edition: First Printing
Printed in the United States of America
Harbor Hill Publishing
Gig Harbor, WA

Library of Congress Control Number : 2020922012

ISBN-13: 978-0-9963805-3-9 (paperback)
ISBN-13: 978-0-9963805-4-6 (epub)

CONTENTS

To forgotten people.
May their voices rise up and be heard.

Dream the dream that never ends
Of a place where known with unknown blends,
Pursue the path each tireless dreamer wends
Until the world, along that arc, tumultuously bends.

Endless Dreams by DL Fowler 2018

THE TURN

a bond that shaped history

CHAPTER ONE

Osawatomie, Kansas—August 1856

For most of William's twenty-odd years he had been like a plowshare. Nose buried in work, always doing Marse's bidding, never a shrug or word of complaint. If not working, keep out of sight, out of mind. Even in his brief time as a freedman, white folks' vision scarcely lighted on him, except to regard his usefulness, or with some purpose of malice or with irritation. It had never been so vital for him to remain inconsequential as it was in that moment.

Three hundred pro-slavery marauders—Border Ruffians—launched volleys of musket rounds into the woods where William crouched beside a fallen oak. He clutched a dead militiaman's musket, a ramrod jammed in its barrel. A stone's throw away in the same thick woods, Captain John Brown's badly out-numbered militia returned the Ruffians' fire. The Ruffians had murdered one of Captain Brown's sons earlier that morning. They would not be content until the abolitionist stronghold of Osawatomie, Kansas, was reduced to embers—until the Captain's body swung from a tree and rigored there under the summer sun.

A whistling shrilled in William's ears, binding him to the refuge of the uprooted oak. His breath caught in his throat. Grapeshot rasped branches overhead. Ruffians charged the woods, howling like a wolf pack swarming helpless prey. Brown ordered his men to retreat north across the river, but desperation tore William in a different direction. Good sense said he would not get there in time to be of any use, but he cast the musket aside and raced toward town like a wind-swept prairie fire. The reek of spent saltpeter gripped his throat as he slashed through brush. Beads of sweat dripped from his coal-black forehead and stung his eyes. His clammy tow-linen shirt clung to his back.

William drew a deep breath, bent over, his palms pressed into his knees at the edge of town. He squinted, straining to focus. A cyclone of smoke rose from rubble, darkening the sky. Town folks scrambled to escape dozens of whooping horsemen. Cries for help were lost in the wrenching wails of Osawatomie crumbling into the throat of an inferno. William wiped his face with the hem of his shirt and patted the pocket of his pantaloons ... his certificate of freedom was still there—bought with the sweat of his older brother's brow.

Horses thundered past. A musket stock rammed William's shoulder, rattling his teeth, driving him to his knees. Pain ran up his neck, down his arm.

A coarse hemp rope tumbled around William's neck. A boot pounded his back, vaulting him forward. A musket stock hammered him until he lay face down in the dirt. A heel pressed into the back of his neck. He could hardly breathe.

A voice rang out. "We ain't lynching this buck."

"Don't plan to. He'll draw a good price down river. Just don't want him running away."

Boots thudded to the ground. Calloused hands wrenched his arms. Manacles clanged around his wrists.

"Get up," one of the Ruffians growled.

The rope tightened around William's neck, tugging and scratching at his Adam's apple. He struggled to his feet. A meaty hand dug into William's pocket and discovered his certificate.

"Well, well. Lookie here."

"Whatcha got?"

"This one's got a certificate. Signed by some Kansas abolitionist judge."

"Won't hold water in Missouri."

The certificate floated to the ground. A boot stomped it, ground it into the dirt.

Resignation shrouded William's thoughts.

"Move it, boy," a Ruffian demanded.

By the time William was loaded into a covered wagon with captured abolitionists and other Negroes, he turned his mind to scheming a way of escape. He whispered, "Anybody seen Grace?"

"Women and children in the other wagon," one of the white prisoners whispered.

A Ruffian shouted, "Shut up."

William and the others held their tongues.

"Just once," the guard bellowed, "I wish one of these abolitionists would sass me."

"They's as docile as them darkies they love so much," the driver replied. "Say jump, they ask how high."

"If it comes to war, all we'll see of them—slave and slave lovers both—is their backsides as they run for cover."

"No use getting worked up about no war what ain't come yet. Gotta get these ones locked away in the county seat before that devil Brown and his vigilantes regroup. Marshal Wood says some New Orleans slave trader is due at the courthouse in a few days to buy some Negroes. Doesn't want us to miss him."

"At least we didn't get stuck with that wench and her whiney young'un. It's time Sam up there drew the short straw."

William closed his eyes. He and Grace were headed to the same place.

* * *

William peeked out at dusk when the caravan looped into a defensive formation. Three wagons on a windswept prairie. No place to run. No place to hide. He and Grace and Maddie would be chased down like varmints scrambling for cover, hemmed in by a pack of ravenous coyotes.

Half a dozen armed Ruffians had already dismounted. One of them dragged Grace to the ground, still shackled and without the baby. Two white women climbed down behind her. The baby wailed inside the wagon. Grace reached for her daughter but was yanked back.

A Ruffian ordered the male prisoners down from the wagons. William and the others maneuvered to the back of the wagon, wrist and ankle chains rattling as they shuffled. Their feet thudded onto the ground. The Ruffians' leader barked, "Take off your boots."

William and Grace exchanged glimpses. He met the panic in her eyes with a flicker of hope.

Someone shoved William. "Start gathering wood for a fire. Then help make supper."

After the evening meal and cleanup, the prisoners loaded back into the wagons for the night. The Border Ruffians rolled out knapsacks and slept around a smoldering fire, taking turns standing guard in pairs. The caravan followed the same routine along two hundred dusty, jarring miles until they pulled into Columbia, Missouri—the Boone County seat. The prisoners unloaded at the courthouse and were transferred to the sheriff's custody.

The white prisoners landed in cells upstairs to await trial for offenses against Missouri's slave laws. In the basement, William and the other Negro men were cast into a packed cell, the air heavy with fetid odors. A few feet away, Grace screamed when her baby was stripped from her cradling arms. The child's shrieks stabbed at her heart. "NO! Maddie!" she yowled. Grace's despair echoed through the basement as little Maddie disappeared from sight. "Gone," Grace wailed. "My baby's gone. Please God, if you're gonna take my child away, strike me dead where I stand!"

Guards shoved the women into a windowless room at the end of the dank corridor. A heavy door slammed shut behind them. The clank of the bolt-lock battered Grace's ears.

William beat his head against the cell's iron bars.

An older prisoner pulled him back. "Won't do no good," the man whispered. "Might as well get used to the way things are."

"But the child needs her mother." Tears streamed down William's cheeks.

"White folk don' see it dat way. Say our women and chillun don' much mine bein' separated. Say it ain't no different den separatin' a cow and her calf when the weanin' time comes."

William did not need to learn white people's ways. His last mistress was a Mormon woman who taught her slaves everything they would need after paying for their freedom. Reading, elocution, posture, a Negro's place in the world, all the ways of the civilized race.

* * *

Days later, William glimpsed Grace on the courthouse steps. Childless, she stood stripped to the waist, her head bowed, hands shackled in front of her. Bile wormed up into William's throat as the auctioneer traced her firm, bronze breasts and touted her teen-aged beauty. The words "fancy girl" rolled off the man's tongue, knifing William's heart.

The gallery of bidders teemed with excitement as the auctioneer called for higher and higher offerings. At a price of $1,600, frenzy gave way to hushed anticipation. "Sold," declared the auctioneer, "to the fine gentleman from St. Louis."

William reeled. His throat seized up. He had vowed to keep Grace and Maddie safe.

Half an hour later, a farmer from Western Missouri shelled out $900 to claim William as human property.

William remained manacled—ankles and wrists—as the wagon rumbled toward his new master's farm. Barefoot, he pulled his knees to his chest and kept his head down. An old Negro riding with him in the back of the wagon enjoyed complete freedom of movement. Slits in his boots allowed his bunioned feet to spread out. He crawled over to William and whispered, "It best to jest let life roll on. Dat what I figger affer all dese years wiff Marse. He ain't as bad as some."

"It's not me I'm worried about," William replied.

"Yous got nutin' else a worry 'bout. Everthin' else is outside yo control. Sooner you figger dat out, easier thins will be."

"You're wrong, old man."

"Name one thing else you gotta worry 'bout."

"You saw that quadroon girl this morning?"

"She none yo bidness anymore."

"She had a child when we got taken."

"Child none her concern no more. Yers, neither."

"I'll find them and free them, if it costs me my life."

"Look, boy. Lemme tell you how thin's is, what goin' happen. Her Marse take yo girl in his house. She serve him, satisfy him. She have chillun by him. When chilluns old 'nough, he work 'em in fields or in house. Maybe he sell 'em. When he marries, if he ain't already, his wife give him little white babies. Yo girl be dere mammy or he sells her to be mammy fer some udder house. Beliefs me. Been there. She forgets 'bout you, and best you do same wiff her."

"That may be good enough for you, but it's not for me."

"I tell you dis one time, boy. Whatever you lets eat you on the inside, don' let any white folk see on the outside."

The shackles binding William's ankles rattled when he turned away from the old Negro. As he looked inside himself, all he found was his uselessness. He had failed, utterly, to keep his sacred promise.

CHAPTER TWO

Western Missouri—Spring 1857

William took care to hide most things inside himself, especially that he loved to read—an offense, if discovered, that would certainly put him under his new master's whip. William had other dark secrets. He could write and speak better than the farmer who owned him, and he had tasted freedom. He had learned the hard way not to trust a white man, no matter how much they wanted you to believe they were kind. Show them any sign of pride or ambition and they would beat it out of you. There was no reason to believe his new master would shrink from using every means of cruelty to break his spirit—put him in his place, make an example for other slaves. Unease festered in William. He'd already said too much to the wrong person.

The old Negro plodded down to the slave shanty on a crisp March morning as he did every morning after receiving work orders from Marse. William had been confined to the farm for the six months since he had been purchased at the auction in Columbia. That morning, though, he was told to load hogs into a wagon and drive them to Butler, Missouri, under the old Negro's supervision.

As they started onto the main road, William slowed the wagon. "Kansas is a few miles west."

"Don' get no crazy notions, now." The old Negro arched his brow.

"If we cross into Kansas, I can sue Marse for my freedom."

"Who fed you dat nonsense?"

"If a Marse takes his slave into a place where slavery is forbidden, the slave is immediately free." William pulled the wagon to a halt.

The old Negro glanced around. "Don' see Marse ridin' back dere wiff dem hogs."

"You're his Negro and that's the same as him taking me."

"Dat might a been law afore. It ain't no more," the old Negro replied. "So, maybe we should get on wiff Marse's bidness."

"Captain Brown told us the Supreme Court said so." William smiled.

"Well, Marse say Supreme Court done change its mind. Da chief judge say we has no rights any white man is bound to respect. Especially, we has no right a sue Marse."

William's grin faded. "When did he say that?"

"Jest weeks ago."

William stared straight ahead.

“’Member dat Dred Scott fella over in St. Louis ... an his wife?” the old Negro said. “Dat judge say dey has a go back to slavin’. Wonder how many suppos’d free Negro folk has dat same fate waitin’ dem.”

William’s shoulders slumped as he prodded the team of horses, directing them away from Kansas and toward Butler.

“Goes a show,” the old Negro added. “A white man always look out for hisself an always come out on top. Laws is made for him, not us. Best a keep yo head low, do what he say, an keep yo mouth shut.”

They rode in silence until they reached the outskirts of Butler. The old Negro pointed to a farmhouse in the distance. “See dat place?”

“What of it?” William asked.

“Woman like her buys Negro babies what gets took from dey mamas an auctioned to St. Louis. Dey raise dos babies an when dey be four o’ five, o’ so, dey sells dem. Gets good money fer dem. Lots more dan dey pays. Das what a Negro life be about. You be a problem o’ a burden, all Marse have a do is buy one younger and cheaper to take yo place. Den he cast yo off wiffout any guilt.”

“Captain Brown is different.”

“Dat so? ’Cordin’ to Marse, dat devil Brown steal slaves jes so he kin sells dem. Den he claim he free a dem so sof-headed abolitionist folk will give him mo money fer doin’ mo mischief.”

“Marse has never even seen Captain Brown. I have.”

“Where do that leave you? Only a fool Negro trusts any white man. No matters how nice dey seem, dey always use you up and casts you aside when dey done.”

William and the old Negro drove straight to Butler, did the business they were sent to do, and returned to the farm before nightfall. As William turned the wagon onto the farm road, he gazed westward. Even if he made it to Kansas, he would wind up in the same mess as Dred Scott. The distance that separated him from freedom had grown a hundred-fold—as had the odds against him keeping his vow to protect Grace and Maddie.

Missouri-Kansas Border—December 1858

Icy wind shrilled between cracks in unchinked walls of the shack William shared with four other slaves. Hopelessness had frozen his spirit to such numbness that no part of him, from bare feet to bare brow, complained of the cold.

William and the other slaves kept the stove's fire low to conserve kindling, and out of fear the heat would draw any remaining moisture from their weathered skin. Because of the howling storm and the biting cold, any slaves who slept, did so fitfully. One hundred yards away, as powdery snow swirled in frigid gusts and collected at the base of fences, Marse bedded down and fell into a quiet sleep in the warmth of his farmhouse.

Near midnight, the shack's door flew open and several men burst in as if catapulted by the violent squall. William and the other slaves gaped at the tempest outside and balked. One of the slaves grabbed a stick of firewood to beat the men away, fearing they were bounty hunters stealing them from Marse to be sold down in sugar country. William threw himself between the stick wielding slave and the intruders. "I know these men," he shouted. "They're with Captain Brown."

"He's right," one of Brown's men said. "We've come to set you free."

Another of Brown's men spoke up. "We've liberated more of you from other farms in the region."

The slaves put on shoes and coats, such as they had, and grabbed what personal things they could carry. As they climbed into a covered wagon, a faint orange glow, appearing to come from Marse's house, flickered in the blowing snow.

Hours after their emancipation, the freed slaves sat with Brown's men, eating a hearty meal in the home of Augustus Wattles across the border in the free state of Kansas. Their laughter drew other houseguests to the kitchen. James Montgomery, leader of Linn County's militant free-soilers asked, "How is this, Captain Brown? Whom have you here?"

"Allow me to introduce a part of my African family, whom I have restored to their natural and inalienable rights." Brown waved around the circle of a dozen newly liberated Negroes.

Montgomery shrugged. "Suppose we should prepare for retaliation from their former owners."

"That storm outside says no one and nothing will be moving for a few days."

"What are your plans with this lot?" Montgomery asked.

"Canada. After the weather clears."

The storm lifted unexpectedly the following morning, offering a window of opportunity for one of Brown's men to load the former slaves into a covered wagon and drive north to Osawatomie. Meanwhile, Brown remained with Montgomery at Wattles' cabin in case the Missourians showed up to extract retribution for the loss of their so-called property.

William fell into conversation along the way with a woman who escaped one of the farms near where he'd been in bondage the past two years. Her exotic voice, her mysterious eyes, gave clues that she was not an ordinary slave.

The woman recounted attending her master on a trip to St. Louis a year earlier. While there, she heard stories of a daring escape by a young quadroon fancy girl who crossed the Mississippi alone one night. Word filtered back to St. Louis through the Underground Railroad that the young woman made it to Alton, Illinois. Before the girl fled, she had talked about establishing her freedom and searching for a child that had been taken when she was enslaved.

"Her name?" William asked. "Did anyone say her name?"

"I don't recollect." The woman shook her head.

"Grace? Could it have been Grace?"

"Yes, could be. That does sound like it."

The woman had planted a seed of hope in William's mind, but doubt crept in and began to squeeze out hope as the wagon crunched on through frozen snow. The woman wasn't certain about the girl's name, and even if Grace had made it to freedom in Illinois, he was headed to a different place—Canada.

William climbed out of the covered wagon when it pulled into Osawatomie and stared at the ground where a Ruffian's musket stock drove him to his knees more than two years earlier. Phantom pain surged through his shoulder and neck. The piercing, frigid wind on his back triggered memories of the farmer's whip cutting into his flesh. Amid the howls of snowy gusts, he recalled Grace's screams, Maddie's wails, and the groans of a town collapsing in upon itself. He drew his woolen coat tight and followed the others into a drafty cabin that had replaced one the Ruffians burnt to the ground.

He fixated on Grace for the next week while he and the other fugitives waited for Captain Brown to arrive and guide them to Canada. He pressed the handful of free-soilers who had resettled Osawatomie, probing for clues that might help him search for her. A couple of whites who were familiar with Illinois sketched a crude map of the least perilous route to Alton. He contemplated rumors of young women who fit Grace's description and places where she may have been spotted. Some possible sightings were as far north as an Underground Railroad safehouse in Ottawa, Illinois. Amid the cyclone of uncertainty churning inside William, two things were for certain. Following well-traveled routes would increase the risk of falling into the clutches of bounty hunters, and a journey alone on foot through the Illinois wilderness during winter could prove fatal.

* * *

The fugitive Negroes loaded into a covered wagon when Brown arrived. One of the militiamen drove the wagon north, tracking precariously close to the Missouri border. They traveled only at night. Brown was not about to raise suspicion by being on the road in broad daylight with a dozen Negroes. He and the driver instructed the Negroes on survival skills—from fishing in frozen streams and foraging, to hiding in plain sight—useful knowledge if they were forced to flee on foot during a Ruffian attack. The driver bragged about the captain's reputation for brazenness, recounting stories from the militia's many exploits. He called the captain a thorn in the side of pro-slavers on both sides of the Kansas-Missouri border.

Brown hid his contraband cargo at a farm outside Lawrence, Kansas, while he went into town to collect rations and clothing for them. That night, they headed west to Topeka where they were joined by several more of Brown's militia and two more wagons loaded with provisions, muskets, and gunpowder. By the time they moved through Holton the next morning, they were a sufficient distance from Missouri that Brown no longer worried about traveling by day.

The caravan arrived in early January at Albert Fuller's cabin, an Underground Railroad stop on Straight Creek. There they hunkered down for a few days due to a wicked storm and high water that prevented them from crossing the creek.

Several days later, one of Brown's men was watering his horse at the stream when two Deputy U.S. Marshals approached. They asked if he had seen any Negroes in the vicinity, and he volunteered to lead them to the Fuller cabin where he heard some were hiding out. One of the marshals accompanied him while the other returned to their posse's encampment.

As the deputy and Brown's man approached Fuller's cabin, the Captain peered out through a slit in a window covering. His man failed to offer an all-clear signal and he dallied at tying up his horse while the deputy looked on.

"I recognize that worthless cuss," Brown muttered. "One of Marshal Wood's deputies."

Brown ordered his men to arm the Negroes, and all waited for the two to enter. The name Wood had become etched on William's mind since he learned the marshal protected Missouri's Ruffians when they raided Osawatomie. William clutched a loaded pistol. He was eager to savor revenge.

Brown's man held the cabin door open while the deputy stepped inside.

"Hands up," Brown ordered.

The deputy raised his hands. His face flushed.

"Been looking for me?" Brown's chiseled face concealed any trace of emotion.

"Everybody's looking to collect that $3,000 reward," the deputy grumbled.

"I won't promise $3,000, but I will let you live to see another day if you give an accurate report on the marshal's position."

The deputy bowed his head. "About a half-mile from here. Hunkered down in rifle pits at the creek."

"How many?" Brown asked.

"About four dozen," the deputy replied.

"I imagine we should go call on them," Brown announced.

Several of Brown's men complained as they filed outside. One argued they were outnumbered by more than two to one and they should wait until dark to detour several miles upstream. They could cross at a shallower, unguarded ford.

"Those who are afraid can turn back," Brown replied, "but the Lord has marked out a path for me and I intend to follow it. The creek is now passable, so we are ready to move." He set his jaw.

"I'm with you, Captain," William declared as he climbed onto one of the horses.

When the horse's owner reached for the reins, Brown intervened. "He who hesitates is lost. The boy earned the mount. You drive one of the wagons, and next time I give an order, do not balk. Just do as I say."

The militiamen mounted and followed Brown toward the creek. The wagons loaded with freed slaves trailed a safe distance behind.

As the abolitionist militia approached the creek, the marshal and his posse were gripped with fear, recalling tales of the terror Brown inflicted on enemies. Many of the Ruffians broke and ran for their horses.

Brown sounded a war cry at the creek bank, and his men charged into the current. The remainder of Wood's posse scrambled out of their pits in panicked retreat. Brown's men spurred their horses.

William and a couple of militiamen peeled off from the charge to round up malingerers. His chest swelled as he cinched knots around the wrists of four prisoners. He relished being the captor, instead of the captive.

From Straight Creek, the party forged north to Seneca where the Topeka group turned back home. They were no longer needed. William wanted to go with them, staying in Topeka until spring when he would seek help from the Underground Railroad to steal through Missouri and cross the Mississippi to Alton, Illinois, where he hoped to find Grace.

Captain Brown learned of William's obsession with finding Grace. He cornered William. "I have vowed before God to deliver the lot of you to the free soil of Canada, and my job isn't finished. You will stay with us for the duration of my mission. After that, you will be free to search for this Grace woman or engage in any other foolishness you desire."

William started to reply, but Brown raised his hand.

February 1859—Southern Iowa

The party pushed against deep snow and icy winds after crossing the Missouri River and passing through southern Iowa. William had been a freedman for six weeks and grew more impatient with every mile of their journey. As they approached Illinois, his misgivings found voice. He complained to other runaways that fleeing to Canada would be the same as giving up on his quest to find Grace.

Brown caught wind of William's continued grumbling and drew his horse alongside the wagon William was riding in. Brown called out William. When William climbed onto the buckboard next to the driver, Brown cocked his head. "Something's been needling me. I keep saying to myself, I've seen so many darkies they all blend together, but there's something familiar about that one."

William shifted on the wooden seat. "I was in the woods the day the Ruffians murdered your son and burned the town."

"Osawatomie?"

"Yes, sir," William replied. "I followed when you and your men went to face the Ruffians that day. I wanted to help somehow. But when hundreds of them appeared, you ordered everyone into the woods. One of your men fell in front of me as we scrambled for cover, blood bubbling from a hole the size of my thumb in the back of his head. I stopped to help, but you shouted at me to pick up the dead man's musket and make myself useful."

"I don't recall the incident you describe, but you seemed mighty at ease handling a pistol and claiming that mount at Straight Creek. I could use your sort in my militia."

"Does that mean you will help me find Grace?" William asked.

"Who's she to you?"

"Do you remember my brother, Thomas?"

"From Osawatomie?" Brown replied.

"He died of fever."

"I recall something of a sickness going around."

"Grace is his widow." William bit his lip. "They had a little girl."

"Why is this woman and her child your problem?"

"The Ruffians took them away when they sacked Osawatomie. I promised my brother I would always protect them." William's throat ached from the memory of his brother's plaintive voice in the moments before he drew his last breath.

"I'm sure you did what you could." Brown scowled. "That's water under the bridge. Now, we have a war to fight."

"I promised Thomas on his deathbed. He bought our freedom."

"Maybe I'm mistaken about you." Brown's steely-eyed glare dispirited William.

"No, sir, I'm honored to be at your service."

"I take care of my people like they were family."

"Thank you, sir."

"All right. It's settled. Welcome to my clan." Brown spurred his horse forward.

As Brown rode ahead, the driver leaned close to William. "You know what you're getting into?"

"He said I'm family. That means he'll help," William replied.

"His mission is everybody's mission."

"His mission is freeing slaves. He's my best hope to find and free Grace."

"In that man's militia," the driver whispered, "you best put this girl and everyone else out of your mind."

William fixed his gaze on Captain Brown riding out in front of the caravan.

The caravan reached Tabor, Iowa, that evening, and even ardent abolitionists gave Brown and his heavily armed men a frosty reception. After shaking off snow from their coats, the party ate a solid meal under a pall of silence and bunked down for a restless sleep. During the next several days, neither the weather nor the chilly mood of the disaffected Taborites thawed. Rumors that Brown's abolitionist militia had murdered slaveholders along the Missouri border dampened their enthusiasm for the captain's exploits. Nothing he said pacified them, so Brown ordered the caravan to continue toward Chicago where they were to catch a ferry to Canada.

For two more weeks they barreled through snow by day and slept overnight at Underground Railroad stops. The weather moderated for the party's arrival at Grinnell, Iowa—home of one of Brown's most loyal allies. Brown sat down with their host, Josiah Grinnell, on the second evening of their stay.

William had learned that Captain Brown was in the kitchen and resolved to make another plea for permission to strike out on his own. He was only a few steps from the passage into the kitchen when he overheard Grinnell. "Tell me about your big plans."

William stopped in the hallway and stepped back to be sure he wouldn't be seen.

"Once the Negroes in my charge are loaded on the ferry to Canada," Brown replied, "I'll head east to lay groundwork for slave insurrections."

"Here's $25 I've collected from your Grinnellian friends. Spend it wisely."

Brown smirked. "Traveling expenses and fire power. Is that wisely enough?"

"You're taking the fight to Virginia?" Grinnell asked.

"Hopefully, Virginia will be the kindling that births an inferno all across Dixie."

"And when the destruction is over?"

"There'll be a provisional government." Brown grinned.

"I suppose you'll be head of state."

"What makes you think I won't be a casualty of war?"

William stole back to his bunk and lay awake. The wagon driver's caution from days earlier dogged him—*his mission is everyone's mission.* Brown's declaration—*now we have a war to fight*—also consumed William's thoughts, like earthworms burrowing in loamy soil. The Captain had no intention of setting him free to search for Grace. William had let his guard down and trusted a white man. He could kick himself.

A few days later, the fugitives climbed into a railcar at the train depot in Liberty, Iowa. When the boxcar doors slammed shut, William stiffened. A loud clang and sudden lurch jolted his frayed nerves. He rolled his shoulders, stretched his neck, and found a seat in a corner.

The boxcar jerked forward and chugged along the iron rails, crossing the Mississippi River into Illinois. William settled and reached into his coat pocket for a map the wagon driver had drawn for him. He studied it in shards of morning light that knifed through gaps in the railcar's siding and around the edges of its doors.

His reading was mostly perfunctory. Embedded in William's mind was the portion of his journey that would begin after the train stopped in Ottawa, Illinois. The covered wagon driver had told him, "Wait until the train pulls away from the station then jump off before it picks up speed. Cross the bridge to the south bank of the Illinois River. Follow the river downstream, staying as close as you can to its bank until you come to the Sangamon River. Follow the Sangamon upstream. It will meander for a long while and lead you to Springfield. If you don't find Grace there, the Underground Railroad can help you get down to Alton."

CHAPTER THREE

Sangamon County, Illinois—July/August 1859

William battled icy winds, torrential storms, impassible terrain, and hunger all spring as he foraged and picked his way along the banks of the Illinois River. When summer arrived, he stumbled through dense underbrush in blistering heat and suffocating humidity. For the last half of July, he followed the snaking Sangamon, his ears trained for flatboat oars slapping and slicing the water and horses' hooves clomping the road that ran beside the river.

Under a scant moon, he exercised what had become a ritual. He dug barehanded in rich, black soil, pausing at the slightest hint of a twig snapping or leaves rustling in the shadows. He kept a sharp rock in easy reach—it would come in handy if he hit hardpan. The hole had to be deep enough to hide a body. His own. A runaway's survival often depended on staying hidden in plain sight. When William finished digging, he undressed, stuffed his clothes in a muslin sack, and nestled in, covering up with branches and moldering leaves to blend his blackness into the nightscape. He clutched the rock, hoping to catch a few hours' sleep without being caught.

He rose at daybreak and waded into an eddy near the riverbank. Goosebumps covered his nakedness as he splashed himself to wash off residue from the previous night's burial. He dressed and continued his journey, carrying his rock in the muslin sack—a makeshift slungshot to defend himself if he was set upon unawares.

If someone told him he would wake one morning and his life would turn, not either bitter or sweet but both, he would pray the sweetness would be finding Grace and Maddie. As for the bitter part, nothing, not even death, could be worse than losing his freedom to a slave hunter. Slave or free didn't matter to hunters, even in a free state like Illinois—so long as your skin screamed Negro and your body could bring a good price at auction. Maybe luck would smile on him, though, and bitter wouldn't be any worse than some sorry cuss just trying to prove there was some poor soul, other than himself, clinging to the bottom rung of humanity's ladder. Funny, how folks take pride in knowing another human is in a more miserable state than themselves.

On that late July morning, he came to a point where the river tweaked up to the edge of the roadway, leaving him no choice but to emerge from the woods' shadows. He had not been long on the road when a carriage pulled beside him and slowed to match his pace. He quickened his stride, kept his head down. Without freedom papers, he was fair game. He tightened his grip on the muslin sack with the rock inside.

The crunching of carriage wheels ceased. His back tightened as he walked on, his heart pounding in his ears, eyes shifting right to left as he calculated his escape. A river too deep to cross on one side, and on the other, a wide-open stretch of prairie grass where he might break his leg in a vermin hole ... or catch a musket ball in the back.

A voice rang out from the carriage. “Haloo, boy.”

He recalled the woman in Brown’s gaggle of liberated slaves who told about a quadroon girl crossing the Mississippi River at night to escape her master. The woman warned of exotic-tongued, dark-skinned Creoles who prodded coffles of African Negroes to flesh markets on wharfs along the river.

“I mean you no harm, boy,” the carriage driver said.

William stopped, his back to the carriage, eyes still scanning side to side.

“Let me give you a ride to town.”

William peeked back at a slight-built Negro wearing a suit and a high hat. He was alone.

“You hungry?” the man asked.

William eased to the carriage, sizing up the stranger. “I don’t take charity, but I’ll give you an honest day’s work for a hot meal.”

“Sounds like a fair trade. By the way, what’s your name?”

“William.”

The man offered William a hand up. “I’m William, too. But folks call me Billy. Billy Florville. Glad to make your acquaintance.”

They had traveled all of a hundred feet when Florville said, “You’re not from here.”

William's stomach tightened. "No."

"Where you hail from?"

William had expected the question to be, where you running from?

Florville continued. "Springfield is a beehive of abolitionist activity. We have a sort of railroad to help fellows like you. Few years back, we had a slave stampede. A dozen runaways from St. Louis showed up in town all at once, slave hunters hot on their heels. Town folks, both white and colored, risked their freedom, maybe their lives. Hid the poor souls until they could be spirited north to Canada. Railroad conductors are friends of mine."

William focused straight ahead.

"How about papers, son? Got papers?"

William poised to jump.

"Whoa." Florville grabbed William's arm. "I know someone who can fix that."

* * *

William stayed in the Florville home after arriving in Springfield. The first evening, Mrs. Florville treated him to a hot meal, drew a bath, and made up a clean bed. William had not enjoyed such indulgences since the raid on Osawatomie. Despite the comfort of his new surroundings, he imagined it would take many more nights before he slept in peace.

After breakfast the next morning, Florville took William to his barbershop near the state capitol. William's eyes lit up. "This is yours?"

Florville puffed out his chest. "Indeed."

"I've never known a Negro who owned much of anything."

"Here is proof anything can be done, if pursued in earnest."

William shuffled his feet. "There's something I want to do."

"Whatever it is you're aiming for, remember—we each have a North Star to guide us. The problem is finding it and keeping it in focus. Now, there's a lesson for us up in the night sky. Most folks think the North Star of celestial fame is the brightest star among a group that looks like a big drinking gourd. It's not. That big celestial gourd points to a star of only common brilliance at the end of a smaller gourd's handle. That, my friend, is the North Star."

"I'm looking for a girl and her child," William said. "We were separated when the Missouri Ruffians burned down our town almost three years ago."

"That's a tall order. They could be anywhere in slave territory by now."

"Grace is her name. I've heard she may have escaped and made it to the Underground Railroad in Alton."

"There was a quadroon girl passed through here by that name." Florville scratched his head. "Maybe twenty years old, or thereabouts."

"That's the right age." William's eyes lit up. "What happened to her?"

"She always blew into town like a prairie wind, then all at once ... *pfft*. She accompanied wagon loads of runaways up from Alton. Full of harrowing stories of encounters with slave hunters from Missouri. She obsessed over children who came through here separated from parents."

"I have to find them."

"It's a big country and half of it you don't want to touch. You may have to wait until freedom comes ... if it does come. Even then you might not find them."

William's shoulders slumped.

"It's a sad plight, but it is reality. Maybe you've got your eyes fixed on the wrong star." Florville handed a broom to William. "I pay sweepers fifty cents a half-day. The job is yours if you want it ... until you figure out where you go from here."

William started to tell Florville more—about how his brother, Thomas, died after buying their freedom, that Grace was Thomas' widow, that her daughter had been stripped from her by slave traders. But the barber sounded too much like Captain Brown—"fixed on the wrong star" was not much different from "his mission is everybody's mission." William held his tongue. No one was going to choose his North Star for him.

William stared at the floor. "Do you think she—"

"Come along." Florville gestured to the door.

They went out to the fairground where nearly 200 of Springfield's colored residents were congregated and speechmaking was already in progress. It didn't take William long to grasp the meaning of the celebration. The first speaker, a barber and friend of Florville's named Presley Donnegan, recalled the emancipation of 800,000 men, women, and children who were enslaved in the West India Colony, now called Hayti. They won their freedom on the first day of August, twenty-five years previous.

Florville leaned into William and explained that he and others in Springfield had immigrated from the Island of Hayti. Many were descended from slaves who had been set free on that occasion, while some of the older folks had been liberated on that actual date.

When Donnegan concluded his speech, everyone took their baskets and retired on the bluegrass lawn to partake of their picnic dinners. William joined the Florville family for their meal and was introduced to Florville's 22-year-old married daughter, Sinette. Her husband, Gilbert Johnson, had served the previous year as secretary of the African American meeting opposing colonization. Gilbert gave his rapt attention as William related stories of Captain John Brown's escapades.

After everyone had eaten their fill, the speeches resumed. John W. Menard, Jr., who came from Belleville, some 90 miles away, employed his strong voice in defense of liberty and equality for all. Menard's theme found fertile soil in William's mind.

Later that evening, sad news struck the Florville family—Gilbert Johnson had died suddenly after the picnic, cut down in the prime of his life by a heart attack. When the immediate shock of his death released its grip on the family, the African community gathered in the cool night air in front of Florville's home, recounting stories of Gilbert's love, kindness, and devotion to the cause of Negro liberty and equality. As each relation, friend, or neighbor spoke in turn, William pondered the lines of a poem written by Henry Wadsworth Longfellow. His Mormon mistress required him and Thomas to memorize the poem as part of their education. The words seemed to fit Gilbert Johnson better than any Negro he had ever known. Of course, the verses fit Thomas, Mr. Florville, and John Menard, Jr., as well. All were staunch men who would not be held down.

Though William had known Gilbert for a speck of time, his emotions were stirred. "If you will allow me," he said, "I would like to honor Gilbert's memory. I have been thinking that a free man should have a name of his own choosing, not one given by a master or mistress. With your permission, I would like to be called William Henry Johnson. William is the name my family called me. Henry is the name of a poet who wrote the lines I want to live by—*act in the living Present! Heart within, and God o'erhead.* And I would like to have the last name, Johnson, in honor of Gilbert's short, but courageous life."

Springfield, Illinois—September 1859

William had been sweeping floors in Florville's barber shop for almost a month when a tall, lanky customer shuffled through the doorway and looped his crumpled black coat over a wall hook. The man pulled a paper from his worn silk hat and passed the paper to Florville before lying back in a special reclining chair that made it easier for the barber to shave folks. The customer's scuffed boots capped a pair of gangly legs that went on forever. His arms hung over the chair, knuckles just about brushed the floor.

Florville instructed the man to sit up straight so he could adjust straps that he pegged to the back and arms of the chair. With the chair set upright, Florville ran his fingers through the man's tangle of black hair.

"William, this is Mr. Lincoln. People say he will be president someday."

"How do, William?" Lincoln said.

William could scarcely believe his eyes, taking in the sight of the man's odd appearance. He studied Lincoln's weathered skin. Not fully white and not the muddy brown of a mulatto or quadroon. More like the putty edges of an approaching storm.

"Boy, what's wrong?" Florville scolded. "Answer the man."

"Sorry," William stammered. "I'm fine, sir. Thank you."

"Excellent," Lincoln replied. "Now, don't let my friend Billy give you trouble. He is not as mean as he sounds."

"Yes, sir," William replied.

Florville turned to William. "Mr. Lincoln here's the best man I have ever known. One frosty evening back in '31, I was on foot approaching the little village of New Salem when I ran into this beanpole. He was returning from the woods in a yellowed tow-linen shirt, carrying an axe on his shoulder. Illinois, being near to slave territory, I was skittish. Before I knew it, though, we fell into easy conversation—him being a storyteller like myself. When he learned I was a barber and about out of money, he took me over to the village tavern to cut hair for the men boarding there. Next morning, my pockets full of money, I set out for Springfield. Been here ever since."

Lincoln let Florville's compliment roll off like spring rain on a pitched roof. "Over twenty years ago when the little village of New Salem was dying out, I removed to Springfield and inquired after old Billy. Was told, 'Sure. Everyone knows Billy. His shop is on the square by the new capitol.'"

Florville laughed. "When you sauntered through the door, I said, 'You come all the way from New Salem to get that mane tamed?'"

Lincoln cut in. "I replied, 'A haircut would be nice, but I'm poor as Job's turkey. Just stopping in to say hello. I'm settling here. Got a room over the general store with a good fellow named Speed.' You told me to sit and gave me a free haircut."

"The least I could do to return the favor you did me in New Salem," Florville replied.

"After you threw in a steaming hot shave," Lincoln added, "you told me I would have to start paying regular fare once I became a rich lawyer. Well, I did become a lawyer. Just not a rich one." Lincoln glanced at William. "Still, he makes me pay the same as he charges the governor."

"Don't let that poor lawyer nonsense fool you." Florville waved the comb at Lincoln. "Folks say he is going to be president. When he is, I shall be happy to cut his hair for free."

"Reckon I'll be paying for haircuts in the foreseeable future." Lincoln chuckled.

"A good many folks think differently," Florville said. "The whole town is abuzz over newspapers across the country publishing that speech you gave in Cincinnati."

"It takes more than a prairie hamlet to elect a president," Lincoln replied.

William's eyes widened as Lincoln rose, unfolding himself as if joined by hinges at points along his frame. Lincoln donned his hat and coat as he thanked Florville.

William followed Lincoln to the doorway and watched him pet a floppy-eared yellow dog.

"Come along, Fido," Lincoln said.

William tracked Lincoln's progress as he ambled down the street with the dog in his wake.

Florville came alongside William and handed him the paper Lincoln brought. "Congratulations. You're a freedman."

William stared at the certificate. It was both a blessing and a curse, like a turn bitter and sweet all at the same time. William was a freedman, but his freedom likely came with a debt owed to a white man, and no white man should be trusted. If he wasn't careful, he would find himself following a North Star that wasn't of his choosing.

Springfield—October 1859

Weeks later, Lincoln perused a stack of mail as he settled into his favorite chair next to the fireplace in the parlor of his home.

Atop the pile he found a telegram addressed to Hon. A. Lincoln.

> *Will you speak in Mr. Beecher's church Brooklyn on or about the twenty ninth November on any subject you please pay two hundred dollars. James A. Briggs.*

Henry Ward Beecher. Brooklyn. New York. Underground Railroad. Harriet Beecher Stowe. *Uncle Tom's Cabin.*

He had read the telegram over and over when Mrs. Lincoln bustled into the room, their two youngest sons in tow—eight-year-old Willie and six-year-old Tad. Without acknowledging her husband, she stopped at the window and planted her hands on her hips. "What is that racket?"

The boys pressed their foreheads against the windowpane, laughing and waving.

Lincoln peered over his steel-rimmed spectacles and laid the telegram aside. He unfolded himself from the chair and joined his family.

A crowd swelled as a band serenaded from the street below. News of Republican victories in local elections had poured in that night from Pennsylvania, Ohio, Indiana, and Minnesota. The results stirred hopes for a possible Republican victory in the presidential vote that was yet a year away, and many folks gave Lincoln much of the credit. They shouted, "Long Abraham, the Giant Killer!" Their cheers were a nod to his unhorsing of the indomitable 5'4" Little Giant, Judge Stephen Douglas, during the United States Senate contest a year earlier. The national fame Lincoln's debating earned him had become a source of pride for all of Springfield.

Shouts and cheers grew louder until the band was nearly drowned out. Mrs. Lincoln replaced her drawn expression with sparkles in her eyes. "Father, they're calling your name."

"Reckon they are, Mother." Lincoln absorbed the scene for a moment longer.

She smiled. "Go. Go be with them."

Lincoln kissed her cheek, stepped out into the chilly night air, and waded into the sea of well-wishers.

William shivered at the back of the crowd. There was no reason for him to get riled up about elections. Colored folks couldn't vote. Most would always scrap and scrape at the bottom of the barrel—unless they were freedmen from birth, like Florville and the late Gilbert Johnson. Even they had to put in ten times the effort and enjoy many times more the good fortune as white men of lesser talent.

Lincoln made up his mind the following morning to accept the invitation to speak at Beecher's church. He supposed folks at Beecher's church already believed the Founders had not intended for slavery to extend beyond where it existed when the nation began. Blind faith never set well with Lincoln, though. He set out to prove the premise with evidence. He camped out at the State Library, combing through stacks of books and *Congressional Journals.*

Before long, he awoke to the reality that he would need more time. The sponsoring committee at Reverend Beecher's church rescheduled the lecture for late February, giving him three additional months. Lincoln figured he could be ready by then if he hunkered down and put aside his duties at home and around the law office.

First, Lincoln broke the news to his law partner, Bill Herndon, who squinted up from a stack of cases on his desk. Herndon's blood-shot eyes suggested he was fighting a hangover. "What of our clients?" he asked.

"You'll take care of them just fine," Lincoln replied.

When Lincoln announced his plans to his wife, her eyes narrowed. "You shall have to get me some help. I cannot manage this house and these boys alone."

Lincoln held his tongue, choosing to keep his powder dry for other battles. He rarely argued with his wife unless the stakes required him to take a stand.

Springfield, Illinois—November 1859

Lincoln trudged through snow-crusted streets to the law office several weeks after accepting the invitation to speak at Beecher's church. He did not bother to remove his coat or shawl.

Herndon peeked up from his work, his eyes again bloodshot. "Am I glad to see you."

Lincoln waved off Herndon's greeting. "Not yet. General Washington said of slavery, 'There is not a man who wishes more sincerely than I do to see a plan adopted for the abolition of it.'"

"So?" Herndon shot back.

"Also, Patrick Henry claimed, 'We deplore slavery with all the pity of humanity. Let Congress examine this Constitution and see they have the power of manumission—in clear and unequivocal terms.'"

Herndon buried his nose in a stack of papers.

"Well?" Lincoln asked. "Where do you reckon I should place those quotations in my speech?"

"Near the beginning."

Lincoln started for the office door.

Herndon called after him. "There is a matter you might want to handle."

Lincoln turned. "Can it not wait?"

"Decide for yourself." He held up a letter from the McLean County Clerk. "You forgot to pay the taxes on Florville's lots."

Lincoln strode over to his partner, snatched the letter from his hand, and sat in a chair across the desk they shared. He wrote to a lawyer friend in McLean County.

> *William Florville, a Colored barber here, owns four lots in Bloomington, on which I have been paying the taxes for him several years. When last at Bloomington, I forgot to pay the recent assessment. Will you please pay all taxes due and send me the receipts? I shall be obliged and will repay you the money by first mail.*

Lincoln tucked the letter under his hat and rushed to post it before going to Florville's shop. When he arrived at the barbershop, Florville and William were alone, standing at the stove warming their hands.

"Billy," Lincoln began, "our friendship means a great deal to me. I hope what I'm about to ask won't drive a wedge between us."

"Sounds serious." Florville turned to face Lincoln.

Lincoln thought it best to avoid the tax matter. He took off his hat and held it at his waist. "It's about your boy, William."

"What about William?" Florville asked.

William continued to warm his hands at the stove.

"I'm up to my eyeballs preparing this big speech."

Florville glanced sideways at William. "How do you expect him to help?"

"Oh, that's not what I mean. Mrs. Lincoln has been on me like bees swarming honeysuckle over things around the house. Chopping, stacking, carrying logs into the house, keeping an eye on the boys, fixing this and that. Between her nagging and Herndon's complaining, I'm half out of my mind. Can you spare William for a few hours a week?"

Captain Brown had taught William how to hide in plain sight, but the way Lincoln was talking right past him, it was as if he was already invisible.

"Maybe you should ask him." Florville eyed William.

Lincoln's shoulders sagged. "Sorry, I don't want to—"

"I know," Florville said. "But I am trying to teach William to be his own man. If he wants to split time between us that's fine, but it should be his choice. I have no problem sweeping my own floor. I have done it plenty."

Lincoln turned to William. "What do you say? Can you make time for me?"

William faced Lincoln, weighing his reply. If Mr. Lincoln was such an important man, maybe he could help him find Grace. With the extra earnings, he could save enough to start searching, buy her freedom when he found her. William answered, "For a fair price, if I can keep learning from Mr. Florville how to be a barber."

"I'm sure we can work out something," Lincoln replied, smiling. "One more thing. Auntie Maria comes twice a week to clean and do some cooking, but sometimes when she's not around I take the boys to the office so Mrs. Lincoln can have some peace. How are you with young boys?"

"I can handle them," William replied.

Florville clapped William's shoulder. "Just do not go embarrassing me, you hear."

"Yes, sir."

After Lincoln left the barber shop, Florville interrupted William's sweeping. "I should warn you," he said. "Mrs. Lincoln can pitch a mighty fuss when she gets a mind to. She can be one hellion—that is for sure."

William discovered Florville's warning to be an understatement when he narrowly missed colliding with Lincoln on the icy street in front of the Lincolns' home. Mrs. Lincoln was hot after her husband—wielding a cleaver—yelling something about coming home with the wrong cut of meat. Again.

William shrunk out of sight, sneaked over the pike fence, and circled to the back of the two-story frame house. He aimed at getting to work chopping and splitting firewood as fast as he could. Not that an axe in hand would deter Mrs. Lincoln if she got it into her mind to give him the what for. It just might settle her a bit to find him working.

William brushed snow off the chopping stump, grabbed the axe handle, and yanked. Not even a jiggle. The axe head was buried in the stump's core. He pulled again. The axe might as well have been grafted to the stump. William recalled Lincoln demonstrating his chopping skills one afternoon. It was rumored that no man could bury an axe deeper in a tree than Lincoln could.

Mrs. Lincoln popped her head out the back door. "When you finish stacking, you must muck out the stable. It smells like no one has touched it in weeks. I do not understand how that man can bear to go in there to saddle his horse."

"Yes, ma'am."

"At last, he has hired some help. The neighbors must think we are too poor to run a proper household." She crossed her arms. "By the way, how much does Mr. Lincoln pay you?"

William released the axe handle. "Twenty-five cents for half days, ma'am."

"Why, that's ... that's ..." She planted her hands on her hips. "He should not be paying you a cent more than fifteen."

William bristled. Florville paid him fifty cents for half days, insisting what's good for a white man should be good for colored folks.

* * *

Lincoln spotted William a few days later as he crossed the square in front of the capitol. "Haloo, William," he called.

William plodded through gritty slush to see what his half-time boss wanted.

"Where you off to?" Lincoln asked.

"Mr. Florville's."

Lincoln scratched the back of his head. "Come to think of it, I might need a haircut, and maybe a shave."

"I'm sure Mr. Florville will be happy for the business."

Florville was finishing another customer as Lincoln arrived with William. Lincoln and the customer exchanged greetings, and Lincoln removed some notes he carried under his hat for safe keeping.

Once the customer was out the door, Lincoln cleared his throat. "Mind if I read you the summation I have prepared for my lecture for Reverend Beecher's church?"

"Go right ahead," Florville said.

William grabbed the broom.

"I reckon you might as well listen, too," Lincoln said, eyeing William.

William leaned on the broom as Lincoln read.

> *Twenty-one of the Constitution's thirty-nine signers confirmed that the Federal Government has the authority*

> *to regulate, even prohibit, the extension of slavery beyond where it existed when the Country was founded. Many of the remaining signers expressed their belief that slavery was wrong.*

"How does it sound?" Lincoln asked.

"Factual," Florville replied. "Should not the end of a speech stir passions?"

Lincoln turned to William, "What do you say?"

William hesitated. His aunt's Bible warned about serving two masters.

"Now William," Lincoln said. "Speaking truth is the highest form of loyalty."

William hesitated. Sweat collected under his collar despite the wintry temperatures. "Mr. Lincoln, I have to say I agree with Mr. Florville."

"I see. I reckon I should have prefaced my question by saying I will be addressing a highly educated eastern audience. I wish to impress them with my logical analysis, so they do not think of me as some backcountry yokel who is easily swayed by emotional appeals."

Florville said. "You can do that in the main part of your speech but arouse them at the end. Incite them to do something."

"Reverend Beecher's church hardly needs an outsider to agitate their passions." Lincoln winked. "The preacher has a reputation for doing the job well enough all by himself."

"You know what's best, I'm sure," Florville replied as he gestured for Lincoln to sit in the barber's chair.

Lincoln expected Florville to trim his hair and shave his whiskers as he always did, but Florville pointed to the scissors and comb. "Hope you don't mind if William does the honors."

Lincoln braced himself. “Not at all.”

William’s fingers twitched slightly as he reached for the barber’s tools.

“First, the cape,” Florville muttered.

William laid the cape over Lincoln’s lanky frame and tucked it around his collar. He paused, his black fingers touching white flesh for the first time.

“Go on,” Florville prodded. “Mr. Lincoln doesn’t bite.”

William held the scissors, mesmerized by the man’s dark rat’s nest of hair.

Florville simulated scissors—*snip, snip.*

William gulped and went to work.

A couple of times, Florville took the scissors from William, ran a comb through Lincoln’s hair, and clipped errant strands. When William reached what he hoped was the end of his work, Florville leaned in for close examination. William held his breath until the barber straightened and gestured toward the shaving utensils.

While Florville readjusted the chair back to a reclining position, William removed the lid from an iron pot on the shop’s wood-burning stove. William pulled out a hot towel and held it for a moment before wrapping and kneading Lincoln’s face. After the massage, William peeled off the towel and returned it to the pot like Florville taught him. As the towel reheated, William rubbed Lincoln’s face with a balm—the barber’s special recipe—then reapplied the wrap. The steaming towel over Lincoln’s face did not stop him from mumbling. William could not decipher the words, but Florville must have, because he laughed.

William wiped the balm off Lincoln’s face, whipped soap into a stiff foam, and worked in the lather with a horsehair brush. He laid the razor against Lincoln's neck and hesitated, wondering how house slaves restrained themselves as they performed such intimate tasks. One slice and the master would be done for—retribution for countless bloody lashes.

William took a deep breath and rolled his shoulders to release the tension in his neck and back. He began shaving with short, precise strokes, swiping away soapy stubble, navigating around moles. He found a rhythm—pinching and spreading skin to access the shortest, finest hairs in the most vexing crevices. When William finished, he stepped back and Florville leaned in.

William's stomach tightened as the barber brushed his hand over Lincoln's face. Florville pointed to the iron pot. "Okay. Wrap him one more time and clean him up."

When all was done, Lincoln said, "Good job, William."

Lincoln stood in the entry hall when he returned home and shook snow from his hat and coat. Mrs. Lincoln eyed him from their parlor. She smiled and approached him. "You went for a haircut without me pestering you. What brought that on?"

"I went to Billy Florville's shop to try out part of my speech." Lincoln smoothed his hair. "Somehow, I wound up sitting in the chair, and William began clipping."

She clutched his chin and turned his head side to side. "That boy did this?"

"Don't be too hard on him. He's just learning."

"Not at all. He did quite nicely," she said.

"Glad you approve."

"In fact," she continued, "this just might be the answer to what has been preying on my mind ever since you were invited to speak at Reverend Beecher's church."

"What's that?"

"A gentleman ought to be attended by a valet."

"A valet?" Lincoln protested. "I'm perfectly capable of handling my own wardrobe and toilet."

"No, I am the one who looks after the details you neglect, but I shall not be with you in New York."

"I will be fine."

"It is decided." She stamped her foot. "I shall not have my husband standing before a hundred witnesses in the house of God in scuffed boots, a rumpled suit, and tousled hair."

Lincoln turned away. "The hotel has servants to take care of those things for guests."

"You should ask Billy Florville. He has the right experience and runs his own clothes cleaning business. He even looks the part. His wife can tend things while he is away. Especially, with that boy William's help."

"Acting as my valet would be an embarrassment to Billy. He exceeds the aptitudes of his race. He's one of the wealthiest men in Springfield.

"What about that other colored barber?" she asked.

"I hardly know Burras. Besides, it would be a greater indignation to Billy if I passed him over for his competitor."

"Whomever you take, he must be able to trim your hair and shave your whiskers properly."

"Billy is the only barber I will ever let touch my head." Lincoln stiffened.

"Why, I do not believe that is so. William gave you a fine haircut just this afternoon."

"Under Billy's supervision."

"He seems to be a quick study," Mrs. Lincoln smiled. "If you will not take Billy, I can have the boy shaped into a reasonable facsimile of a valet in a week's time."

"Mother, I said no. I will not have a valet shadowing me from place to place."

"It is exactly what you must do to make the impression that you're a man of culture and fit to be president."

Lincoln pinched his brow. "But I will be indistinguishable from the slaveholders who carry their human property with them everywhere they go."

"Husband, you are impossible. Go ahead. Throw away whatever chance we may have to live in that grand old house in Washington."

Springfield, Illinois—December 1859

William emptied the last wheelbarrow load of horse manure onto the Lincolns' composting pile on a chilly December afternoon. Mud and dung coated his boots. His stiff, achy hands wore a layer of grime from neglected corners and crevices of the stable. Mrs. Lincoln insisted he clean it spotless. He stowed the wheelbarrow against the stable wall and scrubbed himself with warm, soapy water from a bucket she had brought him. She also left William some cast-off clothes and shoes that belonged to 16-year-old Bob Lincoln, who was back east at a boarding school.

Mrs. Lincoln called out from the backdoor. "William, are you about finished with that stable? I need you inside with the boys."

"I'll be there right away, Mrs. Lincoln." He finished lacing Bob's boots and crossed from the stable to the backdoor. As William stepped into the kitchen, Mrs. Lincoln was prepared to leave, a scarf around her neck, her coat buttoned, and her hat snug on her head.

She scowled. "If you cannot work faster, I shall have to reduce your wage."

He stared at the floor. "Sorry. I'm doing my best."

"Well, your best is not close to good enough. We pay Auntie Maria half of what Mr. Lincoln insists on paying you, and she cooks and cleans and gets twice as much done."

"Yes, ma'am." He glanced into the parlor where Willie and Tad were rough housing. "Should I tend to the boys so you can be on your way?"

Mrs. Lincoln huffed out of the house as William asked the boys, "What will we play today?"

"We'll be musketeers and you can be Planchet," Willie answered.

"Again?" Tad whined. "William can be Old John Brown. I'll be the hangman and, Willie, you can be a soldier."

"Why do you get to be the hangman?" Willie scowled.

"Wait a minute." William's face warmed. "Who said there's going to be a hanging?"

Tad snatched a newspaper off a table next to the rocking chair. "Pa read it. Says they're going to hang Old John Brown."

"Let me see that." William grabbed the newspaper.

> *A different measure of justice has been meted out ... Brown can only look forward to execution.*

William was staring at the article when Lincoln walked into the parlor from the kitchen.

Lincoln smiled. "Nice job on the stable, William."

Willie and Tad ran to their father, yelling, "Pa, now we have three musketeers."

"Whoa, boys," Lincoln replied. "No time for play today. I just came from the office to get something I forgot."

William's voice trembled. "It says they are going to hang Captain Brown."

Lincoln's smile dissolved. "Yes, Old John Brown will likely be executed. Even though he agreed with us about slavery, we cannot excuse violence, bloodshed, and treason."

"What about this man they talk about named Walker. He was acquitted even though he did the same kind of thing."

Lincoln ran his fingers through his hair. "Walker is a devilish filibusterer and he should hang as well. If he's allowed to continue spreading slavery by violence, it will consume every corner of the land and it won't stop there. Everything from the top of Maine to the lowest reaches of South America will be swallowed up by the slave power."

William glared up at Lincoln. "They should hang Walker and let the Captain keep freeing slaves. He freed me, and whatever he does to set people free is the right thing to do."

Lincoln drew a deep breath. "The right thing to do is to obey the laws, but that is not a popular notion these days. Our brothers in the south say if the Black Republicans elect a president, they won't stand for it. Now, if we shall constitutionally elect a president, and brethren in the south undertake to destroy the Union, it will be our duty to deal with them as Old John Brown will be dealt with."

William turned to Willie and Tad. "We're not going to play musketeers and we're certainly not going to hang Captain Brown. But I will read to you."

"May I suggest a book?" Lincoln asked.

William shrugged.

"Upstairs, you'll find a copy of Mr. Dickens' *Bleak House.* If you read it lively enough, you can keep them entertained."

CHAPTER FOUR

New York City—February 1860

Lincoln sat exhausted and alone on the ferry from New Jersey to New York City's Courtland Street terminal. Mrs. Lincoln stayed home as usual, and he refused to take William along as his valet. He switched rail companies five times in three days, meandering over the 1,200 miles after leaving Springfield. At some stops, passengers were rousted from their sleep in order to change trains in the middle of the night.

He stared, pasty-eyed, at two men in earnest conversation about whether New York City's bankers should throw fuel on the secessionist fever that smoldered in the south. He champed at the bit to join in but thought better of it.

One of the men, silver-haired and clean-shaven, hoped the city's politicians would have the backbones to break from the Union if southern states bolted. "After all," the man explained, "northern banks have more than $200 million invested in the southern economy."

The younger of the two declared secession was treasonous.

His companion countered, "Let each go their own way. Holier-than-thou abolitionists in the north can still buy cheap cotton for their textile mills, and southern men will continue to add to their fortunes. That is the path that has created great wealth on both sides of the sectional divide."

The other man rebutted. "What of advancements in agriculture that displace the need for labor—the cotton gin, mechanical reapers? The slave is already rendered useless in many cases."

"*Pfft*. Machines will never harvest sugar cane," the silver-haired gentleman responded. "That's why my money is on the eastern plantations. Our economic energies should focus on breeding slave stock to meet the demand for cheap labor as the slave economy pushes into the sugar region. If secession succeeds, the slave economy will dominate everywhere below the Ohio River, from the Atlantic Ocean to the Pacific, all the way down to Terra del Fuego. Imagine the prosperity this city will enjoy. Every banker and textile manufacturer will be a millionaire several times over."

Lincoln disembarked the ferry when it docked on the New York side of the river, ruing he hadn't given the two gentlemen passengers a strong rebuttal. He lugged his trunk for several blocks, navigating potholes, bleak shanties, and bands of vagabonds warming themselves at open fires. Scrawny curs barked as a brittle icy wind cut up from the river. A few blocks later, he plunged into the tide of hustle, bustle, and ear-splitting noises on Broadway.

At Astor House, a grand six-story hotel, Lincoln laid down two dollars for his first night's lodging and grabbed a copy of the *New York Tribune*. An announcement on page four reported he would be speaking at Cooper Institute in downtown, instead of at Beecher's church in Brooklyn. He palmed the back of his neck. A downtown audience would include Democrats and southern sympathizers, bankers, tycoons, and bluebloods. He would have to rewrite his speech.

Two wintery evenings later, 1,500 people paid twenty-five cents admission and jammed into the Great Hall at Cooper Institute. As Lincoln trailed William Cullen Bryant, the white-bearded, 77-year-old newspaper editor, onto the stage, lines from Bryant's poem, *Thanatopsis*, echoed in Lincoln's mind.

So live, that when thy summons comes
Thou go not, like the quarry-slave at night,
Scourged to his dungeon,
But, sustained and soothed by an unfaltering trust,
Approach thy grave like one
Who wraps the drapery of his couch about him,
And lies down to pleasant dreams.

When Lincoln was seated, he spotted Horace Greeley, the bespectacled editor of the *New York Tribune*, near the front row. Greeley, regarded by many as a king maker, supported Stephen Douglas's victory over Lincoln in the Illinois Senate contest two years earlier. Greeley's silver hair flowed to his shoulders like a lion's mane. Grisly white neck whiskers billowed up from under his collar, giving the impression that his round, clean shaven face floated on a cloud.

Lincoln glanced down at his scuffed-up, weather-worn boots. Worse yet, one pants leg hung shorter than the other. He reckoned Greeley was gloating over the spectacle on stage—his defeated former rival, ill-dressed and perched on an undersized chair with his gangly limbs wrapped around its legs. Mrs. Lincoln would scold him if she caught him in public like that. Sweat collected under his collar.

Over the course of two hours, Lincoln lectured on the facts he mined during long days of research, making his case that the Founders intended to prohibit slavery's expansion and see it die a natural death. He took to heart the advice given by William and Florville. He closed by exhorting his audience—

> *Neither let us be slandered from our duty by false accusations, nor frightened from it by menaces of destruction to the Government, nor of dungeons. Let us have faith that right makes might, and in that faith let us to the end dare to do our duty as we understand it.*

People rose and cheered, waving their hats and handkerchiefs above their heads. James Briggs, the event organizer, proclaimed, "One of three gentlemen shall be our standard bearer in this year's canvass for president—the eloquent Senator William Seward, the able Salmon Chase, or the unknown knight from the prairies of Illinois, Abraham Lincoln."

Lincoln's chest swelled.

New England—February-March 1860

Bob Lincoln, dapper as always, greeted his disheveled father in the biting cold at the Exeter, New Hampshire, train depot.

Bob enrolled at Phillip Exeter Academy—a prestigious New England preparatory school—because he failed his entrance exams for Harvard College. He was preparing for a second try at admission to Harvard, but he had another ambition, as well. When not studying, Bob exploited every opportunity to rub elbows with the upper crust of eastern families. His uncouth, yarn-spinning father might not lead him out of the social wilderness, but a young man could raise his status by riding the coattails of aristocracy.

Bob smirked. "You look like you rode in on a dust devil."

Lincoln let his son's criticism pass over without hitting its mark. He recalled his own boyhood—the back of his father's hand knocking him from his perch on a fence for being overly familiar with strangers passing by. From his earliest days of fatherhood, Lincoln vowed never to be cross with his own sons. He replied, "I reckon news of my New York speech hasn't reached Exeter."

Bob rolled his eyes. "It has. They want you to give a speech here."

"That's good. You can hear what's got those New Yorkers so wound up."

"Should be splendid."

"Do you have plans for supper?" Lincoln asked.

Bob eyed his father from head to toe. "Let's freshen up, first."

While Lincoln wrangled himself into a form that might meet with his son's approval, Bob posted a letter to his mother—

> Father is unkempt—an embarrassment. His suit badly wrinkled. Hair sticking out like rooster feathers. His arms protrude well past the sleeves of his baggy coat.

> How will he manage the remainder of his carnival tour? I cringe at what my friends will say when he speaks here on the Third. At least, he has no chance at becoming president. When he's done with this nonsense, let's hope he will not make any further spectacle of himself.

* * *

Bob and his classmate, George Latham from Springfield, lagged behind Lincoln at the Exeter depot the next morning. All three held tickets for the train to Concord, New Hampshire, where Lincoln was to speak later in the day. As a result of his New York speech, Lincoln had accepted invitations to address ten more audiences across New England.

Bob muttered to George, "You're a trouper for coming."

"What are friends for?" George whispered. "Besides, maybe he will become president."

"I have to see this circus firsthand so I can be prepared," Bob muttered. "When he returns to speak here in a few days, he's certain to find a way to mortify me."

Lincoln was several strides ahead of the boys. "Hurry up," he called.

In the early afternoon, when Lincoln arrived at Concord's Phenix Hall to deliver his speech, a throng of several hundred had already packed into the auditorium. The color drained from Bob's face. He pulled his father aside, smoothed wrinkles in his new black suit and tugged at the sleeves, knowing nothing short of magic could make them the right length.

Bob leaned toward George when they took their seats. "I do not understand why Mother neglected to send a valet to keep him presentable."

"You probably want someone to stand next to him whispering lines in his ear," George scoffed. "Relax. People will forget his appearance once he starts speaking."

"Do not make me sound like a prig. This is not the prairie. If he uses one of his folksy stories, I will die right here in my seat."

Halfway into the speech, Lincoln strained to illustrate a point.

> *If the Republicans, who think slavery is wrong, get possession of the General Government, we may not root out the evil at once, but we may at least prevent its extension.*
>
> *In the same way, if I find a venomous snake lying on the open prairie, I seize the first stick and kill him at once. But if that snake is in bed with my children, I must be more cautious. I shall, in striking the snake, also strike the children, or arouse the reptile to bite the children. Slavery is the venomous snake in bed with the children. But if the question is whether to kill it on the prairie or put it in bed with other children, I think we'd kill it!*

Laughter rippled through the audience.

"Did my father just lay an enormous egg in front of all these people?" Bob slinked down in his seat.

George snickered.

"Mother would die a thousand deaths if she knew he told an uncouth story like that to an eastern audience. By morning, he will be the laughingstock of all New England."

Despite the warm ovation Lincoln received, Bob scarcely uttered a word after the speech. And when the two boys boarded the train back to Exeter, father and son exchanged stiff goodbyes. Lincoln waited for the boys' train to pull away before boarding his train to Manchester, New Hampshire, the second stop on his itinerary.

* * *

Bob was on high alert when the day came for his father's speech in Exeter. At breakfast, one of the upperclassmen taunted Bob, saying his father would make a bad impression with his lanky figure and awkward gestures. Another classmate reported that girls in town had giggled over how unfortunate Bob was to have such a homely father.

With the 800-seat Exeter town hall filled to capacity, Bob and George chose seats near the back so they could make a quick exit when the carnival sideshow ended. A young man groaned in the row in front of them. He complained, "I wish I had known what a freak he is. Have you ever seen such a melancholy visage?" The young man added, "What a darned fool I've been to walk for miles through the mud to hear this man speak."

Sentiments changed by the time Lincoln finished his address. The young man who had slogged through mud turned to Bob, wide-eyed. His demeanor had transformed. "You must be so proud. Every part of his speech fitted into the whole argument perfectly. I know it captured all of us. Your father spoke nearly an hour with no coarseness, no uncouthness of speech or mannerisms, and there has never been such applause in this hall."

Bob's jaw dropped at the sight of his classmates crowding onto the platform to shake his father's hand. He turned to George. "I am not sure I like where this whole affair is headed."

Lincoln spent the next day touring Exeter with his ill-humored son, and the following morning he boarded a train for his next engagement.

Springfield, Illinois—March 1860

Mrs. Lincoln wadded Bob's letter and tossed it into the iron cook stove. As the letter burned to ash, she dispatched her two younger sons with a note to Billy the Barber.

> Mr. Florville:
>
> Please see me at your earliest convenience. Kindly call at the back door.
>
> Cordially, Mrs. L.

When the boys returned through the front door and raced into the kitchen, Mrs. Lincoln asked, "Did you not wait for his reply?"

"He came," Tad blurted.

Willie pointed to the back door. "He's standing there."

She pulled off her apron and smoothed her hair as she went to the door. "Hello, Mr. Florville, thank you for coming."

"What can I do for you, ma'am?" Florville asked as they sat at a small table strewn with meal preparations.

"Mr. Florville, my husband is in a pickle and I am hoping you can be of assistance."

"How so?"

"You see, he's on a trip ... giving speeches." She glanced at her hands, folded in her lap. "I was unable to go with him to attend to ... certain matters."

"I understand he's due to return soon."

"Yes. However, he has been invited to give speeches in other places and shall be traveling for another week. It is a well-known fact that he is not the tidiest man."

"But his speeches seem to have made him a popular man." Florville shifted in his chair.

"I received a letter from our son. It seems Mr. Lincoln is in urgent need of an attendant."

"And you would like me to refer someone?"

"No." She leaned forward and flattened her hands on the table. "I would like for you to be that someone."

"I'm sorry," Florville replied. "I cannot do that."

"And why?"

"Ma'am, I'm a businessman. I cannot just pick up and leave."

"If my husband does not make the right impression," she tilted her head, "he will never get those eastern men to support his nomination."

"I understand your concern, ma'am, but by the time I put my affairs in order and collect everything I need, he will be home."

"You must be on the next train. I shall pay the fare and provide enough money for you to purchase everything you need on your arrival."

"Please," Florville protested, "what you are asking is not practical."

She daubed her eyes with a handkerchief.

"Mrs. Lincoln," he pled. "It's too late to do anything about the present situation. But I have an idea of how we can fix things for the future."

"Too late? When did my husband ever say it was too late to help someone in need?"

"You said young Master Robert wrote you. When was his letter posted?"

"On the first, I believe. Why does that matter?" she asked.

"It's now the fourth," Florville replied. "Even if we knew exactly where Mr. Lincoln will be speaking next, it would take nearly a week to catch up with him. By then, he will be somewhere else or on his way home."

She buried her face.

"Mrs. Lincoln," he said. "Let me see what I can do."

Florville returned to the barbershop, aiming to enlist William in a plan to help Mrs. Lincoln.

William asked, "Do I have a choice?"

"You certainly have a choice," Florville replied. "But why would you not want the job? How many boys have a shot at being the valet for one of the country's leading citizens?"

"He's not president yet," William muttered.

"No, he is not. Though, he is the only man you know who might become president someday. And even if that day never comes, what is there to lose?"

William had better sense than to tell Florville what was on his mind—that Springfield had turned out to be a dead end in his search for Grace. Reports from Alton showed little promise as well. Some accounts suggested Grace had moved on to a new life of freedom in Canada. Maybe she had found Maddie, as well. Maybe he should go there, find them. If he spoke his mind, William feared Florville would tell him his mind was set on the wrong star.

"What if I don't want to be another man's man?" William asked. "Maybe I'm tired of pretending to be invisible, my voice falling on deaf ears. What if I want to be my own man, pursue my own hopes, like you did?"

"Have a seat." Florville indicated the stool he rested on between customers. "I was placed in an orphanage after my parents sent me to Baltimore from our native Hayti during a rebellion against our king. An Orphan Court decided I was old enough to work, so they bound me over as an apprentice to an old barber. One of the barber's customers was a young doctor—Elias Merriman—from a well-to-do family. You've seen him a few times sitting here." He patted the barber's chair.

"You said Dr. Merriman was in Baltimore."

"He was, and so was I. Now we are both here. Providence is a funny thing. In Baltimore, Dr. Merriman took a liking to me and probably felt sorry for me. He hired me to work mornings and evenings under his butler's tutelage. Mind you, I had to continue my indenture for the old barber by day."

"Fine." William slid off the stool. "But how did you get to be a barber with your own shop?"

"Life does not always take a straight line. After the old barber died, I was freed from my indenture. I heard about a place called New Orleans where my native French language was spoken. Many people of my origin had settled there. So, I went. But the place was full of danger. A teenaged slave was hanged for defending himself from his mean-spirited master's attack. Maybe he had been just like me once—freeborn and not carrying papers—but he was seized and bartered on the block. So, I ran off to Illinois where I heard folks like us could live in peace, unmolested." Florville drew a long breath. "Here, I discovered Dr. Elias Merriman had settled ahead of me. He helped me establish my barbering business."

"So, if I become Mr. Lincoln's valet, will he help me follow my own star?" The question on his heart was, if I become Mr. Lincoln's valet, will he help me find Grace?

"I always figured you for a smart young fellow."

William furrowed his brow. "Even if Mr. Lincoln becomes president in America, how could he be of any help in Canada?"

Florville was pondering his answer when Willie and Tad ran into the shop, sent by their mother to fetch William.

William stood moments later at the backdoor to the Lincoln residence, his mind already made up that his wages would be cut, probably in half. To his surprise, Mrs. Lincoln wore a smile as sweet as the honeysuckle that, in summertime, wove its way along the backyard fence. She invited him in.

He was barely three paces inside when she announced, "William, I have a marvelous opportunity for you. I would like to increase your responsibilities, and of course your wages, as well."

William was tempted to pinch himself to be certain he wasn't dreaming.

"Speaking of responsibilities—" Mrs. Lincoln paused.

William braced himself.

"Leading men in all parts of the country are beginning to whisper that Mr. Lincoln should become our next president. Which means there will be many details he simply will not have the time to attend to."

"Yes, ma'am," William said. "Mr. Florville has been telling me—"

"Excellent. So, what do you say? Are you ready to begin your lessons?"

"I ... I—"

Mrs. Lincoln interrupted. "I understand how you would be nervous. But you will find me an excellent tutor. I was raised in a great house in Lexington, Kentucky. My father was a dear friend of Mr. Henry Clay, one of our country's leading men."

William was unprepared for the onslaught of ideas competing for attention in his head. Canada. Dead ends. Maddie stripped from Grace's arms. Auction blocks. Mr. Lincoln. Barbering.

Mrs. Lincoln gestured to the dining room. "We shall start with proper table etiquette."

Springfield, Illinois—Late March 1860

Florville paused and breathed warmth into his hands before opening the door to his barbershop. He glimpsed a grizzly figure who leaned into the icy breeze as he angled up the street toward the barbershop. The man was no stranger. The slave hunter in pursuit of blood money showed his face in Springfield far too often. Florville retreated inside the shop and joined William at the stove. "Get your coat. You best get out of here for a while. Does Mrs. Lincoln have some work for you?"

"I suppose—"

"This is one time you truly want to be overlooked. Take the alleys to Mrs. Lincoln's place. I will come and fetch you when all is clear."

As William ducked out the back way, Florville grabbed a broom and started sweeping. A moment later, the slave hunter barreled through the front door, swaggered over to the stove, and shook off the cold. Without looking at Florville, he said, "I hear tell you have a boy that does that sweeping for you."

Florville continued sweeping. "Sometimes."

"Where can I find him?"

"Which one?"

The bounty hunter unfolded a copy of a reward poster. "This one."

Florville studied the handbill. “Could be just about any of the young colored boys around town. Freedman, every one of them. Seeing that this is Illinois, not Missouri.”

“I’ve been poking around. Seems there’s a particular one what works for you.”

“I have an apprentice barber. Young fellow. Bright. Reads and writes. Quick study. He has papers.”

“You don’t say.”

“I do say,” Florville replied.

“So why didn’t I find his certificate over at the County Clerk’s?” The bounty hunter cocked his head.

“This is Springfield. Our ways are different. Besides, if he could not prove his freedom, he would have headed straight to Canada. He would have been a fool to stop short of the border.”

“Maybe he is foolish. He’s a nigger, ain’t he?”

Florville did not respond.

The bounty hunter flashed a grin and tossed his poster onto the barber’s chair. “You have a good day, now,” he said before swaggering out the door and onto the street.

That night, Lincoln returned from speechmaking in the east and collected his trunk at Springfield’s train depot. He eyed a reward poster tacked on the wall. A bounty hunter was on the prowl for a healthy twenty-odd year-old Negro answering to the name William—runaway from Missouri. Lincoln hated the law that required authorities in free states to aid in returning escaped slaves to their owners. Nevertheless, it was the law and he had argued both sides of it in the courts.

Lincoln did not hang his hat and coat or kiss his wife hello when he arrived home. “Mother,” he asked, “when did you last see William?”

"He was here this morning, splitting wood," she said.

He told her about the slave hunter's poster.

"Why, William is a common enough name," she replied.

"Yes, and it will not matter to the slave hunter which William he hauls back to Missouri. Nor will the slave owner care, especially if the William he gets is healthier and stronger than the one that ran away."

"I suppose some people will say anything to achieve an end, especially when money is involved."

No sooner than the words were out of her mouth, there came a knock at the front door.

"I'm going to bed," she said. "I cannot summon the vigor to endure company."

Lincoln hesitated long enough for his wife to retire to her bedroom before answering the door to find his law partner on the front stoop flanked by Florville and Sheriff John Smith.

"Hello, boys," Lincoln said. "Come on in out of the weather." He hung their hats and coats and added in a low voice, "We'll have to keep it down. Mrs. L. has turned in for the night." On the way into the parlor, he added, "I just arrived on the train. How did you know I was back?"

"We had someone keeping an eye out for you," Herndon replied. "Since early this afternoon."

As they sat, Lincoln glanced at Florville who was uncharacteristically quiet. The overdue taxes on Florville's Bloomington lots crossed his mind. Matters could get sticky for coloreds who bought property. Technically, they were not supposed to. They were always at risk of having it stripped away. All it took was the slightest hiccup—like being late paying your taxes. Lincoln asked, "Whatever's up, it must be important."

"It's William Johnson," Herndon said.

"What about William?" Lincoln asked.

"He's been detained," Sheriff Smith replied.

"Why?" Lincoln asked.

"We've had a bounty hunter in town the past few days," Sheriff Smith answered. "Been looking for a runaway that fits your William's description. Someone sent him over to Billy's shop, saying a Negro boy called William was sweeping floors for the barber. Recalled the boy turning up here a couple of weeks after the hunter claims a slave owner in Missouri reported his boy ran off. Early this afternoon, the hunter showed up at my office with his catch, wanting me to hold him in a cell while he packed to take the boy back to Missouri. Law says I have to accommodate, so I did. Of course, the law doesn't stop me from alerting you folks."

Lincoln chose to be coy. The sheriff was likely unaware of the truth about William's freedom papers. He turned to Florville. "You know William better than anybody. What can you tell us about him?"

"The boy did show up here about that time," Florville replied. "I've seen his papers."

Lincoln stood up and paced, his hands clasped behind his back. The others refrained from disturbing him. Their efforts would have been futile as he immersed himself in deep thought. After a time, he paused at the fireplace and rested an elbow on the mantle. "Did he record the certificate with the County Clerk?"

"You know that's not how we do things here," Florville said.

"The bounty hunter insists he has the right boy," Smith interjected. "If William has papers, he'll insist they were forged by abolitionist sympathizers."

Lincoln turned to Herndon. "I reckon we better see Judge Power and let him sort this out. Do we have a writ prepared?"

"Yes."

"Who has the boy's certificate?" Lincoln pinched his brow.

"Florville brought it to the office after the boy was arrested." Herndon replied. "It's in my desk,"

"You best go collect it and meet us at Judge Power's place. We better hope we don't have to raise him from a dead sleep."

* * *

William sat on the jail cell floor, his knees drawn to his chest, head down, ears on alert, eyes peeled. Memories of iron shackles tugged on his wrists and chafed his ankles. His back itched from old scars left by lashes from the Missouri master's whip. A cockroach stalled an inch or so from his toe.

Voices filtered through a crack under the door that separated the cells from the sheriff's office. An angry voice demanded to take his client's property, no more dodging the issue. William recognized the other voice—the lawyer who worked with Mr. Lincoln, the one who smelled of whisky. The lawyer yelled at the sheriff about a *corpus* and fugitive slave laws be damned. He said Mr. Lincoln would return soon and make everything right.

William edged his toe closer to the cockroach. The pest remained still. Brave, defiant, or scared out of its wits. Maybe it thought by freezing in place it could hide in plain sight. William had practiced the same defense through most of his life. The roach would probably skitter away when Mr. Lincoln opened the cell door. Then again, Mr. Lincoln might not make it back before the hunter prevailed and got his *nigger*.

Dry, crusty bread and tepid beans sat untouched on a tray on the cold dank floor. Night fell, and Mr. Lincoln did not come. The cockroach was still there. It had darted in and out of shadows along the wall. It ventured out again and climbed onto the tray. Sniffed the beans. The bread.

William supposed Negroes and cockroaches were about the same. They ate from the same trays, laid in the same beds, and sat in the same seats. They got stomped on by the same boots, left to rot in the same earth. No one cared if either had families. There was one difference. Nobody ever owned a cockroach, except God.

* * *

William found no measure of security in the slave hunter's empty-handed return to Missouri. The man's parting words rang in William's ears. "Enjoy your freedom, boy, while you can. Not everyone around here is a nigger lover." Gossip around town concerning the exploits of William Walker, the filibusterer, further jangled William's tattered nerves.

Curiosity sunk its fangs into William one day when he was perusing a bookshelf in the Lincoln's upstairs parlor. He should have been picking out a book to read to Willie and Tad, but the title, *The War in Nicaragua*, and the author's name, William Walker, were too tempting.

He had left the boys to their own devices far too long as he became engrossed in reading Walker's book, especially after he encountered an ominous passage—

> *The true field for the exertion of slavery is in Tropical America; there it finds the natural seat of its empire and thither it can spread.*

Mrs. Lincoln's voice rang out from downstairs. "William?"

He grabbed the copy of *Bleak House* he once read to the boys and raced downstairs. He took it, not because the boys enjoyed it, but because it was handy. When he reached the landing, he held out the book. "I went to fetch a book for them."

She gestured toward a fort made of chairs and sheets and pillows. "Was all this accomplished in the time it took you to find a book?"

"No, ma'am," he said. The true answer was, yes, because he had neglected his duties for longer than he was willing to admit. "We were going to have it cleaned up before you returned home."

"As you see, I am home now." She hung up her coat and scarf. "But it is just as well. The children can use it to entertain themselves while we resume your lessons in the kitchen."

Since Mrs. Lincoln forbade him from speaking during lessons—setting a proper table and serving a fine cup of tea—he waited until they were finished to ask for permission to raise his concerns.

"How will being in service to you and Mr. Lincoln help me find Grace?" William asked.

"What does this girl mean to you?"

"She is my brother's widow."

"Oh, yes. I recall you mentioning she was captured in a raid and put into slavery. Poor, poor girl."

"She may have run away. That's why I'm trying to find her."

"She also might have been recaptured." Mrs. Lincoln tilted her head to one side. "If she is as beautiful as you say, and I have no reason to doubt it, she's likely serving in some elegant house and out of harm's way."

"Or she could be in Canada."

"Either way, you will need help from people such as Mr. Lincoln and myself. You cannot possibly search such a vast continent alone, and if you could, there are many places you dare not go. You could wind up being returned to bondage yourself. It is best that you trust my guidance in these matters."

The old farm Negro's voice echoed in William's head—*only a fool Negro trusts a white man.*

That evening, as William helped Florville at the barber shop, he stopped sweeping and leaned on the broom. "Mr. Florville," he said, "neither Washington nor Springfield are safe these days. Maybe it's time I thought of going on up to Canada."

"What makes you say that?"

"Only a few dozen miles of wilderness and a river separate us from slave territory. This place is not so different from Kansas. And I hear Washington is slave territory. Why would I want to be in either place?"

Florville's eyes widened. "In case you missed it, when that slave hunter was here, folks stepped up and defended you. If you are lucky enough to go to Washington as Mr. Lincoln's valet, he will protect you with an entire army. But if you go up to Canada, do you imagine bounty hunters do not cross the border? What friends will you turn to then?"

"Haven't you noticed things changing around here?" William asked.

"Such as?"

"White folks are starting to look at us like we're ink stains on fine linen. We used to walk down the street without notice. Now, we're told to cross over to the opposite side and stay out of white people's way. All this is going on right here in

Springfield—the home of the man who's supposed to stop slavery in its tracks."

"You're just being sensitive," Florville scoffed.

"Have you ever heard of the Knights of the Golden Circle?"

"Those folks are down in Dixie. They don't bother us here."

"There's thousands of them in the southern part of this very state." William's eyes narrowed.

Florville frowned. "Who's filling you with such nonsense?"

"Dozens of folks here in Springfield have joined the Circle. We probably shave and groom some of them. Do you know what the Circle is trying to do? They plan to build an empire on the backs of slaves. From Cuba to the Pacific Ocean. The heart of it will be in Dixie, Mexico, Central America."

"You're talking about that Walker and his grand scheme." Florville waved him off. "It will never happen. He gets stomped down every time he raises his fool head."

William palmed the back of his neck. "I'm starting to think the only place colored folks can go and be safe is Canada. Who knows? Maybe Grace—"

"You just might think yourself out of the best opportunity that ever comes your way, and Grace could be anywhere. Now, finish sweeping and when you're done, stoke the fire."

Springfield, Illinois—June 1860

As summer arrived, William turned up fewer and fewer leads to Grace's whereabouts, and none offered any more substance than a mirage dissolving in waves of heat on a dusty road. The resulting disillusionment fed his anxieties after Lincoln won the Republican nomination for president. The only good news was Lincoln did not require the services of a valet—yet.

Tradition dictated that presidential candidates refrain from traveling and making speeches after their nomination was official. Anyone who wanted a personal encounter with a candidate had to travel to him. Lincoln advocated the Republican cause by writing letters to friends, political allies, and newspapermen.

William helped Lincoln cram two desks into a makeshift campaign office using a room in the Governor's suite on the second floor of the State House. The quarters were so tight the door couldn't be shut for formal meetings. If Lincoln met with more than a couple of people at a time, he and his visitors had to stand in a reception area that was shared with the Illinois Superintendent of Schools.

Often, the line of well-wishers, political allies, and office seekers who came to visit Lincoln extended down the staircase to the front entrance of the courthouse. Lincoln spent many days only greeting visitors. It grieved him to turn anyone away. He hired young John George Nicolay to be his private secretary. Nicolay's steely eyes caught Lincoln's attention when they met out on the Circuit a few years earlier. In those days, Nicolay worked at the Pike County Free Press as a printer's apprentice. Pale, lean, and nearly a foot shorter than Lincoln, Nicolay was a hard fellow to put one past.

Nicolay had a knack for sniffing out opportunists. He ferreted out those who would only waste Lincoln's time. In addition to greeting visitors, Lincoln dispensed with as many as eighty letters in a day. Nicolay decided which ones merited responses and usually wrote the replies. Lincoln reviewed the ones Nicolay declined to answer, and occasionally vetoed his decisions.

Springfield, Illinois—August 1860

When Republicans from across the state descended on Springfield for a rally in Lincoln's honor, 22-year-old Colonel Elmer Ellsworth, leader of the United States Zouave Cadets, became the center of attention. Folks pushed, shoved, and jostled for autographed handbills featuring Ellsworth in his exotic Zouave uniform. Many behaved as if they were battling for the last scoop of grain in the midst of famine. Chief among Ellsworth's admirers were Willie and Tad Lincoln.

If Lincoln spoke that day, few remembered his words, but no one soon forgot the precision maneuvers of the Zouave drill team from Chicago in their flashy uniforms—red kepi hats, red chasseur trousers with white gaiters, and open-fronted, beaded, blue blouses with yellow waist sashes. Many observers went away saying there was no greater military spectacle outside of West Point.

That evening, as Colonel Ellsworth sat at the Lincoln's dinner table, Willie and Tad were under strict orders to remain silent unless spoken to. Compliance with orders of that sort was uncharacteristic for them, but their obedience on the occasion was reinforced by the threat of removal to the kitchen to eat with William and the cook.

When Ellsworth recounted stories of the Zouaves' travels through the Midwest and Northeast, Willie and Tad were mesmerized by his descriptions of the large awestruck crowds. He captured Mrs. Lincoln's heart with his passion for temperance and piety. The Victorian standards he held himself to—no consumption of alcohol, no cavorting with prostitutes, no gambling, and no billiard playing—he also enforced on the Zouaves.

Ellsworth story struck a chord with Lincoln. He grew up poor in Mechanicsville, New York, and was penniless when he moved to Rockford, Illinois, at the age of seventeen to work as a clerk. He fell in love with the daughter of a wealthy family in that city, and her father insisted he find more suitable employment if the young couple hoped to marry. That's when Ellsworth moved to Chicago and began clerking at a law firm.

On discovering Ellsworth's interest in the law, Lincoln offered him a clerkship at Lincoln & Herndon. Mrs. Lincoln invited Ellsworth to board with them if he accepted her husband's invitation. He would have a wonderful influence on her sons. Ellsworth accepted, to everyone's delight. Willie cheered, and Tad exclaimed they finally had a third musketeer.

The boys' jubilation landed like a gut punch on William, as he listened from the kitchen.

* * *

Ellsworth's popularity was a boon to Lincoln's candidacy. The young five-and-a-half-foot Colonel traveled the state, making speeches to rally Illinois men behind the giant from the west. Newspapers carried Ellsworth speeches to eastern audiences, which compared his oratory to that of Senator Stephen Douglas, one of Lincoln's opponents in the presidential race.

One evening when Lincoln kept late hours at the law office and Mrs. Lincoln retired early, Ellsworth and William fell into deep conversation. They had turns reading to Willie and Tad until the boys fell asleep.

William asked, "What is it like to have strangers swooning over you all the time?"

"I try not to notice," Ellsworth replied. "I focus on my task."

"I do my tasks without drawing notice." William rubbed the backs of his hands. "That's my lot in life."

"It doesn't have to be that way."

"Maybe you haven't noticed. My skin is black."

"Tell me, William. What is your greatest dream?"

"Can I trust you to keep a secret?"

Ellsworth pulled out his penknife and handed it to William. Ellsworth rolled up his sleeve to expose the underside of his wrist.

"What are you doing?"

"Cut me," Ellsworth replied.

"Are you crazy?"

"No. We're going to make a pact. We'll mingle our blood and promise to keep each other's secrets."

William clasped Ellsworth's hand with one of his own and held the knife in the other. He laid the blade on Ellsworth's wrist and drew it across, making a small incision. Ellsworth took the knife and cut William's wrist, and they pressed their wounds together, letting their blood mix.

"I promise to keep your secrets as a sacred trust," Ellsworth said.

"I promise to keep your secrets as a sacred trust," William repeated.

When they had bound their wounds, Ellsworth asked, "What did you want to tell me?"

"Mrs. Lincoln is the only person who knows what I'm going to tell you, and I'm sure she won't tell Mr. Lincoln. I don't know what he would do if he knew. But I want something from him."

"What is it?"

"You don't need to know the particulars, but I lost someone and need to find them. Mrs. Lincoln says he might help me."

William shook his head. “I’m not sure. He’d have to free all my people, but it doesn’t sound like he will do that.”

“And you think if he knows your secret, he will think you only serve him out of self-interest and will sack you.”

“Something like that,” William replied.

“Your secret is safe with me, but I’m sure that kind of secret would not get you sacked. It may not even be big enough to warrant a blood pact.”

“It’s all I have, right now.”

“Since we don’t want to waste our blood, we’ll have to make it a friendship pact on top of being a secrecy pact.”

“That may be good in principle but the practice of it may not work out so well.” It was a phrase William had heard Lincoln use, and it seemed like a proper response. Then he added, “After all, I’ve never been friends with a white man.”

Ellsworth grinned. “Nor I with a colored man.”

“I guess that makes us equals, at least in one regard.”

“Yes, and that’s where we’ll start.”

Springfield, Illinois—November 1860

Lincoln hunkered down on election night in the cramped, second-story telegraph office to wait for results from around the country. A young handle-bar mustached operator, John Wilson, handed him the first news from Thurlow Weed, one of the Republican king-makers in New York. “All is safe in this state.” Lincoln was unsure whether the dispatch meant he had won the state’s electoral delegation, or that there had been no violence in the city.

Within minutes of Weed’s report, a telegram from Alton, Illinois, declared, “Republicans have checkmated Democrats’ scheme of fraud." On hearing the latter news, Lincoln strolled down to Watson's Oyster Saloon where Springfield's Republican faithful had gathered to await election news.

The telegraph operator rushed into Watson's after midnight and handed Lincoln a scrap of paper. Lincoln gazed around the room at the expectant faces. Mrs. Lincoln's face was more anxious than all the others. Lincoln's pulse thundered in his ears. He stood and read aloud, "From Philadelphia. The city and state for Lincoln by a decisive majority." Before anyone could let out a cheer, Lincoln pointed in the air and proclaimed, "I think that settles Pennsylvania. Let's hope the news from New York continues to be good."

Shouts and huzzahs rang out from around the room. A crush of friends pressed around Lincoln, offering congratulations. Men fell into each other's arms dancing and singing. Women and men burst into tears, then laughter. Crying and laughing continued all around the room.

A few minutes later, Lincoln slipped through the sea of well-wishers and headed back to the telegraph office, his throat parched. Soon, a dispatch from New York came over the wire. Lincoln read it aloud to a handful who were too eager to wait at Watson's.

> *We tender you our congratulations upon this magnificent victory.*

The tiny room erupted in applause as the message was passed around. Lincoln sank into a chair and buried his face in his hands. Lyman Trumbull—the man who six years earlier won the Senate seat Lincoln had coveted—laid his hand on Lincoln's shoulder. Lincoln stood, and as they embraced, Trumbull shouted, "Uncle Abe, you're the next president."

"Well, the agony is mostly over," Lincoln replied. "Soon we'll all be able to go to bed." He left the telegraph office, ambled downstairs, and paused on the street under a gas lamp. He drew a deep breath, filling his lungs with cool air. His steadfast companion, old yellow floppy-eared Fido, nudged him.

William stepped out of the shadows into the illumination of the streetlamp. He had been unable to sleep, straddling the horns of a dilemma—president's valet or striking out to search for Grace on his own. His throat ached as he offered Lincoln his congratulations.

Church bells began to peal throughout the town, drawing Springfield's sleepy residents to their windows. A cannon fired in the distance. Word of the Republican victory began spreading rapidly. Soon folks of every variety spilled into the streets and filled the courthouse square.

As Lincoln walked home, a parade of friends and jubilant citizens joined him. Fido was not rejoicing, however. The bells and cannon terrified him. William lagged several yards behind the procession.

Despite the chilly night, Eighth Street outside the Lincoln residence became awash with people blowing whistles and horns, singing, dancing, and quelling Lincoln's plans for a good night's sleep. Mrs. Lincoln, who ordinarily would have been mortified over the poverty of her cupboards, beamed as she invited everyone inside for refreshments. William, who had been conscripted into service as a butler by the stubborn hostess, absorbed the brunt of everyone's disappointment when they were offered nothing but water.

When the last guest left, Lincoln climbed the narrow stairs to bed and lay awake deciding whom to pick for his Cabinet.

Springfield, Illinois—December 1860

Over the course of several icy weeks, Lincoln hid away for a time each day—with Fido as his only company—and scribbled out a manifesto to be his guiding star as the nation's Chief Magistrate. When he was satisfied with what he had written, he read it to Florville and William.

> *Without the Constitution and the Union, we could not have attained—but even these, are not the primary cause of—our great prosperity. There is something back of these two things, entwining them more closely about the human heart. That something is the principle of "Liberty to all"—the principle that clears the path for all, gives hope to all, and, by consequence, enterprise and industry to all.*
>
> *The expression of that principle in our Declaration of Independence was most happy and fortunate ... but no oppressed people will fight and endure as our fathers did, without the promise of something better than a mere change of masters.*
>
> *The assertion of that principle was a word "fitly spoken" which has proved an "apple of gold" to us. The Union and the Constitution are "the settings of silver" framed around the principle. The frame was made, not to conceal or destroy the apple, but to adorn and preserve it. The setting was made for the apple—not the apple for the setting.*
>
> *So let us act, in a way that neither setting nor apple shall ever be blurred or bruised or broken.*

Florville stroked his chin. “Certainly, trading one kind of oppression for another wouldn’t be any kind of freedom worth fighting for.”

“I understand that part,” William said. “But the end isn’t exactly true, is it? I mean, even though the apple promised ‘all men are created equal,’ the setting guarantees slave owners the right to make some men into property. So, how does it adorn or protect the apple?”

“Be more respectful,” Florville scolded. “Mr. Lincoln is our country’s new leader.”

Lincoln replied, “I reckon I have told the boy; honesty is the highest form of loyalty. I will consider what you have said, William. If it needs some polishing up, I will make it right.”

CHAPTER FIVE

Springfield, Illinois—February 1861

William stood at the train depot ticket window and glimpsed Mrs. Lincoln approaching with Willie and Tad in tow. William pulled his cap down to hide his face.

"William." Mrs. Lincoln beckoned.

He counted out his fare.

"William. I am speaking to you. Have you gone deaf?"

"Boy," the man in the ticket window said, "the lady's talking to you. Has no one taught you to show respect?"

William retrieved his money and moved away from the window. "Sorry, Mrs. Lincoln, I didn't—"

"Never mind that," she replied. "What are you doing here?"

William stared at his shoes. "I'm buying passage to Chicago."

"What on earth for? The train to Washington leaves in a few days, and your passage already should be arranged."

William kept his head down. "Yes, ma'am."

"Why is Mr. Lincoln sending you to Chicago?"

"He isn't sending me. I've decided to go north to Canada."

"Mr. Lincoln has spoken to you, has he not?"

"Not about going anywhere, ma'am."

"Has he not offered to take you as his valet?"

William glanced up at her. "No, ma'am."

"Well, we shall see about that. But for now, you're coming with me."

She angled her way to the ticket window, smiling at the ticket agent as she cut in front of another customer. "Excuse me. I am Mrs. Lincoln, soon to be Mrs. President of the United States. My servant requires passage to Chicago."

"Yes, Mrs. Lincoln," the agent replied.

"We're off to do some shopping while my husband prepares to leave for the inauguration in Washington City. We shall meet his train in Indianapolis after we finish our business in Chicago."

William tensed the way he had on the roadway the morning he first encountered Florville. This time there was no use contemplating escape. He had learned from experience that once Mrs. Lincoln's mind was set, her will was iron-clad.

Chicago—February 1861

While Mrs. Lincoln and her two young sons settled in at Chicago's Tremont House, a uniformed mulatto led William through the servants' entrance at the rear of the hotel and down a narrow stairway. They passed the kitchen, the ironing stations, and a row of caldrons before arriving at William's basement quarters—a sparse room next to the laundry. After William dropped his threadbare carpet bag next to the bunk, his escort surveyed him as if inspecting damaged merchandise.

"Change into your uniform and wait here," the escort said.

"I'm wearing the only uniform I own," William replied.

"That will not do."

"I'm not really a servant."

"What is your purpose in being at Tremont House?" the escort asked.

"I'm traveling with Mrs. Abraham Lincoln."

"We'll see about that. Stay put until I check with the cashier."

The escort closed the door behind him as he left. *Click.* The doorknob jiggled. William was locked in. He sat on the bunk and stared at his scuffed shoes. Just when he had chosen his own star and headed to Canada in search of Grace, his life rolled backwards. It was a foolish notion. He knew nothing about Canada. She could be anywhere up there or nowhere at all. For all he knew, she was breaking her back on some sugar plantation along the Mississippi. Maybe she was nursing white babies in a mansion in Washington City—where Mrs. Lincoln was determined for him to go be the president's valet. It was possible she was right. Washington might be the logical place to start.

A skeleton key slid into the keyhole. *Clack.* The doorknob rattled, turned. His escort reappeared in the doorway. "Your mistress has called for you. Follow me."

William followed him up a back stairway to Mrs. Lincoln's third floor suite.

Willie and Tad sat at a table set for dinner. Mrs. Lincoln smiled. "In the morning you will be here at seven o'clock sharp to dress my sons and serve breakfast. After that we will pay a visit to Cooley, Farwell & Company on Randolph Street. Their junior partner, Mr. Marshall Field, has agreed to teach you how to fit and care for Mr. Lincoln's new wardrobe. I will be purchasing him a frock coat and silk hat for starters. Oh, and you will be measured for a valet uniform."

"But I don't—"

"I understand. This young woman you have told me about—your brother's widow?"

"Yes, ma'am, Grace is her name."

"And a child," Mrs. Lincoln folded her hands in front of her.

"Maddie," he said.

"You intend to charge up to a foreign land and find them all by yourself. But you must see how unwise that would be. Soon my husband will have the power and the wherewithal to help you like no one else can. Imagine how much easier it will be to find them if he brings freedom to all your people. Draw close to him. Make him your ally. Providence has opened a door for you, and I am its doorkeeper. Do as I say. You shall thank me when you see her lovely face again."

"Mr. Lincoln will help me find them?"

"Maybe not instantly." She wrinkled her forehead. "He will have grave responsibilities that affect our whole nation. But if you are patient and do not burden him with your individual troubles, I am certain you will not be disappointed in the end."

William exhaled a long breath.

"There is another thing we will work on, young man." Mrs. Lincoln draped a neatly folded server towel over William's forearm. "I say this for your own benefit. As a household servant, it will never be your place to display your emotions or draw attention to yourself. You must remain unheard and for all practical purposes, invisible, unless directed otherwise."

William had learned that lesson well from the stern instruction of his Mormon mistress. He didn't need to be told to stay out of white folks' way, keep his nose down, and let his work do his talking. If that was what he had to do while he waited for Mr. Lincoln to help him find Grace, it was the way things would have to be.

Springfield, Illinois—February 1861

Jamieson Jenkins, a colored neighbor, helped Lincoln tie up and label his trunks and deposit them at Cherney House, an old hotel in Springfield. Jenkins was a drayman with a daring past. Ten years earlier he helped hide a dozen runaway slaves from a posse of bounty hunters. When the posse left town, he transported the fugitives to Bloomington—the next stop on the Illinois Underground Railroad. Fifteen years before that, Jenkins fled slavery in North Carolina.

When they finished with Lincoln's luggage, Jenkins drove him to the law office and waited under an awning while Lincoln went inside to confer with Herndon. After they reviewed the office books and discussed plans for resolving various open cases, Lincoln threw himself on the old sofa and lay there staring at the ceiling.

After a long silence, Lincoln asked, "How long have we been together?"

"Over sixteen years," Herndon replied.

"We've never had a cross word in all that time."

"No, indeed we have not, except regarding my appetite for whisky." Herndon neglected to mention their differences over abolition—him being the radical and Lincoln a fence straddler.

"Others have tried to supplant you." Lincoln's voice cracked. "They hoped to secure a law practice by hanging onto my coattails. Despite your faults, which I've criticized only privately, I have valued your trustworthiness and loyalty too much to be tempted by any of them."

"You've been like a father."

"And you, like a son." Lincoln rose from the sofa and gathered a bundle of books and papers to take with him. At the door, he paused. "That signboard down at the foot of the stairway—let it hang where it is, undisturbed. Give our clients the understanding that the election of a president makes no change in the firm of Lincoln and Herndon. If I live, I am coming back, and then we will go right on as if nothing ever happened."

Herndon stood erect. "I have always considered it an honor to have my name beside yours."

Lincoln lingered for a moment, dabbing a tear before he turned and took a last look at the old quarters.

The following morning, Jenkins brought his wagon through muddy streets to Cherney House and helped Lincoln load his luggage in a drizzling rain. On their way to the train depot, they stopped at Florville's shop for a visit. Lincoln and Florville agreed to not say good-bye, the expression had too much of a final ring to it. Instead, they reminisced about their long friendship and laughed about the times Lincoln and colleagues—including rivals like Stephen Douglas—gathered in the shop to tell stories or argue into the night. Florville promised to care for Lincoln's house until he returned from Washington.

Lincoln paused on his way out the door. "Billy, have you seen William lately?"

"You mean he did not pay his respects before he left?"

"Left for where?"

Florville scratched his head. "Said he was going off to follow his star."

"What on earth did he mean by that?" Lincoln asked.

"Heaven only knows what goes through young men's heads these days."

"Well, I'm sorry I didn't get a chance to bid him farewell."

Florville cupped the back of his head. "Maybe he was afraid Mrs. Lincoln would try to talk him into going along as your valet."

"I'll have to admit, once she sets her mind on something, she often gets her way. But just the same."

"Water under the bridge now," Florville cut in. "Just take care of yourself back in Washington."

They shook hands, and Lincoln boarded Jenkins' wagon.

Presidential Special—February 1861

John Nicolay and John Hay, Lincoln's secretaries, waited on the platform when Lincoln arrived at the depot to board a special train to Washington City. Lincoln's old friend from the Circuit, Hill Lamon had joined them along with Bob Lincoln and Elmer Ellsworth. Lamon, a mountain of a man who stood nose-to-nose with Lincoln, was going along as Lincoln's principal bodyguard.

Lincoln ascended the platform and made a brief farewell speech to the friends and neighbors who had gathered at the depot. After the speech, he and his party boarded the three-coach *Presidential Special.* Lincoln shook his head as he inspected the private car provided for the exclusive use of his family and guests. He found the special car, fitted with individual sleeping berths, too luxurious for comfort. Its crimson walls were decorated with star-studded blue silk panels, and the black walnut furniture was upholstered in Mazarin cloth and trimmed with colored braids and gold tassels.

As the *Presidential Special* pulled away from Springfield, Lincoln and Nicolay left the private coach and sat in one of the two common cars filled with newspapermen and politicians. Lincoln patted Nicolay's knee. "I will soon take an oath to preserve and protect the Constitution, but already, the Union and its foundations are being rocked and its bonds ripped apart." Lincoln stared out the window, his eyes misting as his beloved countryside rolled past. Memories, some joyful and others laced with pain, consumed his thoughts.

The train pulled into the Indianapolis depot at five o'clock in the afternoon, and Mrs. Lincoln arrived with Willie and Tad on the ten o'clock train from Chicago. When Mrs. Lincoln strode into the hotel lobby, she made a beeline to Bob and looped her wrist over his arm. "My dearest boy," she said. "It's wonderful to see your bright smile. Come, show us to our suite. I'm sure your brothers are as exhausted as I am." After a few steps, she turned back to her husband. "Oh, William is outside tending our luggage. You two need to talk."

"William?"

"Must I repeat myself? And settle with the driver."

Outside the hotel's front entrance, William stood with his shoulders pulled back, donning a new vested black suit, black shirt, and derby. Lincoln paid the driver and tipped the waiting bellman who had already stacked Mrs. Lincoln's trunks on a baggage cart.

Lincoln turned to William. "Do you mind telling me what's going on?"

"I was at the depot in Springfield on my way to Canada when Mrs. Lincoln walked up and insisted that I go with her to Chicago. I'm not sure how, but she talked me into accompanying you to Washington. She even bought me these clothes."

"Why were you off to Canada?"

"To look for someone I promised to protect, but I don't think it was a wise plan, at least not for now."

Lincoln arched his brow. "What does Mrs. Lincoln plan to do with you in Washington?"

"She has the idea that I'm to become your valet."

"My valet?"

"Yes, sir."

"I can dress myself."

"I know, sir. But she said you can't trim your own hair and that scruffy beard needs some attention."

Lincoln stroked his chin. "I reckon it might be nice to have someone trim these new whiskers."

"I don't want you thinking this is going to be permanent," William lowered his head. "I have plans of my own."

"As you should." Lincoln pinched the bridge of his nose. "Now, go settle in downstairs. I will make arrangements with the cashier and turn in for the night."

"Should I see you upstairs and help you get ready for bed?"

"For Heaven's sake, no. And you do not need to rush upstairs in the morning. We have a long way to Washington. That gives us time to figure out how to make this arrangement work."

CHAPTER SIX

Presidential Special—February 1861

The *Presidential Special* stood by at the Buffalo, New York, train depot, preparing for the Lincolns' departure to Albany. Springfield was six days and dozens of stops behind them.

Pre-dawn shadows tracked the open carriage as it creaked and skidded through empty, snow-laden streets along the route to the station. Lamon and Ellsworth rode with the driver. William stood on the footboard, bracing against the frigid air. He studied a clear black sky, wondering if there was a North Star anywhere with his name on it.

Mrs. Lincoln huddled with Willie and Tad, a coarse woolen blanket draped across their laps. The boys tormented each other, unnoticed by their mother, who remained groggy from a too-short night's sleep. Mrs. Lincoln's gloved hand caressed the blanket in an unconscious rhythm, smoothing its wrinkles. Her pale face bore the countenance of an undertaker accompanying a corpse to its burial. Bob and his father sat opposite them. Lincoln's left eye drifted while his good eye focused on Bob, who plucked at nubs of pilling on the blanket he shared with his father. Bob's tightly drawn lips telegraphed his dismay over the rickety carriage that reminded him too much of his father's coarseness.

Mrs. Lincoln and her sons settled into sleeping berths upon boarding the train. Willie and Tad ignored their father's hushed warning to leave the others in peace. When Lincoln scolded them, Mrs. Lincoln rebuked him for his impatience. He failed to understand what he had done to provoke her. She confounded him almost as much as the southern men whom he had vowed repeatedly to leave unmolested, yet nonetheless, they railed against him.

Lincoln went through to the forward car. A cloud of cigar smoke mixed with locomotive fumes stung his eyes and burned his lungs. He held his breath, stifling the urge to cough. Journalists and political dignitaries, packed tighter than a barrel of cured pork on its way to market, jostled for seats on benches. All the way from Springfield, they had swarmed Lincoln like piglets on a sow's teats, rooting for secret details of the new administration's plans or angling for favors for themselves, friends, and relatives. That morning, however, they listed about in a fog, as if hung over from a night of hard drinking.

Nicolay shooed away the men sitting beside him on a rear bench and beckoned Lincoln to the newly vacated spots.

Lincoln gestured for Nicolay to stay seated as he stepped past and assumed a defensive position by the window.

"You should be resting." Nicolay glanced back at the passage to the sleeping car.

"There's no peace back there."

"You're a little hoarse. Can I get you something?"

Lincoln rested his head against the window. "You keep the wolves at bay." His eyes fell shut. Images of the first several days of their journey filled his mind. Crowds pressing in ... open carriages ... pelting rain, stinging snow, biting winds ... impromptu receptions ... hurried wardrobe changes ... deafening shouts from throngs of thousands ... roaring artillery salutes ... assassination threats ... radical militias lurking ... detours ... dark tunnels ... blocked tracks ... a gun misfiring, shattering the window of an inn one evening as they dined, shards of glass raining down on his wife.

After a few moments, Lincoln opened his eyes and watched snow fall in the fields as they rolled past. In his youth, his father sent him into snowy woods to check traps. Undaunted by the specter of punishment, he loitered in a secluded vale, cloaked in silence, mesmerized by curtains of glistening crystals flitting earthward and kissing the pristine carpet laid by those that had fallen before. His boyhood days having passed, his only refuge had become a sanctuary in the catacombs of his mind.

A delicate flake caught the window beside him ... fluttered for a moment in the train's draft ... slid to the sill ... its path like the trail of a tear. He recalled lines from his favorite poem, *Mortality* by William Knox. He carried a copy wherever he went, though after many years of reciting it, he knew every line by heart.

Yea! Hope and despondency, pleasure and pain,
Are mingled together in sunshine and rain;
And the smile and the tear, the song and the dirge,
Still follow each other, like surge upon surge.

At every stop, crowds clamored to know whether there would be union or disunion, war or peace. They demanded assurance he would stand firmly against the extension of slavery and preserve the victory Republicans won at the ballot boxes. He was allotted only a few minutes in each place to greet the citizenry and imbue them with inspiration of which he was in short supply.

He would readily trade a year of his remaining life for each day by which the time until Inauguration Day could be shortened. Until sworn in, he could only wring his hands and hope that foes and friends alike might embrace the words he spoke at Cooper Institute a year earlier.

Let us have faith that right makes might, and in that faith, let us dare to do our duty as we understand it.

A commotion at the other end of the railcar drew Nicolay's attention. He nudged Lincoln. The *New York Tribune* editor, Horace Greeley, had been bantering with other journalists since he boarded the train at the last minute in Buffalo. Suddenly he was elbowing his way in their direction.

Greeley stopped in the aisle next to them. "Mr. President-elect."

Lincoln gestured for Nicolay to surrender his seat. "It's still Lincoln and no amount of pomp will change that."

"As you wish, but you are the leader of Republicans across this land. Soon you will be installed as the Chief Magistrate of the nation, and you have many of us worried. Only days ago, with calamity pressing in on every front, you declared before a throng of 60,000 in Columbus nothing is wrong, no one is suffering. The next day at Cleveland you addressed a vast number gathered in driving snow and asserted the crisis threatening the very existence of our Union is an artificial one." Greeley shook his head. "The truth is nothing is going right."

"When our train stopped in Cincinnati," Lincoln responded, "I told a host of German men, 'I deem it my duty to wait before I express decidedly what course I shall pursue.' And until the inauguration, I shall continue to perform that duty."

Greeley's eyes narrowed. "May I remind you, sir, seven states have approved bills of secession. The Union is disintegrating. Our ships, our forts are attacked. For God's sake, our flag has been fired upon. An enemy who is intent on our destruction has seized property duly belonging to the government. We are already at war. It would seem that your duty is to declare your intention to put down this rebellion and to do so quickly."

"No one needs to remind me of the present state of affairs." Lincoln glared at him. "Nor do they need to point out that any misstep could ignite a firestorm, which currently I have no power to put out. The government can have only one Chief Magistrate, and right now that is Mr. Buchanan. Fourteen days hence, when the mantle of authority passes onto my shoulders, these difficulties shall be resolved. Until then, I must leave the pot unstirred."

Nicolay returned from the other end of the car. "We're arriving at Batavia."

At half past six o'clock in the morning, Lincoln stepped onto the railcar's rear platform and offered a few words of greeting to a small crowd. While he was speaking his last words, the train pulled away from the station and proceeded toward Rochester.

Exhausted, Lincoln returned to the private coach and reclined on one of the brocaded sofas. With his eyes closed, the half-hour passage seemed like only a few minutes.

"Sir?" William shook Lincoln.

"Yes?" Lincoln sat up, rubbing his eyes.

"It's just after seven o'clock. We're pulling into Rochester Station."

"Very well."

William handed Lincoln his hat.

"Father?" Mrs. Lincoln called down from her berth, still in her nightclothes.

"Yes, Mother."

"Cover yourself with a shawl or you will catch your death of cold ... and for Heaven's sake, leave that tattered old hat here. It's an embarrassment."

"Please, do as she says," Bob added from his berth.

Lincoln kept a firm grip on the brim of his hat. "Yes, Mother."

William draped a grey shawl over Lincoln's stooped shoulders.

The train rolled slowly past the depot for nearly a block before coming to a stop. A wave of people pressed in around the rear of the car. After being introduced, Lincoln gave a short speech, and within six minutes the train started out toward the next stop. He retreated to the sleeping car and tried again to take a short nap.

William woke Lincoln on the train's arrival at Syracuse. Once more, he stepped onto the rear platform to the cheers of a wild congregation. They insisted he step over to a makeshift stage that had been cobbled together hastily. He replied,

> *I see you have erected a handsome platform for me, and I presume you expect me to speak from it. If I should go upon it, you will also expect me to deliver a much longer speech than I am prepared to give. I mean no discourtesy. But, while I am unwilling to go upon your platform, you are not at liberty to infer that I am not bound by that other Platform with which my name is connected.*

The audience responded with mixed emotions. Lincoln imagined many only wanted to hear the words "Repeal the Fugitive Slave Law." He gritted his teeth. If he gave them the words they wanted to hear, he would ignite a flame he was yet powerless to extinguish.

The train pulled out of Syracuse and rumbled toward Utica as snow began falling again. Nicolay handed Lincoln a telegram. Lincoln's throat tightened. Jefferson Davis had been inaugurated leader of the secessionists. The country had two presidents. The news compounded Lincoln's fatigue and darkened his mood.

The advice of a doctor came back to him—one whom he consulted many years earlier concerning his spells of melancholy. The doctor advised him to avoid idleness. Lincoln left the sleeping coach and went forward to join journalists, politicians, and friends. He occupied himself for the remainder of the hour-and-ten-minute jaunt telling stories and swapping jokes.

Lincoln returned to the private car on his way to the train's rear platform on its arrival in Utica. He found a new broadcloth overcoat and a hatbox laid out for him. Mrs. Lincoln grumbled that she was tired of his uncouth appearance and had purchased a new hat and coat while in Chicago. During the previous stop, she instructed William to take away the tattered old hat and coat and bring out the new ones. Like it or not, Lincoln acknowledged he would have to start behaving in a manner consistent with his new rank in society.

As William followed Lincoln onto the rear platform, Lincoln whispered, “Mrs. Lincoln does not understand the bond a man forges with his hat, especially during long months on the Circuit. But I'm willing to suffer the discomfort of being gentrified if it keeps the peace in our home and country.”

“Yes, sir.” William replied. “She can be a hard one to please.”

“Don't judge her harshly,” Lincoln cautioned. “Providence has been unkind to her and she possesses a delicate disposition.” Lincoln handed the new top hat to William. “I reckon I will be bonding with you over the days to come, as well as with that new hat. A man needs a good barber to keep his secrets.”

The stop in Utica lasted fewer than ten minutes.

New York City—February 1861

Lincoln's nerves were raw from a tortured two-day stop in Albany, New York, when Mrs. Lincoln began harassing him over a patronage position for her brother-in-law, William Wallace. Lincoln dabbed clammy sweat from his forehead and escaped to the passenger car to join Nicolay on a bench.

Nicolay handed him copies of the latest New York newspapers and explained, “High water on the Hudson River is forcing us to take several detours. The train's crew will have to change engines for three different railroads. They also plan to add additional cars. Even so, our arrival in New York City should be on schedule. And we'll still make those six quick stops along the route for you to greet crowds."

Lincoln opened Thurlow Weed's *Albany Journal*, holding it up to deter anyone who might try to engage him. Weed's headline read, "President-elect's chaotic visit to Albany last evening." Lincoln agreed it was chaotic—club-wielding militiamen descending on riotous crowds at the Albany depot, then politicians plotting to leverage the nation's tensions for their own financial gains. Lincoln turned the pages to find something entertaining.

On one of the back pages, John Wilkes Booth, a young actor, received better reviews for his appearance in the New York State Capital than Lincoln did. Lincoln was not surprised by Booth's success. The rising star came from a family of gifted actors. The *Journal* called Booth's Gayety Theater performance in *The Apostate* brilliant and declared him one of the finest young actors the country had ever produced. If it had not been for the governor's dinner on the same night, The Lincolns would have attended the show.

He set aside the *Journal* and picked up the *New York Herald*. Its editorial, in advance of his arrival, was unkind.

> *What will Mr. Lincoln do when he arrives? Will he kiss our girls and give a twirl to the whiskers he has begun to cultivate? Will he tell our merchants, groaning under the pressure of the greatest political convulsion ever experienced in America, that 'nobody is hurt' or that 'marching troops into South Carolina' to its fortresses is 'no invasion'?*

Lincoln slammed the newspaper down on the bench. He had made his intentions clear for decades. Slavery must be contained and allowed to die out on its own. It had not been that long ago that he had warned:

> *The world expresses apprehension that the one retrograde institution in America is fatally violating the noblest political system the world has ever seen. Let us re-adopt the Declaration of Independence. If we do this, we shall not only have saved the Union; but we shall have made it forever worthy of the saving.*

Moments later Lincoln's old friend and bodyguard, Hill Lamon, stood next to him, arms folded across his massive chest. "May I join you two?" he asked.

Lincoln gestured to Nicolay, and Nicolay slid toward the aisle to make room.

Lamon picked up the newspapers and squeezed between Lincoln and Nicolay. "We've had a pretty tame ride so far, but from now on, we might as well be behind enemy lines."

"In case you've never noticed," Lincoln replied, "I can be quite persuasive."

"It's one thing to charm a room full of abolitionists or a jury, but an angry mob armed with pistols and knives?" Lamon tucked the newspaper under his arm.

"New York City is a long way from South Carolina or Tennessee," Lincoln added. "I doubt any of those southern pistols can carry a shot long enough to reach us here. Besides, the railroad superintendent insists they have taken precautions."

"Informants tell me New York is crawling with rebel spies," Lamont countered. "And the city's administration can't be trusted to protect you. Hell, the mayor would have his city secede if he thought the governor would back him with militia. Even the bankers are murmuring that your death is the only thing that can keep them from financial ruin."

"They presume they alone suffer abuse," Lincoln said. "I once endured a tedious trip on a steamboat from Louisville to St. Louis. On board were ten or a dozen slaves, shackled together with irons. That sight has continued to torment me, and I see something like it every time I touch the Ohio or any other slave-border. How is it fair that I must tolerate a thing which continually exercises the power to make me miserable? The great body of Northern people crucify their feelings over slavery just as I do, in hopes of maintaining the Constitution and the Union." Lincoln gazed out the window. "As for the danger that awaits us out there, who am I to stand in the way of Providence? If she dictates that I should be struck down before inauguration, then so be it."

"Providence be damned," Lamon growled. "She will have to fight through me to harm a single hair on your head."

Lincoln rested his head against the window and closed his eyes. Words of advice from former President Fillmore ran through his mind.

> *The ways of Providence are inscrutable. As mortals we bow to his awful dispensation without murmur. Our duty is not to inquire, but to submit. Maybe calamities come to teach humility and moderation, to soften the asperity of political warfare, and chasten the inordinate longings of ambition.*

The *Presidential Special* arrived on time at Hudson River Station in New York City where a rush of spectators collided with police lines. The blue-clad constables fought doggedly to keep the platform clear so Lincoln's party could disembark.

William appeared in the aisle, holding Lincoln's coat, shawl, and hat. He gaped at the spectacle.

Lincoln turned to Lamon. "Is there no receiving committee?"

"Thank God, no," Lamon muttered. "That would only complicate matters. There are likely a dozen assassins in that horde, each waiting for confusion to set in to make their move."

Scores of well-wishers crashed through a breach in the police line and blocked the platform.

Lincoln grimaced. "Well, they have their confusion." He told Ellsworth, Nicolay, and William to hold back a few moments with Mrs. Lincoln and sons while he distracted the crowd.

Lamon grabbed Lincoln's arm. "What the hell are you thinking?"

"I'll create a diversion ... give them a chance to lead Mother and the boys to our carriages."

"Did you hear anything I just said?" Lamon gripped tighter.

"It appears you are the one not listening." Lincoln broke free. "Now help me make a way for them."

On Lincoln's signal, Lamon launched himself into the mob and blazed a path to the platform. Close on Lamon's heels, Lincoln began shaking every hand he could grasp. He was nearly swept away by the men and boys pushing, elbowing, and grabbing at his hands and coat. Cold sweat dotted Lincoln's forehead. The brave words he spoke earlier to Lamon taunted him.

Before calamity struck, several Republican partisans emerged from the crowd and surrounded Lincoln and his family. They locked arms, forming a wedge, and pressed against the sea of humanity to blaze a path to three shabby, open-topped barouches. Lincoln's family and Ellsworth boarded one of the carriages while Lincoln's secretaries took the second one. Lincoln, Lamon, and William climbed into the third. An escort of mounted policemen formed around their carriages.

While porters scrambled to gather and load the presidential party's luggage, the Lincolns' shivered under a crisp, blue sky. Mrs. Lincoln complained they would catch their deaths of cold in the frigid air if they didn't get to Astor House at once. When the last of the Lincolns' trunks was found and loaded, the parade marshal cracked his whip and goaded his horse forward. Hundreds more conveyances of all types slowly fell in behind the Lincolns and formed a double line. A throng of hundreds followed on foot, giving half-hearted cheers.

An eerie hush greeted the procession as it turned onto Broadway. The avenue was clear—all traffic had been detoured onto cross streets. Reticent spectators filled doorways, balconies, and windows while a continuous fringe of subdued humanity lined the rooftops.

Lincoln nudged Lamon. "What do you make of this quiet?"

"They're sizing you up. I'll breathe easier once you're settled in at the hotel."

When the Lincolns arrived at Astor House, Lincoln stepped onto the sidewalk and stared up at the granite edifice looming above them. The hotel where he stayed on his previous visit to the city stood as a welcoming friend among suspicious strangers. Lincoln stretched his arms and legs then turned around. While he had been surveying the grand hotel, a silent horde of tens of thousands hemmed in around him. Unlike crowds at other stops, no one clamored for a speech. At least they spared him that.

A small boy ogled him, and the father eyed Lincoln the way one would measure a tree for felling in the woods. Lincoln tipped his hat, turned, and walked through to Astor's lobby. He released the breath he'd been holding and hoped Lamon would never know how relieved he was that no pistol-brandishing or knife-wielding assassin sprang out of the crowd.

William unloaded the trunks for the bellman then circled to the back of the hotel in search of the servants' entrance.

* * *

Thurlow Weed drove Lincoln the next morning to the opulent Fifth Avenue home of Mrs. Julia Irving Bowdoin. The city's most prosperous merchants had gathered there for breakfast and to greet the president-elect. Mrs. Bowdoin's father, Moses Grinnell, was a shipping magnate, influential campaigner for the Republican cause, former Congressman, and New York Chamber of Commerce president.

Lincoln had barely removed his coat when several political opponents of New York Senator William Seward cornered him, pleading that the senator be left out of the incoming Cabinet. One of the men clasped Lincoln's shoulder and drew him close. It was a gesture designed to reduce Lincoln's advantage of stature. Almost in a whisper, the man boasted, "There are likely one hundred millionaires in this room."

"Is that right?" Lincoln said. "I'm a millionaire myself. I got a minority of a million votes last November."

Some of the men who overheard Lincoln's reply glared. Like predators on the scent of fresh blood, they gathered around him and began talking all at once, leveling the same questions he had been asked at every stop on his journey. What was the new administration's plan regarding the nation's troubles? Why had he not provided guidance to the Peace Conference that was meeting in Washington to avert disunion and possible war?

Lincoln addressed the entire gathering.

> *Many years ago, when I was a young lawyer, and Illinois was little settled except on her Southern border, I, with other lawyers, used to ride the Circuit accompanied by a judge, journeying in quest of business from county-seat to county-seat. Once, after a long spell of pouring rain had flooded the whole Country, transforming small creeks into rivers, we encountered some of these swollen streams and crossed them with much difficulty. Still ahead of us was Fox River, larger than all the rest. We could not help saying to each other, 'If these streams give us so much trouble, how shall we get over Fox River?'*
>
> *Darkness fell before we had reached that stream. We all stopped at a log tavern, had our horses put out, and resolved to pass the night. Here, we fell in with the Methodist Presiding Elder of the circuit, who rode it in all weather, knew all its ways, and could tell us all about Fox River. So, we gathered around him, and asked him if he knew about crossing Fox River. 'Oh yes,' he replied. 'I know all about Fox River. I have crossed it often, and understand it well, but I have one fixed rule with regard to Fox River—I never cross it until I reach it.'*

"So that is what I have to say. I never cross a thing until I reach it."

A large number of the guests walked away, murmuring.

That evening Lincoln attended a new Verdi opera while Mrs. Lincoln hosted a reception at Astor House. When he returned to the hotel, he found her sitting on her bed, sobbing. He could make out only a few of her sputtering words—Belmont ... interloper ... unfit. As Mrs. Lincoln calmed, he learned that Mrs. August Belmont, a leading figure in society, was conspicuously absent from Mrs. Lincoln's reception. Mrs. Belmont had broadcast to all of New York society that the Lincolns were interlopers from the Middle West and were unfit to take up residence in the nation's mansion.

Lincoln tried to console his wife, but her rage grew hotter. She stood and snatched the gloves he had just worn to the theater and shook them in his face. "Indolent fool!" she exclaimed.

Lincoln stepped back.

"Where are the white gloves I had William lay out for you?" Her eyes narrowed. "Tell me you did not wear these black ones to the opera."

"They're the best pair I own," he replied.

"I can imagine what people must be saying about us tonight," she screamed. "My husband dresses like an undertaker to go to the opera. No wonder people call us 'interlopers from the Middle West.'"

Lincoln grabbed the gloves. "These are a perfectly fine pair of gloves."

"Gentlemen wear white gloves to theater," she shouted. "Surely, yours were the only black ones in the house, and I can promise you everyone took notice. We shall certainly be the juicy gossip about town tomorrow. That is how people will remember your visit to this great metropolis. You can rest assured I shall set William straight, as well. He ignored my instructions."

Lincoln slinked out of his wife's suite and found William waiting in the hallway. "How much of that did you hear?" Lincoln asked.

"Enough to know I'll be in all kinds of trouble in the morning." William shook his head.

"Don't fret," Lincoln said. "She's had a hard evening and her nerves are delicate. The storm will pass as it always does. Now, if we are to form a bond, we must be each other's watchman."

Lincoln paced the floor into the early morning hours, weighed down by the double duty of holding the Union together and keeping his wife happy. William lay awake in the basement servants' quarters, wondering how many slipups Mrs. Lincoln would tolerate before she closed the door Providence had opened.

CHAPTER SEVEN

Philadelphia—February 1861

Lincoln nudged Lamon in the seat next to him as the *Presidential Special* left New York City and rumbled toward Philadelphia the next afternoon. "I told you we would escape with our hides intact. Not a single pistol or knife presented in our direction."

"You're impossible," Lamon complained. "You should find someone else for my job. Someone you'll take seriously."

"There is not a man in the world I trust more than you." Lincoln patted Lamon's knee. "I reckon I take liberties because I know you will keep me safe."

"I'll do my best not to let you down. But don't tempt Fate. Her patience may run out."

"When I crossed over to New Jersey earlier this morning and addressed their legislature," Lincoln replied, "the majority did not think I am the right man for the office. Yet they greeted me as the constitutional president of the United States. That gives me hope that our tradition of solving differences without violence can be sustained."

Lamon stood and jostled his way to the front of the passenger car.

Lincoln held a copy of Weems' *Life of Washington* in his lap. It was the first book he owned as a boy. He traced the edges of its binding with his long fingers. A lump formed in his throat as he turned to Weems' account of young Washington consoling his mother after a fire destroyed the roof of their house.

> *We can make a far better roof that, if kept together well, will last forever, but if you take it apart, you will make the house ten thousand times worse than it was.*

* * *

In Philadelphia, Lincoln and his party checked in at the Continental Hotel. He ate dinner with his family and stood in a receiving line for nearly two hours. By half past ten o'clock, his achy, gloved hands were damp with sweat. Norman Judd, one of the Republican leaders from Illinois who journeyed with him from Springfield, rescued him from the crush of well-wishers. As Judd escorted him upstairs, Lincoln coveted a long bed and an uninterrupted night's sleep. Instead, they went to a room where a bearded, derby-wearing Scotsman waited.

Judd started to make introductions, but Lincoln interrupted. "Mr. Pinkerton and I are already acquainted from railroad business." He extended his hand to Pinkerton. "Good to see you again, Allan. I will be happy to discuss your patronage request tomorrow. Say, after the flag raising?"

Pinkerton shook Lincoln's hand. "Good evening, sir."

"You need to hear the detective out," Judd said.

"You're here on detective business?" Lincoln assessed Pinkerton's deep-set eyes.

"Yes," Pinkerton replied in a thick brogue. "Rumors persist that there is a great deal of unrest between here and Washington City. The railroad company hired me to uncover threats of sabotage against the line. I have found nothing of the kind, but I did turn up evidence of a plot to assassinate you as you pass through Baltimore the day after tomorrow."

"We have a security man from the railroad, Mr. William Wood," Lincoln replied. "Is he aware of this?"

Judd nodded. "He's been informed."

"I appreciate your concern," Lincoln said. "But my man Lamon often raises alarms over rumors like this. All have turned out to be groundless."

The detective listed names of conspirators and described taverns and brothels where his agents posed as secessionist sympathizers. He detailed the manner in which the deed would be carried out.

Judd and Pinkerton sat silently as Lincoln rose and paced the floor, his hands clasped behind his back. Images swirled in Lincoln's head. A box thought to be a bomb ... runaway slaves attacking in the night, intent on murder ... sister Sally, precious Annie gone too young from this world ... laying mother in a narrow pine coffin ... rain pelting his back as he lay prostrate on their graves ... his lungs burning ... almost drowning in a raging creek.

Pinkerton broke the silence. "We strongly suspect Baltimore's chief of police is complicit in the plot. At the least, he cannot be counted on to ensure your safety. You must leave quietly for Washington tonight."

"No." Lincoln stopped pacing. "I have promised to raise the new thirty-four-star flag at Independence Hall tomorrow, honoring Kansas's admission to the Union. Her path to statehood has come at a dear cost—her soil stained with the blood of a thousand martyrs. Who am I to value my life over theirs? Each died to thwart slavery's spread across this continent and all the way down to Tierra del Fuego."

"You can do the people of Kansas and millions of others a greater service by taking every measure of safety," Judd said.

"Tomorrow afternoon, I am to address the legislature in Harrisburg." Lincoln ran his fingers through his hair. "This afternoon we settled a great flap over Senator Cameron's place in the Cabinet. With recent divisions now mended, I will not break my promise. I will not give Pennsylvanians any further cause for grievance against the new administration."

"Is there a way to keep Mr. Lincoln's appointments," Judd asked, "and spirit him away tomorrow night?"

"If it has to be," Pinkerton replied, "I will find a way."

"Make up a plan," Lincoln said. "If I see fit to follow your advice, Mrs. Lincoln and Lamon will have to be told."

Around eleven o'clock, Lincoln left Pinkerton and Judd. As he approached his room, Lamon's voice rang out. "Halloo, Lincoln. I've been looking all over for you."

"Good. I need to talk with you, too."

Lamon's face turned somber. "Young Fred Seward has been waiting in your room for close to an hour. He has some secret letters from his father."

"More bad news?" Lincoln asked.

"You've gotten bad news?"

"We can talk about it after I'm done with young Seward." Lincoln rubbed his eyes.

"He seems anxious," Lamon said.

"I reckon the Peace Conference has found a new plan for giving away everything Republicans gained in the election. They're hell-bent on waving the surrender flag even before the new administration takes over."

Lincoln's voice drew Seward into the hall. Lamon directed him back into Lincoln's room, and they sat at a table under a gas lamp where a packet from Senator Seward lay open.

William stood by with tea service.

Lincoln perused the packet's contents. The more he read, the deeper worry lines grew on his face. One letter was from Winfield Scott, General-in-Chief of the Army, another was from Senator Seward, and the third was from General Scott's aide.

Lincoln read the aide's letter a second time. His throat tightened. Thousands of men, many armed, would be massing in Baltimore to prevent him from reaching the Capital alive. The scheme was uncovered by New York City police detectives who had been working undercover in Baltimore at the request of men inside President Buchanan's administration—men who had lost patience with Buchanan's inaction over the national crisis. Among the details, one of the detectives heard men declare that if Mr. Lincoln was to be assassinated, they would like to pull the trigger. The aide's letter concluded—

> *All risk might easily be avoided by a change in the traveling arrangements which would bring Mr. Lincoln and a portion of his party through Baltimore by a night train without previous notice.*

William offered the men tea, but they declined.

Lamon held up his hand. “Shouldn’t he step outside?”

They all turned and looked at William.

“William needs to hear this. We have no choice but to trust one another.” Lincoln turned to Seward. “Do you know how this information was obtained?”

“Yes, sir.”

“Have you heard the name Pinkerton?”

“No, sir.”

Lincoln rose and stared out the window. His shoulders knotted. All Philadelphia was celebrating in the streets below with bands and fireworks.

Lamon studied the letter as Lincoln gazed on the scene below.

“What do you make of it?” Lincoln asked.

Lamon replied, “What does Pinkerton have to do with this?”

“He told me that southern sympathizers and paramilitary groups are at work in Baltimore. Their aim is to prevent my inauguration. He gave names of men who plan to kill me.”

Lamon dropped the letters onto the table. “The reports validate each other. I say we heed their advice.”

Lincoln snatched up the letters. “If different persons, not knowing of each other's work, pursued separate clues and reached the same result, there may be something in it. On the other hand, if this is only the same story filtered through two channels, then it does not make the case any stronger.”

“Why take chances?” Lamon asked.

“I shall consider the matter well and try to decide it right. You will have my answer in the morning. Until then, say nothing to Mrs. Lincoln.”

After Lamon and Seward left, Lincoln turned to William. "What do you make of this?"

"It's not for me to say, sir."

"I'm not asking you to decide. I'm asking for the truth as you see it."

"There's plenty of folks that take on greater risks every day in pursuit of freedom. At least you have men around you who are willing to give their lives to protect yours."

* * *

In morning twilight outside the Continental Hotel, Tad climbed aboard a waiting carriage while William held the team of horses steady. Lincoln stood on the boardwalk, conferring with Judd and Pinkerton. When Lamon joined them, he drew a pistol from his coat and offered the butt end to Lincoln.

Pinkerton reached for the weapon. "I'll take that."

Lamon pulled it back. "He should carry it for protection."

"I'll be damned if he's going to enter the nation's Capital like an armed mugger," Pinkerton growled.

"He's right," Lincoln locked eyes with Lamon. "If a president must arm himself to assume power, he has none."

Lamon grumbled as he returned the revolver to his pocket.

"Stay and look after arrangements for tonight." Lincoln placed his hand on Lamon's shoulder. "Tad and I will be plenty safe at the flag raising."

Lincoln joined Tad in the carriage, and William climbed up next to the driver. They proceeded to Independence Hall, escorted by Scott's Legion—a unit of Mexican War veterans carrying a ragged banner they had borne from Vera Cruz to Mexico City.

When they entered the Assembly Room at Independence Hall, Lincoln knelt to be eye-to-eye with Tad. "Son, this is where the Founders gave birth to a new nation, conceived in liberty and dedicated to the proposition that all men are created equal."

"Some," Tad said. "But not all."

"You've been coaching him." Lincoln peeked up at William.

William shrugged. "As the good book says, 'out of the mouths of babes.'"

Lincoln rose and took Tad's hand. He muttered, "Honesty..."

William completed the mantra as Lincoln stepped past. "Is the highest form of loyalty."

William remained at the doorway as Lincoln and Tad inspected the alabaster likeness of George Washington and the cameos of other Founding Fathers. Father and son stopped at the Liberty Bell and traced the long crack with their fingers. A lump formed in Lincoln's throat. He stood on the same floor planks that great patriots had tread upon.

Although Lincoln had not prepared a speech for the occasion, a compulsion came over him. He turned and addressed the members of Philadelphia's Select Council who were gathered in the Hall to meet him.

> *I am filled with deep emotion at finding myself standing here in the place, where were collected together the wisdom, the patriotism, the devotion to principle from which sprang the institutions under which we live. All the political sentiments I entertain have been drawn from the sentiments which originated and were given to the world from this hall.*

> *I have never had a feeling politically that did not spring from the sentiments embodied in the Declaration of Independence. I have often pondered the dangers which were incurred by the men who assembled here and adopted that Declaration of Independence. I have pondered the toils that were endured by the officers and soldiers of the Army, who achieved that Independence. I have often inquired of myself, what great principle or idea it was that kept this Confederation so long together. It was not the mere matter of the separation of the colonies from the mother land; but something in that Declaration giving liberty, not alone to the people of this Country, but hope to the world for all future time.*
>
> *If this Country cannot be saved without giving up that principle ... I was about to say I would rather be assassinated on this spot than to surrender it.*
>
> *Now, in my view of the present aspect of affairs, there is no need of bloodshed and war. There is no necessity for it. I am not in favor of such a course, and I may say in advance, there will be no bloodshed unless it be forced upon the Government. The Government will not use force unless force is used against it.*

The room erupted in applause.

> *I did not expect to be called upon to say a word when I came here. I supposed I was merely to do something towards raising a flag. I may, therefore, have said something indiscreet.*

In unison they shouted, "No. No."
Lincoln continued.

> *I have said nothing but what I am willing to live by, and, in the pleasure of Almighty God, die by.*

Everyone went outside when he finished the speech, and Lincoln's chin quivered as the thirty-four-star flag unfurled in the breeze. He trembled not from the cold, but from recalling the sacrifices of brave men and women who died to keep Kansas's soil free from the scourge of slavery. With the flag waving overhead, the military band played *The Star-Spangled Banner* and dedicated the playing of *The Stars and Stripes Are Still Unfurled* to Mrs. Robert Anderson who was present on behalf of her husband, the commander of Fort Sumter in Charleston Harbor.

At the conclusion of the ceremony, Lincoln greeted Mrs. Anderson, who hailed from southern aristocracy, as did her husband. Lincoln took her hand. "General Scott is prepared, immediately upon my inauguration, to do whatever necessary to hold the forts in the south, or, if they have already been taken, to take them back."

Mrs. Anderson squeezed his hand and thanked him.

Harrisburg, Pennsylvania—February 1861

An unruly crowd—held at bay by soldiers who outnumbered civilians—met Lincoln and his party when they arrived by train in Harrisburg. Not one man in a hundred cheered when Governor Curtin greeted the president-elect.

After giving a short speech to the state legislature, Lincoln met Lamon and Judd. Judd explained, "Tonight, you'll catch a train back to Philadelphia with Lamon. On your arrival in Philadelphia, Pinkerton will have a carriage waiting to take you across the city to meet the eleven o'clock outbound train to Baltimore. You, Lamon, and Pinkerton will board the train along with the detective's female agent. She will pretend to be your sister attending her invalid brother. In Baltimore, your railcar must be pulled across town by teams of horses where it will be connected to the Washington train."

Judd paused. "Your family and the rest of your party will leave Harrisburg for Philadelphia tomorrow morning. From there, the *Presidential Special* will take them through Baltimore to Washington City according to the original plan."

"Will they be safe?" Lincoln asked.

"There's no threat against the line itself," Judd assured him. "As for Baltimore, Pinkerton's agents are certain the assassins do not intend to harm anyone but you."

"What if his agents are wrong? My family's railcar will be drawn through the town by horse teams the same as mine, but in broad daylight. They will be sitting ducks. Is there not a safer route for them to take?"

"Mr. Wood, who speaks on behalf of the railroad, says he can arrange for the train to stop a few blocks above President Street Station to let your family off. They will go under guard to a safe place while their railcars are pulled across town. Once all danger has passed, they will arrive at Camden Street Station to board the train to Washington."

Judd continued. "Tonight, all the telegraph lines except one between this region and Baltimore will be cut. No one will know you are passing through. Once Pinkerton assures us you are out of Baltimore, the rest of the lines will be restored. In the morning, we will broadcast the news that you are not aboard the *Presidential Special*. The threat of violence to your family will be greatly reduced."

"We inform Mrs. Lincoln." Lincoln's stomach knotted.

"I talked with her this morning," Judd said. "I thought it best to gain her approval before we proceed, and she agrees. We must protect you at all cost. If she and the rest of your suite continue to behave as if all is going according to the original schedule, your chances of escaping danger are best."

"Lamon is to stay with my wife and sons."

"Mrs. Lincoln wants Lamon to go with you." Judd folded his arms across his chest. "She refuses to have it any other way, and she assured me that Mr. Wood's presence will have a calming effect on her."

"Yes," Lincoln replied. "She does respond well to him. But I must demand that Ellsworth and William remain with her and the boys at all times. I have no idea how Wood will react in an emergency. Ellsworth and William, on the other hand, have my complete trust."

"We already decided that your man should not travel with you," Judd said. "It is possible spies have made note of his description and circulated it. If he is seen about the hotel here tonight, they are likely to assume you are still here."

"That makes good sense," Lincoln replied.

* * *

William and Lamon were waiting after dinner that evening when Lincoln returned to his room after saying goodbye to his wife and tucking in Willie and Tad. He had wanted to tell Bob to be vigilant and to take care of his mother and brothers, but his eldest son was nowhere to be found.

William handed Lincoln an overcoat, muffler, and low-brimmed wool hat to serve as his disguise.

"Does Mrs. Lincoln approve of my evening attire?" Lincoln winked.

"Don't take any unnecessary risks tonight," Lamon admonished. "Be careful, for once."

Lincoln gestured to a carpetbag he had packed with just enough to keep him until William and Mrs. Lincoln joined him in Washington City. "All that's missing is the old gripsack with my inauguration speech. Bob has been keeping it for me."

"Even though he lost it once already?" Lamon's eyes widened.

"All the more reason to give him another chance to earn back my trust. He would not dare lose it again."

"The little prig probably thinks you won't be able to embarrass him if you don't have a speech to give."

"If a boy cannot have pride in a father who's elected president, what *could* make him proud?" Lincoln dropped the disguise on the bed, and all three set out searching for Bob. As time drew close for the train's departure to Philadelphia, they caught up with him sitting with a young woman in the hotel lobby.

"Bob," said Lincoln. "Can you fetch the gripsack?"

"I left it in good hands." Bob pointed across the lobby to a clerk at the reception desk.

"I gave you the job of watching after my speech."

"I thought a well-trained hotel clerk would be better suited to look after luggage than a Harvard man." Bob glanced at his companion. "The college doesn't give us classes on that subject."

The girl giggled.

"Sorry, young lady. You can have him back when I'm finished." Lincoln pulled Bob to his feet.

William and Lamon followed as Lincoln marched Bob over to the reception desk and commandeered the clerk's attention. "Excuse me. My son, here, says he left you in charge of an old gripsack. Can you find it for us? It's urgent."

"This way, sir." The clerk led them to a closet full of luggage. "It should be in there. I would help you sort through, but I'm not to leave my station for more than a minute."

As the clerk walked away, Lincoln turned to Bob. "Be quick about it."

Bob sneered. "You would think a drudge like him could show the country's president a little courtesy."

"Said the son who cannot show his father any respect," Lamon muttered.

"You should have given the job to your man." Bob pointed to William. "Is not that what servants are for?"

Lamon pulled Bob back. "I think you need a man to do a job this important." He waded knee deep into the pile of baggage.

Lincoln opened his watch. "We've no time to spare."

Lamon lifted a sack just like the one with the speech and handed it out.

Lincoln fumbled his luggage key.

Lamon pointed to the gripsack. "I checked. It's unlocked."

As Lincoln opened it and peered inside, his heart sank. It contained soiled clothes and a bottle of whisky.

Lamon waded deeper into the luggage, tossing aside anything that didn't fit the description of Lincoln's gripsack. William joined him.

Lincoln checked his watch again. "Time is almost up."

William handed out a second bag identical to Lincoln's. Lincoln fumbled the key once more, dropping it to the floor.

Bob knelt and grabbed it. He returned it to his father, his face flushed with embarrassment. Lincoln opened the sack and staggered backward, relieved. His speech.

Lamon checked the time. "We best be going."

"You get the carriage," Lincoln said. "I will join you shortly." He turned to William. "Come up to the room with me. Folks will suppose you are getting me ready to turn in."

Back in his hotel room, Lincoln donned the overcoat, muffler, and low-brimmed hat. He told William, "Wait a while before you leave for your quarters. It will give the impression I am simply a visitor who has taken my leave."

"Yes, sir."

"And ... take good care of my family."

William stood straight. "I'll protect them with my life."

Upon boarding the carriage with Lamon, Lincoln slinked down in the seat, hoping not to be observed. The route from the hotel was jammed with drunken revelers, oblivious to the clandestine mission speeding past. On occasion, a leering eye from some roustabout raised doubts in Lincoln. Someone would surely discover him sneaking through Harrisburg.

Philadelphia/Midnight Train—February 1861

Pinkerton drove Lincoln and Lamon by carriage across Philadelphia to the Wilmington & Baltimore Station. He parked out of view at the edge of a cedar grove a safe distance from the train. Pinkerton whispered that they must remain secluded until the last moment.

The rustling of branches nearby quickened Lincoln's pulse. Variations of shadows in the undergrowth prompted him to peer intently, searching for the sound's source.

"Nothing there but the wind," Pinkerton said.

Five minutes before the clock struck eleven, a figure sprinted toward them. Lamon thrust his hand into his coat pocket, clutching his pistol. Pinkerton told him to relax.

In short order, the detective's agent reached the carriage and handed over a pouch containing tickets for their passage.

"Is everything ready?" Pinkerton asked.

"You have berths at the back of the car," the agent replied. "The rear door is open. The porter has been alerted to expect the late arrival of an invalid who does not wish to be carried through the narrow aisle of the crowded car."

The agent climbed aboard the carriage next to Pinkerton, took the reins, and brought the carriage up close to the train. When the carriage stopped, Lamon jumped off to help Lincoln down. Lincoln draped his arm over Lamon's neck, feigning frailty as they boarded the railcar. Pinkerton followed. The female agent, disguised as Lincoln's traveling companion, welcomed him with an embrace and whispered, "For tonight I'm your sister, Kay."

Lamon lifted Lincoln into his sleeping berth and drew the curtains. The railcar lurched, and Kay stood close by Lincoln as the train picked up speed. The train's wheels clanked on the iron rails, eventually settling into a monotonous rhythm. With each passing mile, Lincoln's anxiety grew. The opening stanza of Fox's *Mortality* taunted him.

Like a swift-fleeting meteor, a fast-flying cloud,
A flash of the lightning, a break of the wave,
Man passeth from life to his rest in the grave.

After a long silence, Lincoln whispered, "Kay, are you there? I think I know the man who intends to murder me."

"Pray tell," she whispered. "The man's name would make our job easier."

"Out on the Circuit, I once encountered a fellow who drew his pistol and pointed it at my face. When I asked how I might have offended him, he replied in a menacing voice, 'I swore if I ever came across a man uglier than myself, I'd shoot him.'"

"How did you disarm the man?"

"I told him, shoot me, for if I am uglier than you, I don't want to live."

She replied, "I wouldn't count on being so lucky if someone catches sight of your face in Baltimore."

Pinkerton joined Kay and whispered into Lincoln's berth that men were stationed at various places along the rails to report anything out of the ordinary. Occasionally during the night, Pinkerton wandered out onto the train's rear platform to observe his agents' signals, returning each time with favorable news. All through the journey, Kay never left her post outside Lincoln's berth, not even to get a wink of sleep.

At half past three in the morning, the train reached Baltimore's President Street Station. One of Pinkerton's men boarded and assured him that "all is right." Lincoln lay still in his berth, scarcely breathing as a team of horses drew the railcar through the quiet streets to Camden Station. More lines from *Mortality* consumed Lincoln's mind.

The hand of the king that the sceptre hath borne;
The brow of the priest that the mitre hath worn;
The eye of the sage, and the heart of the brave,
Are hidden and lost in the depth of the grave.

As he lay in the berth with curtains drawn, wrapped in a scheme hatched to thwart a plot, Lincoln contemplated a bullet piercing his skull—searing pain, anticipating his final breath. He decided he did not want to be warned of any further plots—living in fear must be more excruciating than death.

When their railcar arrived at Camden Station, the sounds of engineers at work shifting coaches onto tracks were the only noises Lincoln could detect. The anticipated mob of secessionist sympathizers, harboring assassins in their midst, had failed to materialize.

Then, a loud banging rang out on the platform.

Lincoln tensed. Lamon and Kay remained alert outside Lincoln's compartment while Pinkerton rushed to a window to assess the commotion. A seeming age passed before Pinkerton reported that a drunkard was pounding against a night watchman's box with a huge club. He was trying to arouse a sleeping ticket-agent.

Soon, the train pulled away from the station, and once they were safely out of Baltimore, Pinkerton signaled to one of his agents perched on a telegraph pole. A message was on its way to Philadelphia, announcing their peaceful passage through Baltimore.

When Lamon pulled back the curtains, Lincoln said, "I never believed I would have been assassinated had I gone through Baltimore as first contemplated, but I thought it wise to run no risk where none was necessary."

"Good." Lamon smiled. "You're beginning to listen."

Lincoln's train rolled into Washington Depot at six o'clock in the morning. He waited in his berth until the other passengers disembarked. Being the last to leave, Lincoln hoped he would pass through the station unobserved. All went well until they reached the exit where a lone man waited partly concealed behind a pillar. Lincoln slumped down and pulled up his muffler to hide his face. The man stepped from behind the pillar and seized Lincoln's hand. In a loud voice he said, "How are you, Lincoln?"

Lamon grabbed the man's arm. Pinkerton raised his fist.

Lincoln stepped between the man and Pinkerton. "Don't strike him. It's Washburne—my friend."

Pinkerton admonished them to keep quiet while Washburne led them to a carriage he had rented to drive Lincoln to Willard's Hotel.

Near the Capitol, they skirted an open canal—the city's main sewer line that flowed from homes, inns, shops, and slaughterhouses. Scant moonlight exposed a dead cat floating in the muck. On the canal's bank, rats scurried for morsels of garbage. Pigs rooted in the fetid bayous formed by debris that built up in the shallows. Despite covering his mouth and nose, Lincoln gagged on the stench.

On their arrival at Willard's, Lincoln, Washburne and Pinkerton dismounted the carriage and headed for the ladies' entrance at the side of the hotel. Lamon drove to the main door to find the proprietor, Mr. Willard.

Senator Seward, recognizable by his short, wiry frame, approached the ladies' entrance. In his distinct husky voice, he applauded the wisdom of their secret passage through Baltimore. He reiterated in strong terms the great danger they so narrowly escaped. When Lamon and Willard joined them, Lincoln thanked everyone for their loyalty.

Willard led Lincoln to Parlor No. 6, a large corner suite on the second floor. He assured Lincoln that he had reserved the best rooms in the hotel for his family to occupy until they moved into the president's mansion. The suite included separate apartments so Lincoln could work undisturbed.

Sleep eluded Lincoln as his mind roiled with visions of the perils his family might face passing through Baltimore. He gave up on his nap and read from a volume of Burns' poetry until Seward returned to collect him for an appointment with retiring President James Buchanan.

On the way to the Executive Mansion, Seward's carriage bounded in and out of deep ruts. Frequently, the driver contested rights-of-way with wandering pigs, cattle, and sheep. The unfinished Capitol dome peeked from behind its scaffolding, and a half-erected marble obelisk—intended to honor General Washington—protruded like a graveyard monument that had been sawed off by cannon fire.

At the Executive Mansion, Buchanan introduced Lincoln to members of his Cabinet, several of whom, according to Seward, were traitors, collaborating with secessionists to capture the city and prevent the inauguration of a Black Republican. A chill ran down Lincoln's spine.

* * *

Lincoln's family and inauguration guests arrived, unmolested, aboard the *Presidential Special* at about four o'clock in the afternoon.

CHAPTER EIGHT

Inauguration Ceremony—March 4, 1861

William had laid out his shaving implements in Suite 6 at Willard's Hotel when Lincoln returned from breakfast. Lincoln unfolded his speech. "Let me read this so you can tell me how it sounds."

William whipped the soap into a lather as Lincoln read. The words *no purpose, directly or indirectly, to interfere with the institution of slavery* set William's hand beating faster.

Lincoln sat when he finished reading and waited for a response.

William remained silent as he draped the barber's cape over Lincoln and tucked the edges around his collar. William's fingers twitched.

"What do you think?" Lincoln asked.

William hesitated.

"Well?" Lincoln said.

"I'm not sure I can put myself in the place of your southern brethren. That's who you're addressing, right?"

"I am trying to assure folks in the southern region that the evils they flee from by seceding are not real."

William began dabbing—almost jabbing—lather onto Lincoln's face.

Lincoln flinched. "Easy."

"Sorry, sir. I am trying to imagine how southern men think."

"The question was, how does it sound?"

William worked the razor on a leather strop. "I'm sure it sounds different to different listeners. As for me, I am not at all reassured. What if a slave hunter were to kidnap me? What would you do? Leave things just as they are? Let the Fugitive Slave Law be?"

"I reckon I already answered that question months ago," Lincoln replied. "Or have you forgotten that slave hunter and your night in jail?"

"That was before you became determined your southern brethren should trust that your government won't accost them."

"Seven states have already backed out of the Union," Lincoln stressed. "That's even before I take the oath. I have not had the chance to do anything to them, but still, they fear what they imagine I will do. My first job is to win them back." Lincoln closed his eyes. "Now, if you do not mind, answer the question. How does it sound?"

"Your words flow as smooth as lard sliding on a hot skillet."

"Okay. Anything in particular you liked?"

"Yes. I'm fond of 'better angels of our nature.' I just wish those angels were a little more partial to folks like me."

Lincoln sighed. "When I last lived here more than a decade ago, I tried to free all the slaves within the city but failed. I don't think folks today are any more inclined to embrace drastic changes than they were then."

"So, things always stay the same." William pursed his lips.

"Progress comes in fits and starts. We did not end slavery back then, but we put an end to slave markets on the streets of our nation's Capital."

"Maybe in the streets, but not in the back alleys. That's what I hear." William wiped the razor clean. "Do you know about the Plummer woman last summer? She was plucked off the streets and held in a pen in Alexandria for two months, then sold down to New Orleans."

"If she was a runaway, that's what the law requires."

"A runaway? From Georgetown district, right here in this city? She was a free Negro on her way home after working late." William draped a warm, damp towel over Lincoln's face and began massaging. "Folks say that's what happens to us. We get caught on the streets after curfew because we are on our way home from working late at some rich Congressman's house ... or the president's house. Before we know it, a bounty hunter slips the sheriff a couple of silver coins and we're on the block to be sold down south." William peeled the towel from Lincoln's face.

Lincoln rolled his eyes. "I reckon progress is never as smooth as words ... or smooth as lard sliding on a hot skillet."

Lincoln finished polishing his speech shortly before noon and was ready when President Buchanan entered the parlor of

Willard's Hotel to escort him to the Capitol for the inauguration ceremony. Buchanan shook Lincoln's hand and leaned in to whisper, "If you are as pleased on entering that old white house as I shall be upon returning to my home in Wheatland, you are the happiest of men."

The outgoing president grinned broadly. Lincoln forced a faint smile. He imagined the mess he was being handed could have been worse—at least Buchanan had not turned over all the government's military properties to the secessionists—Forts Sumter and Pickens remained under federal control. He also had not been allowed to purchase Cuba, which would have saddled the new administration with all the attendant headaches, including a heavy load of debt.

Buchanan took Lincoln in arm, and they walked out to a waiting carriage on Fourteenth Street. Senator Ned Baker of Oregon—an old friend from Lincoln's early Illinois days—occupied the rear-facing seat with Maryland Senator James Pearce. Buchanan and Lincoln climbed on board and sat opposite them.

After two blocks, the buggy turned onto the broad, tree-lined Pennsylvania Avenue and joined a long procession led by Cavalry Colonel Charles Stone on his stallion. Horses' hooves slopped through mud holes—sunshine had replaced the early morning hail and rain—and carriage wheels clunked over well-worn ruts. Lincoln tensed as the parade passed whitewashed sentry boxes that were scattered among homes, shops, empty buildings, and vacant lots.

Sharpshooters in plain sight occupied rooftops, jangling Lincoln's nerves. A thousand more soldiers with fixed bayonets on their muskets lined the street, another reminder of the danger that lurked in every corner of the city. Some in the crowd hurled insults and shook their fists. Halfway along the route someone called out, “There goes the Illinois ape! Bet he won’t live to see sunset.”

Lincoln recoiled.

Colonel Stone spurred his horse. His blue-clad cavalrymen did the same, exciting their mounts to prance and close in around the president’s carriage.

Lincoln glanced over his shoulder toward the place where the heckler had shouted his insult.

Ned Baker leaned forward and patted Lincoln’s knee. “We’re in good hands. No harm will come to you.”

The knot in Lincoln’s back unwound a notch. He glanced at Buchanan. “That heckler triggered the memory of when I first met your attorney general, Mr. Stanton, not too many years ago.”

“Why does that remind you of Stanton?” Buchanan asked.

“Stanton called me ‘that Illinois ape’ and took me off a case. Now, I reckon it is me putting him out of a job.”

“If only I had possessed the nerve to do the same when he first caused me trouble,” Buchanan replied. “I pray your attorney general will not be the problem Stanton has been.”

Almost an hour later, the procession arrived at the east portico of the Capitol. Tens of thousands of spectators already filled the grounds. The crowd erupted in cheers when Lincoln and Buchanan paused at the doorway of the rotunda. Lincoln drew a deep breath before descending the stairs to a wooden canopy where Chief Justice Taney waited. Lincoln lost considerable respect for Taney four years earlier when the court’s radical pro-slavery decision was handed down in the Dred Scott case. The outrage that consumed him back then revisited him momentarily, but he reined in his emotions.

A multitude of dignitaries crammed around the canopy, including foreign diplomats, members of Congress, and Supreme Court Justices. Senators Douglas, Chase, and Baker sat under the canopy, as did Bob, who occupied the seat on his father's right. Ellsworth, Nicolay, and Hay were next to Bob. Mrs. Lincoln sat to her husband's left, a few seats away. She was accompanied by her cousin Lizzie Grimsley, with Willie and Tad tucked between them.

Goose bumps rippled down Lincoln's spine as Senator Baker rose to address the throng. Lincoln's mind retraced the long years of their friendship. The Lincolns' second son, Eddie, now in Heaven, had been named after Baker. Thoughts of Eddie pinched Lincoln's heart for an instant until Baker's baritone voice rang out. "Fellow citizens, I introduce to you, Abraham Lincoln, President of the United States."

A loud roar erupted from the crowd as Lincoln stepped forward, and when the cheers subsided, a few catcalls and boos followed. Lincoln took off his hat and searched for a place to set it. Senator Douglas, who was only of few steps away, came forward and took the hat. As Douglas moved back to his seat, he glanced over his shoulder and quipped, "If I cannot be president, at least I can hold his hat." Those who heard him snickered.

Lincoln gazed over the vast crowd. Trees, fences, and statuary on the grounds below served as perches for men and boys intent on gaining a better view or a more convenient spot from which to hear. His focus locked onto the statue *America*, the central figure in Crawford's *Progress of Civilization*—a collection of sculptures designed for the yet unfinished Capitol. Lincoln's pulse quickened. The sculpture provided excellent cover for a secessionist marksman to take aim.

Lincoln put on his steel-rimmed glasses, unfolded the speech, and cleared his throat. He began by reminding men of the south that the benefits, memories, and hopes embodied in the Union were certain and true. Any experiment to destroy the national fabric was fraught with greater hazards than those they faced as part of it.

> *Physically speaking, we cannot separate. We cannot remove our respective sections from each other, nor build an impassable wall between them. The different parts of our Country can only remain face to face. Intercourse between them must continue, whether amicable or hostile.*
>
> *Suppose you go to war, you cannot fight for all time; and when, after much loss on both sides, and no gain on either, you cease fighting, the same old questions are again upon you.*

He concluded by saying:

> *In your hands, my dissatisfied fellow-countrymen, and not in mine, is the momentous issue of civil war. The Government will not assail you. You can have no conflict without being yourselves the aggressors. You have no oath registered in Heaven to destroy the Government, while I shall have the most solemn one to "preserve, protect, and defend it."*
>
> *I am loath to close. We are not enemies, but friends. We must not be enemies. Though passion may have strained, it must not break our bonds of affection. The mystic chords of memory, stretching from every battle-field and patriot grave to every living heart and*

hearthstone all over this broad land, will yet swell the chorus of the Union when again touched, as surely they will be, by the better angels of our nature.

Upon repeating the oath of office, Lincoln bowed his head and kissed the Bible.

Executive Mansion—March 4, 1861

William had remained at the hotel, barred from witnessing the inauguration ceremony due to his race and entrenched customs. He ground his teeth as thoughts churned in his head—forbidden, voiceless, faceless. So-called freedom and bondage were almost the same thing for a Negro.

William carried his sparse belongings into the white-painted brick-and-stone president's mansion by way of the backside basement door. The basement housed the laundry, kitchen, and servants' quarters and was not visible from the front. William imagined the grounds were designed to slope that way in order to hide the mansion's underbelly from view by arriving white guests. The front door, through which white folks entered, was guarded by Edward McManus, an old Irishman, who had served as doorkeeper of the mansion since Andrew Jackson's administration.

William had entertained visions of grandeur whenever Mrs. Lincoln spoke of the great mansion in the nation's Capital. He certainly expected something different from the cramped, grimy servants' quarters in hotels along the route from Springfield. Instead, a foul, dank odor filled his nostrils as he passed through the basement's central corridor. Splotches of mildew—covered by a thin coat of dingy paint—

clung to the walls of his windowless room. The bed and small wardrobe left just enough space for him to turn around.

While William unpacked, Old Edward began a tour of the mansion for the Lincoln family and others who would live there with them—Ellsworth, Nicolay, Hay, and Lamon. They were joined for the tour by family and friends who had traveled from Springfield for the inauguration. The main floor included three parlors, a large ballroom, the State dining room, and a private dining room for the president's family.

Mrs. Lincoln, in her youth, extracted a promise from Kentucky's venerated statesman, Henry Clay, that he would invite her to the Executive Mansion if it ever became his home. When Clay did not realize his ambition, she resolved to marry a man who one day would become president. At the parlor known as the Blue Room, Mrs. Lincoln stopped in the doorway and exclaimed, "It's mine! My very own. At last, it's mine."

Lincoln ducked his head as they ventured into the low-ceilinged basement. Mrs. Lincoln covered her nose and mouth, complaining, "The place has the atmosphere of an old and unsuccessful hotel. I would not be surprised if it is infested with rats." Old Edward apologized for the offensive conditions and vowed to get to the root of the problem. He sent the Lincolns along to explore the second floor on their own. William joined them.

The upstairs hallway ran east and west and was dark, lined with heavy mahogany doors and wainscoting. The rooms on the western half were family living quarters, including a family parlor, a bath, and bedrooms. The east end housed offices and two bedrooms for staff. Mrs. Lincoln peered into the president's office and declared, "These shabby furnishings look as if they have survived a good many presidents."

"Nonsense," Lincoln countered. "It's furnished well enough. Better than any office I've ever worked in."

"Rubbish!" she replied. "It would be a degradation to subject visitors to such surroundings."

William bit his tongue. If only she knew the hovels some folks called home. Or maybe she knew but didn't care.

Before Lincoln could answer his wife's complaint, bells began ringing violently in every corner of the house. Nicolay and Hay wheeled around and searched for the source of the clamor. Hay insisted the mansion was bewitched.

Old Edward rushed up the stairs and gasped for breath as he paused at the landing. "Coming," he wheezed.

"What's that infernal racket?" Lincoln asked.

The bells continued clanging at a furious pace.

Old Edward huffed. "The bell system, sir. It's used to summon servants and your staff. But you should only ring a single bell for whomever you wish to call."

The bells persisted.

"No one rang anything," Lincoln said. "How do we stop it?"

Old Edward led them up a stairway into the attic to the yoke of the bell system where young Tad sat yanking away on cords. Willie looked on.

Nicolay grabbed Tad by the collar and pulled him away from the bells. Ellsworth gripped Willie's shoulder. Old Edward wagged his finger and warned the two boys to stay off the bells.

"All right, boys." Lincoln palmed the back of his neck. "You best mind Mister Edward. These are his bells. Only to be touched with his permission."

As the group filed back down to the second floor for an inspection of the family quarters, Ellsworth took charge of Willie and Tad. Edward remained in the attic with William.

"What are you doing here?" the doorkeeper asked.

"I'm attending Mr. Lincoln, as his valet."

Old Edward pursed his lips and eyed William from head to toe. "We'll have to see about that."

Executive Mansion—March 5, 1861

Joseph Holt, formerly Buchanan's Secretary of War, waited grim-faced in the president's office early on the morning after Lincoln's inauguration. Holt waved off Lincoln's invitation to explore their Kentucky roots and handed him a packet.

"What is this?" Lincoln asked.

"Sir, it is correspondence from Major Anderson and his officers at Fort Sumter. I have included my letter summarizing the matter. Getting straight to the point, Anderson and his men are in dire straits."

Lincoln ripped open the packet and read its content, tossing pages aside as he read. Halfway through Anderson's letter, Lincoln gasped. "Major Anderson says rations will soon be exhausted? The need to reinforce is urgent?"

"Sir, an expedition has been quietly prepared and is ready to sail from New York on a few hours' notice."

"Then we should proceed at once."

"Our chances for success are dubious, sir."

"My God!" Lincoln threw Anderson's letter on the table. "He says he would not stake his reputation on the success of a mission of fewer than 20,000 men. If we sail such a force into Charleston Harbor, war shall be on us before you can say, *Hail Columbia*. The world will say we are the instigators."

"Sir, the southern confederacy knows our government's intentions even before orders are given. The rebels have prepared for our next step. They have closed the harbor entrance." Holt face flushed. "Once you decide to resupply, they shall close the remaining channels in the harbor."

"How is it possible I have not heard any of this before?" Lincoln's eyes narrowed. "When was this dispatch received?"

"It was sent from Charleston on February 28, received here yesterday morning."

"Damn Buchanan! Damn him! I should drag him back here from Wheatland, stand him before one of Scott's cannon. I'd have the mind to light the wick myself. How did it take four days to deliver an urgent dispatch from Charleston?"

Holt pointed to the envelope. "Major Anderson's letter arrived by post. It—"

"For Heaven's sake," Lincoln interrupted. "Why the post? Why not the telegraph?"

"There is no telegraph in the city."

"What?" Lincoln gripped his forehead. "We've had telegraph out on the prairie for more than a decade. How can there be no telegraph in the nation's Capital?"

"The closest telegraph office is in Maryland."

"The fool." Lincoln walked to the window and gazed into the distance, wringing his hands. "Buchanan gave away more than a dozen federal forts and arsenals. He surrendered a quarter of the soldiers we had deployed in Texas. Now he has left Major Anderson in peril at our most important southern fortress. Only yesterday I told an anxious nation we need not have any bloodshed or violence. In the same breath I promised the power entrusted to me would be used to hold, occupy, and possess property belonging to the government without any invasion or use of force. Now, to fulfill my obligations I must dispatch thousands of troops to invade a southern harbor."

Lincoln turned back to Holt. “Had I seen this before my speech yesterday, I could have found other words. Words that would not make me into either a coward or a liar.”

Nicolay stepped into the office. “Sir, I have a message from the Senate. They are ready for your Cabinet nominations.”

After Holt left, Nicolay closed the door. “I also have a letter from Senator Seward. He has dropped his demand that Senator Chase be kept out of your Cabinet and is willing to go in as Secretary of State.”

Lincoln fumbled through papers on his desk. His mind was so distracted by the news from Sumter that he could not focus. “Nicolay, where’s the list with Seward and Chase’s names?”

When Nicolay retrieved the list, Lincoln instructed him to take it quickly to the Senate and await word of their confirmation.

Nicolay hesitated. “But we haven’t told Chase his nomination to head Treasury is going forward.”

“We do not have time to stand on ceremony. He will have to learn of it when Hamlin reads the list to the entire Senate.”

As Nicolay crossed the threshold, Lincoln called to him. He collected Holt’s packet and handed it to him. “Take this to General Scott and tell him I need to know his views at once.”

Nicolay returned within the hour with General-in-Chief Scott’s response—"evacuation is almost inevitable.”

Lincoln pressed his palms to his brow.

* * *

Senator Salmon Chase wasted little time calling on Lincoln that afternoon when the Senate was done with its business for the day. He strode into Lincoln’s office. “Mr. President.”

"There's no need for formality. Call me Lincoln."

"Sir." Chase rubbed his balding head. "I was perplexed on hearing my name read before the Senate as your choice for the Treasury post."

"I thought that was our understanding."

"Until you dropped me to appease Seward," Chase replied.

"Seward and I were in a little cock fight. At the last minute, my rooster came out on top."

"Even so, sir, I presumed it went the other way. After all, he aims to be premier with you as his puppet. I would be an impediment."

"I reckon it will take a little time for us all to sort out a few things. Please, sit with me for a moment." Lincoln proceeded to tell a story.

> *An ant, nimbly running about in the sunshine in search of food, encountered a dull-looking chrysalis that was near its time of change. "Pitiable animal!" cried the ant. "While I can run hither and thither at my pleasure and ascend the tallest tree, you lie imprisoned here in your shell, with power only to move a joint or two of your scaly tail."*
>
> *The chrysalis did not reply. A few days after, when the ant passed that way again, nothing but the shell remained. Wondering what had become of its contents, the ant felt himself suddenly shaded and fanned by the wings of a beautiful butterfly.*
>
> *"Behold me," said the butterfly, "your much-pitied friend! Boast now of your powers to run and climb." Saying that, the butterfly rose in the air and was borne along by the summer breeze, until it was out of sight forever.*

Lincoln met Chase's bewildered stare. "It may appear at the moment that I'm a pitiable chrysalis, but the people of this land elected me to be their leader, and I intend to rise to whatever challenge lies before us. Will you do likewise?"

"Sir, you have put me in an awkward position."

"I apologize for any discomfort," Lincoln said. "Nonetheless, I need you in the Cabinet, and it will cripple this infant administration if you decline."

Chase fidgeted with his coat button. "I will tender my resignation from the Senate forthwith."

"Thank you, Senator. I am most grateful. The first Cabinet meeting will be conducted this afternoon."

As Chase left, Nicolay appeared in the doorway and announced, "We're under siege." He handed Lincoln a list of ten state delegations waiting to call on him and explained, "The upstairs hallway is jammed all the way to the family quarters. The staircase leading down to the vestibule is full as well."

Lincoln laid his hand on Nicolay's shoulder. "Yesterday evening, a vanguard of four state delegations invaded us and intruded on the family living space. Mrs. Lincoln was irate, and I don't blame her. We must do something."

"She left in a huff with her cousin," Nicolay said.

"When? Where did they go?"

"A short time ago. I believe to the Soldiers' Home that Mr. Buchanan spoke of after the inauguration."

"I see." Lincoln peeked into the hallway and turned back to Nicolay. "Can we put up a small gate to block the public from meandering into the family's suites?"

A caller approached them and cleared his throat.

"Excuse me." Nicolay guided the man away from the office door. "The president will be available shortly."

Lincoln called Nicolay back into his office. He pointed to the interior wall that separated his office from the family parlor. “Do you think we can punch a hole here and make a passageway to my personal quarters?”

“It’s possible,” Nicolay replied. “And we should add a second gate in the corridor to keep visitors from wandering unannounced into our offices.”

“Who do we talk to?” Lincoln asked.

“Mr. Buchanan said something about a Superintendent of Buildings. I’ll find out who it is.”

Lincoln shook his head. “It’s a shame he did’t tell us more.”

“At least Old Edward told us a few things, like the water from the right-hand well is better than the left one.”

“When was that?”

“On the tour, down in the basement.” Nicolay replied. “He was going on about how inconvenient it is that water isn’t piped into the building, that the servants must use bathtubs as reservoirs to avoid making constant trips out to the wells.”

“Where was I?”

“You were with us, sir.”

“I was?”

“Yes, and in case you missed it as well, for toilets, we must use the outhouses on the east side of the mansion.”

Lincoln scratched his head. “Have you seen William?”

“No, sir. Shall I have Hay look for him?”

“That won’t be necessary. I’m sure he will turn up.”

* * *

The next morning, Lincoln saddled his horse and rode three-and-a-half miles north of the city to the Soldiers’ Home. When

Mrs. Lincoln returned from visiting there the previous day, she insisted he inspect it immediately.

A chilly breeze brushed Lincoln's face as he stood on the back porch of one of the property's residences. The vast compound, once owned by one of Washington's elite bankers, was purchased by the government to house disabled soldiers. Its secluded, pastoral setting and cooler elevation made it ideal for convalescence, and President Buchanan used the estate as a summertime retreat.

Lincoln gazed into the distance, surveying the outline of Washington City nestled along the Potomac River. The unfinished Capitol dome peeked back at him.

On Lincoln's return to the mansion, the swarm of petitioners was already spilling onto the north portico. He guided his horse to the stable where William met him.

"Good morning, sir. Do you have time for a word?"

Lincoln dismounted. "Of course."

"You've made a big mistake, making me your valet."

"How so?" Lincoln asked.

"The mansion staff say my skin's too dark to be a president's valet. If I don't quit, they're sure to give me my comeuppance."

"We cannot have that. Let me talk with Mrs. Lincoln. I know politics of the country pretty well, but she knows how to run a big house like this one."

Lincoln found his wife in the upstairs family parlor with Cousin Lizzie, who had come to Washington for the inauguration festivities.

Without looking up from her reading, Mrs. Lincoln accosted her husband over a patronage appointment for her friend, Mr. Wood. "You remember him," she said. "He was the railroad superintendent on our journey here on the *Presidential Special.*"

Lincoln replied that he had thousands of such requests.

She slammed her book shut. "But only one wife."

"Fine. I shall tend to it."

She fingered a bolt of red fabric Lizzie had been examining.

"Mother," he continued. "I need your help on something. William came to me and complained the lighter-skinned staff think he should not be my valet."

She ran her hand over the fabric.

"They tell him there is something of a pecking order here based on the darkness of a fellow's skin."

"Father, such prejudice does not exist only in this house. Any great house follows the same protocol. Take my new seamstress—"

Lizzie nudged her cousin. "I just remembered. Is she not supposed to deliver you a dress for tonight's levee?"

"Why no, dear." Mrs. Lincoln patted Lizzie's hand. "I told her I do not need it until Tuesday evening when I host my first dress reception. Tonight's levee is informal."

Lincoln pinched the bridge of his nose. "You were saying."

"Oh, forgive me, Father. Yes, I was saying, do you think women like Senator Jeff Davis' wife or Captain Lee's wife would have hired Miss Lizabeth to sew for them if her skin were as dark as coal? These customs are essential for maintaining order. I suppose you shall have to hire a seasoned butler and find the boy a suitable position in one of the government's departments."

"That's hardly fair."

"Unfair or not," Mrs. Lincoln replied, "it is something you must abide for the greater good." She returned to her book.

Lincoln threw up his hands and walked out of the parlor into the hallway to search for William. He had only gone a few paces when Nicolay intercepted him. "Sir, the heads of the army and navy are waiting in your office."

"I reckon I better see them. Find William and let him know we need to talk when I've finished with Neptune and the generals."

General-in-Chief Scott and the army's chief engineer, General John Totten, sat stiff-backed at the long table in Lincoln's office. Secretary of Navy Welles, whom Lincoln nicknamed "Neptune," sat opposite the generals next to his top assistant, Silas Stringham.

Lincoln suggested they skip pleasantries and asked who wished to lead the dance.

Scott's voice was gravelly, weak. "President Buchanan would not allow any plan regarding Sumter to go forward while he negotiated with South Carolina's commissioners. Their bargaining ended without success, and two peaceful missions using merchant ships were laid out. Later, those plans were scuttled."

Welles fidgeted.

Scott continued. "New proposals were offered, one using warships fighting their way to the fort. The other relied on Major Anderson to bombard and bring-to any merchant vessels passing his way, helping himself to their cargo."

Welles smirked.

"The warships were approved," Scott added. "But before they could be arranged, new commissioners arrived from South Carolina, causing further delays. When those deliberations dissolved, I ordered four small steamers belonging to the Coast Survey to sail with provisions to

Charleston. I have no doubt the venture would have succeeded, but it was held back by a new truce between President Buchanan and a number of secessionists in the Senate." Scott slouched in his seat.

Totten interceded. "During a long delay caused by the negotiations, the harbor's defenses were greatly strengthened. Powerful new land batteries were constructed. Hulks were sunk in the channel, making it impractical to access Fort Sumter by sea."

"Impractical?" Lincoln blurted. "Is that the test we apply to the question of one hundred men's welfare or the question of our duty to hold and defend the government's property?"

"Impossible," Scott wheezed. "Unless we have a large enough fleet and 25,000 troops with several months training."

"We believe it would take much less," Welles insisted.

"Based on what facts?" Totten's eyes narrowed.

"Based on the fact we have a new administration, unwilling to pander to traitors," Welles replied.

Lincoln pounded the table with his fist. "All right." "Saturday evening, we will put the question before the Cabinet. In the meantime, General Scott, I will give you some interrogatories to answer."

As the military men left, Nicolay stepped into the office. "William is waiting in the basement. He says Old Edward warned him not to venture upstairs."

Muffled voices filtered up from the musty basement as Lincoln descended the stairs. He paused on the bottom step as a single voice became clear. Old Edward continued his tirade, his back to the stairwell.

As Lincoln stepped closer Old Edward glanced over his shoulder then glimpsed again and turned to face Lincoln.

"I will take it from here." Lincoln glared at Old Edward. "William and I need to talk. Please excuse us."

Old Edward took his leave.

Lincoln clasped his hands behind his back. "I talked with Mrs. Lincoln about our predicament."

William lowered his head.

"It seems the customs of great houses such as this one are exactly as the others have told you."

"Yes, sir. I don't want to be a burden. You have enough troubles without having to worry about me."

"No. I did not bring you out of Egypt to abandon you in the desert."

"It's not your fault," William said. "I was on my way up to Canada when Mrs. Lincoln dragged me out of the ticket line at the train station. I let her talk me into coming here."

"Yes, she can be a hard one to say no to."

"So, if she's not inclined to hold me here, I might as well pack for Canada."

"What draws you to Canada?" Lincoln asked.

"Sir, compared to the business of the whole country, it's a trivial matter and I will not add to your woes."

"Let me be the judge of that," Lincoln replied.

William recalled what Mrs. Lincoln told him in Chicago—*it is never your place to display your emotions or draw attention to yourself.* "Sir, I peeked in on you the night after you learned about those men at the fort in Carolina. You were stooped, pacing like you carried the weight of the world."

"Then, I will be the one to say no. I refuse to let you go."

"Sir, I am no longer a slave. I come and go of my own free will."

"I would not shackle you," Lincoln replied.

William locked eyes with Lincoln.

“Go ahead if you have something to say.”

Words churned in William’s head—you could free men whom other men have shackled.

Nicolay appeared at the foot of the stairs. “Sir, a messenger just arrived with General Scott’s answers to your interrogatories.”

Lincoln patted William’s shoulder. “Do not go anywhere just yet. Give me time to find a solution. In the meantime, I’ll see to it that Old Edward leaves you alone.”

CHAPTER NINE

Executive Mansion—March 1861

Lincoln's eyes, sunken and reddened, bore witness to many sleepless nights. Volleys of pain stung his temples. His voice rasped as he addressed the Cabinet assembled around the long table in his office. "My opinion is no state can, in any lawful way, get out of the Union without consent of the others. If I am correct, we must take any measures necessary to preserve the government's property, without regard to where it sits."

Several ministers shifted in their seats. Seward studied each in turn, calculating their dispositions.

Lincoln continued. "When I heard months ago that Mr. Buchanan intended to surrender Fort Sumter, I declared if that is true, they ought to hang him! Let not that be said of us." He paused. "On my way here from Springfield, I encountered Major Anderson's wife at a solemn ceremony in Philadelphia. I assured her that upon my inauguration, General Scott's orders would be to hold the forts or retake them if they had already been surrendered."

Lincoln put on his spectacles and picked up General Scott's reply to his interrogatories. "General-in-Chief Scott has given me a dismal report regarding the Sumter situation. It appears the tug has come." He read from Scott's report.

> *In respect to subsistence without additional provisions, Major Anderson and his men may hold out twenty-eight to forty days.*
>
> *The besiegers are about 3,500 men, now somewhat disciplined. They have four powerful batteries on land and one floating battery, all with guns and mortars of large caliber and of the best patterns.*

Lincoln continued.

> *Fort Sumter—being defended by fewer than 100 men, including common laborers and musicians—might be taken at any time by a single assault. More easily, if previously harassed for many days and nights.*
>
> *A fleet of war vessels and transports would be required, which in the current scattered disposition of our Navy could not be collected in fewer than four months. The venture would require 5,000 regular troops, and 20,000 volunteers.*

Secretary Chase, a hero of the radical Republicans, gasped as Lincoln went on.

> *To raise, organize, and discipline such an Army—not considering the time to pass necessary legislation—would require from six to eight months. As a practical military question, the time for securing Fort Sumter has passed. A surrender under assault or from starvation is merely a question of time.*

Lincoln peered over his spectacles at Scott. His weak eye twitched. "What is our current military strength, General?"

"Sir, our ground army stands at about 16,000, spread over 2,000 miles of frontier. All the navy's ships are deployed, either patrolling distant waters or laid up for repair. The strongest armed forces in the country are the militias of the seceding states. Those militias have been maintained in constant readiness in order to contain the slave population."

Lincoln's headache grew more intense as he waited for someone to respond. A few groaned. Others grimaced.

Postmaster Blair, an abolitionist of southern roots, weighed in. "We must stand against these insurrectionists."

"I am astonished," Attorney General Bates kneaded his brow. "Fort Sumter must be evacuated, and the leaders of our army concur in that opinion. I can hardly believe Sumter has been left so poorly provisioned and unable to defend itself."

Welles spoke. "I was of the same mind days ago. But I am forced to admit, this assessment leaves little room for hope."

"Gentlemen," Seward said. "We should not act rashly. I have rapport with Senator Davis, who leads the confederacy, and with others in the south. They are reasonable men with whom we can bargain in good faith. I ardently encourage this administration to adopt a policy of patience and conciliation. Such a policy will deny the disunionists any new provocation and will prove their apprehensions are groundless."

All the men at the table, save Blair, agreed with Seward.

Lincoln recoiled. Seward had labored hard to worm those notions into all of their minds. He pounded his fist on the table. "I am not of the mind to negotiate with Jeff Davis or his alleged government. We shall not give any claim of legitimacy to these so-called confederate states." He folded up General Scott's report and laid his spectacles aside. "The sentiment appears to be against holding Fort Sumter. It is not a view that I am inclined to share, but I shall mull it for a few days."

Postmaster Blair took Lincoln aside as the Cabinet filed out and proposed he meet with Gustavus Fox. Fox was Blair's brother-in-law and a former navy man who served under the late Commodore Matthew Perry, Father of the Modern Steam Navy. According to Blair, Fox had valuable information about earlier plans to relieve the fort.

Lincoln glimpsed William lingering in the doorway, ready to groom him and lay out his attire for the evening's festivities—the first formal reception of the new administration. He agreed to interview Fox in the morning and followed William down the hallway to his bedroom to get ready. Mrs. Lincoln's heightened anxieties had been on display for the better part of a week, and he should not make her late. The city's luminaries and their wives would soon fill the East Room and pass judgement on his wife's performance as hostess.

While William worked up lather for Lincoln's shave, Lincoln insisted, "When we get back to Springfield four years hence, I do not want you breathing a word of what I am about to say, because I shall deny every word of it. I enjoy your haircuts every bit as much as Billy Florville's."

"Maybe that's because it's the only pleasure you're allowed these days," William replied.

"I am certain there is more to it than that. You're one of the few around me I've come to trust without reservation."

"Your secrets are safe with me."

"Good." Lincoln sighed. "I need someone to keep my secrets. You will do me and the country a great service if you accept the arrangement I am proposing. I will find you a job in another department with the understanding that you will work for me as I require, whether as a fireman, messenger, bootblack, barber, bodyguard, or whatever. You can keep your room here in the servants' quarters. How does that sound?"

"What will Old Edward and the others think?"

"That's where we shall compromise. It seems their objection rests on the custom that the president's butler is the head of the domestic staff. They will never accept you in that role, just as many southerners have refused to accept a Black Republican as their president. Fortunately, in our household—unlike in our government—we can keep the peace by finding a leader the majority will accept."

Later, when Lincoln looked in on his wife, her cousin Lizzie was pleading with her while an olive-skinned woman held out a dress for inspection.

Willie and Tad raced up and clung to Lincoln's legs. As the boys dragged him toward the sofa, he laughed and began pulling on his gloves. He hoped his wife's mood would improve on noticing his gloves were the right color and style. With a theatric flare, Lincoln collapsed on the floor and let the youngsters pile on as he recited lines from Shakespeare's *Taming of the Shrew*.

Mrs. Lincoln ignored their play and complained to Cousin Lizzie seated next to her on the sofa. "I have no time to dress, and, what is more, I shall not dress and go downstairs."

“I am sorry if I have disappointed you, Mrs. Lincoln,” the olive-skinned woman said. “I intended to be in time. Please let me dress you. I can have you ready in a few minutes.”

“No.” Mrs. Lincoln stamped her foot. “I shall not be dressed. I will stay in my room. Mr. Lincoln can go downstairs by himself and enchant all the ladies he pleases.”

“But there is plenty of time for you to dress,” Cousin Lizzie pleaded. “Let Miss Lizabeth assist you, and she will soon have you ready.”

“Mrs. Lincoln, this dress will be the highlight of the evening,” Miss Lizabeth assured. “I should know. My girls and I have sewn every gown you will see tonight. I made certain yours outshines all the rest.”

“Are you absolutely certain about that?” Mrs. Lincoln’s eyes narrowed.

“Absolutely, Mrs. President,” Miss Lizabeth replied.

“We had best get to it then.” Mrs. Lincoln patted the dress.

When his wife was dressed, Lincoln quoted more lines from Shakespeare.

At last, though long, our jarring notes agree,
And time it is when raging war is done
To smile at ’scapes and perils overblown.

Mrs. Lincoln turned to her husband. “You seem to be in a poetical mood tonight.”

“Yes, Mother, this shall be a poetical occasion. You look charming in that dress. Miss Lizabeth has met with great success.”

On their way downstairs for the reception, Mrs. Lincoln stopped. “My handkerchief. Has anyone seen it? I must not go down without it.”

They returned to Mrs. Lincoln's bedroom and while they searched, Willie and Tad planted themselves on the sofa. Tad grinned, a glint of mischief in his eyes.

Miss Lizabeth stopped in front of the sofa and stood over them, her hands on her hips. "Master Tad, you will kindly hand over your mother's kerchief."

He giggled as he pulled it out of his pocket.

Mrs. Lincoln fumed as Miss Lizabeth pinned the handkerchief in its proper place.

"Now there, Mrs. Lincoln." Miss Lizabeth patted the handkerchief. "Take your husband's arm and show those folks downstairs who is the great lady of the People's House."

Mrs. Lincoln's calm was restored, and she descended the stairs on her husband's arm. As they reached the first landing, Mrs. Lincoln said, "I almost forgot. Miss Lizabeth has important news for you."

"Can it not wait?" Lincoln asked.

"No." She beckoned Miss Lizabeth to share her news.

"I might be able to help you, sir," Miss Lizabeth said.

"How so?" Lincoln asked.

"Mrs. Lincoln tells me you are in need of a butler to replace young William."

"That is not my choice. It's an unfair burden that is dropped in my lap, just like the mess I inherited from my predecessor in this office."

"Yes, sir," Miss Lizabeth replied. "I might have a solution for your domestic problem. I am acquainted with a refined colored gentleman, Mr. William Slade. He is an elder in the church where I worship. A man of high credentials and skin light enough he could pass for white, if a person did not examine too closely."

"I reckon this Mr. Slade would be worth talking to," Lincoln replied, "as long as he understands William will continue to attend to my beard and haircuts, and other tasks as needed."

"Thank you, sir. Shall I talk with Mr. Hay or Mr. Nicolay to arrange an appointment?"

"Yes. Please do, and thank you for your help, especially the fine job you do with Mrs. Lincoln's wardrobe." He hesitated. "And for calming her spirits when she becomes anxious."

"It's an honor to help in any way I can."

As Miss Lizabeth retreated up the stairs, the Lincolns proceeded down to the East Room to greet their guests.

* * *

Gustavus Fox called on Lincoln before dawn the next morning and laid out a plan for relieving Fort Sumter. "We can sail several small warships and a transport steamer to Charleston Harbor from New York."

"How do you propose getting troops and provisions into the fort?" Lincoln asked. "I understand there are obstructions in the channel that must be passed over."

"I propose shallow-hulled launches towed by light-draft steam tugs."

Lincoln frowned. "They would have to pass within range of rebel land batteries on Morris and Sullivan Islands."

"A well-armed warship anchored at the entrance to the main channel should be enough to give them cover," Fox replied.

"You seem to have planned this well, Mr. Fox. I shall present it to the Cabinet."

"Sir, I am confident it will work."

After Fox departed, Lincoln stood at the mirror in the water closet, assessing the gaunt face that peered back at him. The question he put to the Cabinet the previous day tormented him. Assuming it possible to now provision Fort Sumter, is it wise to attempt it?

Whichever choice he made regarding Sumter, many would say he lacked character—he was either deceitful, or he could not remain true to his word.

Lincoln splashed water over his face. Two decades earlier, he lamented losing his only valuable possession—his character. He had broken his promise to marry Mrs. Lincoln. In the aftermath of that regrettable choice, melancholy deluged him, and he wished to die. It was not the first time he had entertained suicide. During an earlier dark episode as a young man, he penned the words—

Hell! What is hell to one like me
Who pleasures never know;
By friends consigned to misery,
By hope deserted too?
To ease me of this power to think,
That through my bosom raves,
I'll headlong leap from hell's high brink,
And wallow in its waves.

Lincoln continued to agonize over the crisis at Fort Sumter as Willie and Tad lay beset with fever in the upstairs parlor. Cousin Lizzie applied cold towels to relieve their flushed faces and bloodshot eyes. Their idol, Elmer Ellsworth, showered them with attention. Over the next week, as measles covered the boys with rashes, William relieved Ellsworth and Cousin Lizzie whenever either needed rest. Each day, William brought lunch to Lincoln in the parlor, and in the afternoons, he served tea as Lincoln lay on the sofa, reading to his sons from Charles Dickens' *Oliver Twist.* When Lincoln nodded off, having paced his office floor throughout the night mulling arguments over Fox's plan, William read to the boys in his stead.

Executive Mansion—April 1861

Rain pelted the window of Willie and Tad's bedroom, their huddled bodies nearly concealed by night shadows. The boys had healed from their bouts with the measles and passed the affliction on to Ellsworth, who had mended as well. Lincoln leaned against the doorjamb at half past two o'clock in the morning, watching them sleep, wishing he could share their tranquility.

His slippered feet ached from hours of treading the office floor. The Cabinet reluctantly agreed to Fox's plan, and it had been six days since Fox's fleet sailed for Charleston to resupply and reinforce Fort Sumter. Not a word had been heard from them. Knots tightened in Lincoln's stomach with each passing hour. Telegraph lines from the south had been cut off by rebels. The only news getting to Washington were reports gleaned by the northern press from smuggled southern newspapers. The previous day, the *New York Times* reported three federal steamers lay at anchor off South Carolina's coast. The report listed some but not all the ships that were under Fox's command. The paper also claimed Sumter had been resupplied without bloodshed, though the report was unconfirmed.

Lincoln carried a chair to the boys' bedside and sat, the rain's *rat-a-tat-tat* at his back.

Hours later, a noise in the hallway pulled him from a deep trance. He checked his fob watch—six o'clock. The storm had receded, and morning's first light subdued the night shadows. Voices at the other end of the hall grew louder, clearer. Lincoln tucked the blanket around the boys' shoulders and went to see about the commotion.

At the gate that kept visitors from wandering into the president's office, Nicolay talked with a messenger from the telegraph office. Lincoln approached as Nicolay's face turned ashen.

"What's the news?" Lincoln asked.

"The *New York Times* is reporting they had it all wrong yesterday," Nicolay replied. "The rebels bombarded Sumter."

Lincoln buried his face in his hands. Hundreds of notions spun through his head.

"Sir," Nicolay said.

Lincoln looked up. "What's the present situation?"

"We do not know. Not until the newspapers get us whatever they learn from their sources."

"Get Hay up to the telegraph office in Maryland. Have him take a couple of clerks and send dispatches to the northern newspapers requesting any information they have. The minute something comes off the wire about Sumter, I want someone to make tracks back here." Lincoln palmed the back of his head. "And summon the Cabinet."

"Sir, the Virginia Commissioners will be here at nine o'clock. What should I do with them?"

"I'll meet with them, but they won't like what I have to say."

Virginia's three commissioners arrived at the appointed hour and sat across the long table, their eyes fixed on Lincoln. One of the commissioners was George W. Randolph, a secessionist and grandson of Thomas Jefferson. The other two, Alexander Stuart and William Preston were former congressmen who served in Cabinets of previous administrations. Stuart represented himself as a Unionist and Preston was a one-time abolitionist who converted to a more moderate view.

Preston opened the meeting by reading a resolution passed by Virginia's legislature.

Lincoln interrupted him. "The Richmond newspapers regularly publish details of the convention's proceedings. I am asked to communicate to the assembly the policy which the federal executive intends to pursue regarding the so-called confederate states. Did I recite it correctly?"

Preston and Randolph exchanged sidelong glances.

Lincoln pushed a paper containing his response across the table. "I stated my policy clearly in my inauguration speech. I must admit that I deeply regret, no ... I am mortified that there is great and injurious uncertainty in the public mind about what I intend to do. I intend to hold, occupy, and possess the properties that belong to the federal government. That includes forts, particularly those in the states that claim to have seceded. However, there will be no invasion, no using of force against or among the people anywhere."

The tension on the commissioners' faces faded.

"Nevertheless," Lincoln continued, "if what we have heard this morning is true, that Fort Sumter has been assaulted, I shall consider stopping the delivery of mail to the states in rebellion against the government. The military posts and property situated within those states still belong to the government. I shall not attempt to collect duties and taxes by armed invasion of any part of the country, but I may land such force as is deemed necessary to relieve any fort under menace. Is there any confusion in your minds as to what I intend?"

"So, you intend nothing like a general war?" Stuart asked.

Lincoln gazed out the office window. Hundreds of miles away, it seemed the question of war was out of his hands. "You are correct, Mr. Stuart. A general war is not what *I* intend."

Once the Virginia commissioners departed, William Stoddard, a new addition to the secretarial staff, interrupted. Stoddard's eyes radiated the vigor of youth. "Sir," he said. "I seek release from my duties so I might join the National Rifles in defense of the Union."

"It seems that a mob of radicals has fired on our flag, but we are not at war," Lincoln cautioned. "If we succeeded in resupplying and reinforcing Major Anderson's garrison, we might be able to pressure South Carolina's officials to deal firmly with the perpetrators."

Stoddard pulled back his shoulders. "The morning news is that Major Anderson has already surrendered. They say war has begun."

Lincoln kneaded his brow. "If the fort has been taken, we shall do what we can to get it back. However, war is not our only recourse. South Carolina threw a tantrum some thirty years ago, but when President Jackson threatened to send an army down to Charleston, they capitulated."

"Just the same, sir—"

"I hope, Stoddard, you're not wanting to join up for the excitement of battle." Lincoln crossed his arms. "If that's your reason, let me assure you that war is no game. It's grave business that should only be entered into as a last resort."

"No, sir. I consider it my sacred duty to offer myself in defense of the Union."

"If it makes you happy, you can go sign up. But nobody is marching off to fight, and your duties in this office take precedence, unless, of course, the city is under attack. Is that understood?"

"Yes, sir."

* * *

Secretary of War Cameron arrived at two o'clock in the afternoon, accompanied by James Gilmore, an author and newspaperman with deep relationships in the south. Lincoln sat with them in his office and asked Gilmore for his impression of southern attitudes towards the government.

"Until recently," Gilmore replied, "the masses have been indifferent to the extension or non-extension of slavery. The large slave-owners, who are a small minority, have been the inciters of the present crisis. The small farmers believe they can raise their crops cheaper using hired labor rather than carrying the burden of keeping slaves. When you were nominated for the presidency, the slavers broadcast word that you are an abolitionist, and worse, that you have Negro blood in your veins. They claim you intend to free the slaves and make them equal to whites politically."

"Do you think the common people believe those absurdities?" Lincoln asked.

"They are intelligent men, but most have never traveled a hundred miles from home, never seen a decent Yankee, and never read anything but what the politicians choose to tell them in southern newspapers. Let a northern army set foot on southern soil, and every man of them will become a soldier. They will fight to the last gasp in defense of their homes. They have no idea of any allegiance to the general government. They have been reared in the doctrine of States Rights, and so when their states secede, they will go with them, feeling sure that they are doing their duty to their country."

A disturbance in the hallway distracted Lincoln. Official word from Sumter was overdue. He looked at Cameron. "Are you expecting news?"

Cameron shook his head.

Lincoln returned his attention to Gilmore. "Would not one good, decisive victory bring them to their senses?"

"No, sir. Not even ten victories," Gilmore replied. "The leaders have gone into this struggle to win at any cost. Those who are not self-seeking scoundrels are fanatics. Words and concessions would be wasted on them. They have planned this thing since General Jackson buried the idea of Nullification nearly thirty years ago, or maybe even from the beginning of the republic. Jackson stood his ground and they capitulated, but he did not kill the notion that states are superior to the nation. That idea has come to life again in the form of secession. The only way to bring the south to its senses is to knock down the secessionist leaders."

"Knock down the leaders?" Lincoln leaned back in his chair. "Did you not say the mass of common men are of the same mind?"

William entered with a tray of tea and began serving.

"They are," Gilmore replied. "However, most southern people do not own slaves. If they employ any, they pay wages to the slaves' masters—the same wages they would pay to freedmen, or more. Although they are indifferent to the slavery question, they fear the general government will make it a policy to put the Negro race on an equality with the white man."

Lincoln interrupted. "Full equality would offend even the staunchest northern man. In many southern districts where Negroes outnumber whites, such a policy would give political control to the colored man."

"Yes," Gilmore said. "That fear is the power their leaders have over them. Whatever course you take, do not go down any path that leads to Negro equality."

William wanted to scream. *No! Don't listen to this man. Equality is exactly the course you should take.* But Mrs. Lincoln's caution echoed in his head—*it is never your place to display your emotions or draw attention to yourself ... remain unheard and for all practical purposes, invisible.* He held his breath, willing himself to be perfectly calm.

"How do you propose we take down the leaders?" Lincoln asked.

Gilmore leaned forward. "A man's wealth in the south is not calculated in dollars, but in the number of slaves. Drive your carriage into any plantation and the first thing you will see is the slave shanties on display, all in rows. It takes little effort for a visitor to estimate the owner's wealth in human property. The leaders of the south have gone into the rebellion to protect their human property. You cannot put down their insurrection until you deprive them of slavery."

Cameron nodded his agreement.

"Go on," Lincoln said.

William had spent countless hours, lying awake nights mulling whether freedom without equality was truly freedom. He reminded himself, *do not display your emotions ...*

"The Abolitionists are right." Lincoln straightened. "Slavery is the root of the whole crisis. But I have no constitutional authority to abolish it."

William gritted his teeth. He wanted to say—*that's what you were chosen to do*—but he checked himself.

"Except as a war measure," Gilmore replied. "Now, seven states have declared themselves independent and have begun a war in Charleston Harbor."

Cameron interrupted. "The Cabinet is not yet prepared to go to war."

"Yes," Lincoln focused his attention on Gilmore. "It does appear that something like a war may be upon us, but whether we've had enough cannonballs flying to justify extreme measures is the question. Tell me, Mr. Gilmore, what would you do if you were in my place, bound as I am by the Constitution?"

"If I were in your place, sir, I would announce to the seven seceding states that if they do not return to their allegiance within a specified time—say ninety days—you will free every one of their slaves. Of course, you will probably end up freeing every slave in the south, but the slaveholders would have brought it upon themselves."

Lincoln pressed further. "Do you reckon the north would sustain me in such a measure? Even if they did, what do you think would be the result?"

"For more than twenty years, I have enjoyed the closest relations with the south. My dearest friends live there, and if we have a war of any considerable duration, four-fifths of all my worldly possessions will go up in smoke. Nevertheless, I would rather see it all go than know my children would inherit a disorganized and disunited country. Other men feel as I do, and they will want you to remove from the nation this seed of perpetual discord."

Cameron clenched his jaw.

"They may," Lincoln ran his fingers through his hair. "If they are brought to see things as you see them. And they would find me willing, you may say, eager to listen. But you must bear in mind that I have no authority to emancipate slaves, except for the preservation of the Union."

A lump rose in William's throat. He recalled Mrs. Lincoln's other words—*if you are patient ...*

"As I said," Gilmore replied, "it must be a war measure, forced upon you by the pressure of necessity."

"Or the overwhelming sentiment of the north," Lincoln said. "Now without touching slavery, how would you put down this rebellion?"

William's hands trembled as he picked up the tea service. One of the cups tumbled to the floor. He and Lincoln exchanged glances.

Cameron whispered to Lincoln. "Had not you dismissed him when he served us earlier?"

"I didn't see the necessity," Lincoln replied. "Mr. Gilmore, please go ahead with your thought."

"Nearly a century ago, the British cabinet had a plan for subduing our revolution. They intended to divide the colonies into three sections and to crush each section separately."

"The principle of divide and conquer." Lincoln smiled.

"Exactly. Deprive them of their slaves. Cut the confederacy into three pieces, and the rebellion will fizzle."

Lincoln thanked Gilmore and walked him and Cameron down the hallway to the top of the stairs.

William lingered in the office, hoping to speak privately with Lincoln.

When Lincoln returned, he studied William for a moment. "Is there something you want to say?"

"Sir, I was just wondering. If it does come to war, will we be allowed to fight?"

"Unlikely," Lincoln replied.

"Who has more to fight for than the people who are oppressed?"

"There are not enough white men willing to fight alongside Negroes to raise an army of any size. Besides, there's not going to be any war." Lincoln sat at his desk and sifted through a stack of papers.

"But, sir."

"That's all, William."

"Yes, sir."

* * *

Telegrams littered Lincoln's desk after another sleepless night. He massaged his temples. Major Anderson had surrendered under a maelstrom of artillery fire. Why, Lincoln wondered, did southern men harbor such malice? Malice toward the Negro. Malice toward those who would elevate the condition of all men. Malice against popular government when it opposed them.

What right did they have to insist that a minority of people could break up popular governments when asked to yield for the greater good? Had he not, in fact, yielded for his entire lifetime, yielded to the necessity of slavery and its benefits to the nation's economic machinery? He fingered the cuff of the linen shirt on his back. Even his shirt was a daily reminder of his concessions to slavery.

Voices in the hallway alerted him to the arrival of Cabinet ministers coming to weigh in on the Sumter crisis.

Once all were seated, Secretary of War Cameron laid out a plan to call for more than 100,000 volunteers. He advocated blockades of southern ports, the capture of Charleston and New Orleans, and freedom to all slaves who deserted their masters to join the Union armies.

Seward argued that such measures would close the door to reconciliation with the seceded states.

Lincoln stood in the breach between the two men. Neither course would allow him to keep his promises. Seward's notion conjured images of a dog chasing is own tail. Cameron's proposal would require ten times the army the government had available. Besides, it was too ambitious and belligerent. Instead, Lincoln wanted the army to focus, on what mattered most—defending the seat of government and repossessing the properties that had been seized by the insurrectionists.

Attorney General Bates cautioned that only Congress, which was not in session, had the power to raise an army or declare war. When asked whether there were exceptions, he cited the *1795 Act for Calling Forth the Militia*, which President Washington used to put down the Whisky Rebellion. The act allowed the executive to call forth various state militias to serve for 90 days, or for up to 30 days after Congress assembled.

The Cabinet agreed to call Congress to a special session. If the people demanded an energetic war, their elected representatives could authorize a half million, or even a million men. By unanimous vote, the Cabinet approved a proclamation petitioning the states for 75,000 militia, in the interim, to defend the government if the secessionists mounted a military invasion of Washington.

B & O Washington Depot—April 1861

Willie and Tad sported wooden swords as they accompanied their parents to see Ellsworth off at the train depot. The boys claimed to be the first Illinois recruits to answer Lincoln's call to arms. Ellsworth teased that he would have been first, but he had to travel to New York to organize a new militia regiment, while his surrogate younger brothers were already in the Capital. Ellsworth planned to recruit New York firefighters for a unit modeled after the Chicago Zouaves. He would call them the Fire Zouaves.

The skids had been greased for Ellsworth's arrival in New York. Thurlow Weed's contacts with the city's volunteer fire companies had set in motion the process of gathering 90-day recruits from the local firehouses. Garment makers were already cutting patterns for regimental uniforms—light gray chasseur-style jackets with dark blue and red trim, gray trousers with a blue stripe running down the seam, and tan leather leggings. Along with their gray uniforms, the Zouaves would wear red kepis with blue bands and don red fezzes with blue tassels.

Ellsworth also carried a personal letter of recommendation from Lincoln.

> *Ever since the beginning of our acquaintance, I have valued you highly as a friend, and at the same time, have had a very high estimate of your military talent.*
>
> *Affectionately yours,*
>
> *A. Lincoln*

Ellsworth turned to William as he ruffled Tad's hair. "Can you handle these two without my help?"

“It won’t be the same,” William replied. “How can they pretend we’re the four musketeers?”

Tad pointed his wooden sword at William. “Just three musketeers and Planchet.”

“Now we’ll be only two musketeers and their servant,” Willie added.

“Hold your horses,” Lincoln teased. “I thought he was my Planchet.”

The conductor’s “All Aboard” call spoiled a light-hearted distraction from the bittersweet hour. Mrs. Lincoln kissed Ellsworth on the cheek as tears welled in her eyes. Lincoln’s eyes misted when the boys hugged Ellsworth goodbye.

CHAPTER TEN

Executive Mansion—May 1861

Mr. Slade—the valet who replaced William—arrived shortly after sunrise, carrying a fresh suit. Lincoln studied him. Hazel eyes, straight chestnut hair, skin so light he could pass for white. The rebellious domestic staff should be satisfied.

"Let's get out of that nightshirt," Slade said.

"I'm capable of dressing myself," Lincoln insisted.

"Yes, sir, I know. But there will be thousands of folks assessing you when you go out. It shall not hurt to have two sets of eyes looking you over before you leave."

"I reckon you have a point." The president fidgeted with the buttons on his new shirt.

"And don't forget, sir. Young Colonel Ellsworth has returned from New York with his Fire Zouave regiment. You will be inducting them into service this evening."

"Will he be joining us for breakfast?" Lincoln asked.

"No, sir. He will be occupied all day with military business."

"Maybe I shall go visit him this afternoon, if time permits. Where is the regiment billeted?"

"I understand they are camped on the floor of the House of Representatives chamber," Slade replied.

"By the way, my wife's dressmaker ... Miss Lizabeth?" Lincoln paused.

"Yes, sir. Mrs. Keckly." Slade stood by with Lincoln's coat draped over his arm.

"So, Miss Lizabeth recommended you."

"Yes, sir."

"Mrs. Lincoln is quite high on the woman."

"As am I." Slade held out Lincoln's tie. "I knew Mrs. Keckly when I lived here in the city prior to moving my family up to Cleveland for a little while. She is well respected in our church community."

"It's a shame how the others treated William." Lincoln put on the tie and began tying a diamond knot.

"Yes, sir. In a dog-eat-dog world, folks seem to find ways to excuse injustice."

"I agree. I reckon you and Miss Lizabeth, being religious folks, are on the side of justice."

"Certainly." Slade adjusted Lincoln's tie. "And that raises a question I suppose I should have cleared up when I was interviewed for this position."

"Go ahead. I'm listening."

"Since Mrs. Keckly is involved in the same matters—and I assume Mrs. Lincoln is willing to tolerate it—I hope you will show the same leniency."

"Spit it out, Slade."

"Sir, both Mrs. Keckly and I are strong advocates of the advancement of Africans in society. You and I may be at cross purposes on some occasions."

"Mrs. Lincoln already enlightened me." Lincoln gestured to chairs next to the window. "Sit with me."

"Thank you, sir."

"You spoke of cross purposes," Lincoln said. "Now, let me tell you a story of an event that occurred when I was a young man. The head surveyor in the county sent a local farmer to tell me he wanted to hire me to be his deputy. Unlike you, I had no training or experience at the job in question. On top of that, it was well known that I was partial to the Whig Party. The surveyor was the opposite—an avid Jackson man. The farmer took notice of my hesitation and asked what was the matter. The job paid $3 a day. Almost half of the salary of the State's governor."

"Sounds like you should have jumped at the chance," Slade said.

"That was the farmer's sentiment. He believed the surveyor probably didn't care about my politics. He was desperate for the help, considering how fast the county was growing. But I wasn't sure the farmer understood politics well enough, so I went to the county seat in Springfield to find out for myself. Without owning a horse, it was nearly a day's walk each way."

"So, what did the surveyor say?" Slade asked.

"Just what the farmer suspected, but I still had doubts. So, I pressed the matter harder. I inquired, 'Why would

President Jackson allow you to give an appointment to a Whig?' The surveyor leaned back in his chair and said, 'Folks tell me you're the brightest, most honest and dependable young man to be had. I assure you that your politics won't matter to President Jackson, and I don't give a hang about your politics, either.' Still not sure, I asked, 'You won't press me to change my views or shrink from speaking forthrightly?' He replied, 'My only concern is having accurate, honest surveys made with all dispatch. As long as that's done, you're free to engage in whatever political matters you see fit.'"

Lincoln stood. "I'm sure you already know disagreement is a big part of my job. In fact, disagreement helps me do the job right. I reckon as long as we can approach any differences with mutual trust and respect, we should not have a problem. After all, William is not bashful about saying what's on his mind ... which by the way brings me to a big point. You will see a lot of William around here. I'm arranging employment for him in one of the other departments, under the condition that I can call on him whenever I see fit. I promised him he can be my barber and run whatever errands I deem appropriate. He will tend to my wardrobe in the mornings and evenings under your supervision. Your main job is to keep this household in good order."

Slade smoothed the shoulders of Lincoln's coat. "There you are, sir. You can rest assured I will do my very best to meet your expectations. As for young William, maybe I can do you both a service by taking him under my wing. Teach him the ropes. Make him into an excellent gentleman's man."

* * *

Lincoln pored over patronage petitions after everyone else had retired for the night. Around ten o'clock, someone bounded up the central staircase to the mansion's second floor. Nicolay bolted out of his bedroom at the east end of the hall and intercepted the unannounced visitor.

Lincoln stepped out of his office into the hallway to find Nicolay listening intently to one of the Zouaves. Nicolay and the Zouave clammed up as Lincoln approached.

William appeared at the top of the stairs. He had been in the basement, unable to sleep as he mulled the differences between freedom for coloreds and freedom for whites. The footsteps on the staircase turned his attention to Lincoln's safety and that of his family.

Lincoln laid his hand on Nicolay's shoulder. "What's up?"

"There's been a shooting," Nicolay replied.

"Let's go into my office, so we don't disturb my family."

Once inside the office, Nicolay explained, "Near the National Hotel, an angry mob of soldiers is threatening to demolish the guardhouse and hang the culprits."

"Sir." The soldier removed his hat. "Word is the victim is one of ours."

"Ours?" The word caught in Lincoln's throat. "A Zouave?"

"Yes, sir. We've dispatched a detail to collect the remains. Captain sent me here. Thought you'd want to be informed."

"Is it? Is it Ellsworth?" Lincoln rocked to one side.

Nicolay gripped Lincoln's elbow.

"We don't know," the Zouave answered. "There was a scuffle between the Metropolitan Police and some militia. Several policemen have been arrested. Military commanders are talking to the Police Chief and trying to get the soldiery settled down."

"Son," Lincoln said. "Go catch up with your detail and bring me word as soon as you know anything more."

William went downstairs to make tea while Lincoln and Nicolay waited for news.

Lincoln's chin quivered as memories flooded his mind—Ellsworth reading points of law, giving stump speeches for the Republican cause, helping shove folks aside to clear a path to the voting window, the exotic uniforms and precision drills.

An hour of agony passed before the Zouave returned to report that Ellsworth was not involved in the shooting. Lincoln slumped forward and buried his head in his hands, pressing back tears of relief.

The soldier explained that the victim was not a Zouave. He was a 19-year-old member of the Washington Rifles—an amiable youth who was the principal support of his orphan sisters. He was shot in the back of the head. The murderer was believed to be a police officer with secessionist sympathies.

Lincoln's relief turned to anger. A patriotic life sacrificed for a cause that no decent man should oppose. Not only that, it easily could have been Stoddard.

Lincoln's ire continued to flame as he paced his office floor alone, resigned to another sleepless night. He stopped his pacing to work at his desk and shuffled papers until hours later when more footsteps clambered up the stairs. His fob watch told him it was half past four in the morning. As Lincoln stepped into the hallway, Nicolay stood in the waiting area, admonishing a young soldier from Ellsworth's regiment.

"What is it this time?" Lincoln demanded.

Mrs. Lincoln appeared in the doorway of her bedroom. She stomped her feet and screamed, "Have you no respect for our privacy?"

"Sorry, Ma'am," the Zouave replied.

"A fire," Nicolay explained. "A large building adjoining Willard's Hotel."

The soldier added, "The Zouaves were called on to put it out."

"Where's the fire department?" Lincoln asked.

"Sitting on their hands." Nicolay replied. "The city is plagued by divided loyalties."

"Damned rebels," Mrs. Lincoln grumbled. "I have a train to catch in the morning. Cannot a person get some sleep in this house?" She stormed back to bed.

The soldier continued, "The municipals were slow responding. We broke into some firehouses to get equipment. Ladders are scarce. Water was coming at a trickle."

"Do we know how it started?" Lincoln asked.

"No, but our boys formed a human pyramid to haul water up to the roof. No sooner than the flames were put out, several more fires started in the basement."

Nicolay lowered his voice. "Willard's is full of Republican dignitaries."

A twinge of headache struck behind Lincoln's eyes. "Was the hotel damaged?"

"Just some smoke and water damage," the soldier answered.

"How about the other building?"

"Gone, sir. But you will be proud. When the fire was at its highest, a small national flag fell from the rear of the building, and a band of secessionists nearby yelled, 'There, there, that's the way they'll all go before long.' A Zouave caught the flag before it hit the ground and waved it amid a cheering crowd of patriots. Mr. Willard ran up two large flags from his hotel, and a Zouave shouted back, 'Our colors shall never be burnt, and they shan't come down.'"

Washington City—May 1861

The Zouaves moved out of their billet on the floor of the House of Representatives chamber after the Willard's hotel fire and set up camp on the heights across the river from the Navy Yard. Two weeks later, William drove Willie and Tad to the regiment's new encampment. The boys exchanged quick hellos with Ellsworth before rushing off to inspect the troops.

With the boys out of sight, Ellsworth's mood turned solemn.

"Is everything all right?" William asked.

Ellsworth invited William into his tent. "I have a secret for you."

"Sounds serious," William cocked his head.

"Yesterday, after Virginia voted to ratify secession, rumors floated about that a movement was to be made against Alexandria. I went immediately to see General Mansfield, the commander at Washington. I told him I would consider it a personal affront if he did not allow us to have the right of the line. It's a right that is due us as the first volunteer regiment sworn in for the war."

"What does that mean?" William asked.

"All I can say is we are preparing for a nice little sail, and, at the end of it, a skirmish."

"You'll be careful." William's eyes narrowed.

"Of course, but we go forward either to victory or death. We shall do nothing to shame the regiment. We intend to show the enemy that we are honorable men, as well as soldiers, and will treat them with kindness until they force us to use violence. I prefer to kill them with kindness."

William locked eyes with his friend. "You sound like you plan to die."

"Plan, no, but I am prepared to do so if that is my lot." Ellsworth placed his hand on William's shoulder.

William stared at the floor of the tent.

"I have a favor to ask." Ellsworth angled his head into William's line of vision.

"Anything," William replied.

"I have two letters I would like posted. One is to my dear father and mother. The other is for my beloved Carrie." Ellsworth placed the envelopes in William's hands.

"I shall ask Mr. Lincoln to let me go with you." William's throat tightened. "This is more my fight than yours."

"You can't," Ellsworth countered.

"Why?"

"You know why."

"So, we're not truly equals." William clenched his jaw.

"I'm going for you and Grace and all the other Graces."

"Come back." Tears welled in William's eyes. "You can meet her when freedom finally comes."

"I look forward to that day. And we must make a trip north so you can meet my Carrie." Ellsworth smiled, bravely. "The highest happiness I look forward to on this earth is my union with her."

"Then you will come back safe."

"I am perfectly content," Ellsworth said, "to accept whatever my fortune may be, confident that He who noteth even the fall of a sparrow will have some purpose in the fate of one like me."

Willie and Tad popped into the tent, their inspection of the encampment complete.

Ellsworth gave each of them a hardy embrace before they climbed aboard the carriage and drove off.

Executive Mansion—May 1861

Folks say that lightning never strikes twice in the same place. Lincoln wished the adage were true. Tears welled in his eyes as he tried to focus on the War Department's announcement of Elmer Ellsworth's death and the memorandum of details that accompanied it. In Lincoln's 52 years, too many whom he loved had died too young—his little brother Tommy, his angel mother, his sister Sally, his sweetheart Annie, his second son Eddie, Ellsworth at age 24—what a grand life he lived.

Lincoln's grief compounded as he stepped into his wife's bedchamber and broke the news. She sobbed, collapsing in a heap on the floor. He knelt beside her, taking her into his arms.

"Do not make me go through this sorrow again," she murmured, tears streaming down her cheeks. "Promise me our Bobbie will not go to war."

Together they wept.

With his voice hoarse from grieving, he told her what he knew. Ten thousand Union troops swarmed into Alexandria. The campaign to take the town and bluffs across the Potomac was necessary to create a buffer between the Capital and Virginia's rebel army. Ellsworth's men were detailed to put out fires during the invasion. As Ellsworth pulled down a rebel flag at Marshall House, the inn's proprietor shot him.

Mrs. Lincoln composed herself as abruptly as her grief had manifested. She dressed in black, with a dark veil pulled over her face, and rode with her husband to the Navy Yard to view Ellsworth's body. On seeing the young soldier's lifeless form, she sobbed anew.

"My boy!" She exclaimed. "Was this sacrifice necessary?"

One of the exotic-uniformed Zouaves approached and placed in Mrs. Lincoln's hands the bloodstained rebel flag that Ellsworth took down at Marshall House. Her tears grew more intense. She thrust the flag into her husband's hands and muttered, "I cannot bare the sight of that thing!"

Lincoln, fighting back tears, gave it over to William and instructed him to hide it away somewhere it would never be seen. William's eyes misted, his throat raw. Ellsworth was the only white person he truly called a friend. He reminded William of a younger version of his own brother Thomas—dedicated, loyal, kind, both taken too soon from this world.

Lincoln returned to the mansion after viewing Ellsworth's body to find Senator Henry Wilson of Massachusetts, a leading radical Republican, waiting to see him. Lincoln's chin quivered as he greeted the senator. "Excuse me," he stammered. "I cannot talk. I will make no apology for my weakness, but I knew Ellsworth well and held him in great regard."

In the early evening, Lincoln drove back to the Navy Yard and arranged for removal of Ellsworth's body to the mansion's East Room—a spacious parlor appointed with rich carpeting and flowing draperies. When the lad's remains arrived, Mrs. Lincoln placed Ellsworth's picture on the casket, along with a flower wreath made with her own hands.

Following Ellsworth's funeral, Lincoln, Willie, Tad, and William escorted the young Colonel's remains to the train depot and watched as the casket was loaded onto a railcar for their friend's final journey to his parents' home in New York.

On returning to the mansion, Lincoln shut himself in his office and locked the door. He dropped into a chair—eyes bleary, head throbbing—and drew a thick veil over his thoughts. William brought tea and knocked on the door. Lincoln didn't answer.

William set the tea service next to Lincoln's office door and tiptoed downstairs to his bed where he wept until morning.

Lincoln rose hours later in hazy moonlight that filtered through his second story office window. He took his shawl from its peg by the door, draped it around his shoulders, and wrote condolences to Ellsworth's parents, Ephraim and Phoebe Ellsworth of Mechanicsville, New York.

> *My acquaintance with your son began less than two years ago, and through the latter half of that time, our association was as intimate as the disparity of our ages and my engrossing engagements would permit. The proof of his good heart is that he never forgot his parents. I intend no intrusion upon the sacredness of your sorrow by sending you this tribute to the memory of your brave and early fallen child. May God give you that consolation, which is beyond all earthly power.*
>
> *Sincerely your friend in a common affliction.*
>
> *A. Lincoln*

* * *

William rapped on Lincoln's office door. He carried Lincoln's breakfast tray and a copy of *Frank Leslie's Illustrated Newspaper*.

Lincoln responded with a terse, "Enter."

William had opened the newspaper to a double-page spread of woodcuts, hoping the illustrations would catch Lincoln's eye. One illustration showed runaway slaves—men, women, and children—crossing a creek under a full moon. Another frame depicted Union General Benjamin Butler welcoming the runaways into Fortress Monroe. The headline declared—

Stampede among the Negroes in Virginia

William set the tray on the long table next to a newspaper Lincoln had been perusing. That paper displayed a headline—

Estimated value of property under General Butler's protection is $500,000–an average of $1,000 apiece at the Southern human flesh markets

Lincoln muttered, "They are supposedly contraband of war."

"Does that mean they're free?" William asked. His thoughts fled to Grace and Maddie.

Slade, who had shadowed William, unnoticed, appeared in the doorway. "No, it does not, but that tongue of yours is running mighty loose."

"Everyone seems to think all I must do is utter some magical incantation." Lincoln waved his hand in the air. "And everyone is free and living in peace. Failing that, they take whatever business they're after into their own hands."

"I think Mr. Lincoln has more important things to do than listen to your jawing," Slade scolded.

"What I do not have time for is the two of you at each other's throats," Lincoln said. "I have enough on my hands with generals in the field running their mouths."

Lincoln pulled the food tray close and picked up the newspaper.

As Slade and William stepped into the hallway, William muttered, "You took my job. What more are you after?"

Slade gripped William's shoulder. William jerked away, clenching his fists.

"Boy," Slade growled. "You need to do something about that chip before someone knocks it off your shoulder."

"Is that a threat?"

"I did not come here to make war. And I did not take your job. As I understand it, some bumptious house Negro did not care for the shade of your skin. It was not me. If you open your eyes you will see that I want to help you. But you have to be willing to be helped."

"You and Mrs. Keckly are friends, right? The other staff started on me as soon as she showed up to work for Mrs. Lincoln. I may be another ignorant colored boy to you, but my brain works as good as yours. So do my eyes. I see what you two are doing."

William tramped down the stairs, gritting his teeth.

Washington City and Vicinity—Summer 1861

Buggies and wagons filled Washington's streets on a bright morning in late July. Jubilant men of every type and station shouted, "Forward to Richmond," as they set out on a three-hour journey to Centreville, Virginia. The Union and rebel armies were set to face off on the banks of a small river called Bull Run near Manassas Junction. Everyone wanted a front row seat to watch General McDowell's army crush the rebellion in a walkover—get the whole thing over in a day. Among them,

Senator Henry Wilson carried a basket of sandwiches to enjoy as he and his friends watched the excitement.

When the day began, Wilson didn't anticipate he would be in Lincoln's office after midnight, dazed and beleaguered, recounting the terror of that afternoon. He and others became impatient with the hour-long delays in receiving updates from the battlefield. From their vantage at Centreville, a few miles from the battle, all they saw were puffs of gun smoke rising above treetops. They ventured closer to the sound of muskets and artillery fire, settling at a spot within a mile of the action. Wilson was passing out sandwiches when the earth rumbled under his feet. He looked up at wagons and horses thundering toward him, followed by a wave of blue-clad infantrymen in retreat, shouting as they raced past, "Turn back! Turn back! We're whipped!" Wilson was almost captured by rebels as he watched a cannon shot demolish his empty carriage. He returned to Washington on the back of a stray mule. At least one member of Congress was not so lucky. He was taken prisoner.

Elihu Washburne, an old Illinois friend of Lincoln's, staggered into the office and added his account. He tried to stop the panic-stricken soldiers from retreating by blocking the road with his wagon but was overwhelmed by a stampede of civilians caught up in the Union army's flight. Another senator who was with him, Ben Wade of Ohio, picked up a discarded rifle and threatened to shoot anyone who didn't turn back and face the enemy.

Lincoln's mind reeled at the horrors the senators described. Images of carnage and chaos dogged him long after the men left. The astounding casualties. The consequences to the nation. The humiliating loss meant the war would be protracted and costly. Ultimate victory was anything but certain.

General Scott barged into the office unannounced at about 2 o'clock in the morning, demanding Mrs. Lincoln and their sons be sent north, far from danger.

Mrs. Lincoln could not help waking as the 300-pound general rumbled up the stairs, shuddering the floorboards of the old mansion. On hearing his demand, she stormed out of her bedroom, dressed in her night clothes and robe, and planted herself in her husband's office doorway. "We will do no such thing," she shouted.

Scott pleaded with Lincoln. "For heaven's sake, if she won't be sensible, command her to leave."

Mrs. Lincoln lunged at Scott, her hands raised ready to pummel the rotund, ailing, 75-year-old. Lincoln caught her and wrapped his arms around her. She flailed at her husband's chest. "Don't make us go," she pleaded with tears in her eyes.

Lincoln replied in a steady voice, "I will neither make you go, nor force you to stay. Whatever you wish to do, I will honor that."

General Scott complained. "I cannot protect them. I have no army—".

"Thank you, General," Lincoln replied. "Your concerns are noted. If you'll excuse us."

Lincoln walked his wife to her suite and continued to comfort her.

At daybreak, the once hopeful Union army, having been reduced to a tattered rain-soaked mob, straggled past the mansion. The lines continued through the afternoon. Along Pennsylvania Avenue, shocked and somber citizens worked at tables set up by the Sanitary Commission to feed haggard soldiers. Doctors and nurses stood by, waiting for ambulances that had been sent to transport the wounded from the battlefield. But most returned empty. Anyone who could not walk away from the fight was left behind to be taken prisoner or to die. Congress sent Lincoln a bill authorizing the enlistment of 500,000 men for up to three years of service.

* * *

Several weeks after the army's debacle at Bull Run, Lincoln found Miss Lizabeth sitting in the upstairs parlor. "Do you have a moment?" he asked.

Miss Lizabeth always found a way to mollify his wife's sullen moods, and Lincoln hoped the dressmaker could help him settle a domestic impasse. Mrs. Lincoln had been trying without success to get her friend, William Wood, appointed to the post of Superintendent of Buildings.

Miss Lizabeth glanced up at him, her reddened eyes betraying her grief.

As she started to stand, Lincoln gestured for her to remain seated. "What's wrong?" he asked.

"Sorry, Mr. Lincoln. I do not need to bother you with my problems." She blew her nose in a kerchief.

"I do not understand." He knelt in front of her.

"My George—" she murmured.

"George?"

She tried to explain through her sobbing. "My sss ... sson."

"Your son?" he asked.

"He's gone. My sweet George is gone." She clutched a scrap of paper in her hand.

"For Heaven's sake, what happened?"

"Killed." She sobbed harder.

"I am so sorry." Lincoln's lips quivered.

She straightened, drew a deep breath, and wiped her tears. "What is it you wanted, sir?"

"It's about Mrs. Lincoln."

"She has locked herself in her room. Shall I try to rouse her?"

"No. It can wait," he answered. "I am truly sorry for your loss. If there is anything I can do, please do not hesitate to ask."

Miss Lizabeth thanked him for his kind words, and he excused himself, allowing her to continue mourning in private.

CHAPTER ELEVEN

Executive Mansion—September 1861

Nicolay followed as William carried the morning newspapers upstairs. They found Lincoln in his office, pacing, agitated over his wife's response to news that her friend, Mr. Wood, faced serious corruption allegations by a Congressional investigating committee.

Lincoln stopped pacing and collected the newspapers from William. He glanced at the first headline. General Frémont had declared martial law in Missouri and issued a proclamation that all rebel property would be confiscated. Slaves would be freed and recruited into the army. Lincoln threw the newspaper across the room. It fell short of landing on his corner desk.

"Could he not telegraph me first?" Lincoln shouted. "I am just learning about this from a newspaper? This is not his decision to make. He has upended months of negotiations with Congress over compensated emancipation and endangered our fragile bond with leading men in the Border States."

"Shall I draft an order rescinding his proclamation?" Nicolay asked.

"No," Lincoln replied. "Europe's governments will lose faith in our resolve to end slavery. They will cave to economic demands by bankers and industrialists to reinforce the south for the sake of the cotton trade. That would be the end of us."

A couple of days later, sweat collected on Lincoln's brow as he read a telegram from Joshua Speed, a long-time intimate friend and the administration's strongest Kentucky ally.

> *I have been unable to eat or sleep... Frémont's foolish proclamation will crush every vestige of a Union spirit in the state ... so fixed is public sentiment in Kentucky against freeing Negroes and allowing them to remain among us ... cruelty and crime will run riot in the land and the poor Negroes will be almost exterminated ... think of this, I implore you.*

Lincoln sent an urgent dispatch to Speed, assuring him that Frémont would revise his proclamation. He would not exceed the intent of Congress's Confiscation Act which passed with unanimous support from the Kentucky delegation.

No sooner than Lincoln replied, a second telegram arrived from Speed. A unit of Kentucky's pro-Union militia threw down their weapons and disbanded upon hearing of Frémont's proclamation. Speed doubted Kentucky could be kept in the Union camp if Frémont's edict wasn't quashed.

Lincoln collapsed in a chair, imagining it would not take Jeff Davis long to smell the opportunity Frémont handed him. Rebel troops would flood into Kentucky, and Speed would be hard pressed to convince his Unionist friends to remain steadfast. Losing Kentucky would be nearly the same as losing the whole game. Kentucky gone, the Union could not hold Delaware, Missouri, or Maryland. With the Border States in the rebel camp, he might as well consent to disunion and surrender Washington, to boot.

The tug-of-war between Lincoln and General Frémont dragged on for more than a week. During that time, Lincoln's advisors battered him on all sides. Some lauded Frémont and warned reversing his policy would push Europe over to the side of the rebellion. Others fretted that bringing Negroes into the fight would undermine public support for the government's call to arms. Northern men might fight for them, but not with them.

William sat in a corner one morning, blacking Lincoln's boots, when Secretary Chase arrived for a meeting. Chase defended Frémont's proclamation. He claimed the rebels made slavery the cornerstone of their cause—every Bill of Secession passed by a seceding state declared so. Chase unfolded a newspaper clipping of a speech given by Alexander Stephens, the rebellion's vice president. "See here." Chase pointed to the speech. "He inaugurated their new constitution by boasting it 'puts to rest forever the agitation over our peculiar institutions—slavery and the proper status of the Negro in our civilization.'"

"I've seen the speech," Lincoln replied. "He also said the agitation over slavery was the immediate cause of the present revolution."

"Of course, it was," Chase insisted. "But that is not my point. Here, he declared that the principles of Jefferson and our Founders were 'fundamentally wrong.' He asserted the confederacy's new government is 'founded on the opposite ideas. Its cornerstone rests upon the great truth that the Negro is not equal to the white man, that slavery and subordination to the superior race is his natural condition.' He boasted their new government is 'the first in the history of the world to be founded upon this great moral truth.'"

"What do you want me to do?" Lincoln asked.

"Leave Frémont and his proclamation in place. Let the Negroes join the fight."

"That would be suicide, both for the Negroes and for the Union," Lincoln retorted. "Not to speak of the fact that the Constitution prohibits the general government from interfering with slavery where it existed when the country was formed."

"I think you are making a grave mistake," Chase insisted.

"You may be correct, but it is my mistake to make. Now, if you don't have anything else for me, I have some things that demand my attention."

After Secretary Chase left, William set down the boots he was blacking. "Is what Mr. Chase said true?"

"Of course, it is." Lincoln sat to pull on his boots. "Just the same, I have decided to rescind Frémont's edict."

"The general has done exactly what the war ought to do."

"Things are more complicated than they appear," Lincoln replied. "Besides, generals don't have the authority to act as he did. Hell, *I* don't have that kind authority. Congress doesn't have it, either."

"So tens of thousands of soldiers are fighting over whether people like me should exchange our old masters for new ones?"

Lincoln recalled similar words he read to William in Springfield as he drafted his manifesto.

> *... no oppressed people will fight and endure as our fathers did, without the promise of something better than a mere change of masters.*

Lincoln cocked his head. "What does one thing have to do with the other?"

"If we're not allowed to fight our own battles, then we're inferior. Someone is over us, same as if they were our masters."

"I have no intention of putting Negroes in the army to carry arms."

Executive Mansion—October 1861

Crisp autumn air signaled winter's approach as Lincoln lounged under a large tree on the mansion's northeast lawn. Senator Ned Baker lay on his back with his hands clasped behind his head. A gentle breeze played with wisps of Baker's gray hair. In their Illinois lawyer days, Baker's grand oratory was said to fill halls like a snarling, silver trumpet.

A few yards away, Willie, Tad, and two of their friends tossed scarlet, gold, and auburn leaves from piles raked up by the mansion's gardener.

Baker gestured to one of the mansion's second floor windows. "Who's that?"

A gentleman who watched from the window was joined by Mrs. Lincoln. She smiled and leaned into him as she waved to Lincoln and Baker.

Lincoln answered, "His name's Wikoff or something like that."

"So that's the Hungarian adventurer all the gossip is about. I suppose he has replaced Wood as her majordomo."

"I reckon she would be more at home," Lincoln conceded, "if she had married a European count instead of the head of a democracy. But she has a big heart." Lincoln pointed to his sons' playmates, Bud and Holly Taft, sons of a former clerk in the Patent Office. "She's written half a dozen letters trying to get a job for those boys' father. It's not easy for a Democrat to find good employment in the government these days." He picked up an errant leaf and twirled it with his fingers.

"She loves holding court, doesn't she?" Baker propped himself on his elbow. "If she could only understand how her schemes hurt the ones she wants to help, not to mention how her indiscretions reflect on you. I can see why people hasten to accuse her of southern sympathies—her infatuation with the trappings of aristocracy and all that."

"Speaking of loyalties," Lincoln said. "I cannot believe you turned down my offer to make you a major general."

"Senate rules forbid me from taking a commission in the regular army, but they don't stop me from keeping my rank as colonel in the state militia. I can continue as your advocate in Congress while I serve my country as a soldier."

"A major general directing troops at a safe distance is much less likely to be maimed or killed," Lincoln said.

"Let old men like General Scott cling to past glories, surrounded by bustling clerks and clacking telegraphs. I'd rather die with my face to the enemy."

Lincoln's heart ached. No more death, he thought.

Baker sat up. "Do you remember that time in the Illinois House when we jumped out a window to keep from voting on the State Bank's charter?"

"The second greatest embarrassment of my life," Lincoln replied.

"And the first?"

"Breaking my engagement with her." Lincoln gazed up at his wife.

They fell silent for a moment.

"I fear the bloodshed will get worse in coming months." Lincoln drew a long breath. "Speed thinks if Kentucky is to be saved, it will take an overpowering force of local men to drive the rebels into Tennessee. If you die in this war, which people say I started ... well ... I would not be able to live with that."

"You worry too much. I'm assigned to a reconnaissance company. We'll only probe the enemy lines. We don't engage them."

"Just the same, every time we go into battle against these rebels, we expect to beat them with ease. Instead, they keep handing us our hats. Today in Missouri, Frémont's army took hard hits at Lexington and Liberty."

Lincoln and Baker resumed reminiscing about the old days in Illinois. They traded different accounts of the same stories, laughing as if the world around them was in perfect harmony. After a time, Baker stood. "I must report to duty."

"Be careful," Lincoln's voice softened. "I need you to come back from the battlefield in one piece. I cannot afford to have that pro-slavery governor of yours replace you with a secessionist Democrat."

"I'll be back the first of December for the new session. That's part of the deal I made with the Senate."

"You better. Or as Commander-in-Chief of the Army and Navy, I shall send the whole lot of them after you."

Baker took Willie in his arms and kissed him.

Mrs. Lincoln joined them for goodbyes and gave Baker a bouquet of flowers.

Baker's eyes grew misty. "These flowers and my memory will wither together."

* * *

Lincoln was ill at ease as he met with Interior Secretary Caleb Smith a few days after Baker's visit, but he couldn't pinpoint why. He doubted his jitters had anything to do with the plan to appease Border States by creating offshore colonies for freed slaves—the subject he called Smith to his office to discuss.

After he finished with Smith, Lincoln trekked a few blocks to General McClellan's headquarters. While he waited for the general, he discussed the afternoon weather with two newspaper correspondents who were there to investigate reports of military maneuvers. The pace of activity in the lobby and the incessant click of the the general's personal telegraph in the adjoining room suggested McClellan's workday would be unending.

A young lieutenant ushered Lincoln into McClellan's inner sanctum a half hour later. "Mr. President," McClellan said, "I can report good news. The confederate advance into central Kentucky appears to have been turned back. We have checked them at every point of attack. In Missouri, General Plummer has routed the State Guard and captured one cannon, a 12-pounder."

"Thank you, General. A great weight is lifted from my shoulders."

"Yes, sir. But there's bad news with the good."

"Go on."

"General Stone's men ran into unexpected trouble at Ball's Bluff on the Potomac north of the Capital."

"And—" Lincoln's pulse quickened.

"At least two hundred of ours are dead." McClellan stared down at the dispatches.

"Two hundred?" Lincoln angled his face into the general's field of vision.

"It appears there was some confusion among our officers," McClellan added. "Many of our men were shot in the back as they retreated across the river. Others drowned when their boats capsized." McClellan's next words smote Lincoln like a tornado plunging to the ground. "Colonel ... I mean Senator Baker died facing enemy muskets as he attempted to scale the bluff."

Lincoln slumped forward, bracing himself with both hands on the telegraph desk. General McClellan continued to speak. Lincoln waved him off. He wheeled around, blinded by tears, and stumbled into the lobby. He wobbled as he stepped onto the street, nearly tumbling to the ground. With his hands pressed to his heart, he staggered toward the mansion.

Lincoln tottered into the mansion, his face ghostly grey. Old Edward called for help. William raced up from the basement, fearing disaster had struck. As he reached out, Lincoln fell into his arms, mumbling, "Surely I am cursed." William's heart wrenched.

After composing himself in a downstairs parlor, Lincoln plodded upstairs and broke the news of Ned's death. Willie and Tad burst into tears. Mrs. Lincoln stood stoic, her lips pursed and her jaw clamped tight.

While the Lincoln family mourned Baker's death, public outrage grew over the catastrophe at Ball's Bluff. McClellan blamed the calamity on poor discipline by generals under General-in-Chief Scott's command. Scott countered that McClellan had sent a unit blindly into the enemy's den and failed to support them. McClellan insisted he ordered only a slight demonstration to discover how rebel troops would react, never intending an attack, and the reconnaissance party was directed to retreat if challenged by the enemy. There were no troops in the area to reinforce in the event of an engagement.

Days after Senator Baker's funeral, 75-year-old General-in-Chief Scott retired, and Lincoln named McClellan to replace him. Two weeks later, with Congress and the public impatient because McClellan had not mounted an offensive against Richmond, Lincoln prodded him to get his army in motion. The new General-in-Chief stuck his hand in his vest and declared he would not be cajoled into battle until the army had sufficient numbers to assure victory. He also scolded Lincoln over a speech given in New York by Colonel John Cochrane, urging the government to recruit and arm former slaves. Secretary of War Cameron stood at the colonel's side, applauding the speech. The general demanded the Cabinet end all talk of enlisting Blacks. He refused to have the "ignorant, lazy, untrainable" lot of them in his army.

Less than a week later, William paused on the upstairs landing while delivering Lincoln's copy of the *New York Herald* morning edition. He strained to catch pieces of hushed banter between Slade and Mrs. Keckly as they stood outside Mrs. Lincoln's bedroom. When Slade glimpsed William listening, he ended the conversation and proceeded toward Lincoln's office.

William muttered as Slade passed, "Plotting again? Who's your next victim?"

"Excuse me," Slade replied.

"Who are you trying to get sacked now?"

"What makes you think I want anyone sacked?"

"I don't know. You two are always whispering, like you're cooking up something. And I talked with some of the household staff. The say Mrs. Keckly convinced Mrs. Lincoln to find a job for you here in the president's house.

"No. No plot. No cooking up anything. We're trying to run this house as smoothly as possible. We talk quietly so as not to disturb the peace of Mr. Lincoln and his family. They, along with the others who work here, and visitors who call on the president carry heavy burdens. They do not need us to add to their difficulties."

William rolled his eyes.

"If you intend on becoming more than a bootblack, you should watch and learn, not snoop and imagine conspiracies."

"I'll never be anything more," William shot back. "Look at me. Mr. Lincoln is supposed to be this big, powerful man. He can only throw me scraps and he has to sneak around the backdoor to do that. He can't even get the people who work for him to give me a job."

Slade clasped William's shoulder. "Let us take Mr. Lincoln his newspaper."

When William and Slade entered the office, Lincoln's brow bore deeper furrows than most mornings. Without greeting his valets, Lincoln tossed aside the telegraph dispatches he had been scouring and snatched the Herald from William's hand. His eyes locked on the front-page coverage of Colonel Cochrane repeating his New York speech in the nation's Capital.

Lincoln slammed the paper down on his desk. "Slade..."

"Yes, sir."

"Have you heard about Colonel Cochrane's speech?"

"Yes, sir. I have."

William braced, anticipating a repeat of the question. It didn't come.

"Cameron promised there would be no more of this talk in the public square."

"At church," Slade said, "it's all folks are talking about."

"What do they say?" Lincoln arched his brow.

"They wonder why you don't enlist colored men. We have more at stake in this war than anyone else."

"There's a very good reason we do not." Lincoln pressed his palms together. "Can you imagine what would happen in Kentucky or Maryland? The specter of armed slaves murdering their masters would invoke horrid memories of past slave rebellions."

Slade leaned forward and straightened Lincoln's collar.

William tracked Slade's every move.

"I can tell you what will happen," Lincoln said. "The Border States will go with Jeff Davis and his rebels. When that happens, France and Britain will consider our cause lost, and will back the insurrection. McClellan will quit."

"Sir?"

"What is it, Slade?"

"Do you want to know what my friend Frederick Douglass says about arming our people?"

"I can only imagine what that firebrand has to say."

"Sir, his sentiments today are the same as what he printed in his paper months ago after the rebels fired on Fort Sumter." Slade took a paper from his vest pocket and unfolded it. "I keep this to remind myself and my friends of the power we coloreds possess, if only we were allowed to do our part." Slade's hazel eyes glistened as he read.

> *A lenient war is a lengthy war and the worst kind of war. Let us stop it on the soil upon which it originated and do so at once. LET THE SLAVES AND FREE COLORED PEOPLE BE FORMED INTO A LIBERATING ARMY to march into the South and raise the banner of Emancipation among the slaves.*

"I reckon he would say such." Lincoln threw up his hands. "He also abetted John Brown's treason. If he had been caught, he would have swung from the gallows alongside Brown. He's the last person this government needs to have on its side."

Brown's name evoked different images in William's mind—powerful sermons, chasing pro-slavers out of Pottawatomie, the raid on Black Jack to free his imprisoned sons, his bravery in defending Osawatomie, emancipating slaves, putting pistols and muskets in the hands of fugitive slaves. The Captain didn't shirk or make excuses. William eyed Lincoln.

"May I say one more thing, sir?" Slade asked.

"Of course," Lincoln replied.

Slade returned the paper to his pocket. "There are some 2 million able bodied colored men in the rebel states. Freedmen, field slaves and the like. They outnumber the rebel army by almost 1 million. Give them the same guns white soldiers carry and the fighting would not last three weeks."

Lincoln rolled out a map on the long table. "This map proves your arithmetic. But I am convinced the thing can be won without arming slaves. When Richmond is surrounded by 100,000 northern troops, the rebels will come to their senses and we can work out a peaceful end to this conflict. Peace will come much easier if slavery is not a stumbling block."

William's eyes narrowed. He asked himself, slavery a stumbling block? He wanted Slade to ask what the purpose was in all the fighting if it wasn't to stop slavery. The question never came.

As Slade and William stepped into the hallway, William posed a question. "Say the rebels don't give up. Suppose they don't trust Mr. Lincoln to leave them and their slaves in peace. Do you think he'll let us fight then?"

"At least we planted a seed and maybe we watered it a little. But let me ask you this—and think hard before you answer—if he does let Negroes in the army and puts guns in their hands, will you put all your dreams at risk and sign up?"

Before William could answer, Lincoln emerged from his office and called out, "William, I almost forgot."

William turned and greeted Lincoln's smile with pursed lips. He wondered why peace needed to come easily when slavery was so hard for so many.

"I have good news." Lincoln beamed. "Mr. Chase has made a position for you over at Treasury. It pays $600 a year on top of what I already pay you. You will work there in the afternoons as his messenger and come here in the mornings and evenings to tend to my grooming and my wardrobe. Any other times I want your assistance, Mr. Chase has agreed to make you available at my request. Mr. Slade will continue to see that the rest of the staff keeps their noses out of your business."

CHAPTER TWELVE

Executive Mansion—January 1862

William parked the carriage in front of the Taft residence as dinner was ending. He had been sent to fetch the Lincoln boys and their playmates, Bud and Holly. Willie and Tad had been to the Tafts' for dinner almost every night between Christmas and the New Year, and Mrs. Lincoln insisted on reciprocating.

The boys jumped out of the open carriage the instant William pulled to a stop at the mansion stables. They headed straight for Willie's pony. A few days earlier, the four playmates had stayed outside in the wintery weather until after dark, riding the pony in slush left behind by recent snow.

William called out. "Madam says you're to play inside."

"To the fort," Tad shouted. He darted toward the basement entrance with the others on his heels.

They raced through the basement, grabbing whatever snacks were handy, up two flights of back stairs to the second floor, up another narrow stairway to the attic, and out onto the flat copper roof. Against the high stone balustrade, they had built a cabin which they called the quarterdeck, from which they peered through a spyglass to monitor passage of any strange ships and boats on the river. They also tracked activity on the Virginia shore. Any suspicious happenings were reported to Mr. Lincoln whom they called the Commodore. The Cabinet were designated as officers, but the boys sailed the *Ship of State.*

William asked permission to board the vessel with a message from Madam. It was time for the boys to go down to dinner. Tad directed William to return to Madame and report they had already eaten dinner at the Tafts'.

When William relayed Tad's message to Mrs. Lincoln, she responded with an ultimatum. William returned to the attic and informed the crew of the *Ship of State*, "The Madam says you must come down."

After Bud and Holly ate a second dinner that evening, William drove them home. They might have stayed the night at the mansion, but Willie complained of a scratchy throat and was generally out of sorts.

Executive Mansion—February 1862

The Atlantic Monthly dressed up its February front page with a poem by Julia Ward Howe. The monthly's founder and chief editor, Ralph Waldo Emerson, waited outside Lincoln's office, accompanied by his escort, Senator Charles Sumner of Massachusetts.

Sumner became a hero of the abolitionist cause in 1856, when Congressman Preston Brooks of South Carolina caned him with impunity in the Senate chamber. The assault left Sumner unconscious—two bloody wounds cut deep enough to expose his skull. In addition to physical wounds, he suffered psychical ones. It was three years before he returned to his duties in the Senate.

When Lincoln invited them into his office, Sumner got straight to the point. "Mr. President, we come to discuss the fate of Nathaniel Gordon."

Gordon was the first slave smuggler in North America to be sentenced to death, and he appealed to Lincoln for a pardon. Even though smuggling slaves from Africa had been a capital crime for half of a century, few smugglers were ever convicted, and no one had ever been hanged.

Lincoln replied, "I reckon there never was a man, being raised where butchering cattle and hogs was a routine part of daily life, who grew up as averse to bloodshed as I am. You cannot imagine how hard it is to know a man will die, when a stroke of your pen could save him."

"I am against capital punishment." Sumner planted his hands on the table. "But I am for hanging that slave trader, just the same."

Lincoln gazed out the window. "A large number of respectable citizens have begged me to spare his life."

"You must show that the government is willing to hang a man who commits atrocities." Sumner's scarred face twitched. "Doing so will deter other slave traders and prove to the world we are committed to a change of policy."

Lincoln replied. “That seems to have been the sentiment of Judge Shipman who determined the sentence in Captain Gordon’s case. He made the point passionately and I have a record of his justification on my desk. He argued the condemned man should not attempt to hide from the enormity of his sins. Instead, he should ponder, for his remaining time, his cruelty and wickedness—thrusting nearly a thousand fellow beings beneath the decks of a small ship to die of disease or suffocation. Those who survived were consigned—they and their posterity—to a fate far more cruel than death. He carried off not only men to such a fate, but women and helpless children as well—because they belonged to a different race which God assigned to them. Not a single one of those poor souls ever did him any harm.”

Lincoln leaned forward. “I agree the nation’s policy regarding slavery must eventually change. Make no mistake. When that hour comes, I shall act, even at the cost of my own life. But this is not the time.”

Emerson smiled. “I can see you are a conscientious man.”

“It is my sincere desire to be so,” Lincoln replied. “I see a great danger in radicalism when great decisions weigh in the balance. Now, you might call Judge Shipman’s decision radical when laid next to similar cases.”

“Passionate,” Senator Sumner interjected.

“Passion, radicalism, revolution. Would you not agree, Mr. Emerson, they are cut from the same cloth?” Lincoln asked.

“I see a connection,” Emerson answered.

“Revolution—that is the sentiment of Mrs. Howe’s poem. Am I wrong?” Lincoln paused, though not long enough to entertain a response. “Or should I call it a hymn as its title claims? Poetic as her words are, they pit one half of this nation against the other based on the battle cry of a holy war. In your publication, you call it a battle hymn."

> *Mine eyes have seen the glory of the coming of the Lord:*
> *He is trampling out the vintage where the grapes of wrath are stored;*
> *He hath loosed the fateful lightning of His terrible swift sword:*
> *His truth is marching on ...*
> *As He died to make men holy, let us die to make men free.*

Lincoln paused to give his next words greater weight. "I see a great danger in turning the present crisis into a revolution against slavery."

Emerson pressed his palms together as if he were about to pray. "Rebellion, whether by man or Nature, is the bitter harvest of oppression. It seems through history, Mr. President, that fires, plagues, revolutions, and calamities of all sorts serve to break up entrenched routines, clear the arena of corrupt contests, and open a fair field to all men. Creation is always preceded by destruction, and in the intensity of conflict and battle, humanity shines ever more brightly."

Lincoln stood. "Those are romantic principles, eloquently spoken—though I do not see how they help me wash the stain of another man's blood from these hands. Do not lose heart, however. I am not satisfied that I grasp all the ramifications of Captain Gordon's case, and I shall study the evidence once more before deciding on the right course."

"All we ask is that you weigh the matter seriously," Emerson said. "And I am convinced you can be trusted to do that very thing."

As Lincoln bid his visitors goodbye, his wife hurried toward him. Worry lines wrinkled her face. When she was a few steps away, she burst into tears.

Lincoln pulled her into his office and closed the door. He put his arm around her. "Now, what's this all about?"

"It's Willie. He is burning with fever."

"*Shhh.* Come. I will check on him with you."

Lincoln found Willie sprawled on his bed—the picture of a lad who had wrestled with an angel, his bedcovers in a heap at his side, his little body fully exposed. Lincoln brushed a strand of brown hair from his son's eyes. The boy's forehead was clammy from fever. Willie moaned as his father pulled the blanket over his shoulders.

"I knew he would catch his death of cold." Mrs. Lincoln gripped her husband's wrist. "They never should have been out in the snow riding that pony. We must cancel the ball and recall all those invitations."

Lincoln stepped back. "But you have sent out hundreds."

"It does not matter," she insisted. "I cannot go through with it. Not with our child in this state."

"I will send Hay for a doctor," Lincoln said. "We can decide about the ball after he sees the boy."

"Send someone to bring Lizabeth."

Lincoln stiffened. "What do you expect Miss Lizabeth to do?"

"Just get her."

"All right, Mother. Calm yourself. I shall go for her. But I will also send Hay for a doctor."

When Lincoln returned with Miss Lizabeth, Dr. Stone had finished his examination and was repacking his medical bag.

"How is he?" Lincoln asked.

"It's just a cold. Give him plenty of water and make sure he rests. He should be fine."

"Do you think it would be wise to recall the invitations for the ball?" Mrs. Lincoln asked.

"No, not at all," Dr. Stone replied. "The boy will be up and playing before you know it."

The doctor's good news freed Lincoln to focus on pressing business. One issue that had him by the nape of the neck and wouldn't let go was Captain Gordon's appeal. The slave smuggler's execution was set for the end of the week and would be carried out if he did not act. Lincoln stood at the end of a blind alley with walls on both sides teetering toward him.

Finally, on the afternoon of the ball, he made up his mind and drew up his decision—

> *I would personally prefer to let this man live in confinement and let him meditate on his deeds, yet in the name of justice and the majesty of law, there ought to be one case, at least one specific instance, of a professional slave-trader, a Northern white man, given the penalty of death because of the incalculable number of deaths he and his kind inflicted upon black men amid the horror of the sea-voyage from Africa.*

He dispatched William to deliver copies to the parties in the case and headed down the hallway to check on Willie. As he passed through the little gate for the receiving area, Dr. Stone appeared at the top of the stairs. They entered the sickroom together and found Miss Lizabeth consoling Mrs. Lincoln at Willie's bedside. Mrs. Lincoln glanced at her husband, her eyes wide with alarm.

"How's the patient doing?" Dr. Stone asked.

Mrs. Lincoln wiped her forehead with the back of her hand. "Much worse. He has stomach cramps, headache, nausea, diarrhea." The stench of dried urine and excrements hung in the room. She pointed to a bundle of soiled clothing and linens. "He's too weak to make it to the toilet on his own."

"William can stand by to carry Willie outside to the toilet," Lincoln said, "and do whatever else is needed."

The doctor retrieved a bottle of Quinine from his bag and forced a dose down Willie's throat. "He may experience some discomfort from the medicine, but it should kill any infection. I will check back in the morning."

Miss Lizabeth leaned into Lincoln and whispered, "Maybe we should set up a sickroom so he can rest in quiet."

Lincoln agreed.

Miss Lizabeth made the sickroom out of a suite at the west end of the hall. The suite became known as the Prince of Wales Room after Britain's crown prince occupied it on a visit during the Buchanan administration. Mrs. Lincoln furnished the room with a six-foot-wide, eight-foot-long, rosewood carved bed. Above the bed hung a purple satin canopy with an American shield embroidered in gold thread at its center.

William moved Willie into the sickroom and read to him from a volume of George Gordon Byron poems while Miss Lizabeth helped Mrs. Lincoln dress for the ball. During the ball, the Lincolns took turns sneaking upstairs to check on Willie. He remained awake, but lethargic. After midnight, the last of several hundred supper guests boarded their carriages, and the Lincolns went to look in on Willie before retiring.

When they paused at the top of the stairs, Mrs. Lincoln wore a tired smile. "Tomorrow's papers will call this the greatest social event Washington has ever seen."

"I'm sure they will," Lincoln replied.

As the Lincolns entered the sickroom, Miss Lizabeth reached halfway across the bed to daub Willie's forehead and chapped lips with a wet cloth. William stretched over from the other side of the bed to hold Willie's hand. He recalled the agony that gripped him as his brother, Thomas, battled for his life against fever. Mrs. Lincoln encouraged William and Miss Lizabeth to retire, but they insisted on staying at Willie's bedside through the night.

Early the next morning, Dr. Stone returned as the Lincolns, Miss Lizabeth, and William hovered over the stricken boy. Willie had complained during the night of dizziness and ringing in his ears.

Mrs. Lincoln pulled up Willie's shirt, exposing his chest.

Miss Lizabeth shook her head. "Typhus."

"When did this start?" the doctor asked. "There was no sign of rash yesterday."

"We just noticed it." Mrs. Lincoln's voice cracked. "He will be okay, will he not?"

"This could be more serious than I first thought," Dr. Stone confessed.

Mrs. Lincoln begged the doctor for stronger medicine.

"Calomel is for the gravest cases. A youngster as fragile as yours may not survive the treatment."

The color left Lincoln's face. He recalled a doctor administering such a mercury compound to help cure his melancholies when he was a young man. The medicine almost killed him. Lincoln vowed he would never again endure such treatment.

Before Lincoln got a word out, his wife blurted through her sobs, "Please, whatever it takes to save my boy."

"But ... but ..." Lincoln stammered.

"But what?" his wife screamed. "I will not lose him because of your timidity. Doctor, I am not letting him go out of this world without a fight. Give it to him."

"We will keep pushing this down him." The doctor opened the vial. "At the point he starts salivating, we will know the bacteria are being expelled from his body."

Willie gagged on the first dose.

Lincoln recoiled. "How much does he have to take?"

The doctor clamped Willie's mouth shut, pushed his head back, and forced him to swallow another dose. After the doctor released his grip, Willie gasped for air, his shoulders heaved.

Lincoln tipped forward. William steadied him.

When the doctor left, Miss Lizabeth convinced Mrs. Lincoln to retire to her chamber while Lincoln and William remained with Willie. Insomnia was normal for Lincoln, but sleepless nights had sapped his wife's energy.

Near noon, Lincoln's eyelids grew heavy. His head listed to one side. Nicolay stood in the doorway and cleared his throat.

Lincoln jerked straight up in his chair. "Sorry. Have you been there long?"

"Only for a moment," Nicolay replied.

Lincoln cupped his hand over Willie's forehead.

Nicolay stepped into the room. "How is he?"

"Holding steady ... I think," Lincoln replied.

William daubed Willie's lips with a cool, wet towel.

"What's up?" Lincoln asked.

Nicolay spoke in hushed tones. "General Grant must think you need some good news. He's captured Fort Henry in northern Tennessee. Soon, the Tennessee River will be open to Union traffic all the way down to Alabama."

Lincoln forced a smile.

Willie moaned something unintelligible. Lincoln squeezed his son's hand. "He says it's time the army did something."

"Commodore Foote deserves much of the credit," Nicolay replied. "His gunboats convinced the rebels to give up before Grant's men fired a shot."

The Lincolns stayed at their son's side constantly as the doctor continued twice daily visits. They were never sure whether the bile and liquids expelled from Willie's body were due to the disease or the cure. William remained close at hand, except when he carried Willie outside to the toilet, hauled soiled bedclothes to the basement laundry, or couriered messages between Lincoln and Cabinet ministers or generals.

Capitol Hill—February 1862

The House Judiciary Committee called Lincoln away in the midst of Willie's illness for an urgent meeting on Capitol Hill. At last, Lincoln had good news to report regarding the war. Navy gunboats gave cover to General Burnside's army division as it captured Roanoke Island along North Carolina's outer banks, gaining access to the inland sounds. The map of slave populations in southern counties suggested the army could run into only slight resistance as it marched inland from the coast to surround Richmond.

The committee chairman, Congressman John Hickman, greeted Lincoln warmly then stiffened. "Mr. President, we have asked you here to make you aware of troublesome information concerning your wife and her possible involvement in inappropriate conduct. One case in point is the leak of your recent annual message to Congress."

Lincoln bristled.

Congressman Hickman continued. “A correspondent for the *New York Tribune* fingered a man who gets news from the White House—from women in your family. The man’s name is Henry Wikoff. He refused to divulge his sources when interviewed by this committee, citing an obligation of strictest secrecy. As a result, he is now in custody.”

Lincoln shifted his weight.

Hickman went on. “We are also aware that Wikoff is a secret correspondent for the *Tribune’s* competitor, the *New York Herald*—the paper that published parts of your message. Wikoff is reputed to be a flatterer, social climber, and close friend ... er ... confidant of your wife.”

“What are you saying?” Lincoln demanded.

“I hope you can see how one might suspect that Mrs. Lincoln was one of Wikoff’s sources.” Hickman arched his brow. “If that be so, he is likely protecting her by refusing to give answers.”

Lincoln asked, “Even if this Wikoff is a scoundrel, what leads you to believe Mrs. Lincoln is in league with him?”

“We are not saying she is. But if she is not, we must have something to pacify those who believe her behavior raises questions. Only a week ago she threw what newspapers have called an ostentatious and unseemly White House ball while soldiers shuddered in the cold without blankets, boots, and pantaloons. There are voices that rail against her proclivity for spending the federal treasury on lavish decorations for the Executive Mansion. I am sure I do not have to remind you that her deep southern roots provoke questions about her loyalties. A brother, three half-brothers, and three brothers-in-law serve in the Confederate army.”

Hickman's insinuations reminded Lincoln of something Cousin Lizzie confided before she returned home from her extended stay in Washington. She explained that Mrs. Lincoln was exasperated beyond measure over constant gossip that she was not loyal, that she was a rebel sympathizer, not in accord with her husband's sentiments. Some even accused her of leaking government secrets to the rebel army. Supposedly, because she hailed from Kentucky and had many relations in the south.

Lincoln clinched his fists. "Enough. You have my unequivocal assurance that no member of my household is involved in any treasonous business nor are any of our friends."

"What can you give us to satisfy—"

"Satisfy doubters?" Lincoln clenched his jaw.

Hickman folded his hands and leaned forward. "You have to give us something."

Lincoln hung his head. "I'm convinced her peculiar behavior is the result of partial insanity, a condition for which I must assume responsibility. Since being installed as Chief Magistrate, I have been too distracted to offer her the attentiveness she deserves. I need you gentlemen to let me take care of my own domestic problems. Please, do not turn my wife's difficulties into a public spectacle. Especially while our boy's life hangs in the balance."

The committee agreed to back away from their investigation into Mrs. Lincoln's alleged indiscretions. Lincoln returned to the mansion to find their youngest son, Tad, also stricken with fever and his wife inconsolable.

Executive Mansion—February 1862

Willie could no longer keep down food of any kind. He vomited water, was constipated, and half of the time he was delirious. The doctor gave him larger doses of calomel to no avail. Lincoln shuttled back and forth between his two sons. He daubed Tad's brow with cool towels. He tried to get Willie to sip water. Lincoln fought back tears as his wife wept incessantly. William was constantly at his side, doing everything he could to lighten Lincoln's burden and rally his spirits.

Tedious mornings dragged into long afternoons. Evening hours folded into sleepless nights. Each day brought more visits from the solemn doctor. Late one evening, as Willie and Tad languished, the War Committee gathered in Lincoln's office, intending to accost Lincoln again over McClellan's inactivity. They came well-armed. The coordinated navy-army successes in Tennessee and along North Carolina's coast had taken the teeth out of McClellan's excuses for delaying an attack on Richmond. Lincoln shielded the General-in-Chief—again—and promised to build a fire under him.

Chairman Wade retorted, "My God! Replace the traitor. Put Halleck in his place. He's not afraid to fight."

The committee's grumbling continued as the members filed out of the office and trundled downstairs. When the last of them were gone, Lincoln walked to the opposite end of the hallway where Willie fought for his life.

Later, Edwin Stanton, Cameron's replacement as Secretary of War, found Lincoln in the Prince of Wales Room with Willie. Stanton, whom Lincoln nicknamed "Mars" after the Roman god of war, asked how the lad was progressing.

Lincoln massaged Willie's hand. "All we have left is hope."

"I have good news." Stanton peeked down at a telegraph dispatch he was holding.

"These days, no news seems good enough. What is it?"

"General Grant reports the rebels at Fort Donelson will surrender unconditionally in the morning. Halleck's regiments now control both the Tennessee and Cumberland Rivers. After clearing the waterways, we can assail the heart of rebel territory."

"What are the prospects for taking Nashville?" Lincoln asked.

"It looks like the entire rebel force in that region is trapped inside Donelson. After they surrender, Nashville will be defenseless. If we pounce before reinforcements move in, the city will be taken easily. Thank God Halleck and Grant run the show down there, and not McClellan."

"I reckon it's good of God to give us something to be thankful for."

"Yes, sir," Stanton replied. "Bells will ring across the nation tomorrow when the news of Fort Donelson's capture is announced. Indeed, we have cause to be thankful."

Lincoln wiped Willie's brow. "I wish I could find it in myself to celebrate."

William sat next to Lincoln at Willie's bedside as Stanton left. William bowed his head and closed his eyes. Neither he nor Lincoln spoke for several minutes. Then Lincoln asked, "Do you believe in prayer?"

William looked up. "When I was little, Auntie taught us it works when nothing else will."

"Do you think prayer will make my boy better?"

"I don't know," William replied. "Sometimes I think it doesn't change anything. It just brings peace."

"Peace. Sounds like a beautiful thing. Do you think it's really possible?" Lincoln folded his hands and pressed them to his lips.

William bowed his head again and silently begged God to bring Mr. Lincoln peace. Lincoln cupped William's shoulder and whispered, "I cannot begin to thank you enough."

Silence resumed its spell.

A few days later, Miss Lizabeth found Lincoln kneeling at Willie's bedside, sapped by lack of sleep and sobbing. She knelt next to him and hummed softly.

"How can I possibly go on?" Lincoln mumbled.

"I have walked in your same shoes." She wiped away her tears.

"I know you have. I'm so sorry. How do you find the strength?"

"In our weakness, God gives us his strength." She continued to comfort Lincoln.

His eyes grew heavy, and the room around him dimmed. He envisioned himself floating over an expanse of dark, quiet waters.

Several hours later, Lincoln awoke to the patter of rain on the window. He was sprawled on the floor and Miss Lizabeth had retired. Bud Taft sat on Willie's bed, holding his ailing friend's hand.

Lincoln rose and approached Bud, putting his hand on the boy's shoulder. "You should go home. I will send word if anything changes."

"He's afraid." Bud kept his eyes trained on Willie. "If I go away, he'll call for me when he wakes up."

"Will you be okay while I step down the hall to check on his brother?"

Bud nodded.

Lincoln hesitated in the doorway. "Did your mother bring you?"

"She's waiting downstairs."

"I'll let her know you can stay, if you like."

Bud nodded again.

When Lincoln returned, Bud was lying across the foot of the bed, asleep. Lincoln covered Bud with a blanket then pulled up a chair and sat with a book in his lap.

Rain showers persisted through the night and into the pre-dawn hours, tapping gentle rhythms on the window. At first light, Lincoln checked Willie for fever. Willie's eyes opened, and he smiled. Lincoln held his hand and Willie acknowledged him with a feeble squeeze.

Bud stretched and yawned. On seeing Willie's bright face, he sat up and smiled.

William arrived with coffee and toast for Lincoln's breakfast. "Go find Miss Lizabeth," Lincoln said. "Have her relay the good report of Willie's improvement to Mrs. Lincoln."

When William returned, he was joined by Mrs. Lincoln, Miss Lizabeth, and Slade. All insisted Lincoln should let William trim his hair and beard to cheer Willie. Lincoln agreed, and William brought in the barber's chair to do the job right in the Prince of Wales Room. When William finished, he drove Bud and Mrs. Taft home.

The War Committee re-assembled in Lincoln's office that afternoon and demanded again that McClellan be replaced as General-in-Chief. Energized by Willie's rally, Lincoln once more refused. After the committee members left, Lincoln confessed to Secretary Stanton, "I'm growing weary of defending the general's stubbornness."

Hay interrupted Stanton's reply. "Excuse me." His voice was edged with alarm. "Mrs. Lincoln is desperate to see—"

Lincoln rushed down the hall and burst into the sickroom, nearly bowling over William who was carrying out a bundle of bile-soaked bedclothes. Lincoln gagged. Willie writhed in his bed, moaning. Lincoln's heart ached. His wife bathed Willie's bare, boil pocked chest with wet towels. Dr. Stone motioned for Lincoln to hold Willie still as he forced medicine down him to temper the seizure.

Willie soon fell limp, taking shallow, sporadic breaths, his pallid face beaded with sweat. As the doctor packed his bag, Lincoln sat next to his wife and draped his arm around her. She leaned into him and murmured, "I cannot bear the thought of losing him."

Lincoln drew her closer. His heart numb, he had no words of consolation to offer her.

The afternoon dragged on with torrents of rain drumming on windows and dark skies closing in around the mansion. Lincoln opened his watch, its second dial clung to each passing mark as if straining to foil the inevitable march of time. As daylight faded, William brought supper, but neither Lincoln nor his wife ate. Several hours later, exhaustion overtook Mrs. Lincoln, and Miss Lizabeth put her to bed. Lincoln encouraged Miss Lizabeth to retire, as well, but she refused. She split her time between Willie's bedside and tending Tad in the boys' bedroom. The younger son's condition was not as severe as Willie's.

William remained at Lincoln's side through the black of night. At times, Lincoln leaned into him, weeping, while William hummed lullabies he learned as a child. By morning, the storm clouds had blown off, and a bright sun took their place. William fetched breakfast, but again, neither Lincoln nor his wife ate.

Near noontime, Willie woke for a few moments and called for Papa and Ma. Each parent gripped one of the boy's hands. "We're right here," they replied together. Willie thrashed in the massive bed, shaking his head and crying, "No. No. I want Papa and Ma. Why won't you let me see Papa and Ma?" As abruptly as he awoke, Willie fell back into a deep sleep. Lincoln's heart could hardly contain his grief.

William rubbed Lincoln's shoulders.

Mrs. Lincoln sobbed as Miss Lizabeth held her and whispered words of comfort. Lincoln urged both women to get some rest. His wife refused, and Miss Lizabeth insisted on remaining by her side. In time, Mrs. Lincoln's nerves settled, and Miss Lizabeth went to check on Tad before retreating to the family parlor to nap. Willie's breathing grew shallower and more sporadic.

Dr. Stone stopped in around four o'clock. When he finished evaluating Willie, the doctor guided Lincoln down the hall to Tad's room. Out in the hallway he paused. "I'm afraid, in Willie's case, we're at the limit of what can be done."

"What are we to do?" Lincoln's parched throat tightened.

"I'm saying that nothing more can be done. It's not likely he will survive the night. Go be with your wife and son. Comfort them as best you can. For your Willie, this ordeal will soon be over. He will be in a far better place than we have the capacity to understand."

Dr. Stone went to see Tad, and Lincoln returned to Willie's bedside to sit with his wife and hold her trembling hand. Willie exhaled his last feeble breath at five o'clock that afternoon. Mrs. Lincoln wailed, begging him to come back. Her pleading grew louder, more desperate. She crawled, sobbing, into the bed beside her lifeless son and buried her face in his chest.

Lincoln laid his hand on her back to calm her anguish. After a few moments of trying to console her, he sent William down the hall to carry the news to Dr. Stone.

William hesitated in the doorway to Tad's room, biting his lip. One glimpse told Dr. Stone everything he needed to know. The doctor stood, and without a word, went to tend to the Lincolns' dead son.

Tad peered at William through watery eyes. "Can you take me to see Willie?" he asked.

William approached the boy's bedside. "Not now. You see, he's sleeping." William knew the road ahead for Tad because he was living it. Both he and Tad were younger brothers who would forever miss the bright star of their youth and would wonder why they had been allowed to survive. He sat at Tad's bedside and told him a story—it was about a boy who became lost but found his way home by following the North Star.

Miss Lizabeth began washing Willie's body while Dr. Stone assisted Mrs. Lincoln to her bed and administered a dose of laudanum to help her sleep. Exhausted, Lincoln padded down the hall to Nicolay's office, not yet ready to face Tad. Every part of him ached from grief.

"Nicolay," he murmured, "my boy is gone."

"Is there anything I can do?" Nicolay asked.

Unable to contain his tears, Lincoln shook his head and retreated to his own office to compose himself. After a time of private mourning, he returned to Nicolay and instructed him to send a carriage for Senator Orville Browning and his wife, Eliza—old Springfield friends. "I would like for them to spend the night, if they are able."

"Should I inform anyone else?" Nicolay asked.

"The Cabinet, I suppose." Then he shuffled down the hallway to the Prince of Wales Room.

Miss Lizabeth stood at the foot of the bed, her eyes reddened and swollen. She had finished washing Willie, dressed him, and covered him. Lincoln lifted the cover from his son's face and murmured, "My poor boy, you were too good for this earth." He leaned and stroked Willie's head. "God has called you home. I know that you are much better off in heaven, but I love you so. It is hard ... hard to have you die!" Tears spilled out of him again as he hunched over the bed, his shoulders shaking uncontrollably.

Once he collected himself, Lincoln turned to Miss Lizabeth and thanked her for all she had done. Her chin quivered. She replied in a soft murmur, "It was my honor. I only wish I had been able to do the same for my own boy."

The aching in her eyes gave Lincoln pause. He swallowed back tears. "Forgive me. When your son died a few months back, I was too consumed with my own petty concerns to ask what happened."

"No need to apologize. You carry the entire nation's problems on your shoulders."

"It was a trivial matter—a small tiff with Mrs. Lincoln over a government appointment for her friend. I should have put my cares aside well enough to console you in your grief. Please allow me to correct my previous rudeness, so I can accept your consolations now in my own time of deep sorrow."

Her voice cracked. "Soon after the war broke out George joined the 1st Missouri Volunteers. He died in his first battle."

"I'm sorry but I don't understand. We have no colored troops in our army, and if we did, we would not arm them."

"His skin was as light as yours." She touched Lincoln's hand. "My father was white. George's father was, too. I had saved up money and sent him to Wilberforce College. But the war broke out and he loved his country. More than that, he wanted to fight for our people's freedom."

"I am doubly grieved to hear of your loss, knowing I am in part to blame." Lincoln wrung his hands.

She blew her nose in a kerchief.

"You come from a long line of freedmen?" he asked.

"Oh, no. I was born into slavery. But at thirty years old, I bought my freedom and my son's."

"You're fortunate."

Her eyes widened. "Fortunate? It is not good fortune when you must pay for what's God-given."

"But you no longer live under a master's thumb."

"Is that how you see it?" she replied. "To this day, I live with the scars and nightmares of those years in bondage. I was four when I was put to work—a mere child, caring for a swaddled infant. One day I accidentally tipped the cradle and that little white baby spilled out onto the floor. I was beaten until blood oozed from my wounds. Four years old I was."

Her words pinched Lincoln's heart. He had called himself a slave and a son of a slave for much less abuse in his youth.

"When I was seven," Miss Lizabeth continued. "Master had just purchased hogs for which he was unable to pay in full. To escape his embarrassment, he sold Little Joe, the son of the cook." Tears welled in her eyes. "The boy came in with a bright face, was placed in the livestock scales and sold like a hog at so much per pound."

Lincoln's stomach turned. Never had he suffered such humiliation, sold by the pound like an animal.

She went on. "The boy's mother was kept in ignorance of the transaction, but when Little Joe started for Petersburgh in the wagon, the truth began to dawn on her, and she pleaded that her boy should not be taken from her. Master quieted her by saying the child was simply going to town with the wagon and would be back.

Lincoln squeezed his eyes shut. Precious Willie and the others he had loved and lost had been claimed by laws of Nature, not by the cruelty and greed of men. A slave auction he had witnessed in New Orleans clawed at his conscience—frenzied bidding for a pale-skinned girl who was yet in her teen-age years ... a mother wailed as her husband was auctioned away, frightened children clung to her legs.

"At fourteen, I was loaned out to my Master's eldest son," she said. "His new bride was wicked and became determined to subdue what she called my stubborn side. When I was eighteen, she enlisted a neighbor's help. The neighbor took me into his quarters and demanded that I undress so he could beat me. I told him, 'You shall not whip me unless you prove the stronger. Nobody has a right to whip me but my own Master, and nobody shall do so if I can prevent it.' He bound my hands and beat me, then returned me to Mistress with bleeding welts on my back."

Lincoln's back stung from the memory of his father's lashes, but with time his welts faded. His back bore no permanent scars as reminders of injustice.

"The next week, the neighbor man flogged me again until his strength was spent and sent me away bleeding. A week after that, the man flogged me once more until he was exhausted. In none of those times did I let him see any tears or hear so much as a groan. Eventually, he gave up trying."

Her voice turned gravelly. “Even before my wounds from those beatings healed, a leading man in town demanded that I give him favors of a certain kind. When I resisted, he raped me. Not once, but over and over for nearly four years. It was not until my flow stopped and my belly began to grow that he quit violating me. But my shame, my suffering, my mortification worsened. Only when I held little George, did the pain subside and my spirit began to heal.”

Lincoln stood in silence.

“Many years later,” she added, “my mother confessed on her deathbed that she endured the same humiliation. My son and I were rejected by our white fathers because of our African blood. Yes, I bought my freedom and my son’s but I cannot escape my years of bondage. Every day, I enter great houses through the back door and am unwelcome at tables served by people who still are regarded as human property. I grieve the loss of my son, who gave his blood for the freedom of millions more to come.”

Lincoln shuddered. Stories abounded of slavery’s horrors but never had it been lived out before him in the tortured eyes, the twisted snarling lips, of one reliving thirty years of vile inhumanity. He took Miss Lizabeth’s hands in his own. “We must never let it be said your son died in vain.”

She straightened a wrinkle in the covering over Willie’s body. “You should go sit with your wife.”

“Yes, that’s a good thought. Let William drive you home so you can get some rest. I will stay with her until Mrs. Browning arrives.”

“I am concerned for Mrs. Lincoln,” she murmured.

“I know. She relies on you, but you will not do her any good if you exhaust your own strength. In the morning, I will arrange for an army nurse to help you look after Mrs. Lincoln and Tad."

By the time Senator Browning and his wife, Eliza, arrived, Mrs. Lincoln was sleeping soundly, thanks to Dr. Stone's laudanum dose. Mrs. Browning offered to sit with her during the night.

Orville Browning and Lincoln went to check on Tad. Outside the boy's room, Lincoln said, "I must depend on you, dear friend, to handle the details of Willie's funeral and burial."

"We can discuss those things in the morning," Browning replied. "For now, you need rest. Should I ask the doctors to give you something to help you sleep?"

"Thank you, no. I can manage without it."

"I'll keep an eye on Tad." Browning patted Lincoln's shoulder. "Why don't you go to bed?"

Lincoln bowed his head. "I reckon I shall just sit in my office for a while."

Lincoln stretched out on the sofa in his office and shut his eyes. His heart ached as a patchwork of memories flooded over him. Willie standing on the terrace of their Springfield home urging passersby to 'Vote for Old Abe' ... giving speeches to playmates after parades ... drawing up railway timetables ... conducting imaginary trains from Chicago to New York with perfect precision ... minstrel shows in the attic.

William kept vigil outside Lincoln's office the entire night, not shutting his eyes for more than a few minutes at a time.

Mrs. Lincoln was up the next morning, ready to greet the Cabinet and their wives when they called to show their respects. Her rally did not last long, and after the visitors were gone, she returned to her suite and demanded another dose of laudanum.

That afternoon, Lincoln checked in on his wife and found Mrs. Browning sitting in the dark, the curtains drawn. Mrs. Browning told him that his wife demanded the curtains be closed and insisted on more medication to help her sleep. As Lincoln opened the drapes, Miss Lizabeth entered the room, accompanied by a mature, plain-featured army nurse named Rebecca Pomroy.

Lincoln took Nurse Pomroy's hand. "I am heartily glad to see you. You will surely be a comfort to us. My wife is distraught over our boy's death, and another son is stricken with fever."

"Sir, I am humbled that Mrs. Dix thinks me worthy to serve your family. But I must confess. I worry over leaving the young soldiers in my ward at the hospital."

"You must not worry." Lincoln offered a weary smile. "Mrs. Dix is a capable administrator. She will see they are tended to."

"Yes," Nurse Pomroy replied. "She's a saint to open her asylum to so many battlefield casualties while still attending to the poor women she set up her hospital to serve."

"Do I understand correctly, she established it as an institution for women who suffer from insanity?"

"She did. You might be able to see it from here. It's a large white building near the river."

"Yes. I believe I have seen it." Lincoln glanced at his wife lying in her bed in a laudanum-induced fog. "Come. Mrs. Browning and Miss Lizabeth can watch my wife while I introduce you to our son, Tad, and the doctors who are attending him." Lincoln led her down the hallway.

That evening before going down to supper, Lincoln checked on Tad again and found him sleeping. Nurse Pomroy reported he had been weeping earlier, calling for his brother, whimpering he could never speak to Willie anymore.

"Yes." Lincoln bit his lip. "They were inseparable." He invited her to join him in the family dining room, but she insisted on staying at Tad's bedside.

After supper, Lincoln viewed Willie in his coffin in the downstairs parlor. As Browning described the revolutionary embalming technique doctors used—a process proven in Europe to keep bodies preserved in nearly perfect condition for a decade or longer—Lincoln again was overcome with sorrow. He rushed upstairs and closed himself in his office, sobbing without restraint. When the clock on the mantle chimed ten, he fixed his gaze on sparse embers nestled among smoldering ash in the fireplace. He reached back in his memory to recover moments since viewing Willie's lifeless form in the coffin, but all was a blur. His thoughts took an abrupt turn to Tad. He leapt from his chair and rushed to his son's bedroom to find him asleep and Nurse Pomroy still sitting at his bedside.

"How is he?" Lincoln asked.

"Little changed."

Lincoln set a chair beside her and leaned to touch Tad's forehead. "The fever has lessened."

"No. I opened a window. The cool night air gives that impression."

They sat in silence for a while then he asked, "Is it Mrs.?"

"Widowed."

"Tell me about your family," he said.

"My father was a sea captain." She folded her hands in her lap. "He was rarely home and died when I was a girl. After that, life was lean. Mother raised us four girls and our younger brother on her own, sewing for folks. Daniel and I married when I was nineteen, and he was sickly almost from the time we were wed. Nearly twenty years. His body finally gave out two years ago."

"I'm sorry. Did you have children?"

"I have one son remaining, George. He joined the army when they first called for volunteers. Our Clara died four years ago. She was nine. Our Willie passed on when he was thirteen. That was the year before Clara died."

"Your Willie was close to the same age as mine. Were you able to say, 'Thy will be done?'"

"No," she replied. "Not at the first blow, nor the second, not even the third. After Daniel died, I drifted through life for the next year and a half, feeble and heartsick. Months after my affliction, God met me when I attended a camp-meeting."

"Watching Willie waste away," he said, "and seeing him laid out in that coffin—it's as if my heart has been ripped out and carved into a thousand pieces."

Nurse Pomroy described the many ways her faith sustained her in her grief and continued doing so. Of God's steadfast love.

"Why? Why?" Lincoln cried out. "This trial heaped on me is more than I can stand."

"But the Almighty will sustain you," she answered. "Thousands of prayers go up for you daily, and for your family."

Lincoln fell to his knees. Tears flowed.

She knelt beside him and sang a hymn, softly.

The next morning when Lincoln failed to show for breakfast, Slade took a tray upstairs to his bedroom. "Sir, shouldn't you be getting dressed for President Washington's birthday ceremonies at the Capitol?"

"I won't be going," Lincoln replied.

"I suppose there are some Democrats who will be pleased not to see you, but your nation needs you. In case you forgot, there's a war going on."

"I will not be going," Lincoln repeated.

"Be that as it may, you look a sight. How do you think young Tad will feel if he sees you in this condition, not to mention Mrs. Lincoln? Your gloom is not going to cheer them in the least. Besides, William is on his way up to trim you."

Shortly after Slade left, William entered the room.

As Lincoln rolled out of bed and sat in the barber's chair, William spoke softly. "I'm so sorry about young Willie. Maybe if we clean you up, the pain will be easier to bear."

Lincoln rubbed his eyes. "I am not sure Merlin the Magician could help me this morning."

William worked the razor along the leather strop. "Now just sit back and try to forget your sorrows."

"I don't—"

"Hush. I didn't say to talk about your tribulations. Just relax and let me freshen you up."

Several times William tried to engage in light conversation, but Lincoln's silence made dialogue impossible. Afterwards, Lincoln went into his office and shut the door.

Rain drummed on the office windows as evening fell, and the truth struck Lincoln that the entire day had passed. He had missed Washington's birthday ceremony. He plodded to the water closet and doused his face before checking on Tad.

As he lingered in the doorway of Tad's room, the sight of Nurse Pomroy at the boy's bedside brought him a modicum of relief. She turned, her eyes bright, raising his spirits as he stepped into the room. He pulled up a chair and sat next to her. "How is he?"

"Stable," she whispered. "He slept all afternoon. No signs of discomfort."

"That's encouraging." Lincoln folded his hands in his lap. "Tell me again how you obtained your faith in God and how He sustained you through your afflictions."

"There isn't much more than what I told you last night."

"Please, tell me again and do not leave out the slightest detail. I am trying as hard as I can to place my trust in the Divine, but I cannot seem to."

She repeated her story, and he interrupted several times, trying to understand. At last he said, "The principles you describe are easily understood. It's the practice that is so difficult." Then he bowed his head and murmured, "Oh, why is it?"

She offered him her hand and whispered, "Simply trust God who does all things well."

"Whenever I lose heart," he assured her, "I will remember what you have endured, and your example will help me weather my sorrows."

* * *

Mrs. Lincoln scrawled a note the next morning to Mrs. Taft, mother of Bud and Holly. Mrs. Lincoln requested that the Taft boys stay away from her son's funeral and never return to the mansion. She confessed to Miss Lizabeth, "It makes me feel worse to see them."

Despite his wife's wishes, Lincoln sent for Bud, the older of the two Taft boys. Lincoln's heart told him at least Bud should be allowed to say goodbye to his playmate and friend—it would be cruel not to. Lincoln's sons had played every day for almost a year with Bud and Holly Taft, either at the mansion or at the Taft's home. Many nights they ate supper together and slept over in one home or the other. They had become the new four musketeers with William as their Planchet.

Bud walked slowly into the Green Parlor where Willie's coffin was open for private viewing. It was a room he had never ventured into the many times he'd been to the mansion. Everything about the room seemed oversized in the eyes of a 10-year-old. When he stepped up to the coffin, he peeked at first, then he gaped at his friend's lifeless form. He slumped and dropped to the floor in a heap, like a rag doll. The new assistant secretary, Stoddard, picked him up and carried him home.

Mrs. Lincoln remained bedridden until moments before the service began when Miss Lizabeth and Eliza Browning helped her down to the Green Parlor, still in her nightclothes, to view her son for the last time. When Mrs. Lincoln gazed into the coffin, she shrieked at the sight of Willie's pale face. Sobbing, she threw herself on the coffin—arms wide as if clutching a life raft in a tempest. Miss Lizabeth and Eliza Browning came by her side, calmed her, and took her back to bed.

All the downstairs mirrors were covered in mourning drapery, their frames wrapped with black and the glass concealed by white crepe. Mirrors were not needed to reflect Lincoln's grief as he viewed his son laid out in his little brown suit. No matter how many times he had buried loved ones, death's dagger pierced his soul as if for the first time. But this time, the fangs of a hundred venomous serpents assailed his heart. He turned stone cold except for his quivering lips and chin. When he mustered the willpower to murmur his final goodbye, an old nemesis—melancholy—cloaked him in darkness.

Nature was unrestrained at that hour. Storm clouds, pushed by violent winds, raced through the sky. The room darkened and windows rattled as if the entire mansion quaked with sorrow. On the portico and out on the drive, torrents of rain pummeled a large crowd. Some fortunate souls avoided the storm by cramming into the lobby. None had any hope of joining the cadre of generals, commodores, government officials, family, and friends who filed into the East Room where the ceremony took place.

The household servants were admitted into the Green Parlor for their turn to bid Willie farewell. Their sobs filled the downstairs. Nurse Pomroy kissed the tips of her fingers and pressed them to Willie's alabaster forehead. Though she never knew the boy, tears trickled down her cheeks as she revisited memories of a son and daughter laid out in their coffins. William's chin quivered and his eyes flooded with grief. Slade's throat tightened as he draped an arm over William's shoulder.

As invited guests settled into seats in the East Room, Lincoln's eldest son, Bob, sat stiff-backed at his father's side. His demeanor was more fitting for a general's aide de camp than a mourning brother. Lincoln slumped forward and bowed his head as tears streamed down his face.

Reverend Dr. Phineas Gurley's words brought little comfort to Lincoln. The eternal blessings Gurley recited were paltry compared to the sorrows that haunted the grieving father. The preacher's words provoked questions for which Lincoln's heart demanded answers. If a tender boy's death, if the deaths of thousands of young men and boys on battlefields across the land, were examples of a Divine who doeth all things well, what hope did heaven hold? Was it not cruel for the Almighty to test virtue with affliction? How could a future ever seem brightened when unbearable misery hung like a perpetual storm over one's remaining days? There could be no rejoicing or gratitude in tribulation. Those promised rewards were difficult enough to accept when offered by women like Nurse Pomroy and Miss Lizabeth, who had suffered life's cruelties. Coming from a man whose business was the Almighty, such sentiments were a bitter pill.

By the conclusion of the ceremony, the rainsqualls subsided, giving way to a monotonous drizzle. Most of the guests in the East Room slogged through sodden streets of the city to Oak Hill Cemetery in Georgetown. Two white horses drew the hearse carrying Willie's coffin, their legs and underbellies collecting layers of grime. Lincoln and Bob followed in a carriage pulled by two black horses with muck splattered coats.

Following a brief ceremony in the intimate cemetery chapel, Willie's casket was carried by workmen to a borrowed vault. Willie was to remain there in the crypt, until the Lincolns returned to Illinois.

Oak Hill Cemetery—February 1862

The thought of Willie lying in the cold, damp mausoleum haunted Lincoln. After hours of tossing in bed, unable to sleep, he went downstairs and out to the stables.

He drew his finger along the side of the presidential carriage as he strolled past. The goats nudged him, and the boys' rabbits rustled in their cages. He stopped and stroked

Willie's pony. "It's not your fault," Lincoln whispered. "I am guilty for letting him play so near that canal brimming with sewage and disease. I should have called him in when the weather turned foul, or at least told him to put on his coat."

As Lincoln saddled his horse, the stable door creaked. He turned.

A familiar "Hello" dissolved his alarm.

"William," he called out. "What are you doing up at this hour?"

"I could ask you the same."

"I am the president. I can do what I want."

"I'm the president's valet. I do whatever he needs."

"If that be so, you best saddle up that pony," Lincoln replied. "Because I am about to take a ride."

"Just don't leave without me." William hefted a saddle from the rack.

A bright moon illuminated the two-mile ride to Oak Hill as frigid air stung their eyes and numbed their cheeks. The image of Willie lying alone in a cold granite vault hung like a millstone around Lincoln's neck.

At the cemetery, a caretaker offered to lead them to the crypt. Lincoln thanked him for the courtesy but reminded him that he knew his own way. The caretaker insisted on serving as their guide. After all, the keys were his responsibility.

Inside the crypt, the caretaker removed a marble marker from the wall and opened Willie's vault. He helped pull out the casket and set it on the ground. William led the caretaker away to give Lincoln time alone with his son. Outside the crypt, surrounded by the specter of death, William shuddered. An image washed over him—Grace and Maddie, their bodies mouldering in a barren field without even a few stones piled together to mark the spot where they had been covered with a few clods of rocky soil. Such was the end of a slave's existence.

Lincoln knelt on the cold floor and caressed the rosewood trim of the child-sized coffin. He glided his palm over the cool metallic lid. His hand came to rest on a latch, his breath caught. He unfastened the lid and raised it gently. He locked it upright. Willie's face. Calm, peaceful, as if he merely slept. Oh, if he were only asleep. Salty tears found the corners of Lincoln's mouth. He reached under the boy, cradled him, brushed a wisp of hair into place.

"Willie," he murmured. "You cannot know how much I wish it was me locked up in this place instead of you. You had so much to offer this world. Your smile, your laughter, your wit, your bright, inquisitive mind. You lifted me. Inspired me. Without you to cheer me, how can I carry the burdens that bear down on me? My load is so heavy. Your brother ... Taddie ... he calls for you every hour ... your Mother ... your dear Mother ... distraught ... almost insane. Oh, Willie! Why did you have to leave us so soon?"

After hours of weeping, stroking his boy's marbled cheeks and silky locks, smoothing his brown jacket, spilling out his heart to Heaven, Lincoln laid his son's lifeless frame back in the casket. With his last measure of strength, he rose and called for William and the caretaker to help him lift Willie's coffin into the vault.

Lincoln continued to mourn without relief in the days that followed. He slogged through his duties. He offered only muted congratulations to Chase when Congress approved the issuance of US Notes as legal tender, alleviating the government's desperation for money to fund the war. He hardly managed to smile when Nashville fell into Union hands without rebel resistance, extending the navy's dominance over vital waterways. He gained little satisfaction from removing McClellan from his position as General-in-Chief and putting him in the field to command the Army of the Potomac.

Part of him envied his wife—shutting herself in her room, dulling her heartache with laudanum, shrouding grief in a mental fog. He didn't begrudge her any of that. He only wished he had some place to lock away his anguish so he could soldier on and bear the weight of the mantle that had been thrust on his shoulders. He recalled King Solomon's lament.

> *Wherefore I praised the dead which are already dead more than the living which are yet alive. Yea, better is he than both they, which hath not yet been, who hath not seen the evil work that is done under the sun.*

CHAPTER THIRTEEN

Executive Mansion—April 1862

April began with the promise of warmer weather until snow fell four days in a row. The resulting gloom and mounting death count from the battle at Pittsburg Landing kept Lincoln bed-ridden until early afternoon when he prepared to receive Reverend Noyes W. Miner, an old friend and former neighbor.

Lincoln found him waiting in the family parlor and clasped his hands. "I am glad you have come from Springfield. It is a relief to see you. I am in such need of consolation in these trying days. I can talk with you as I cannot with anyone else."

"I regret not coming sooner," Miner said.

"Have you visited the city before?" Lincoln asked.

"This is my first time."

"Then I shall have someone bring the carriage around so we can take a grand tour."

As Lincoln's carriage turned onto Pennsylvania Avenue, Miner braced against an icy breeze. The frosty air lost its grip on him when a thunderous clamor erupted behind them. Lincoln's driver pulled tight on the reins and brought the carriage to a stop.

Reverend Miner gawked as an artillery battery rumbled past.

"There's no cause for alarm," Lincoln assured him. "Our boys are drilling for battle. In this city, we live with constant reminders of war's horrors and inevitable sadness."

"Yes, sadness," Miner said. "You have been visited by far more than your share. Christian people all over the country are praying for you, as they have never prayed for mortal man before."

Lincoln shook his head. "I am also aware of the millions of Christians below the Potomac who raise up prayers daily for my failure, if not my death."

"Their prayers are of no concern to God," Miner insisted. "Nor should they be to you. They have no foundation in righteousness."

"When I look at the wasteland around me, it is hard to see the Almighty's favor. My sweet Willie gone from this earth more than a month now. The rebellion's resilience. People across the land abandoning hope. Were it not for a few humble examples close at my side who demonstrate genuine Christian faith, I fear I would abandon hope."

"I am deeply concerned for Mrs. Lincoln," Miner confessed. "There was a hardness about her when I called on her a day or so ago. She has two brothers who were at Shiloh. She hoped they were either dead or taken prisoner. When I showed surprise at her remark, she claimed they would kill you if they could and would destroy our government. She repeated herself—she hopes they are either dead or taken prisoner."

"The night after that battle," Lincoln said, "I walked the floor till morning, never closing my eyes except to squeeze back tears. I hope with God's blessing, once these times are over, we can go back to Illinois and pass the rest of our lives in quiet."

"I hope that for you as well."

"We had some happy days in Springfield, but misery visited us there, too. When Eddie was born, I gave Mrs. Lincoln a downstairs bedroom and added a pantry. Three years later we lost him, and she couldn't bear to sleep in that room anymore."

"Dwell on the happy times," Miner replied.

"Willie was our Christmas gift that year."

Miner smiled. "I think Willie was everyone's favorite."

"With losing our darling Willie, the awful destruction of life, the loss of dear friends, the ugly fractures between members of the same family, it is as if the poet's words were meant for me—

> *What evil looks had I from old and young. Instead of the cross, the Albatross about my neck was hung.*

"Ah, yes," Miner said. "*The Rime of the Ancient Mariner.* Quite morose. You should not be so hard on yourself."

"My wife's dream as a young girl was to live in the president's house." Lincoln pinched his brow. "But tragically we have had a hard time of it since coming here, and none of the difficulties have been of her making. It is all my doing, even her loneliness, her desperate cries for attention. It is as though she has lost a husband among all her tragedies. I would do anything to see her well again, but this great conflict consumes me." Lincoln paused. "I have made inquiries about committing her to an asylum for a time."

Silence fell over them until Miner asked, "Do you not think we shall be able to put down this rebellion?"

"Relying on the Almighty for help and believing that our cause is right, I think we shall conquer in the end. Nonetheless, the struggle will be protracted and severe, involving a fearful loss of property and life. What strange scenes are these through which we are passing. I am sometimes astonished at the part I am acting in this terrible drama and I often ask myself, when shall I awake and find it all a dream?"

"Many are happy you were given by God to shepherd our nation through these dark hours," Miner replied.

"If I could, I would gladly take my neck from under the yoke. Nonetheless, it has pleased almighty God to place me in my present position. And looking to Him for wisdom and Divine guidance, I must work my destiny as best I can."

When the carriage pulled up to the War Department building, Lincoln escorted Miner inside where he turned him over to a young officer for a short tour. As Lincoln bid Miner goodbye, he reminded his guest that Mrs. Lincoln expected him to join them for dinner, promptly at six o'clock.

Back outside, Lincoln instructed his driver to wait for Miner and return him to the mansion by dinner time. Lincoln pulled his shawl around his neck and trudged across the snow to the mansion. Upstairs, he shut himself in the Prince of Wales Room to mourn.

At supper, Miner pointed to an extra place setting. "Are we expecting another guest?"

No sooner than the words were out of his mouth, Lincoln's favorite Tabby cat strolled in and jumped into the vacant chair. Lincoln took the gold fork from the extra place setting and offered Tabby a taste of his supper.

Mrs. Lincoln scowled. "Mr. Miner, do you not think it is shameful for Mr. Lincoln to feed Tabby with a gold fork?"

Without giving Miner a chance to reply, Lincoln answered, "If the gold fork was good enough for Buchanan, I think it is good enough for Tabby." He continued to feed the cat for the remainder of the meal.

After Miner returned to his hotel, Orville Browning called on Lincoln at the mansion. Lincoln took the opportunity to solicit Browning's views on the closing of a letter he had written to General McClellan.

> *... it is an indispensable necessity for you to strike a blow if you are to maintain your character before the country.*

Browning agreed with the letter's message and tone, saying it was about time Lincoln brought the hammer down. Lincoln thanked him for his support but complained of a severe headache that began to assail him. He asked to be excused so he could retire for the night.

William had gathered Lincoln's wardrobe from the laundry and was waiting outside his office when Browning left. He had been sitting in the reception area during most of Browning's visit and had something he wanted to get off his chest.

"What is it?" Lincoln asked.

"I heard you from out in the hallway when you told Mr. Browning the army needs to strike a blow."

"It's not a government secret that I'm getting impatient with General McClellan." Lincoln chuckled.

William pulled back his shoulders. "You wouldn't have to be waiting around for the army to get moving if you let colored men fight."

Lincoln's eyes narrowed. "No, I will not recruit Negroes into the army."

"Why not?" William asked.

"As a lot, they are unfit for the task, indolent, uneducated, unequal to the rebel soldiers they would face."

"Sir, as Mr. Slade said, no one has more to fight for."

"But will they fight for it?" Lincoln replied. "I think not. If they had a stomach for it, they would have rebelled long ago."

"Where would they have gone after they rebelled?"

"You are exactly correct. Society has no place for them, but as hundreds of so-called contrabands cross our lines, claiming to be free, we must make a solution for them."

"You mean the colonies you talk about," William responded.

"There must be a place for them to raise themselves up freely, without the burdens so often placed upon minority classes. Once their equality is demonstrated, they can come back and live among us peaceably."

"But, sir—"

"William, please. I am quite tired tonight and for a change I have it in my mind to get a full night's sleep.

"Yes, sir," William muttered. "I see a little scuff on your boot. I best be taking care of it if you will kindly take them off."

Lincoln rolled his eyes and removed his boots.

William carried Lincoln's boots to the basement and shut himself in his room. He rubbed polish into every crease and crevice. The more he thought about what Mr. Lincoln said, the harder he rubbed. Finding Grace and Maddie already bordered on the impossible and none of Mr. Lincoln's plans would make it easier, only harder. Mr. Lincoln's freedom was nothing more than bondage dressed up in a fancy suit. It reminded him of Mr. Florville, Mrs. Keckly, and Slade. Anything they owned could be snatched away by the rap of a judge's gavel. No court would allow them to speak on their own behalf—if they were sued, only white folks could come to their defense. Any freedoms Negroes imagined they might gain from a white man's war were like mirages on a parched prairie road.

William Slade Residence—April 1862

On an unseasonably warm morning in late April, Tad jumped from the carriage the instant William brought it to a stop in front of Slade's Fourth Ward home—a two-story brick house on Massachusetts Avenue, one mile from the Executive Mansion. William remained parked on the street, waiting for Slade. The duty had fallen on William to deposit Tad at the Slades' boarding house a couple of mornings each week before his afternoon shift at the Treasury Department.

Slade's younger children—Andrew, Jessie, and Nibbie—became Tad Lincoln's favorite playmates after he recovered from the fever that claimed his brother's life. With the Taft boys banished, Tad's rambunctious behavior exhausted the domestic staff's patience, raised the ire of Lincoln's secretaries, and drew complaints from visitors who came to the mansion on official business. Mrs. Slade, on the other hand, delighted in having Tad around to keep her children occupied while she tended to her boarders.

In the beginning, William held carriage rides with Slade in the same regard as having a stone caught in his shoe and not being able to shake it out. Over time though, a bond began to form, filling a void William didn't realize had existed.

Slade climbed aboard the carriage wearing a broad grin. "Freedom at last! At least Congress has made it official here in the city. I never thought I would see the day."

"Excuse me," William replied. "No one's free this close to slave territory. Any one of us could get snatched off the street, like *poof*… and sold down south."

"I overheard Mr. Lincoln and Mr. Browning talking about nullifying the Fugitive Slave Act." Slade rapped his knuckles on the wood trim on the driver's seat. "With any luck they will get it through Congress. Problem solved."

"But if Mr. Lincoln has his way, freedom means we all have to pack our bags—assuming we get to take along anything but the shirts on our backs—and hop a boat to somewhere far from America. He talks about Hayti, Africa, or Panama."

"Any freedom is a step forward," Slade said.

"People aren't free if they don't have rights. Like owning property, voting, defending themselves."

Slade crossed his arms. "Mr. Lincoln is doing what he can."

"All he ever talks about is keeping Kentucky happy. When that Speed fellow bends the Tycoon's ear, he is like, yes suh, whatever you wants suh."

"I will have you show more respect for our president."

William snapped the reins. "Tycoon is what his secretaries call him behind his back."

"Since when do you model your behavior after those who have no manners? If you wish to continue your present service, you will do better."

"Fine. But I heard him with my own ears. He told Mr. Browning he is the only person who can free all the slaves, and he's not going to."

"Patience, William. Rome was not built in a day."

"Patience?" William spit the word out of his mouth. "Men. Women. Children. Bound like oxen to carts. They need freedom now. If Mr. Lincoln wants them to be patient, maybe he should be shackled with them while they wait."

"How do you propose he do things any faster?"

"He can let Negroes join the fight," William replied.

"Tell me boy, why are you so eager to join the freedom fight?"

"I have my reasons, but I prefer to keep my business to myself."

Executive Mansion—May 1862

Slade stepped into Lincoln's office. "You wanted to see me?"

Lincoln gestured to the chairs by the window. "Close the door and come sit with me."

As they sat, Slade asked. "What can I do for you?"

"I've been wanting to talk with you about William."

"Is there something the matter?" Slade asked.

"That's my question. Is something eating at him?"

"I suppose you could say he was a bit irritable when he dropped off Tad at my house just now."

"Did he say anything in particular?" Lincoln asked.

"Oh, he was running at the mouth about colonies and Negroes joining the army."

"I was short with him the other night." Lincoln rubbed his forehead. "It wasn't his fault. My patience was worn thin."

"If I may, sir, the young man does have something of a point. Our people have demonstrated a readiness for equality."

"A readiness in part, I would agree. But if I'm a juryman, I am not yet convinced they are prepared for full equality. Until they are, it falls on me to find a way to protect them. Colonization is part of my plan to do just that."

"As you have said before," Slade leaned forward, "disagreement is a big part of your job and it helps you do the right thing."

"Since you understand my case, can you help me smooth things over with William?"

"I'll do my best, sir."

"That's all I can expect of anyone," Lincoln replied. "You should know that I'll be taking William on an excursion soon. It's hush-hush. So, keep it to yourself. William won't even know until we're ready to leave. If you can deal with him in the meantime, maybe the trip will go more smoothly than it might otherwise."

Slade nodded. "I will speak with him later today."

Secret Destination—May 1862

William collected Nurse Pomroy from the Columbian College Hospital and delivered her to the mansion. Mrs. Lincoln had relapsed into a severe state of anxiety, which meant the nurse would be staying for a while to attend to her. Lincoln directed William to put her trunk in the Prince of Wales Room and to come back for additional instructions.

When William returned, Nurse Pomroy had already gone into Mrs. Lincoln's chamber. Lincoln took William into his office and closed the door. "You will be joining Mr. Chase and a couple of others with me on a little journey tonight, but you must not breathe a word of this to anyone."

"Yes, sir." William arched his brow.

"We'll be leaving straight away, so go downstairs and get packed. Meet me at the stables."

* * *

Stiff winds and pelting rain set in at the Navy Yard around nightfall, as Lincoln, Secretary Chase, and William boarded the revenue cutter *Miami*. Lincoln and Chase sat at a table and waited for the rest of their party while William went to the galley to check on supper.

Secretary Stanton and an army engineer came down the gangway at about eight o'clock. They shook the rain from their coats and sat with Lincoln and Chase. Stanton pressed his palm to his forehead. "McClellan has been fooled again."

"What this time?" Lincoln asked.

"He claims he's outnumbered," Stanton replied.

Lincoln slammed his hand on the table. "When the whole affair started, he had Magruder outnumbered four men to one. He should have gone on the attack."

"To be fair," Chase said, "his spies reported much greater numbers on the rebels' side."

Stanton shook his head. "He still had plenty of men to take the fight to them. Instead, he pulled back and laid siege, shelling Yorktown with heavy cannon fire. He's been at it for a month now."

"What is the current situation?" Lincoln asked.

"He's not going to advance until the city is leveled and there's not a rebel soldier left breathing."

"Oh, they shall be breathing when he's done." Lincoln sneered. "And they'll be laughing at us in Richmond. Of course, there will be twice as many in their lines and we will have exhausted a month's store of gunpowder."

Stanton grinned. "At least he is too occupied to interfere with us during the next few days."

After dinner aboard the *Miami*, William cleared the table and Lincoln raised the topic of possible routes for an attack on the rebel harbor at Norfolk, Virginia. Considerable discussion ensued. About ten o'clock, they bedded down for the night in a nineteen-foot cabin below deck that was set up with four cots. William retired to a cot in the passageway outside the cabin.

By noon the next day, the ship was tossing on choppy waters in Chesapeake Bay. Lincoln hunched over and gave up his lunch almost as soon as he had swallowed the first bites. The others poked fun at him and continued to eat until their own plates and cups tumbled off the table and rolled around on the floor. As William cleaned up the mess, Chase laughed, insisting the table was under the spell of a spiritualist.

Eventually the water calmed, and the party went on deck to chat under a canopy. Stanton recounted a story about the government's recent dealings with the industrialist Cornelius Vanderbilt. "I wired Commodore Vanderbilt asking how much he would charge to destroy the rebel ironclad *Merrimack*, or at least prevent her from coming out of Norfolk's harbor. Rather than wiring back, Mr. Vanderbilt rushed to Washington to meet with Lincoln and me. He told us he could stop the iron monster with his fastest and largest vessel, assuming she were properly manned and outfitted. He offered his yacht, the steamer *Vanderbilt*."

"I asked how he was sure it could be done," Lincoln said.

Stanton continued. "He insisted that no vessel had been or could be made by the rebels to withstand the concussion of *Vanderbilt*'s weight—more than 3,300 tons."

Lincoln added, "I inquired of him again, how much he would charge."

Stanton laughed. "To which Vanderbilt complained he was not one of the vampires who profit from war. He offered to donate his steamer to the Union navy, provided he could control its preparations for battle. Lincoln did not so much as draw a breath before blurting out, 'I accept her.'"

"In four days' time," Lincoln said, "the Commodore stood on the deck of the new warship as it sailed into Hampton Roads waterway. He had installed a steel ram on her bow."

Hours later, just past nine o'clock in the evening, the *Miami* tied up at Fortress Monroe's lower wharf. Almost immediately, the fort commander's staff officer, Colonel Le Grand Cannon, boarded. "Sir," Cannon said, "we had no notice that you were coming."

"We did not want to risk our plans falling into the wrong hands," Stanton responded. By the wrong hands, Lincoln imagined Stanton meant McClellan's hands.

"Very well," replied Cannon. "If you do not mind waiting, General Wool will want to come aboard and welcome you in person. He should be the one to escort you up to the fort."

"Thank you, Colonel," Stanton replied. "We shall do as you suggest. By the way, we've been without telegraph for the past day. Do you have any word on McClellan's movements?"

"The rebels put up quite a fight at Yorktown," Cannon replied. "It took most of the day and maybe as many as 2,000 casualties for McClellan to dislodge them."

"Two thousand total, or just ours?" Lincoln asked.

"Just ours, sir," Cannon replied.

"My God!" Lincoln gripped his forehead. "He has dallied for a month, and we still pay dearly. All to the rebels' benefit. He should have hit them when they were at their weakest."

When 77-year-old General Wool joined them aboard the *Miami*, Lincoln told him they had to find a way to move the rebels out of the Hampton Roads waterway. Wool, reputedly one of the army's most tenacious and capable officers, responded, "I cannot do it without Flag Officer Goldsborough's help. We need the navy's guns to give our troops cover to land on the rebel side of the waterway. But he refuses. The rebel ironclad inflicted too much damage on his vessels during battle a couple of months ago."

"We must convince him our navy is up to the task." Lincoln insisted.

"Unfortunately, McClellan agrees with him," Wool replied.

"McClellan's opinion should not matter," Lincoln insisted. "He has no authority over troops under your command. You may be equal in rank, but you have more time in grade. When he visits your fort, it is his duty to defer to your judgment." Lincoln turned to Stanton, whom he dubbed Mars. "Mars, what do you think? Am I not right?"

"You are absolutely correct," Stanton replied.

"Fine," Lincoln declared. "Let's go see the admiral."

"Mr. President," Wool replied. "I believe we should wait till morning to call on Goldsborough. Colonel Cannon's quarters up at the fort will be at your disposal during your stay."

"I am thankful for your generous accommodations," Lincoln said. "But that can wait. I prefer we proceed directly to Admiral Goldsborough's flagship to continue our discussions."

"At this hour?" Stanton asked.

"I see no reason to delay," Lincoln replied.

"It's nearly midnight," Chase complained. "We will all be fresher in the morning."

Lincoln picked up his tall hat and slammed it down on the table. "I insist."

Once aboard the *Minnesota,* flagship of the Atlantic Blockading Squadron, Lincoln's party went below deck where they found the thick-bearded Admiral Goldsborough in his cabin. At Lincoln's request, Goldsborough spread out charts of Hampton Roads—the broad waterway where Chesapeake Bay joins with the Atlantic Ocean at the mouths of the James and Elizabeth Rivers. Goldsborough indicated the positions of Union land batteries at Hampton, Newport News, and Fortress Monroe. He also pointed to the Rip Raps—a manmade rock island on which Castle Calhoun stood—a third of the way between Fortress Monroe and rebel-held Sewell's Point.

Goldsborough boasted that Union artillery gave the navy control over traffic passing through the waterway. Government land batteries also protected the Union fleet's blockade of rebel traffic in and out of Richmond by way of the James River. He marked the locations of rebel land batteries at Sewell's Point and Craney Island, protecting the entrance to Norfolk Harbor. Goldsborough jutted out his chin. "Their guns don't have sufficient range to touch our warships in Hampton Roads, but they do prevent us from attacking Norfolk."

After spending a few moments studying the charts, Lincoln indicated the shoreline directly across the channel from Fortress Monroe. "Can we not take troops over to that beach under the cover of our guns and march them directly down to Norfolk? What is that ... eight or ten miles overland?"

"No place to land along that shore," Goldsborough replied. "They would have to sail around the cape and approach from the other side. It would be a long and difficult operation."

"Are you positive there is no landing place?" Lincoln asked.

Goldsborough scratched his head.

"Have you tried?" Lincoln pressed.

"No, sir. I have not."

"What I am wondering, Admiral, is why don't we learn what we need to know? Our army's chief engineer has long advocated that the best way to stop the *Merrimack* from menacing our navy is to deprive her of her port at Norfolk. Push her farther south. Let's find a way to do it. Silence the rebel batteries and land our troops without any worries."

"I have studied the charts," Goldsborough replied. "The water is too shallow for our transport ships to get close enough for the army to safely unload its men."

Lincoln turned to General Wool. "What's become of all those shoal-draft canal boats McClellan was unable to use during his pontoon bridge fiasco at Harpers Ferry?"

"They're stored at Fortress Monroe, sir."

"Problem solved," Lincoln declared. "Our warships can carry troops until the water becomes too shallow, and the canal boats can be used in some fashion to get them ashore."

"Yes," Stanton agreed. "It's time we do something."

"Admiral, do you have any objections to putting on a little demonstration in the morning?" Lincoln asked.

"Even without their land batteries," Goldsborough answered, "there's still the matter of their ironclad."

Lincoln replied, "I would like to see your guns do some damage to those rebel land batteries and draw their *Merrimack* into open waters. If we're lucky, our new *Vanderbilt* can make a run at her. With their ironclad out of commission and their land batteries destroyed, nothing would stop us from sailing troops directly into Norfolk."

"If that's what you wish, Mr. President. I am sure we can put on a show for you," Goldsborough said. "I will have members of my staff prepare accommodations for you on board to stay the night. Your man can bunk with our coloreds down in the engine room."

While Stanton and Chase slept, Lincoln paced the floor in his cabin, turning over recollections in his mind of the charts Goldsborough had shown them. The Rip Raps, the locations of rebel batteries, the depths of shoals extending out from beaches where the government troops might land, overland routes from the beaches to Norfolk.

The clunking, clanking, and hissing of steam engines in the ship's bowels where William was berthed made sleep impossible. He also figured Lincoln would not sleep any better on the ship than he often did in the mansion. He took Lincoln tea service from the ship's galley, and Lincoln described his ideas about using the canal boats to land troops. He recounted his riverboat days as a young man, the things he had learned about the subtleties of currents, shorelines, and shoals, and his invention of a ballast system for shallow-hulled boats that earned him a patent.

William repeated what he learned from the ship's colored sailors whose job it was to man her big guns. Their greatest fear was that the rebels' iron monster would slip under the ship's guns and out maneuver the *Minnesota* in open waters. They worried the *Vanderbilt* would fare no better.

"All the more reason," Lincoln said, "for us to put an end to its reign of terror."

After a short night, Lincoln rose early and climbed the companionway to the *Minnesota*'s broad deck to survey the waterway firsthand. Sunrise was less than half an hour away when Goldsborough joined him and pointed out landmarks, barely visible in the morning twilight. "For reference, that's Fortress Monroe, and that mound of rock is the Rip Raps."

Lincoln eyed the admiral. "Let's not have another Sumter."

"Not on my watch," Goldsborough replied.

"Out there." Lincoln gestured. "Vanderbilt's yacht?"

"Yes. She's a beauty."

Lincoln squinted at a gunmetal object floating in shadowy water, silhouetted by the predawn sky. "There, just in front of the yacht. Is that a raft? It's hard to make out. Looks like a log resting on a half-sunken cheese box."

"That's our *Monitor* with her twenty-two-foot turret."

"Fascinating. Where did she and the rebel ironclad duel?"

Goldsborough guided Lincoln astern and indicated a jut of land at the mouth of the Elizabeth River. "Between here and that point."

"And where are those rebel batteries we need to silence?"

"On each side of the mouth of the river. Sewell's Point is closest to us, Craney is on the opposite bank."

"What's the range of their guns?" Lincoln asked.

"They can't reach us here, but we can hammer them with our guns all day long."

"What if their ironclad gets under our guns?"

"If that happens, *Monitor*'s job is to engage her and take pressure off," Goldsborough replied. "But a couple of months ago when that happened, we lost a valuable warship and sustained severe damage to this one. We only recently finished repairs. Better not let it happen again."

Lincoln gazed across the channel at the rebel batteries. "I would like to return to Fortress Monroe."

"We can have a tug ready to transport you over to the *Miami* after breakfast."

"I prefer going at once. We have urgent business to discuss with General Wool."

"As you wish, Mr. President."

After instructing Wool on preparations for attacking Norfolk, Lincoln spent the remainder of the morning reading Shakespeare in Colonel Cannon's quarters. As he read, Colonel Cannon passed the open door, and Lincoln called to him, "You have been very busy, Colonel. Come in here and rest. I'll read to you."

Lincoln's voice became tremulous as he read from Shakespeare's *King John*—the part where Constance bemoans the loss of her son.

And, father cardinal, I have heard you say
That we shall see and know our friends in heaven:
If that be true, I shall see my boy again;

Lincoln paused. "My greatest wish is to see my dead boy again, but here's the part that wounds my soul."

There was not such a gracious creature born.
But now will canker-sorrow eat my bud
And chase the native beauty from his cheek
And he will look as hollow as a ghost,
As dim and meagre as an ague's fit,
And so he'll die; and, rising so again,
When I shall meet him in the court of heaven
I shall not know him ...

William was carrying a message to Lincoln from Chase when he heard Lincoln's plaintive voice carrying into the hallway. He held back a few steps from Cannon's quarters.

"Such a thing might be true of my poor Willie." A lump formed in Lincoln's throat. "I shall not recognize him when my time comes to join him on the other side. If so, my lament shall be the same as that poor mother's."

> *Grief fills the room up of my absent child,*
> *Lies in his bed, walks up and down with me,*
> *Puts on his pretty looks, repeats his words,*
> *Remembers me of all his gracious parts,*
> *Stuffs out his vacant garments with his form ...*

Lincoln laid down the book and asked Cannon, "Did you ever dream of some lost friend, and feel that you were having a sweet communion with him, yet have a consciousness that it was not a reality?"

"I think all of us have those experiences," Cannon replied.

"That is the way I dream of my lost boy Willie." Lincoln began weeping.

Cannon choked back tears at the sight of Lincoln with his head bowed, grieving.

William's throat tightened. If his hope for finding Grace and Maddie was in vain, and someday they met in heaven, he wondered if they would recognize each other. He considered the same about Thomas. He stepped back a few feet farther from the doorway, struggling to maintain his composure.

Inside Cannon's quarters, Lincoln wiped his eyes and thanked Cannon for sitting with him and enduring his anguish.

"It was my honor, sir," Cannon said.

Lincoln checked his watch. "I reckon it's about time for Admiral Goldsborough's demonstration. I'd better gather my party."

Lincoln followed Cannon into the hallway. On discovering William just outside the doorway, Lincoln said, "I was just coming to find you. I want you to collect Mars and Chase and our army engineer. We're going over to Castle Calhoun to watch the demonstration Admiral Goldsborough has planned for us."

"Yes, sir." William fingered the note from Chase.

"Is that for me?" Lincoln asked.

William handed over the message.

Lincoln put on his steel-rimmed spectacles and read. He peered over the rims at William. "I reckon you already know what it says."

"Yes, I do."

"How did Chase react when he learned about Hunter's order?" Lincoln asked.

"He stormed around the room and complained that you or Mr. Stanton should have answered General Hunter months ago when he asked permission to enlist freedmen in his department."

Lincoln grimaced. "Chase must be worried he won't have enough labor to run the plantations he confiscated in the Sea Islands."

William tilted his head to one side. "The message says General Hunter plans to conscript any Negroes who don't enlist willingly. If Mr. Chase can't spare any laborers, maybe the general should find other Negroes to put in his army."

"This will not do." Lincoln hesitated. "However, I cannot deal with Hunter right now."

"Yes, sir," William replied.

"Norfolk and that monster *Merrimack* are all I have time for at the moment. Mars will have to take care of General Hunter when we return to Washington."

"May I—" William fidgeted with his sleeve.

"I know what you're going to say. I am not changing my mind." Lincoln said. "If or when slaves are freed and put into the army, I am the one who will decide it. Neither Congress nor any general is going to sneak behind my back and do my job."

Lincoln and his party stepped off the tugboat at Castle Calhoun in time to watch Union warships begin firing 11-inch shells at the rebel batteries on the mouth of the Elizabeth River. Acrid white smoke from the ships' guns and black belches from the stacks painted the sky grey. When a Union volley sheared off an enemy flagstaff at the far battery, one of the rebels climbed onto the ramparts and waved a new flag. Another shell exploded yards away and chased him to cover.

The Union ironclad *Monitor*, dwarfed by the other ships, joined the bombardment. A burst of smoke from its turret was followed seconds later by a distant thunderous explosion. Guns from the Rip Raps joined the fight as well, and the rebel batteries fell silent. Lincoln muttered just loud enough for William to overhear him. "Why was Goldsborough afraid to do this sooner?"

At that moment, a large puff of black smoke plumed over the woods behind Sewell's Point. Nearby soldiers pointed and yelled, "There comes the *Merrimack*."

William gripped Lincoln's forearm. "Let's go."

Lincoln pulled away. "This is what I came to see."

"You can watch from a safer distance," William contended. "We can't risk exposing you."

"Fine." Lincoln glanced around for the rest of his party. They had already headed to the tug.

"Now, sir," William insisted.

Lincoln grabbed a nearby soldier by the sleeve. "Send a message to Admiral Goldsborough aboard the *Minnesota.* Say the president orders him to keep the wooden ships out of any battle with the *Merrimack*. Let the *Monitor* and *Vanderbilt* do the job."

Once aboard the tug, Lincoln went astern and kept a keen eye on the *Merrimack*. William joined him.

When the rebel ironclad retired to her harbor without engaging the Union warships, William asked Lincoln, "Are you disappointed?"

"I came here to see her destroyed." Lincoln tightened his grip on the boat's railing.

"But now, I suppose you'll have to go home and wait for someone else to finish your fight." William cocked his head.

"No." Lincoln slapped the railing. "I shall go straight over there and take away her home port."

"Some folks aren't given the choice to fight for what they want." William braced for Lincoln's reply.

Lincoln glared at him.

* * *

Lincoln wasted no time after returning to Fortress Monroe. He broke into a grin as the canal boats arrived at the fort's wharf and immediately set about lining up transportation for troops and artillery.

The civilian steamer *Adelaide*, filled with passengers and freight destined for Baltimore, was the first vessel conscripted.

A half dozen other civilian steamers were likewise put into military service. In each case, Lincoln questioned the ship's captain regarding the vessel's draught. He wanted to be certain it could carry men and equipment close enough to shore for safe landing.

As Lincoln monitored troops loading onto the transport ships, William asked, "Why can't you understand that when two are yoked together they must carry burdens equally?"

"Of course, I understand it. It is a time-honored principle."

"So, you must see," William argued, "that if I am not allowed to carry the burden equally, I am not truly free."

"If you want a taste of war, you can have it." Lincoln ran his hands over his head. "Go on the march tomorrow with Chase but stay out of harm's way."

William was prepared to throw more of Lincoln's own words back at him. For instance, carrying the load equally meant Negro troops should "strike a blow." That's what Lincoln told General McClellan to do if he wanted to earn the people's respect. But William held his tongue.

William's impatience yielded to exhilaration the next morning as the pre-dawn light painted waters grey around Fortress Monroe's wharf. He was going to war, even if only as Secretary Chase's armor bearer. He followed Lincoln and Chase aboard the revenue cutter *Miami.*

The big guns from Castle Calhoun thundered a new round of shells at the rebel batteries—a precaution to hold the enemy at bay while the *Miami* crossed to the landing site that Lincoln had personally reconnoitered. There was no response.

Chills ran down William's spine as they approached the opposite shore where the fleet of troop transports lay at anchor, loaded with 6,000 infantry and cavalrymen, their horses, cannon, and materials of war. The fleet had steamed across during the night under cover of darkness.

Around seven o'clock, Wool, Chase, and William boarded a rowboat and went ashore. Troops disembarked their vessels, hitting make-shift ramps that were constructed during the night by lashing together canal boats and arraying them lengthwise along the shore. As units assembled on land, they marched off to Norfolk.

Lincoln stood on *Miami*'s deck, taking in the spectacle, but his focus never strayed from William and Chase mounting their horses and joining the procession. When the two of them rode out of view, he whispered a quick prayer that all would go well, all would be safe.

William's heart pounded as he and Chase rode ahead of Wool's main body of soldiers to join a squad of dragoons that had gone off before the main column. In about five miles, they caught up with the dragoons. William's pulse raced faster as artillery thundered close by. An officer told Chase the rebels had set fire to a bridge about half a mile up the road and their artillery was deployed on the other side. As a precaution, Union guns were battering the suspected rebel positions.

When General Wool's formation caught up with the dragoons, he gave orders to detour north around the bridge. The march proceeded, discovering along the way that the enemy was in retreat, destroying everything of value in its wake. On entering the charred works that had been the center of operations for the rebel navy, Wool's troops cheered wildly. William's chest swelled over being part of the victorious military campaign. He also rejoiced for Lincoln, who accomplished his mission of capturing the rebel ironclad's home port.

Lincoln's mood remained anxious throughout the day as he awaited news at Fortress Monroe. Wool's failure to send updates evoked trepidation over the darkest possibilities. There would certainly be more death. He should not have allowed Chase and William join the march.

Around nine o'clock, Cannon convinced Lincoln and Stanton to retire for the night, having promised to awaken them with any news that arrived. Later, he went outside the fort to the wharf and waited in moonlight. After a couple of hours, the splashing of paddlewheels in the distance broke the night's silence. Cannon peered, straining to make out a form in the water. Beyond the moon's reflection, the splashing grew louder. Finally, a gunboat appeared.

Once the small vessel tied down, General Wool, Secretary Chase, and William jumped off. All three wore broad grins. Wool gave Cannon the news that Norfolk was taken without resistance and proceeded to the fort to tell Lincoln.

As General Wool approached the wall of the fort, a guard called out, "Who goes there?"

"General Wool," he bellowed.

The commotion drew Lincoln's attention. He rushed to the window and yelled, "What's going on?"

"I've come to present Norfolk," General Wool replied.

"Someone wake Mars," Lincoln ordered. "And General Wool, come up here."

While Wool, Chase, and William went to see Lincoln, Cannon roused Stanton.

Without dressing, Stanton rushed to Lincoln's quarters and threw his arms around Wool, hugging him.

Lincoln shouted, "Look out, Mars! If you don't release him, the general will throw you."

"This is the most important capture that has been made," Stanton declared. "You should proceed to Norfolk, Mr. President, and issue a proclamation on rebel soil."

Lincoln eyed William. He had never witnessed him consumed with such delight. It was a bittersweet vision.

Cannon found a robe to cover Stanton's nightclothes and the Secretary sat down to write Lincoln's proclamation.

The next morning as Lincoln and Stanton were crossing over to Norfolk, a great explosion caught everyone off guard. Momentarily, a signalman announced the rebels had blown up the ironclad *Merrimack* in open waters to prevent her capture. Secretary Chase greeted reports of the *Merrimack*'s demise by declaring, "So has ended a brilliant week's campaign of the president, for I think if he had not come down, the rebel monster would be as much a terror as ever. Now, the whole coast is virtually ours."

CHAPTER FOURTEEN

Washington City Vicinity—May 1862

The five-story stone Columbian College building loomed over an array of white hospital tents. The college, nearly two miles north of the Executive Mansion, had become the home of Camp Carver. Lincoln promised Nurse Pomroy he would visit her there after he returned from his secret mission and greet her boys—wounded soldiers. As Lincoln's carriage approached—unannounced—William rode next to the driver.

Nurse Pomroy had her nose buried in patient medical cards at her desk in the main building when she was called to the lobby. When Lincoln greeted her, the embarrassment on her face drew a chorus of laughter from the assembled surgeons, stewards, cadets, and nurses.

After the nurse introduced Lincoln to each staff member, they all went out to the tents where wounded and sick soldiers were called out and arranged in a straight line. Even the lame, faltering, and feeble insisted on straggling out.

Lincoln took off his hat and shook hands with each one, asking his name, his home state, and the name of his regiment and company.

Before Lincoln left, Nurse Pomroy led him to the kitchen and introduced three colored staff. "This is Lucy, formerly a slave in Kentucky. She cooks the nurses' food."

Lincoln shook Lucy's hand and turned to the men on Mrs. Pomroy's left.

"This is Garner and Brown," she said. "They are serving their country by cooking the low diet for our sickest boys."

Lincoln shook their hands. "How do you do, Garner? How do you do, Brown?"

William overheard the whispers of two surgeons standing nearby. "The gall of that woman," one of them sneered. The other replied, "Hell will freeze over before you catch me shaking a Negro hand. Freedom is one thing, but her brand of equality is too much."

William clenched his jaw. He did not regard himself to be an expert on much, but he figured he knew Lincoln's sentiments almost as well as he knew his own. As Lincoln told him on the train from Springfield, "A man forms a bond with his hat and his barber." Lincoln may have shaken some colored folks' hands, but he was no threat to the surgeons' way of thinking. He was against putting Negroes on an equal basis with whites.

Executive Mansion—May 1862

William pushed the barber's chair into Lincoln's office while Nicolay was reading aloud a draft of the order to rescind General Hunter's emancipation of slaves in South Carolina's Sea Islands.

Lincoln sat in the barber's chair. "Good morning."

William grunted a response.

"Someone's cheerful this morning," Lincoln said.

William slapped the razor against the leather with uncharacteristic *oomph.*

"Be careful with that."

"I know how to shave. I've been doing it for almost two years now."

"If something's eating at you, spit it out." Lincoln jerked the towel from his chest.

"You won't care for what I have to say."

Lincoln walked over and shut the door. "I've told you before. In private you can say whatever's on you mind."

"I have ears. You're stopping General Hunter's emancipation order—"

A knock on the door interrupted them.

Before Lincoln answered William, Nicolay re-entered the office. "Sir, the Maryland delegation is downstairs, waiting."

Lincoln folded the towel and handed it back to William. "Let's continue this conversation when you come back this evening."

William collected his shaving implements and left.

Later the same day, Lincoln found Mrs. Keckly in the upstairs parlor. She stood when he entered the room.

"Please sit," he said.

She resumed her seat. He sat opposite her in an armchair.

"Madam Elizabeth. That's what polite folks call you, am I right?"

"Yes, sir."

"May I call you that?"

"Of course," she replied, smiling.

Lincoln pressed his palms together. "I want to thank you for your service to my family during these very trying times."

"It's my honor, sir."

"Not only have you ministered to my wife during periods of nervous exhaustion, but you have been a God-send for little Tad."

"I would have done as much for any family that employs me," Mrs. Keckly replied.

"I am sure that is true. Nonetheless, if there is anything I can ever do for you, you have but to ask."

"Thank you very much." She folded her hands. "I suppose there is one small thing. Small for you probably, but it would be a large thing for me and the girls I employ."

"Then it is done." Lincoln clapped his hands.

"We would like to be treated with respect." She straightened.

"We have always tried to do that," Lincoln replied, "but if we have failed in any way, it will be fixed. Just tell me what we must do."

"When I tend to Mrs. Lincoln's wardrobe, I do so as a businesswoman, not as a servant. In my view, respect would mean entering this building through the front door. The same should be true for Mr. Slade's daughter, Josephine, and my other girls."

"What's the matter with you people?" Lincoln sputtered.

"We people?"

"I am trying my best." Lincoln raked his fingers through his hair. "With all the responsibilities this office has heaped on my shoulders, please do not ask me to reverse centuries of customs all at once."

"You could at least not stifle progress once it has been gained," she replied.

"William keeps accosting me with this business about equality. Are the whole lot of you conspiring against me?"

"No, sir." She raised her chin. "But apparently, we are all agitated about the same thing."

"Does your agitation have anything to do with the business over General Hunter's proclamation?"

"In part," she replied.

"I do not know why I must keep repeating myself," Lincoln replied. "Whether it shall become an indispensable necessity for the maintenance of the government to declare the slaves of any state free, or to enlist freedmen into military service, such decisions are my responsibility alone as Commander-in-Chief of the Army and Navy. I cannot feel justified in leaving those decisions to commanders in the field."

"I suppose we have said our peace." Mrs. Keckly stood.

Lincoln rose. "All I ask for is your understanding."

"You shall have that and more. Know that our prayers are with you, and I am certain there is likely no other man who will make those decisions more prudently than yourself."

"Thank you, Madame Elizabeth. And if I may prevail on you, which I ask humbly, knowing I cannot at this time give you what you have asked of me, will you please talk to William? See if you can soothe him for me."

"Sir, I will do my best."

Soldiers' Home—June 1862

Oppressive June heat and grief over Willie's death drove the Lincoln family north to the Soldiers' Home, nearly four miles out of the city. An elevation change of only a couple hundred feet was enough to offer cooler air for evening pleasure and comfortable sleep. A dozen wagons loaded with personal belongings and much of the family's furniture followed Lincoln's carriage and a second one carrying household staff.

Mary Cuthbert, the Lincolns' housekeeper, rode with Slade and William in the second carriage. She shut her eyes as they drove past a row of whorehouses and taverns. She shook her head when she opened her eyes to signs directing passersby to a racetrack. Back home in Ireland, on paydays her father rarely made it home sober, and his pockets were empty, except for chits reminding him of debts he owed on lost wagers. The atmosphere changed for the better as the caravan left the city behind and passed through lush woods.

Almost an hour from the mansion, the wagons pulled to a stop in front of a large two-story stucco house. William climbed down, mesmerized by the diamond-shaped windowpanes and gingerbread trim.

Slade clapped William's shoulder. "Unloading is a young man's work."

Tad jumped from the family's carriage and ran to the front door. Mrs. Lincoln called him back as Lincoln helped her down. In her second breath, she gave instructions to the men who came along to help with the move.

Lincoln's focus was captivated by rows of white markers in a field north of the house a few hundred yards. Three teams of workmen busied themselves with shovels.

Lieutenant Colonel Thomas L. Alexander, acting governor of the Soldiers' Home, greeted Mrs. Lincoln. "Welcome. We've prepared the main cottage to serve as your residence."

"I cannot believe we're here at last," she said.

"Cottage?" Tad asked. "Why not this big house?"

She laughed. "Son, that is the cottage. It was built for a rich man."

"Is Papa rich?" Tad asked.

Mrs. Lincoln patted Tad's head. "The government bought it from a rich banker, and now we get to use it for a while."

Alexander indicated an imposing stone structure with a massive tower only a few yards away. "You'll be sharing the grounds with 150 inmates who are in residence at Scott Hall. Many are crippled."

Tad tugged his mother's skirt. "Look, Ma. A real fort. Can Nibbie and her brothers come and play?"

"Perhaps on occasion. But Colonel Alexander has sons you shall be able to play with anytime you want." She filled her lungs with fresh air. "I have not tasted air so sweet since we left Springfield. Like many of those poor men, I am certain I will find comfort here that I have not known in a long while."

Lincoln joined them and pointed to the field he had been observing. "Those grave markers?"

"Twelve hundred battlefield dead brought back here and buried," Alexander replied.

"And I reckon there are tens of thousands of men left behind and buried at battlefields where they fell." Lincoln palmed the back of his head.

"Hardly a day goes by when we aren't burying a few more. Today we had three—one from Ohio, one from Virginia, and one from Minnesota."

"Is the Virginia boy one of theirs?" Lincoln asked.

"All are ours."

Lincoln stared at the second story windows of the cottage. "I would like that room for my office, if that's all right."

"I think you'll be more than satisfied when I show you what we have planned."

The colonel led Lincoln upstairs with William and Slade close on their heels. Tad bounded ahead of them. Mrs. Lincoln followed, studying everything she passed. From the second-floor landing, everyone proceeded to the west end of the house. Lincoln paused at a large, north-facing window and gazed across the grounds to the cemetery. Alexander gave Lincoln a moment to absorb the view then led him through a doorway into an equally large adjoining room with a southern exposure. "This room," the Colonel said, "gives you a view of the Capitol in the distance."

"And the room we just passed through?" Lincoln asked.

"The lighting is better in here," Alexander replied. "But the home is large enough that you can keep that space open to insure privacy."

"That should be fine enough."

"Shall I show you the rest of the house?" Alexander asked.

"I am sure Mrs. Lincoln would like that, and Mr. Slade, too," Lincoln replied. "He will be supervising our housekeeper and cook. But I need to set up my quarters so I can begin working. William can help me."

* * *

On a Sunday after the family finished unpacking their belongings at the Soldiers' Home, Lincoln found a newspaper from the previous fall. A kindly editor published a poem Willie had written following Senator Baker's death. A lump formed in Lincoln's throat as he read the lines.

He laid the newspaper aside, walked out of the cottage, and entered Scott Hall. An orderly directed him to a stairwell that led to the top of the tower. He had been told Union soldiers used the tower to observe rebel troop movements on the other side of the Potomac. It also served as a signal platform to send semaphore messages to Smithsonian Castle, to be relayed to the mansion and the War Department only blocks away.

Lincoln stood atop the tower and faced southwest, bracing against the parapet. He drew a spyglass from his coat pocket and peered into the horizon. There it was. Oak Hill. Willie's crypt was cradled under mature oaks in a draw over the crest. Tears welled in his eyes, obscuring his vision. He put down the spyglass and wept.

Footsteps nearby forced an early end to his mourning. He blinked his eyes into focus and found William standing at his side.

"Are you all right, sir?" William asked.

"Of course not."

"I'm sorry to interrupt, I just—"

"Thank you. But there's no cause for concern. I was visiting with my little boy's spirit."

"Then I'll leave you," William replied.

"No. I have found what I was looking for. Though I reckon in the future, it would be good if you came along and guarded the stairway, so I am not disturbed."

"Yes, sir."

* * *

On the nation's eighty-sixth birthday, Lincoln rode alone on horseback from the mansion toward the cottage. He had endured a tortuous day in the city—a fitting end to ten days from hell. General McClellan had put 130,000 men in the field against General Lee's 90,000. Union casualties had exceeded 16,000, including dead, wounded, and missing. The number 16,000 haunted him. He could not fathom such a dreadful scene. Memories flooded his mind—glimpses of smaller scale carnage he witnessed as a soldier in the Black Hawk War. Bodies in a row on the ground. The crown of each head, a bloody patch. A dead boy with buckskin breeches like his. Flies swarming, a dozen disemboweled, beheaded carcasses. A detached head, its cloudy eyes still open, and its mouth agape as if death seized its soul mid-scream.

A youthful voice rang in Lincoln's ears, bringing him back to the moment. An ambulance wagon crunched along next to him—part of a long train of wagons carrying battlefield wounded to military hospitals on the city's outskirts. A soldier, his head bandaged and bloody, eyed him. "You're Uncle Abe," the soldier blurted.

"Yes. I reckon I am. How are you, son?"

"Banged up, but alive."

"Yes, I can see you are. Thank you for your devotion to our country."

"They was a hornets' nest of screaming rebels. Wish we coulda gone into Richmond and finished 'em off."

"Thank you, just the same." Lincoln tipped his hat. "With hard-fighting boys like you, we're sure to get there soon."

Lincoln spurred his horse and met up with the next wagon in the train. He heard more about hard and disappointing battles. He continued along, riding a distance with each ambulance, offering words of encouragement and gratitude. When the line of ambulances turned off the main road toward one of Washington's many military hospitals, he rode on to the cottage.

His thoughts turned to William, who had chosen to remain in the city for the night. He wished there was some way the young man could be made to grasp the ugly realities of war.

Contraband Camp—July 1862

The sun beat hard on a Saturday afternoon in mid-July. Contraband Camp and Hospital had been open for a week. Several hundred runaway slaves moved to the refurbished wood-framed barracks on filled-in swampland a mile north of the Capitol. Compared to the cramped, disease infested, dilapidated tenements at Duff Green's Row where they had been living, the Camp offered promise—like a rainbow in the summer sky. Everything was shiny and new—at least new in the eyes of the newcomers—except for a blight that was easily overlooked by those who looked the other way. Washington City's fetid open sewage canal ran right past the camp. The compound, bordered by 12th, 13th, R and S Streets, was once known as Camp Barker and had been abandoned by the army.

Contraband Camp's population burgeoned with daily arrivals of hundreds of escaped slaves seeking their "New Jerusalem" in the recently emancipated Capital. The hospital wards filled quickly with sick and fatigued patients. White people were nowhere to be found in Contraband Camp, unless they were doctors, chief nurses, military guards, or smallpox sufferers. A rampant smallpox epidemic was the closest thing to equality the city knew. The only color boundary was an invisible line drawn on the floor of the smallpox ward—whites on one side and coloreds on the other.

Slade and Mrs. Keckly beamed as they passed through the entrance to Contraband Camp. They led contraband relief efforts within their spheres of influence. Slade was an elder in the Fifteenth Street Presbyterian Church and president of the Social, Civil, and Statistical Association—a mutual aid society that advocated citizenship for Africans. Mrs. Keckly was a prominent member of the Fifteenth Street Church, also, and was a force to be reckoned with.

William tagged along on their visit to the new camp. Since there was little chance—though not little enough to give up trying—that he would be allowed to go to war, time had come for him to do something. Anything. No matter how small.

As they inspected one of the tented female hospital wards with special permission from the camp superintendent, a 17-year-old patient sat up in bed, hugging her knees to her chest. Her eyes were not trapped in a vacant stare. She gazed over everyone's heads, as if assessing a far-off destination and calculating how to reach it. She escaped her master's Virginia estate the very day news sped from plantation to plantation that emancipation had come to Washington City. Her introduction to freedom was a searing fever that infected her at Duff Green's Row. The fever broke earlier that morning.

William stole glances at her as he trailed Slade and Mrs. Keckly through the ward. He glimpsed again when they reached the exit, and he stumbled into Slade.

"Whoa," Slade said. "Watch your feet."

"Sorry," William replied.

A few steps outside the ward William asked, "What happens next? Where do these people go from here?"

"Some go to Heaven," Mrs. Keckly replied. "As for the rest, that's up to Mr. Lincoln."

Executive Mansion—July 1862

Worry lines grew deeper by the day on Lincoln's weathered face after Molasses McClellan's Army of the Potomac stalled near Richmond. Lincoln fretted it would be only a matter of time before General Lee's army cinched the rebel noose around the Union's throat. If the tide did not turn soon, Kentucky, Maryland, and Delaware would decide to throw in with the rebels. Lincoln called together senators and representatives from Border States and made his final attempt to bind them to the Union cause—irrevocably. He read from a speech he had prepared.

> *Let the States in rebellion see they can in no way convince you to join their proposed Confederacy ... and without you, they cannot win. But you cannot divest them of that hope so long as you are determined to perpetuate the institution of slavery within your own States. The bell has already tolled. It is no longer a question of whether slavery will end, but of a matter of how. If the war continues long, the institution in your States will be extinguished by the mere friction and abrasion of war.*

Lincoln surveyed their faces.

> *I do not speak of emancipation at once, but of a decision at once, to emancipate gradually. The Government is prepared to compensate you fairly for your lost property. Room in South America for colonization can be obtained*

> *cheaply and in abundance. When a large enough number of the freed people open their eyes to the immense benefits of creating their own places in the world, the remainder will not be so reluctant to go. You will be free of the burden you imagine they would be by living among us.*

He pressed his palms together as if in prayer.

> *You are patriots and statesmen. Our common Country is in great peril, demanding the loftiest views and boldest action to bring it speedy relief. Once the burden of this conflict is lifted from our shoulders, our form of Government will be saved as a beacon to the world, our beloved history and cherished memories will be vindicated, and our happy future will be fully assured.*

The senators and representatives around the table remained silent. Many glanced away when he tried to read their eyes. Some sat tight jawed. He thanked them for their courtesy and exchanged small talk with a few as they filed out of his office. If he were able to draw any conclusion at all, it was that, as a whole, they were fence-sitters who could be blown one way or the other by the next stiff wind.

Lincoln confessed his gloom to William the next morning as he sat in the barber's chair waiting to be groomed. Not only was the war going from bad to worse, but he he would be returning to Oak Hill Cemetery that afternoon. Secretary Stanton's son was being interred a short distance from the crypt where Willie lay. William was relieved he would not be going along to the cemetery. It was as if Lincoln's grief was contagious. The more of it William breathed in, the worse it infected him.

When the dreaded hour arrived, Lincoln was handed an urgent message as he stood on the mansion's drive, waiting to board his carriage with Seward and Welles. A flash of pain struck like a lightning storm—not the kind that unleashed its bolts in rapid succession, but as if all the strikes fused into a single terrible flash. On top of everything that pressed in on him, the message carried the news that Colonel Alexander's two-year-old son died earlier that morning. Lincoln knew the parents' pain all too well.

The carriage rattled along for a few blocks before Lincoln told the others, "Gentlemen, we are about at the end of our rope. We have played our last card and must change tactics or lose the game."

"What are you saying?" Welles asked.

"Bondsmen are a strength to those who have their service, and we must decide whether that element should be with us or against us."

"What about the Border States?" Welles pressed. "How will they respond if we meddle with slavery? It is the foundation of their customs, the source of their wealth."

"We've been barking up the wrong tree," Lincoln said. "Fretting over their sensitivities. The Border States are determined to do nothing on their own, but they can be moved by decisive and extreme measures on our part."

"What do you propose?" Seward asked.

"If we want the army to strike more vigorous blows, we must set an example. Strike at the main principle of the rebellion. We must free the slaves or be ourselves subdued."

Seward shifted in his seat. "I understand the sentiment but let us not forget. There's the not so small matter of the Constitution."

"The rebels cannot at the same time throw off the Constitution and also invoke its aid," Lincoln replied. "Having made war upon the government, they are subject to the calamities of war. The laws of war clearly give the president full belligerent rights as Commander-in-Chief to seize enemy property, which according to the rebellion's own view includes their slaves. This right of seizure and condemnation is harsh, as are all proceedings of war. Admittedly the tactic is extreme, but it is nevertheless lawful. I have determined that emancipation has become a military necessity, absolutely essential to the preservation of the Constitution and the Union."

Steward furrowed his brow. "But every time one of our generals has given an order regarding slavery, you have revoked it."

"Their orders were not within their authority. According to the Constitution, the question of military necessity is vested in me alone."

"What do you plan to do with this seized property once the fighting ends?" Welles asked.

"We must not waiver. The rebels must be convinced that our seizure will be permanent. Whatever becomes of the freed slaves, this government will not allow them to be re-enslaved."

Contraband Camp—July 1862

William returned to Contraband Camp while Lincoln attended the funeral for Stanton's son. An obsession gripped William that he could not shake loose. He prayed. Luck was too fickle to be trusted in matters so important. Besides, he had used up all the luck anyone with skin as dark as his could expect.

He had met Billy Florville out on that road near Springfield. It easily could have been an encounter with a slave hunter. Florville introduced him to Mr. Lincoln. Mrs. Lincoln pulled him out of that train station ticket line. Mr. Lincoln kept him on at the mansion, despite objections from the rest of the domestic staff. Slade became like a father. William never knew a father's wisdom.

The guard should not have let him through the gate. A pass was required, but he claimed to have a message from the president's wife for Mrs. Keckly. The truth was Mrs. Lincoln had gone to New York—an item of information that would have been published in the newspapers. Also, it was only a guess on William's part that Mrs. Keckly would be at the Camp that Sunday afternoon.

The location of the ward where William had seen the young woman was etched in his memory. So was the position of her bed. However, except for special circumstances, like a tour by leaders of the relief movement, no men were permitted inside the women's ward or barracks unless they were surgeons, all of whom were white. He'd been working all morning on excuses to get around that obstacle.

"William?" someone called as he approached the ward.

He recognized the voice. "Mrs. Keckly."

"William, what are you doing here?"

William looked at his feet. It was impossible to out-pray a woman who was regarded a saint by an entire congregation. Especially, the Fifteenth Street Presbyterian Church.

"Does this have anything to do with the young lady who caused you to stumble into Mr. Slade?" She laughed. More like an auntie's hoot than a gentlelady's muted snicker.

William couldn't call up a response.

"I'm afraid she's gone."

"Where?" Necessity unlocked his voice.

"One of my customers inquired about finding domestic help. I told her about Mariah."

"Mariah?" he asked.

"Yes, her name is Mariah. Anyway, Mariah now works for Mrs. Cosgrove in exchange for room and board and a little extra spending money. In a few days, she will start volunteering here at the Camp, as well."

William's heart raced.

Mrs. Keckly's eyes narrowed. "I suppose you want me to arrange an introduction."

"I could never thank you enough, Mrs. Keckly."

"Gratitude will not be all you shall owe me, William. You shall start by lending a hand around here. In a land of equality, the hands that clip the president's hair and trim his whiskers can do the same for these poor souls."

"Whatever you say, Mrs. Keckly."

* * *

As William drove Mrs. Keckly to Contraband Camp the following Sunday afternoon, he could not pinpoint a specific spot where his heart pinched.

Mrs. Keckly interrupted their silence. "Today you'll be working the laundry."

William held his tongue.

Later, as William stumbled into the laundry and dumped a bundle of soiled blankets on a bench, sweat dripped down his back.

"Not there," a female voice scolded.

William turned and planted his hands on his hips. "Where then?"

No sooner than the words left his lips, he wanted to reel them back. Her piercing brown eyes stopped him cold.

"There." She pointed to a tub of soapy water.

His mind reeled, but the rest of him seized up.

She sneered. "What? Now you got the lockjaw?"

Meeting Mariah for the first time had been different in his daydreams.

She collected the soiled blankets and dumped them in the washtub. "So, what do they call you? I mean besides useless."

"William," he stammered.

"I'm Mariah."

"I know."

"That so? Then folks should call you snoop."

"I … I …"

"Aye yourself," she scoffed. "I can see by that fancy vest your flesh ain't never been beat raw by no overseer's whip. Stop dawdling." She pointed to the door. "I'm sure that wasn't all the nasty blankets they've got down in the men's ward."

William shuffled out the door.

Mariah returned to kneading soiled blankets, towels, and stained bedclothes on the washboard.

An older woman rinsed Mariah's wash in a tub of scalding water. "Um, um. That fine lookin' boy's got eyes for you."

Mariah scrubbed harder. "Be that as it may, I got no time for nonsense. Besides, Mrs. Cosgrove won't stand for no bucks sniffing around her back door, leading her girls astray."

"Alls I's sayin'—"

"Doesn't matter. If he comes back with foolishness on his mind, I'll nip it in the bud before it gets started."

The rest of the afternoon William carried laundry back and forth between the wards and the laundry, always careful to cut Mariah a wide berth.

On the drive back to the mansion, Mrs. Keckly asked, "Well, did you meet your young lady today?"

"In a manner of speaking," William muttered.

"How did it go?"

"About as much fun as a castration."

"Then I shall have a conversation with Mrs. Cosgrove."

Cosgrove Residence—July 1862

Mrs. Keckly made a habit of keeping promises before dust could settle on them. Consequently, William knocked at the servants' entrance to Mrs. Cosgrove's federal style mansion only a few days later. He stepped back and clung to the bouquet Mrs. Keckly fixed for him. In his vest pocket he carried a letter of introduction from Mrs. Keckly.

A matronly woman wearing an apron answered the door. She crossed her arms and asked in an Irish brogue, "What's your business, young man?"

William removed his hat and handed her the letter.

"As if I can read. Who's this for?"

"The mistress of the house."

She eyed the bouquet. "And those?"

"For her, as well."

The woman took the bouquet. "Wait here."

William drummed his fingers on his thigh. His throat grew dry. He puckered and sucked, trying to moisten it.

Faint footsteps padded across the floor toward him, accompanied by heavier footfalls. By the time Mariah reached the doorway—with the matron in her wake—the words he had rehearsed were jumbled in his head. They remained there, on the wrong side of the gap between his mind and his lips.

"Come in," the matron grumbled as she marched them to the kitchen. "I haven't got all day."

William and Mariah sat across from each other at a table where preparations for dinner were spread. The woman stood at the end of the table and pulled a small hourglass from her apron pocket. "You have twelve minutes." She set the hourglass on the table and picked up a cleaver. With a series of hard whacks, she chopped off the feet of three chickens.

Mariah jabbed a finger at William. "If you mean to—"

The matron interrupted. "She has an hour of free time each evening between seven and eight. Saturdays she's off. Sundays she goes to church and to Contraband Camp. Send Mrs. Cosgrove a note the day before you intend to call."

Mariah lowered her head. "You can come to church."

Again, the matron intervened. "In case you're not familiar with the custom, men and women sit on opposite sides of the church. So, don't get any ideas."

"Mrs. Keckly offered to chaperone," William replied.

Mariah gritted her teeth.

The woman sorted onions and carrots on the table. "I would assume you have a master, or at least an employer, who governs your free time?"

"Yes," William replied. "I spoke with Mr. Lincoln this morning."

Mariah's eyes widened.

"President Lincoln?" The matron sputtered.

"He said he can spare me now and then in the evenings and on weekends. Mr. Slade offered to fill in for me, if needed."

The matron waved her cleaver at William. “I will not put up with such nonsense in this house. Mrs. Cosgrove reveres the man. Heaven only knows why, but the long and short is that tall tales have no place in a Christian house. You are warned, young man. The truth first and always. That’s the rule. No making up stories to seduce young girls. Not under this roof.”

“But ... but,” William stammered.

“Stop. You’re dark as pitch. Only a fool would believe the likes of you could be the president’s barber. Why, Mr. Buchanan—God bless the man—didn’t have any darkies on his domestic staff—fair-skinned mulattos at worst.”

“I am telling the truth.” William pulled an envelope out of his vest pocket. “I’m to deliver this to Mr. Seward after I leave here. See? It has the president’s seal and it says Mr. Seward.”

The matron snatched the hourglass off the table. “All I have to say is, the next time you call, you better bring a note from Mr. Lincoln, himself. But now, your time is up.”

Executive Mansion—July 1862

Lincoln sifted through papers on his desk at the mansion. He fingered a letter his close friend Joshua Speed had written after he was elected president almost two years earlier.

> *As a friend I am rejoiced at your success—as a political opponent I am not disappointed. But all men and all questions sink into utter insignificance when compared to the preservation of our glorious Union. Its continuance and its future will depend very much upon how you deal with the inflammable material by which you will be surrounded.*

Lincoln laid the letter aside. If only he had understood then what a tinderbox he was stepping into. He picked up the tattered manifesto he had written during his last days in Springfield.

> *Without the Constitution and the Union, we could not have attained the result, but even these, are not the primary cause of our great prosperity. There is something back of these, entwining itself more closely about the human heart. That something is the principle of "Liberty to all"—the principle that clears the path for all, gives hope to all, and, by consequence, enterprise and industry to all.*

He checked his watch. William was late again.

Slade appeared in the doorway, carrying William's grooming implements.

"Where's William?" Lincoln arched his brow.

"I rousted him a few minutes ago. He will be up shortly."

"That's the second time this week. What is he up to?"

"He's afflicted." Slade winked.

Lincoln cast a sidelong glance at Slade. "Sick?"

"Lovesick, I'm afraid."

"I reckon that has to happen at some point in a young man's life. I know I was smitten badly once."

"Mrs. Lincoln, I presume?"

"I suppose her, too." Lincoln chuckled. "So, I must have been love-struck twice."

"What was her name, if I might ask?"

"The prettiest blonde girl. Eyes as blue as a prairie summer sky. Smart too, like Mrs. Lincoln. Her name was Annie."

"You had a falling out, I suppose?" Slade asked.

"Yes, on account of my stupidity. But that was not the reason our youthful romance ended."

"What happened?"

"I reckon you can say I am cursed when it comes to love." Lincoln rubbed his temple. "Providence charts its own course. What can we do but tag along?"

William rushed in, tucking his shirt tail into his trousers. "Sorry, sir. I lost track of time."

"Just remember," Lincoln warned, "once is a mistake, twice is a problem, the third time a thing becomes a habit."

"Yes, sir."

Slade handed William the razor and strop. "Will you be needing me further, Mr. Lincoln?"

"Yes. Now that I have both of you here, I might as well read a proclamation I intend to issue. I would like to hear what you think." Lincoln reached for the draft he had been working on.

William fidgeted.

At the end of the reading Slade said, "'Shall then, thenceforward, and forever, be free' are compelling words. Almost to the point that the rest gets lost."

"The rest isn't lost on me," William replied. "He says freeing slaves is up to their masters, and the proclamation only frees slaves in places the government can't touch."

Slade eyed William. "I think he's announcing how he intends to implement the new laws Congress recently passed."

William cocked his head. "Then he forgot to put in a part about letting Negroes join the army."

"Thank you," Lincoln said, laying aside his draft. "It seems I need to work on how I read the thing. And William, trust me. I am doing all I can in the circumstances I've been handed. Besides, this is not the only tool in my work shed."

A few days afterward, Lincoln read the proclamation to his Cabinet. No one jumped out of his seat and clapped. Some worried it was too radical. Seward had little to say about the content, but he warned it should be kept private until the government could enforce its provisions.

"What would that ability look like to you?" Lincoln asked.

"A victory on our side," Seward answered. "We've had a dismal summer in the field. McClellan was supposed to be our salvation, but he got himself whipped miserably by Lee. Now he's retreating from the peninsula, and Richmond is safe from any threat by us. If we issue your proclamation now, it will look as if we are grasping at straws."

CHAPTER FIFTEEN

Soldiers' Home—September 1862

The summer had been brutal. A committee of Negro leaders rebuffed Lincoln's plan to organize offshore colonies for freed slaves. Their cooperation would have been key to convincing the teetering Border States—Kentucky, Maryland, Delaware—to disavow slavery. Any declarations of the sort would quash the rebellion's hope for more disaffections from the Union. But the whites in those regions feared a race war would erupt after any large-scale emancipation. Lincoln was hard-pressed to disagree on that point.

Lincoln massaged his temples. He had paced the floor at the cottage most of the night. A string of August losses weighed on him. Six defeats in Virginia alone. Not a single victory. Routed in Kentucky. Twice beaten in Missouri. Lee's army on the march toward Maryland. If Baltimore fell, Washington would be next. The whole game lost. He'd have to make plans to get his family to safety. Europe, maybe. His shoulders drooped, like a condemned man climbing the gallows steps.

The morning light had failed to bring new perspective to the array of telegrams, letters, and memorials in a pile on his desk. On top, a dispatch from the War Department—General Pope beaten at Bull Run. Only able to hold his men in defensive positions. No advance possible. The idea of a general holding his men at bay stuck in Lincoln's craw. He brushed the telegram aside.

He shuffled more papers—complaints from Chase and Seward charging McClellan failed to reinforce Pope out of spite. A telegram from Governor Ramsey, lamenting Minnesota's failure to meet the draft quota on account of war with the Sioux. Nicolay's telegram from Saint Paul reported 2,000 Sioux warriors attacking over a 200-mile line. Hundreds of white settlers massacred. Equipment and supplies urgently needed—six 12-pounder mountain howitzers with arms and accoutrements, horses and equipment for 1,200 cavalry, 5,000 or 6,000 guns with 500,000 cartridges to suit, medical stores for three regiments, and blankets for 3,000 men.

Lincoln fingered a petition from Central American governments protesting colonization of freed slaves inside their borders. More bad news for the Border States.

He itched to make something happen, but there was the matter of a promise he made to Mrs. Lincoln. She enlisted Slade and Madame Elizabeth to help wear him down, and he capitulated. Just like he caved in the previous week when

General Saxon insisted on recruiting freed slaves in the Sea Islands. This time, Lincoln allowed it only in Saxon's department and only out of military necessity. His concession to Saxon was met with more than a raised eyebrow from William.

William rapped on the partially open door.

"Come in." Lincoln barked.

"Mrs. Lincoln says we should start getting you ready." William cradled his grooming supplies.

"I reckon it's not a good idea to get her riled up."

"No, sir. That would not be good."

Lincoln leaned back in the barber's chair. "How are things progressing with that girl of yours?"

"We're doing fine, sir."

"Do you mind if I give you some advice?" Lincoln asked. "Lessons I learned in my youth."

"You always say Mrs. Lincoln pursued you."

"That is partly true. But she was not my first sweetheart."

"Are you going to tell me I should sample fruit from several different trees to see which is sweetest?" William asked.

"No. What I recommend is, do not make rash promises. At times, I have found myself in a tight spot by doing so. Keep any promise you make. I broke a sacred promise that almost ruined my life. Only good fortune intervened to save me. Another thing, never test love which is sincerely offered."

"I don't understand that last one." William prepared the lather for Lincoln's shave.

"When I was young, I fell in love with the most beautiful, brightest young lady. I loved her and she loved me sincerely. But I worried I didn't deserve her, so I put her love to the test."

"What happened?"

"I succeeded in stirring her ire," Lincoln replied. "We fell away from each other and did not make amends until she lay on her deathbed. To this day, I consider those days of alienation to be one of the greatest losses of my life."

"Did you ever put Mrs. Lincoln to the test?"

"I am not the most attentive husband, especially of late. In that way, I think I have tested her greatly. Our earliest years were different. She was my greatest champion."

When William finished grooming Lincoln, they went downstairs and joined Mrs. Lincoln for a carriage ride to Contraband Camp. Some of his Cabinet members would join them there. Mrs. Lincoln planned to return to the cottage afterwards, while Lincoln rode on to the mansion with William.

Contraband Camp—September 1862

A bugler called the residents of Contraband Camp to a former parade ground that had become their meeting area. Women and girls came in threadbare dresses. Men and boys sported castoff blue uniforms, and a few wore pieces of gray ones collected from rebel corpses abandoned on battlefields. Old folks huddled in the same corner as always.

A buzz rose from the assembly when it was announced that the president was due to arrive. He would be accompanied by family and friends. That explained the flags decorating a small platform some of the residents helped cobble together earlier that morning. A collective gasp greeted word that the president wanted them to sing.

The camp's song leader, a young runaway named Mary Dines, took charge and directed a short practice session, after which folks were encouraged to change into their finest clothes. Few of the men wanted to change out of their military uniforms. Many hoped they would get to wear new blue ones of their own one day.

By the time most of the residents reassembled in the meeting area, a cavalry unit appeared at the camp's gate. Behind the soldiers, a carriage pulled to a stop and a lanky figure in a tall hat and black suit stepped out to help his wife down. Everyone cheered as the president and his party approached. William's eyes lit up on seeing Mariah in the crowd. He gave her a tentative wave. She blushed.

When the program began, the camp commander called on Uncle Ben, the eldest in camp, to come to the platform and lead in prayer. Uncle Ben could certainly preach and pray and make everybody wake up when he began to moan and groan. He was called a spirit preacher because he couldn't read a jot. He just preached the gospel as God had taught it to him. Folks joked that he had been with Moses on the mountain when God gave the Commandments. Supposedly, he wasn't mentioned in scriptures because he was Moses' footman, neither to be seen nor heard. That morning when Uncle Ben prayed, he called upon every saint he ever heard of, or possibly met, to bless President Lincoln and his good lady.

At the conclusion of the prayer, the camp commander signaled for everyone to stand for the singing of *My Country, 'Tis of Thee.* Lincoln, who was already standing, took off his hat and sang along with the rest.

Mary Dines tittered when she was called to the platform to lead everyone in singing a few pieces they had rehearsed earlier. She couldn't believe they were singing for President Lincoln. Mary sang the stanzas of *Nobody Knows What Trouble I See, but Jesus* all by herself. Everyone else joined in on the chorus. Lincoln wiped tears from his cheeks as she introduced the next piece, *Every Time I Feel the Spirit.*

The camp commander had announced that Mr. Lincoln could not stay long, but Mary added more songs. *I Thank God that I'm Free at Last* was a camp favorite, so they sang it several times. The old folks lost all inhibition and began to yell and shout. Lincoln took in the words and music, his head bowed in silence. He recalled a riverboat trip when he battled melancholy. A coffle of slaves broke out in joyful song, and he couldn't fathom where they found such joy and strength.

Mary closed with *John Brown's Body.* William figured a bunch of Negroes lamenting John Brown's body mouldering in the grave would be what Slade would call going beyond the pale. William smiled when Lincoln joined in on the chorus and sang the words as loud as anyone else—"Glory, Glory, Hallelujah ... His soul goes marching on." A couple of times Lincoln's voice strained as he surveyed the crowd and witnessed the joy in many people's faces.

When the program concluded, residents pressed in around Lincoln. He reached out and grasped the hands of as many as he could, thanking them for their well wishes and listening earnestly to their stories. William angled through the crowd and ushered Lincoln to the entrance of the men's hospital ward. Mrs. Keckly guided Mrs. Lincoln to the women's ward.

After the hospital tours, Mrs. Lincoln and Mrs. Keckly met Lincoln and William in the walkway between the men's and women's wards. Mariah joined them. Lincoln reached to take her hand. "Am I to assume, young lady, you are—"

"For Heaven's sake," Mrs. Lincoln huffed. "At least give some pretext that you are a gentleman. Thank goodness we have Mr. Slade around the mansion to set a proper example."

"Excuse me," William interrupted. "I would like to introduce someone."

"We would very much like to meet your friend," Mrs. Lincoln replied, smiling.

"Mr. and Mrs. Lincoln, this is Mariah. She volunteers here at the camp."

"What a delight to meet you." Mrs. Lincoln fanned herself with her kerchief. "Madame Elizabeth has told me about the good work your people are doing. What is it that you do?"

"I work in the laundry, ma'am," Mariah replied.

"And sometimes she helps me," William added. "She brings me hot towels when I shave the inmates."

Lincoln laughed. "I did not know I gave you that much free time. Am I going to have to start coming here to get trimmed?"

Mrs. Lincoln arched her brow. "One of the nurses we met mentioned something about a smallpox ward in the camp. I hope you are not exposed to any of those poor souls."

"But Mr. Lincoln risks his life," William replied. "You should have seen him at Norfolk."

"I am sure he used appropriate precautions." Mrs. Lincoln eyed William. "Just the same, he would miss you greatly if you should fall ill and die."

"There's no need to worry, ma'am," Mariah assured. "Those patients are quarantined, and the laundry doesn't handle any of their things. It's all burned."

Executive Mansion—September 1862

Lincoln ordered General Boyle to send troops from Kentucky to shore up defenses at the Capital. Boyle complained the units were needed to defend Louisville.

Lincoln sent a dispatch from the War Department's new telegraph office.

> *Where is the enemy you dread in Louisville? How near to you?"*

Lincoln knew the answer. Louisville was in no danger.

Later that evening, Pennsylvania's Governor Curtin demanded 80,000 disciplined troops to defend his state. Lincoln was polite, if sarcastic.

> *We do not have 80,000 disciplined troops on this side of the mountains. The best security for Pennsylvania is putting the strongest force possible in the enemy's rear.*

Lincoln's last dispatch that night was to McClellan.

> *... hearing nothing from Harper's Ferry or Martinsburg today, affirms my fear that the enemy is re-crossing the Potomac. Please do not let him get off without being hurt.*

Lincoln woke in a sweat the next morning. He had dreamt of battles. Lee tightening the noose around the Capital. New dispatches deepened his anxiety. Stonewall Jackson's rebel army was advancing on the Union garrison at Harpers Ferry. The specter of surrendering Harper's Ferry to the rebels, yet again, turned his stomach. Lincoln also learned McClellan's army was in a foot race through the South Mountain passes, hoping to cut off one of Lee's columns headed for Sharpsburg, Maryland. Lincoln winced at the thought of McClellan in a foot race with anyone. Nonetheless, if McClellan could keep the rebel force divided, his 102,000 Union soldiers could shatter the backbone of Lee's much smaller army.

William appeared in the office doorway as Lincoln closed the gripsack he used for carrying the proclamation between the mansion and the cottage. "Sir, will you be spending the night here again, or returning to the cottage?"

"I need the tranquility of the cottage tonight," Lincoln replied, eyeing the thick book William clutched to his chest. "What are you reading?"

"The title is French, but the story is in English. Nicolay ordered it for me from the government's library. It's new, and the title means the miserable ones. It has something to do with a rebellion in France. A man named Hugo wrote it."

"Let me know if you learn anything." Lincoln drew a long breath. "I reckon these American rebels have me vexed."

Contraband Camp—September 1862

Lincoln guided his horse off the turnpike that evening on his way back to the cottage. He tipped his hat as he passed through the gate at Contraband Camp. The guard saluted.

Lincoln followed the aroma of evening meal preparation wafting from a building slotted between the barracks and the hospital. His stiff joints ached as he dismounted and handed the reins to a boy of about twelve. Foggy memories of his own childhood gave way to images of Willie and Tad gaily riding their pony on the mansion lawn. Doubtless, the boy tending his horse had not enjoyed the same kind of carefree days.

"Where can I find Miss Mary Dines?" Lincoln asked.

The boy pointed toward the kitchen.

Lincoln smiled wearily and followed the boy's gesture. When Lincoln stepped inside, he spotted Mary. She sang softly. Lincoln asked, "Miss Mary, is it all right if I interrupt?"

"Oh my!" she sputtered. She straightened her apron and smoothed her hair.

"I hope I have not startled you. I need you to do me a favor."

"Oh my." Mary cupped her cheeks.

"I can wait if this is a bad time." Lincoln gestured to the meal fixings spread out on a table.

"No, sir. It is never a bad time for you."

"You're sure now?" he asked.

"Absolutely."

"May we sit?" He gestured to a couple of chairs at a table.

Mary nodded.

Lincoln placed his hat on the table. "I've been thinking about you all since I left here and am not feeling so well."

"What's the matter?" Mary asked.

"It seems that all the cares of the world are on my shoulders, and times come upon me when I am not sure I can take any more."

"We pray for you constantly, sir. I know God will give you the strength you need."

"I pray as well," he replied, staring at the ceiling. "But I am not sure it does any good. How can we ever know what the right thing is?"

"We just keep on and hold fast to the promise that this too shall pass."

"There is something you can do for me. I think it will help."

"What could I possibly do but pray?" she asked.

He wore a tired smile. "Mary, what can the people sing for me today?"

She burst out laughing and clamped her hand over her mouth. Her laughter cheered him. She answered, "Whatever you want, Mr. President."

Camp residents wasted no time gathering in the meeting area to serenade Lincoln. Many arrived carrying candles. When

Mary led them in song, Lincoln joined in. His voice grew louder and more cheerful through *Swing Low, Sweet Chariot*; *Go Down Moses*; *Didn't My God Deliver Daniel?*; *I Ain't Got Weary Yet*; and *Steal Away*. Tears welled in his eyes as they droned the words, "I've been in the storm so long, you know I've been in the storm so long, Oh Lord, give me more time to pray, I've been in the storm so long." After they closed with *Praise God from Whom All Blessings Flow*, Uncle Ben prayed.

Soldiers' Home—September 1862

Lincoln sat at his desk in the cottage, staring at his hands, after visiting Contraband Camp. Memories from decades earlier haunted him. A fair-skinned fancy girl. A river flat boat ... a coffle of slaves shackled together ... all would drown if one fell in the current.

William's words echoed in his mind— "If I am not allowed to carry the burden equally, I am not truly free." Lincoln was no longer sure he knew what freedom meant. He took out a pen and paper and wrote:

> *September 13, 1862*
>
> *The will of God prevails. In great contests each party claims to act in accordance with the will of God. Both may be—and one must be—wrong. God cannot be for and against the same thing at the same time. In the present civil war, it is quite possible that God's purpose is something different from the purpose of either party—and yet, the human instrumentalities, working just as they do, effect His purpose. I am almost ready to say that this is probably true—that God wills this contest, and*

wills that it shall not end yet. He could have either saved or destroyed the Union without a human contest. Yet the contest began. And, having begun He could give the final victory to either side any day. Yet the contest proceeds.

He prayed, not even sure whether the Almighty dealt in bargains. Maybe God only did things his own way—no compromise. There was one way to find out. Lincoln promised Heaven he would issue the proclamation emancipating slaves if Lee and his army were driven out of Maryland.

Executive Mansion—September 1862

Lincoln rose before daylight two days after bargaining with the Almighty. He saddled his horse and left the cottage before anyone else was awake. At first light, he stopped and watched the smoke rise from Contraband Camp's kitchen stoves. The lyrics from a song they had sung rolled through his mind. "I've been in the storm so long, Oh Lord, give me more time to pray, I've been in the storm so long." He lifted his eyes, gazed at the stars, and begged for a speedy end to the war.

Later that morning, McClellan's ten o'clock telegram reported rebel losses were estimated at 15,000. General Lee was possibly among the wounded. If McClellan was right, bells would soon peal in every quarter from Boston to San Francisco—Lee whipped at last, the rebellion crushed without a fatal blow to slavery. The southern peculiar institution could be dealt with peaceably and the proclamation would be his negotiating lever.

He sat at his desk with celebratory tears moistening his eyes as he scrawled a message to McClellan.

> *Your despatches of to-day received. God bless you, and all with you. Destroy the rebel army, if possible.*
>
> *A. LINCOLN*

He beamed as he wrote an Illinois friend, Jesse Dubois.

> *I now consider it safe to say that Gen. McClellan has gained a great victory over the great rebel army in Maryland between Fredericktown and Hagerstown. He is now pursuing the flying foe.*
>
> *A. LINCOLN*

Lincoln's optimism fizzled in late afternoon. A dispatch reported "the infernal screech owls of rebel cannon came hissing through the air, plowing great holes in the earth" at Harper's Ferry that morning. Colonel Miles, the Union commander, ordered his soldiers to raise white flags across their defensive line. Moments later, a shell exploded near the colonel, killing him. Harper's Ferry and the garrison defending it—all 12,700 troops, 13,000 arms, and 47 pieces of artillery—were surrendered to General Stonewall Jackson's rebel army.

News of Miles' surrender resounded in Lincoln's head as if the Almighty had thundered, "No Deal!" in response to the bargain he had proffered.

Lincoln telegraphed McClellan for updates. He received no reply through the remainder of the day and evening.

Near midnight, Lincoln sent John Hay to the telegraph office with a dispatch to Governor Curtin in Pennsylvania.

> *What do you hear from Gen. McClellan's Army? We have nothing from him to-day.*
>
> *A. LINCOLN*

Once Hay left the room, desperate scenarios spun through Lincoln's mind. He snatched a stack of papers from his desk and threw them. The pages scattered around the room. As he watched the papers fall to the floor, the swirling in his head slowed. He knelt and began retrieving them.

He was on his knees collecting the papers when William arrived with a pot of tea. William surveyed the scene, set the teapot on the long table, and stooped to help.

Lincoln waved him off.

William picked up a few of the pages, anyway. The words *A Proclamation* stood out on one of them. He peered at Lincoln. "Does it say we can fight?"

"Do you not realize you cannot be yoked equally with white soldiers? If we put colored troops in battle, leaders of the rebellion will make it their policy to execute them on surrender or sell them into slavery."

"Then we shall have to be victorious or fight to our deaths." William handed him the proclamation.

As they were getting back to their feet, Hay entered the room with Governor Curtin's answer to Lincoln's telegram.

> *We have no definite news. Our telegraph operator at Hagerstown reports that a battle is progressing near the Potomac, between Sharpsburg and Williamsport. What success did McClellan meet with yesterday? We have not heard, and should know, in order to use our forces that are now being pushed into Maryland.*

Hay handed Lincoln another telegram. Governor Richard Yates of Illinois wrote:

> *Your despatch to Col Dubois has filled our people with the wildest joy. Salutes are being fired & our citizens are*

relieved from a fearful state of suspense. We thank you for the welcome news.

Lincoln considered an immediate response to Yates, retracting his earlier dispatch, but elected to wait until morning.

After William and Hay left, Lincoln sifted through the papers he and William had gathered. He muttered to himself, "I have a general who does not fight and a Negro valet who wishes for nothing more than the chance to do so."

The next day near dusk, when Lincoln rode out of the mansion stables and returned to the cottage, the best he could say was that General Lee's advance in Maryland had been stalled—at a great cost of lives. The battle near Sharpsburg had settled into an uneasy lull. Both sides were hunkered down near Antietam Creek where the fighting began at dawn.

Soldiers' Home—September 1862

When Lincoln arrived at the cottage, he dismounted and sauntered over to the soldiers' cemetery. Colonel Alexander told him two mornings earlier that a boy from Pennsylvania had been one of the new arrivals. There was some confusion about the soldier's name. Lincoln counted seven new graves dug in the two days he had been gone. A list of the newly buried was probably waiting on his desk upstairs. The total number of markers in the graveyard approached 2,000.

Later, Slade brought a light supper to Lincoln who was hunched over at his desk, pen in hand.

"What are you working on, sir?" Slade asked.

"I am just doing a little fixing up of this proclamation."

"That means you have good news from General McClellan."

"Things are still unclear. I want to have it ready, just in case," Lincoln replied.

"What will you do with all the slaves once they are freed? Put them in the army and finish this nasty war?" Slade asked.

"That would certainly put an end to William's nagging."

"You know how young men can be. Slade shook his head. "They conflate bravery and foolhardiness."

"It's not that I disagree with the young man," Lincoln confessed. "But Mac does not want Negroes in his army. He would quit if we did that. I cannot afford to let him go, especially if he has won a victory at Antietam."

"I understand. The Union comes first."

"The Union's the only weapon that can stop slavery in its tracks," Lincoln insisted.

CHAPTER SIXTEEN

Executive Mansion—September 22, 1862

Lincoln called the Cabinet to his office and began the meeting by reading *High-Handed Outrage at Utica*—a short piece by humorist, Artemus Ward, *nom de plume* for Charles Farrar Browne.

The satirical story was about a traveling carnival that featured wax figures of *The Last Supper*. According to the story, a burly spectator, thinking the statues were alive, was offended by Judas Iscariot's presence in his town. He pummeled the statue of Judas, caving in the traitorous disciple's head. The assailant was charged with arson in the third degree.

Lincoln let out a belly laugh at the conclusion of his reading while members of the Cabinet sat stone-faced. He chided them. "Why don't you laugh? With the fearful strain that is on me night and day, if I did not laugh, I should die. You need this medicine as much as I do."

Without waiting for responses, Lincoln told them he had been thinking a great deal about the relationship of the war to slavery, but unlike Artemus Ward, he had been unwilling to bash in Judas's head to end the war. Lincoln confessed he had been wrong, and the nation could ill afford to persist in making that mistake. The time had come.

He wished it were a better time. He wished the army had won a greater victory. Even though McClellan had allowed Lee's army to slip away and regroup, the rebels were driven out of Maryland, and Pennsylvania was no longer under threat of invasion.

He was not seeking their approval. He had made a bargain with the Almighty, which he must keep. He was simply inviting suggestions to improve the proclamation's wording. The new proclamation declared that slaves within areas in continued rebellion against the United States on January 1, next, were thenceforth and forever free. Military officers were forbidden from returning fugitive slaves to their owners. Assuming Congress appropriated funds, slaveholders might be compensated for loss of property, including slaves—so long as they proved their unbroken loyalty to the government and their states returned to a proper relationship with the Union.

Surprise disarmed everyone around the table—the unexpected Sunday morning summons, Lincoln's seemingly inappropriate attempt at humor, his rebuke, the timing he chose for announcing the proclamation, the cataclysmic shift in the document's tone from the first reading two months earlier. While the earlier draft relied on authority provided under prior Acts of Congress, the new version was an executive edict, not subject to Congressional approval. The Cabinet's opinions on the main principle were unsolicited, unwanted, unnecessary.

The Cabinet members sat perplexed. Some ventured minor word changes which Lincoln accepted. Then he handed over the proclamation to Secretary Seward to be published.

William didn't need to wait for the proclamation to become public. Lincoln had read it to him and to Slade as he refined it during the week after the battle at Antietam Creek. There was no mention of military service for Negroes.

The next day, the preliminary draft of the *Emancipation Proclamation* became public, and the burden of keeping it secret was winched off Lincoln's shoulders. Another weight was lifted as well. News arrived that volunteer regiments in Minnesota had overwhelmed and defeated the Dakota Sioux. The Indian insurgency was over.

Antietam Creek, Maryland—October 1862

William entered Lincoln's bedroom, carrying his grooming supplies, and found Slade helping Lincoln pack.

"No time for a trim, William," Lincoln said. "Go downstairs and get ready. We're going up to McClellan's headquarters at Antietam Creek for a visit."

"Yes, sir. How long will we be gone?"

"A few days."

"How soon are we leaving?" William asked.

"When you're packed."

"But—" William started.

Lincoln closed his carpet bag. "Is there a problem?"

"No, sir. It's just … I promised Mariah."

"I thought you would want to visit another battlefield."

"I just need to let her know."

"Slade can give her a message, but you had better hurry. The train will leave on time, with or without you."

William took a pen and paper from the table beside Lincoln's bed and scribbled a note.

The note was delivered by the time Lincoln's entourage arrived at Harpers Ferry—the garrison and surrounding heights having been abandoned by the retreating rebel army.

* * *

The presidential party spent the remainder of that day and most of the next reviewing Union troops in the region. Afterward, they proceeded to Antietam Creek, arriving just before nightfall at Grove's Farm where much of McClellan's Army of the Potomac was camped. The general greeted them warmly and directed his staff to show the visitors to their tents. He promised Lincoln there would be much to do the following day. As they left McClellan's tent, Lincoln whispered to William, "With Little Napoleon, everything is tomorrow."

The next morning after breakfast, Lincoln returned to McClellan's tent and found the general sitting at a table poring over reports and maps. He sat across from McClellan and asked the question that burned in him since learning General Lee's army escaped what should have been total destruction while retreating back into Virginia. "What do you intend to do now?"

"You've been informed of our losses?" McClellan asked.

"I have," Lincoln replied.

"Then there should be no surprise we have reorganizing to do. We also need reinforcements if you can arrange it."

"I understand General Lee's losses were as great as ours and we had him outmanned from the start."

"We had no great advantage, and still do not," McClellan replied.

Lincoln studied McClellan who returned his attention to a stack of reports. "I wish to call your attention to a fault in your character." Lincoln paused. "A fault which is the sum of my observations of you in connection with this war. You merely get yourself ready to do a good thing—no man can do that better. You make all the necessary sacrifices of blood and time and treasure to secure a victory. But whether from timidity, self-distrust, or some other motive inexplicable to me, you always stop short—just on this side of results."

McClellan grabbed some letters from a pile on his desk and offered them to Lincoln. "Here. These letters are from friends who serve in the opposing army. They urge me to make myself dictator of the nation and negotiate an end to the war. My refusal to yield to their pleas is proof of my loyalty."

As Lincoln was about to respond, a prominent war photographer, Alexander Gardner, appeared. "Mr. President," he said, "would you do me the honor of posing for some photographs?"

McClellan smirked. "I am sure we will have time to continue our conversation later. I understand Mr. Gardner's camera can be quite temperamental if its demands are not met in a timely fashion."

Lincoln rose, glaring at McClellan.

"Please stay seated," Gardner said. "I'll start with the two of you as you were. Let me arrange a few things, first."

While Gardner's assistant unloaded the camera from a wagon that served as a traveling darkroom, the photographer removed a folded rebel battle flag from the table behind Lincoln and placed it on the ground at Lincoln's feet. He stepped back and surveyed the arrangements, then he picked up the rebel flag, unfurled it, and dropped it on the ground at the head of McClellan's bed.

After Gardner finished photographing Lincoln and McClellan, he invited Lincoln to wander through camp and pose for more pictures. When Gardner mentioned he would be photographing Allan Pinkerton's spies, Lincoln agreed and dispatched William to invite other members of his party to join them.

William delivered the message to as many in the entourage as he could find then ducked inside Lincoln's tent. He checked the top button on his white shirt and smoothed his black vest. He turned up the brim of his hat on one side like he had seen soldiers doing and creased the fold to keep it upright. Even if his hat wasn't official, at least he was doing his best to look the part of a soldier.

As William approached Pinkerton's tent, Gardner pointed to him and said, "You."

William's mouth opened, but nothing came out.

Gardner turned to Pinkerton. "You have a colored spy?"

"Not him." Pinkerton pushed his hat back on his head.

"But word is you do use them," Gardner said.

The detective shrugged.

"Over there." Gardner pointed to an open space in the line of spies he had arranged for his next photograph. "You'll be his stand in."

William took his place and gawked at the camera.

"Wait." Gardner approached William and gave him a towel. "Stick this in your belt. It's part of your disguise."

The word disguise unnerved William. Though by the time he realized the towel draped over his belt made him appear to be a servant, instead of a spy, the photographer had returned to his camera and captured the image he wanted.

As the group headed out to photograph soldiers in camp, Gardner's attention locked onto members of an Indiana regiment seated on the ground. One was a general who clung to a bottle of wine, and several of the other men were puffing on cigars. In the middle of the group, a servant, muscular with skin as dark as a field slave, stood holding a pitcher.

William supposed General McClellan didn't object to colored servants on a battlefield, not even ones with skin so dark they would never be considered for duty as house slaves.

When Gardner asked permission to take photographs, the Indiana soldiers agreed without hesitation. Gardner and his assistant unloaded the camera from the wagon, and after the first picture was made, the photographer rearranged the scene. He collected a high-back wicker chair from the Grove's farmhouse and centered it behind the soldiers.

Gardner pointed to the chair as he eyed the Negro servant. "Sit, please."

The servant tensed.

"Sit," Gardner repeated.

The general who held the wine bottle glimpsed Lincoln standing a few feet away. "It's okay, Edward," he muttered to his colored servant. "Do as the man says."

Edward eased over to the chair and sat.

Gardner gestured to the ground in front of the servant. "Okay fellows, find a comfortable spot at the boy's feet."

The men followed the photographer's instructions, some glared, others grumbled.

William's pulse raced. He speculated on consequences the enthroned servant might suffer once the photographer left—consequences a Negro wouldn't have to endure if one of those Indiana militiamen fell in a hail of musket fire, if that Negro rescued him and carried him to safety.

* * *

On the following morning, Lincoln mounted his horse and rode through a light mist to Pry House. He had been told General McClellan stood on a chair and monitored the great battle from the attic window. While at Pry House, Lincoln showed his respects to one of his generals who lay severely wounded in a second story bedroom.

The fog had burned off by the time Lincoln headed back to Grove's Farm. Already the sun warmed the fields where more than 5,000 dead were buried—many in shallow graves where they fell. A faint odor of decomposing corpses wafted from the ground and hung in the air. Another 15,000 lay wounded in field hospitals, many of them maimed, limbs blown off, skulls or chests cratered. Lincoln warred with his melancholy nature.

When Lincoln returned to McClellan's camp, he insisted the general join him in visiting sick and wounded rebel soldiers in the Grove's farmhouse, a make-shift hospital. William and other members of the presidential party joined them.

Inside the house, a large blood-stained table occupied the center of what had been a dining room. The floorboards bore deep puce reminders of mangled torsos, amputated limbs, and gushing arteries. The subtle fragrance of chloroform lingered on the edge of more pungent odors. One of the surgeons reminded McClellan their supplies were running low.

William eyed a wheelbarrow coated with gelatinous dregs from countless loads of discarded body parts. A large, toothy saw hung on the wall—purple stains on its wooden handle. Bile wormed into William's throat. Lincoln leaned toward him and whispered, "There is nothing glorious about war."

Lincoln fought nausea as he asked for William's benefit, "What do you do with the limbs?"

"We stack them out back," the surgeon replied, "until a burial detail gets around to digging a trench. The wait's not so long now that we're caught up on burying the dead. They could stack up again, though. No telling how many of the poor boys in this place are not going to make it or how fast the ones who don't are going to die."

William rushed outside, only to be assaulted by the rank odor of rotting limbs piled against a fence. He gave up his breakfast. Contraband Hospital had its share of disease and death, even an occasional amputation, but the scale of misery he encountered there was small compared to what took place inside the farmhouse.

By the time William rejoined the others, Lincoln stood at the cot of a wounded rebel soldier. The young Georgian's face was drained of color, his restless eyes shifted abruptly from one visitor to the next.

"Are you in great pain?" Lincoln asked.

"Yes, sir. My leg is gone. I am sinking from exhaustion." There was a tug to the soldier's gaze—as if locking onto another's eyes could hold him back from the throes of death.

"Would you shake my hand if I were to tell you who I am?"

"There should be no enemies in this place," he replied.

"I am Abraham Lincoln, President of the United States."

The soldier's eyes widened. He made a great effort to smile and extended his hand.

Lincoln clasped the soldier's hand in both of his own and held it for some time.

Anger, awe, pity battled in William's heart and mind.

Lincoln raised his voice so everyone in the room could hear. "The solemn obligations which we owe to our country and posterity compel the prosecution of this war. It has followed, therefore, that many have become enemies through uncontrollable circumstances. Nevertheless, we bear no individual malice and are able to take each other by the hand with sympathy and good feeling."

Each patient who was able to walk rose from his cot and went forward to shake Lincoln's hand. When he had greeted each of them, he and General McClellan passed by those who were too wounded to leave their beds, bidding them good cheer and promising that every possible care would be taken to nurse them to good health.

Soldiers' Home—October 1862

Lincoln sat at his desk upstairs in the cottage as the evening turned chilly. When he left Antietam two days earlier, he prodded McClellan to pursue Lee's ragged, retreating army. McClellan still had not budged. Impatience gnawed at Lincoln like a ravenous cur on a bone.

Footfalls in the adjoining room belonged to William who was loaded down with wood for the fireplace—his last chore before heading back to the city.

"What are you working on?" William asked.

Lincoln put down his pen. “A reminder to General McClellan that we’re fighting a war.”

“Colored soldiers wouldn’t need a general to get them moving,” William said.

“I am not in the mood, William.”

“I was just saying—”

“How’s Mariah?” Lincoln asked. “Has she forgiven me for keeping you away so long?”

“It’s not you that’s got her riled.”

“What have you done now?” Lincoln asked.

“Doesn’t matter,” William replied. “You’ll take her side.”

“That again. Wish her luck for me. If what you saw at Antietam did not dissuade you, I am not sure anything would.”

“Good night, sir.”

“Good night, William. Take the carriage back to the mansion. That way nobody will bother you for being out alone this late. I’ll ride my horse into the city tomorrow.”

“Yes, sir.”

Lincoln took up his pen and signed the note he had been writing to his new General-in-Chief Henry Halleck. *Send a dispatch over your signature to McClellan—say cross the Potomac and give battle to the enemy or drive him south.*

Cosgrove Residence—October 1862

William drove around to the back of Mrs. Cosgrove’s house and found Mariah on the bench, tapping her foot on the ground. As he climbed down, her glower gave him pause. The bouquet of flowers in his hand might as well have been ragweed.

“Where’d you steal those?” She crossed her arms and legs.

He offered them to her. “From Mr. Lincoln’s conservatory.”

"Flowers ain't gonna fix things."

"I'm sorry." He sat next to her.

"Sorry for wantin' to go to war, or 'cause you slipped and said so?"

"When he takes me to those places—"

"Next time, tell him you can't go."

"It's my job," William protested.

"It could be Mr. Slade's job if you let it be."

"He has a family."

She snatched the bouquet and threw it back in his lap. "Well thank you Mr. Johnson for clarifyin' where we stand."

"That's not what I mean."

"Oh. It's what you mean all right." Her stare grew icier.

"I mean when I see those white boys losing arms or legs or eyes or dying, fighting our fight, I feel like less of a man."

"How would bein' dead or maimed make you more of a man?" Her chin quivered.

He sputtered.

"Stop. Here's what makes me feel like less of a woman. Knowin' you'd rather die in place of one of them than live for me. Want to know what I think? They're the ones what stole our freedom. They can pay the price to buy it back." She stood and stomped into the house.

William got up to follow but froze. The matron blocked the doorway, a smirk had replaced her normally dour countenance. She had been eavesdropping on their argument.

Executive Mansion—October 1862

William moped for most of the month like a sad-eyed hound struck dumb, unable to bay at the moon. It took a *New York*

Times headline to restore his voice. The First Kansas Colored Volunteers "fought with desperate bravery" at Island Mound in Missouri. His people had proven their courage in battle. Outnumbered two-to-one in hand-to-hand combat—eight killed, eleven wounded—they turned back the attacking rebel guerillas.

William laid the newspaper on Lincoln's desk and cleared his throat. "Sir?"

Lincoln glanced at the article and snapped at William. "Do not say a word."

Lincoln did not have to be told the army needed more soldiers like those colored volunteers. He was still fuming over a report from the War Department—only 60,000 of the 140,000 troops on General John Pope's payroll could be found. When McClellan took the field at Antietam, he could not account for more than 45,000 of the 93,000 who returned from the aborted march on Richmond. Lincoln reckoned that some of the missing men permitted themselves to be captured so they could be paroled by the rebels. Parole meant they could return home if they promised not to take up arms again.

It was no mystery to Lincoln as to why McClellan was all the time calling for more troops. Deserters and furloughed men on the army's rosters outnumbered those in the field. To fill up the army was like shoveling fleas.

Lincoln vented his frustration in an exchange of dispatches with McClellan. When the general complained that his horses were sore-tongued and fatigued, Lincoln replied—

> *Will you pardon me for asking what the horses of your Army have done since the battle of Antietam that fatigue anything?*

Lincoln followed with another biting message to McClellan—

> *Stuart's cavalry out-marched ours. Will not a movement of our Army be a relief to the cavalry? But I am so rejoiced to learn you began crossing the river this morning.*

* * *

William learned, days later, that McClellan—recently demoted from General-in-Chief—had also been sacked as commander of the Army of the Potomac and would be kept off the battlefield all together. He strode around the basement like a peacock in mating season.

Slade drew William aside. "Do not gloat when you go in to groom him this morning. He's as irritable as I've ever seen."

"But I can't help myself. The general was the biggest reason our people have been kept out of the fight. Now that he's gone—"

"I said, mind your tongue." Slade set his jaw.

"I've held my tongue for weeks. Since Mariah—"

Slade sneered. "She has not spoken to you since, right?"

"She has not," William conceded. He had begged for Mariah's forgiveness a dozen times since their argument. She quit helping him shave refugees and patients at Contraband Camp. She refused to acknowledge his greetings when they passed each other going in and out of the laundry.

"That's because she can smell it on you, and so can he. Your manhood is more important to you than the whole world, them included."

William bit his lip.

"What are you waiting for? Go groom the man."

Executive Mansion—November 1862

While William waited in the lobby of the War Department, carrying a message from Lincoln to General-in-Chief Halleck, he overheard a conversation between Secretary Stanton and a short, compact man Stanton addressed as Professor Lieber. At first, William's interest was piqued by the man's European accent, but he became fully engrossed when the professor said, "The president insists that rights and privileges of a freedman belong to such persons."

Stanton replied, "The president wants General Halleck to review your work to be certain nothing conflicts with the proclamation he intends to issue."

William strained to catch every word. He wanted to find out who the professor meant by *such persons*. His mind churned. *Rights and privileges … proclamation*—those words were spoken in the War Department. Something clicked in his mind. Lincoln had become secretive about the old leather gripsack he used for carrying the proclamation. He had stopped reading the document aloud to him and Slade whenever there were changes.

William's eavesdropping ended when an army officer asked, "Is that for General Halleck?"

"Yes, sir," William answered, clutching Lincoln's message.

"Fine." The officer plucked the message from William's hand. "You'd best be on your way."

When William returned to the mansion, he pushed the barber's chair into Lincoln's office. "Ready for a trim, sir?"

Lincoln tossed aside the papers he was examining and threw up his hands. "Is there no end to the calamities that assault this office?"

William held his tongue and scanned the room for the proclamation gripsack. It held its usual place on the corner desk. If Lincoln had been working on it that morning, he had moved on to other business.

Lincoln sat in the barber's chair, laid his head back, and closed his eyes. "Didn't we just do this this morning?"

"No, sir. That was yesterday." William worked up lather as he eyed the gripsack.

"But why are we at it so late today?"

"You sent me off on an errand," William replied.

"I should be more attentive. Having you groom me is the singular pleasure of my existence these days."

William fixed his mind on conjuring a scheme to get into the gripsack. He had to know if anything important had changed—at least anything that was important to him.

Lincoln took a long breath. "Maybe I should go off in the middle of the night the same way I arrived here. Return to my simple life in Springfield."

William continued to hold his tongue.

"I'm sure they would follow us," Lincoln mused. "They would even find us across the mountains should we go as far as California. Running away would be of no use."

"Sir, I know my troubles aren't as great as the ones that weigh you down. But sometimes I imagine running away, too. I just can't think of anyplace safe, except maybe Canada."

"My advice is to stay away from Minnesota." Lincoln chuckled.

"What's wrong with Minnesota?"

"Everything, it appears," Lincoln replied. "On the table are letters from clergymen, telling me of the evils this government perpetrates against Indians in that region. Next to them are stacks of case files of Sioux warriors convicted of murder for rebelling against those supposed atrocities. Three hundred and thirty-three of them. Each sentenced to hang."

"What are you going to do?" William wiped the razor clean. Unlike Negroes, Indians were allowed in the army. They were even armed. William imagined if it had been Negroes rebelling, there would not have been trials of any kind.

"I do not yet have an answer," Lincoln replied.

"What if they were secessionists, instead of Indians?" William asked.

"That's the knotty puzzle I am trying to solve. What distinguishes civilized people from savages?" Lincoln took William's towel and wiped his face.

William followed Lincoln to his desk. All he wanted was a peek at the proclamation.

Lincoln opened the gripsack as he sat.

William lingered, peering over Lincoln's shoulder.

"That will be all." Lincoln closed the gripsack.

* * *

Mrs. Keckly went to Lincoln's office before supper that evening to comb his hair as she did when her schedule allowed. A ragged edge in Lincoln's voice betrayed his anxiety. "What's cooking downstairs, tonight?"

"Mrs. Lincoln thought you would enjoy a terrapin soup."

"Yes. I do like a good terrapin soup, but I am not in the mood to enjoy such delicacies these days."

"I suppose not." She ran the comb through his hair.

"Well, it's time we buckled down and struck a big blow to Jeff Davis's so-called government."

“Yes, I would agree it’s about time,” Mrs. Keckly replied.

“I am fixing up the proclamation some more.” Lincoln arched his brow. “It’s bound to shock some folks.”

“They could certainly use some shocking.”

“We’re going to do some amending of our Constitution,” Lincoln added. “Payments to States that free the slaves. Payments to loyal slave owners whose slaves gain freedom by the chances of war. Authority for Congress to appropriate money for colonizing free Negroes. Those amendments, alongside the proclamation, should end this rebellion.”

“If you permit me, it sounds like a lot of bribery to folks who should just do what’s right.”

He turned in his chair and faced her. “Sometimes, you have to swallow some nasty medicine to cure what’s ailing you.”

“I suppose, if you can stop all this fighting and free all the people, spending that money would make good business sense.”

He ran his fingers through his hair. “I hope enough folks will see it that way.”

“But when freedom finally comes,” she said, “there can be no backsliding.”

“If there is,” Lincoln replied, “we shall take it back.”

“It will take more than that.” Mrs. Keckly held up the comb as if to punctuate her point. “Equality is the bedrock of freedom. Repression cannot be allowed to replace oppression. If that be the case, it will be only a matter of time before the violence returns.”

“That’s why I need your people to get behind the colonization idea. Not only will we remove their shackles, we will send them somewhere they can exercise those new muscles of freedom among people who are their equals." He took her hands in his.

She recoiled. "Are you saying, in God's sight we are not equal to the people we already live and toil amongst?"

He shook his head. "The unfortunate truth is that you will not be treated as equals, at least not for some time. Establish your freedom and prosper where you are truly free, and someday your people can come back and thrive among us, peaceably and recognized as equals."

"My." She glanced at the clock on the mantle. "If I make you late for supper, Mrs. Lincoln will be furious. Besides, I have customers who need to know they are not forgotten."

"If I were not late for supper, Mrs. Lincoln would find something else to be angry about. But before you go..."

"Yes?" Mrs. Keckly asked.

"What is eating at William? This morning he said he sometimes considers running away. Do we not treat him well?"

"You should speak to him but let me talk to Mariah first."

"You think that would help?" he asked.

"It might." Mrs. Keckly put away Lincoln's brush and comb. "If I turn her thinking a little and you encourage William to give it another try, maybe they can patch things up."

Cosgrove Residence—November 1862

Mariah sat across the table from Mrs. Keckly in Mrs. Cosgrove's kitchen. "Do you love the boy?" Mrs. Keckly asked.

Mariah stared out the window. "Does he love me?"

"Did you ask him if he loves you?"

"He says he loves me, but he wants to go fight in the war."

"But it's your freedom he would be fighting for."

"No, he'd be fightin' to prove his manhood." Mariah crossed her arms. "I don't need someone showing me they can lord it over people. I've already been under a master, and never again. When you let people treat you like property, the only thing that happens is you get used."

"If he says he loves you, give him a chance to show it."

"Why?" Mariah demanded.

"Where there is love, there is hope."

"Hope for what? A broken heart?"

"Love is messy. Sometimes it hurts." Mrs. Keckly searched Mariah's eyes, hoping to find a window into her heart.

"What would you know about love?" Mariah's eyes narrowed. "You're all alone."

"The man I loved and called father was not my true father." Mrs. Keckly folded her hands on the table. "My mother's master raped her. I sprang from his seed—nothing more than a crop planted in her belly. But my mother's husband loved me the same as if I were his. I bore a son in the same circumstances as my mother and loved the little one with all my heart. This damned war took him from me." She paused.

"Yes, I was married," Mrs. Keckly continued, "but not to my George's cruel white father. I loved and was loved by a kindhearted man. But over time, he was broken by bondage. He gave himself over to alcohol and indolence as a result. I had to choose between loving him and protecting my son. I know about love's messy parts. I know how much love can hurt."

"Then why should I want to have any part of it?" Mariah asked, her eyes softening.

"Love also has sweet parts. They make the messiness and the hurt worth it. If you are lucky, you only taste its sweetness, but if you never love, all you ever taste is loneliness."

“You’re telling me I should marry William, savor his sweetness for a little while and let this war steal him from me, leaving me with a lifetime of sorrow.”

“You cannot control Providence.” Mrs. Keckly reached across the table to take Mariah’s hands. “All you can do is give yourself over to it and make the best of its good parts.”

“The good parts. That’s the problem.”

“What do you mean?”

“He’s too good.” Mariah’s eyes misted. “That’s what scares me. He’ll put everything else ahead of us. You should see him when he works in the camp. He loses himself bringin’ them small comforts. I could just see him goin’ off to war and throwin’ himself in front of a bayonet to save someone else’s life—some white man’s life. Then where would that leave me? Slaving away, scrubbin’ floors in some other white man’s house just to get by—because the darkness of my skin says I’m not good enough for anything more.” Mariah sobbed.

Mrs. Keckly stood, went to Mariah’s side, and stroked her hair. “The bigger question is, where will you be if you deprive yourself of the love he can give you, even if it’s only for a season?”

“Tell William he can call on me if he wants.” Mariah wiped her eyes.

CHAPTER SEVENTEEN

Executive Mansion—December 1862

In early November when military tribunals sentenced 303 Sioux fighters to hang after the recent uprising in Minnesota, Lincoln insisted on reviewing each of the trial transcripts. His deliberations were completed in a little under a month, and he applied the same treatment to each that he would give to any white soldier. He commuted sentences of 264 of the prisoners and braced for backlash from every quarter. He explained his reasoning to the Senate.

> *Anxious to not act with so much clemency as to encourage another outbreak on the one hand, nor with so much severity as to be real cruelty on the other, I caused a careful examination of the records of trials to be made,*

in view of first ordering the execution of such as had been proved guilty of violating females.

Contrary to my expectations, only two of this class were found. I then directed a further examination, and a classification of all who were proven to have participated in massacres, as distinguished from participation in battles. This class numbered forty and included the two convicted of female violation. One of the number is strongly recommended by the commission which tried them for commutation to ten years' imprisonment. I have ordered the other thirty-nine to be executed on Friday, the 19th instant.

Lincoln handed William the message to deliver to leaders of the Senate then offered him some advice. "Go make amends with Mariah before it's too late."

"How do I prove I love her?"

"Save some money. Find a home for the two of you and move out of the basement. Give her a way to see your love is permanent, even if, God forbid, you're someday called away to fight in this war."

"Do you think it will come to that?" William's eyes widened.

"Come to what?"

"Calling us to fight."

Lincoln clasped William's shoulder. "That's not the kind of talk that will win her back."

"You said, 'if I'm called away to fight in this war.'"

"I also told you to go make amends."

"You told one of your callers that you will man Fort Sumter with Negroes when you take it back. I was right here in the office when you did."

"I said, if we take it back, and I was blowing off steam. I am allowed that now and then, am I not?"

* * *

On New Year's Eve, Lincoln gathered his Cabinet in his office and announced—

> *After the commencement of hostilities, I struggled nearly a year and a half to get along without touching that institution which is the source of our present conflict. At last, when I conditionally determined to touch it, I gave a hundred days' fair notice. By simply again becoming good citizens of the United States, they could avoid a peremptory proclamation, which I announced on what appeared to me to be a military necessity. They chose to do otherwise, and being made, that proclamation must stand.*

Lincoln held up a copy of his revised proclamation. "You are familiar with the provisions of that preliminary order. Now I submit changes I have made after weeks of careful deliberation. You will see as I read the final document, there are three principal differences from the earlier versions. First, the proclamation stands solely as an exercise of executive authority under the Constitution, rather than relying on Acts of Congress. Next, I declare and make known that emancipated persons of suitable condition will be received into the armed service of the United States to garrison forts, positions, stations, and other places, and to man vessels of all sorts in said service."

Whispers were exchanged among the wide-eyed Cabinet ministers.

"Finally, I enjoin upon the people hereby declared to be free to abstain from all violence, unless necessary for self-defense, and I recommend that, in all cases when allowed, they labor faithfully for reasonable wages."

"What will be done regarding colonization?" Blair asked.

"It is my hope that Congress will follow the model of an experiment I am putting together." Lincoln removed his spectacles. "Tonight, I intend to sign a contract with the promoter of a freedmen's colony to be set up in Hayti."

Welles stiffened. "That would be like holding out a prize to get them to fight then taking it away once we claim victory."

"While being yoked together in war is a matter of present necessity," Lincoln contended, "permanent equality can be more expediently achieved by separation of the white and Black races. The plan is voluntary. Any who chooses to go can raise themselves up freely, without the burdens so often placed upon minority classes. Once their equality is demonstrated, they can come back and live among us peaceably."

The Executive Mansion—January 1, 1863

The mansion doors were thrown open to hundreds of official visitors the following morning at ten o'clock. Members of Congress, Supreme Court justices, diplomats, military officers, and other dignitaries filed past, greeting President and Mrs. Lincoln, exchanging best wishes for the New Year. Many commented on Lincoln's bright disposition. They had not witnessed him so cheerful since he arrived in Washington.

By late morning, all of the smiling, forced conversation, and constant press of people wore on Lincoln. His bones ached and his posture became slouched.

William crossed from his station next to the parlor doorway and whispered, "Sir. They've gathered in your office. It's time."

Lincoln excused himself and went upstairs. His private secretaries and members of the Cabinet stood with solemn expressions around the long table. A carefully prepared official document lay waiting for him.

Music blended with the buzz of conversation and filtered up from the East Room festivities. The guests were oblivious to the way in which the war was about to take a turn. At least, Lincoln hoped that would be the result.

Lincoln sat and took up a pen that had been placed next to the document. His hand quivered. He closed his eyes and laid down the pen, not wanting to make his signature with an unsteady hand. He must leave no room for posterity to speculate over his resolve. He was taking a daring step. He raised the pen again and signed the proclamation with a bold stroke.

William stood just inside the doorway, wearing a smile.

Executive Mansion—February 1863

Vice President Hannibal Hamlin, who called himself the fifth wheel of Lincoln's administration, requested an urgent meeting. When Hamlin arrived in Lincoln's office, he was accompanied by several young army officers, including his son, Captain Cyrus Hamlin. Each officer asked for a colored regiment to lead in battle.

"You realize what you're in for?" Lincoln asked. "Blacks in arms incite the ugliest passions, both among our people and people in the south."

"Yes, sir," they replied in unison.

"Have you heard of Jeff Davis's order—that white officers who command colored troops, if captured, are to be turned over to the States to be tried and executed?"

Hamlin's son replied that they had seen a broadside to that effect from the *Richmond Enquirer* and had read every word.

"Is it still your wish to serve as officers with colored regiments?" Lincoln asked.

They all agreed it was.

"I want to look each of you in the eye as you tell me so for yourself, not as a group," Lincoln insisted. He went down the line, stopping before each one, examining their faces for any signs of hesitation as they answered. When he finished, he turned to the elder Hamlin. "What is your best judgment?"

"Will you write the order at once?" Hamlin asked.

Lincoln sat at his desk and hurriedly wrote an order to Secretary Stanton to form a brigade of colored recruits. "Here. Take this to Mars without delay and watch out. He's likely to become unhinged when he sees it. He has accosted me for months over my hesitation to put Africans in arms."

Vice President Hamlin and the young officers rushed to the War Department and delivered Lincoln's order to Stanton.

"No, it cannot be true!" Stanton declared as tears rolled down his cheeks.

Vice President Hamlin threw his arms around Stanton, gripped him tight, and replied, "It is true."

"Thank God for this," Stanton shouted.

* * *

Lincoln braced for William's reaction to the news that a colored regiment was to be organized, and his anxiety hit a high point when William showed up an hour earlier than usual that evening. Lincoln set aside the *Richmond Enquirer* broadside he had been studying and turned to face William. "Did something happen over at Treasury today?"

"No, sir," William replied, "Mr. Chase left a couple of hours ago and dismissed me early.

"I see."

There was a brief silence.

William's pulse quickened. "Sir, I hear Mr. Stanton is over the moon about getting permission to form colored regiments."

"Yes. I suppose he will put together a few thousand freedmen down in the southern region."

"I was wonder—"

"It's nothing that concerns you," Lincoln snapped.

"I beg to differ, sir." William pulled back his shoulders.

"Were you not trying to patch things up with your sweetheart?"

"Yes." William replied. "We're working things out,"

"And you suppose resurrecting your interest in soldiering will help that?"

"We're working things out. That means coming to an understanding. She doesn't want to be under anyone's thumb. I agreed, as long as I am not tied to someone's apron strings."

"That sounds more like an impasse than a compromise."

"I have to join up," William insisted.

"Do you know what Jeff Davis says he's going to do with colored troops?"

"I've heard rumors."

"Our spies in Richmond have discovered exactly what he will do." Lincoln picked up the broadside. "What he has already done."

"It doesn't matter," William averted Lincoln's eyes.

"Last November," Lincoln continued, "a rebel vanguard landed on Saint Catherine's Island where they encountered six Africans armed with muskets and wearing federal uniforms. The Africans were part of the Sea Islands brigade General Saxton cajoled me into allowing him to form. Two Negroes were killed and the other four captured. One of the captives was a boy named Manuel. He was taken to slave brokers for sale. A rebel general ordered him removed from the brokers and put in jail until Richmond gave permission to make examples of all four by way of execution. Jeff Davis replied they should be treated as slaves in flagrant rebellion against their masters. Under the laws of every slave-holding State, such slaves are subject to death."

"Every man who goes to war knows he may die," William replied.

"Yes. And it is my fervent prayer that you shall not meet such a fate."

"If I'm a freedman," William argued, "I should be allowed to make the same choice Captain Hamlin and his friends made."

"My answer is no. I will not allow the army to recruit Negroes beyond the scope of Mr. Hamlin's request. That is final." Lincoln returned to his desk and sifted through papers.

Cosgrove Residence—February 1863

William sat next to Mariah on Mrs. Cosgrove's back porch. They shared a coarse woolen blanket to fend off icy, biting gusts. William draped his arm over her shoulders.

"Somethin's on your mind." She leaned into him.

He cradled her head and drew her close. “I’ve been trying to find a new position. Something more permanent.”

“But you like working for Mr. Lincoln.” She pulled away.

“I do, but I’m always going back and forth between two bosses. I want to settle in one place.”

“Have you asked Mr. Lincoln for more responsibilities?”

“He has too much on his mind to care about me. Besides, he won’t be president forever.”

“Won’t he be taking you back to Springfield when he’s done here?” she asked.

“He’s been having me spy on Mr. Chase. The secretary wants to be president. If he wins the election, I might stay.”

“I thought—"

William shook his head. “This war is eating at me. It’s not going anywhere. I’m burning inside to see everyone truly free.”

“What?” she demanded. “You’re still wanting to go fight?”

“I’m not saying I would go. I just want to be free to make the choice. But he’s only authorized one brigade of 5,000 and I doubt they’ll even get to fight.”

“If you could go, would you?” she braced for the answer she knew was brewing inside him.

“There’s something I haven’t told you. I know I should have brought it up before.” He averted her eyes.

“What haven’t you told me?” She tilted her head.

“I made a promise to someone before we met. A vow to protect them. A vow I don’t think I could possibly keep until all our people are free, everywhere.”

“Are we talking about another—?”

“It’s not what you think.”

Mariah threw off the blanket. “What I think is, it’s high time you figured out what you want.”

"I know what I want. It's just, no one wants me to have it."

"Exactly what do you want, William?"

"I don't want to spend the rest of my life looking over my shoulder, fearing every white man I see could be scheming to snatch me off the street and sell me down south. I want the freedom to keep my promises."

She stood. "Just who is it that's stoppin' you from doing what you want?"

"Seems like everyone." He buried his head in his hands.

"If that's what you want, don't let me be one of those everyones that's holding you back."

"I wasn't talking about you."

"Is that so? Well, it sounds like it."

"Mariah, I love you." He opened his arms. "I want you to be at my side, whatever I do."

"Exactly. At your side. Like an old carpet bag."

"It's not like that."

"Oh, it *is* like that. You turn from hot to cold to hot again, like a man with a fever. That's sickness, not love." Her words ran him through like a bayonet.

"No," he protested.

She stormed into the house.

William returned to the mansion basement and lay awake all night.

He called on Mariah a few days later. He had cut another bouquet of flowers from the mansion conservatory and bought her a bracelet. The matron turned him away, told him Mariah was done with him. Told him to move on.

On Sunday he arrived early at church and lingered by the door, hoping to catch Mariah's eye. When she spotted him, she detoured around to the back of the church and entered through another door. That afternoon at Contraband Camp, he tried to catch her attention several times, but she always found ways to dodge him.

Every Sunday for weeks thereafter, he kept up the same routine, but couldn't find a chink in her armor. She wouldn't even glance his way.

He wrote love letters. She never replied.

He asked Mrs. Keckly to carry a message to Mariah and brimmed with hope when he learned Mariah had accepted it.

Contraband Camp—April 1863

William's thoughts strayed off track without warning. One moment he would be tying a perfect diamond knot in Lincoln's tie, then he'd be lost in distraction. When he snapped to, Lincoln would be undoing the knot and tying it himself. There were razor nicks above Lincoln's lip, unevenly trimmed patches of hair, wrinkled trousers. Late one evening as William was sprawled out on his bed, fully dressed, he found in his pocket an undelivered message from Lincoln to a senator.

When Mariah avoided William during those weeks her throat pinched. She had to remind herself that he never loved her. At least, he didn't love her as much as he loved someone else or as much as he loved a kind of freedom no Negro would ever be allowed to have.

She had almost made a turn from regret to hostility one Sunday afternoon when she saw William bolt out of the men's hospital ward, slopping through mud with two Negroes chasing him. She froze.

The two pursuers—whose brother was fighting for his life after being assaulted by a mob protesting Black enlistments —

tackled William and pummeled him. By the time camp guards intervened and corralled the assailants, William lay on the ground, coated with mud, bloodied, and dazed. Mariah rushed to his side, cradled his head in her lap, and began wiping blood from his face with the sleeve of her blouse.

"We'll take it from here." A guard gripped her arm and pulled.

"No," she growled.

"Listen, these bucks need to be taught a lesson. We don't allow fighting in this camp."

"He wasn't fighting. He was running."

One of William's pursuers, restrained by three burly guards, shouted. "Damn right he was running—while the rest of us is volunteering to fight for our freedom. As if we wasn't meant to have our freedom in the first place."

One of the guards landed a blow on the pursuer's jaw.

"This man is the president's valet." Mariah glared at the guard looming over her and William. "I'll take him to the president's house. Mr. Lincoln will see that he's looked after."

"Get up woman." The guard yanked her mud slicked arm.

She slipped out of his grasp.

William murmured, "My pocket—"

She thrust her hand into William's pocket. As the guard pulled back his fist to bring it down on her, she held up a piece of paper. "Read this."

Another guard snatched the paper from her hand and unfolded it. "Well boys, this looks like the genuine article. I suppose we shouldn't risk making Mr. Lincoln mad. We'll see what he has to say about this."

Executive Mansion—April 1863

Lincoln sat at the long table with Stanton, General-in-Chief Halleck, and Professor Lieber. As Lincoln finished reading the professor's report, Nicolay entered the room. "Sir, we have an urgent matter. It involves William."

"Excuse me, gentlemen." Lincoln rose, worry lines deepened on his brow.

Nicolay led Lincoln into the hallway where William stood, grimy, battered, and bruised. A smatter of blood stained his white shirt.

"My God. What happened?" Lincoln asked.

"This boy says he works for you," one of the guards answered.

"He does indeed, but that does not answer my question."

The guard started to speak. Lincoln held up his hand. "William, are you okay?"

"I'm sorry, sir. I didn't mean to cause you any embarrassment."

"Tell me you did not get into a fight over that girl of yours." Lincoln placed his hand on William's shoulder.

"No, sir. We're not together anymore. It was about a patient at the hospital."

"Guards, thank you for bringing William home. We will take care of getting him cleaned up." Lincoln turned to Nicolay. "Send Hay for a doctor."

"I'm fine," William insisted. "Just a little banged up."

"We shall let the doctor decide, but first, I have something to show you. Come along."

When Lincoln returned to his meeting with William, he said, "Professor, this is an example of the import of your business. William, here, wants nothing more that the privilege of fighting for his people's freedom. He also has the notion that freedom and equality are somehow intertwined."

"Here. Here." Stanton clapped his hands.

"That's enough demonstration, Mars." Lincoln picked up Lieber's report. "The professor deserves our congratulations. This paper does the job just as I had hoped. He has made a fine case for our Emancipation Proclamation under the laws of war and laid out why those laws apply equally to our colored combatants." Lincoln turned to William. "You see, we are making progress."

Contraband Camp—June 1863

Stifling summer heat, late autumn storms, and blowing winter snows had plagued Contraband Camp and Hospital over the months since it opened. The onset of spring was unkind, as well. Arid, icy March winds turned fields into dust that an April blizzard whisked into a dull grey powder. In May, torrential rains turned remaining patches of snow into a dingy slush.

Thousands of refugees had migrated through camp. At times, a dozen would be crammed into a single moldy room or tent, without heat or dry bedding. What was thought to be fresh water was tainted by the nearby sewage canal. Disease permeated the camp and recovery was often hindered by the lack of food, medical supplies, and sanitation.

When Major Alexander Augusta became surgeon-in-charge, Mariah and others had hoped conditions would change. However, William doubted any colored officer could make a difference. Augusta sympathized for the residents and patients, but sympathy would not make up for the fact that he was a Negro, and only a major at that. Not a general, not even a colonel. William trod lightly, though, when folks spoke in Mariah's presence of the camp's backward slide or complained about her favorite Major Augusta.

William was quick to praise Mariah's efforts under Mrs. Keckly's tutelage—improving her elocution and adopting other refinements that would increase her prospects for employment by members of white society. Their rekindled romance started picking up steam once he reassured her that he was no longer determined to join the army. He promised she would always be first in his heart. She let him kiss her. Once. On the cheek. He replayed the kiss in his mind and resolved if he got another chance, he'd plant one on her lips.

A boy, about 7 years-old, sat in the barber's chair at Contraband Camp and told William, "Shave me jus' like Mr. Lincoln."

William laughed.

Mariah smiled at the boy's bold demand. "You heard the boy." She grabbed the shaving mug, whipped up some lather, and nudged William with her hip.

He winked at Mariah as he stroked the razor along the whole length of the strop. The sparkle in her deep brown eyes egged him on. She sidled up to him. No nudge this time. She leaned into him with her whole body. William's heart raced. Her eyes locked onto his.

"Do you make Mr. Lincoln wait this long?" the boy blurted.

"Just a minute." William grabbed a towel, dipped it in a pan of water and covered the boy's face. Without hesitating, he grabbed Mariah, pulled her close and planted a kiss. His lips parted, ever so slightly. She kissed him back.

Soldiers' Home—June 1863

Death—especially death of the Union—consumed Lincoln's thoughts in early June when he and his family returned to the cottage to escape the city's summer heat. The first evening back, he stared out the north-facing second-story window toward the cemetery—a thousand new markers in the seven months they had been away. Hundreds of thousands more troops had been thrown into battle, and Lee's Army of Northern Virginia was marching toward Pennsylvania. The Capital was more vulnerable than ever. There would be more death.

Lincoln walked downstairs, crossed over to the cemetery, and wandered to a section of freshly dug graves to greet the new arrivals. Among them, a Robert from New York. Interred nearby was a Thomas from New Jersey. Tears streamed down his cheeks and a stitch of pain pricked his voice as he recited lines from William Collins's verse—

> *How sleep the brave, who sink to rest, by all their Country's wishes blest!*

Not far from those two were an Edward and a William. Another William rested a few plots away. Lincoln fell to his knees and sobbed.

Dusk gave way to the black of night as Lincoln wept over tens of thousands he had sent to their graves. He prayed their deaths would not be in vain.

Contraband Camp—June 1863

News from Port Hudson in Louisiana spread across Washington like an unexpected rainbow spanning the western horizon. Even those who supported recruiting colored troops had calculated it would take months before those regiments saw battle, much less performed at a level approaching the proficiency and bravery of white soldiers.

Reports in northern newspapers caught everyone by surprise and fanned an ember William had not doused out, no matter how hard he tried. Captain Andre Cailloux, a Black officer shouting commands in English and French, led his men forward—two African regiments, the 1st and 3rd Louisiana Native Guard. Rebel heavy artillery battered their front. The rebel 39th Mississippi's light artillery and muskets assaulted them from their left. From their right along the Mississippi River, heavy guns and infantry rifles rained down. After Captain Cailloux fell in a hail of gunfire, his men surged forward, hurdling their own dead and wounded. Only when their ranks were decimated and their annihilation was all but certain, did they turn back. Despite their retreat, they gained the nation's respect. Doubts about the courage and determination of colored troops began to dissipate.

Ten days later, the fire in William's belly burned hotter. Union Colonel Herman Lieb's 10th Illinois Cavalry engaged rebel troops at the Tallulah railroad depot near Milliken's Bend, Louisiana. During the skirmish, Lieb held his African Brigade in reserve. He doubted their readiness to fight. As his cavalry withdrew, the rebels gave chase. To protect his cavalry's rear, Lieb was forced to put the colored soldiers into the fight. They held the line and helped disperse the enemy.

General Grant's praise of Lieb's African Brigade swelled William's pride. A War Department declaration sent him over the moon. Assistant Secretary of War Charles Dana announced,

> *The sentiment of this army with regard to the employment of Negro troops has been revolutionized by the bravery of the coloreds in the recent battle of Milliken's Bend.*

William didn't have to say anything when he was near Mariah. She tasted his smugness in every breath she inhaled. His gloating fed her agitation. When William barged into the hospital ward where she was stripping bedcoverings from mattresses, his whooping and hollering broke the tenuous bands that held her anxiety at bay.

"Can't you leave these ailing men in peace?" she shouted.

"It's a time for jubilee," he answered, waving a newspaper.

She strode toward him.

"It's what we colored folks should have been doing all along," he announced for everyone in the ward to hear.

She snatched the paper from his hand and threw it at him.

"Whoa," he said. "A Negro woman led more than 300 colored soldiers on a raid in South Carolina. They freed 800 of our people from bondage."

"How many did they lose?" she spat back.

He glared at her. "Not a one."

"What makes me think you wish there was at least one casualty, and it had been you?"

"Oh, Grace ..."

"What?" She planted her hands on her hips.

"It's not what you think."

"You called me by another woman's name."

"Let me explain," he begged.

"It doesn't need explanation."

"She was my brother's wife." His shoulders sagged. "When he died, I vowed to protect her and their little girl. But I failed."

"So that's what's burning inside you. You want to punish yourself." She pursed her lips.

"No." Tears welled in his eyes. "What I want is for all our people to be free. To force folks to treat us as equals. At least that way, even if I never find them, their nightmare will be over. They can have the life my brother tried to give them ... and me. He worked himself to the bone to buy our freedom. Mine, Grace's, their daughter's, even his own. But his body broke from all that toil, and when the fever came it took him."

Mariah picked up the newspaper and studied the photograph on the front page. The tension in her back and limbs faded. "Is this the woman who led the raid?"

"Yes," William replied. "Her name is Harriet Tubman. We should all be Harriet Tubmans."

"You know your brother's name." Her eyes locked with his. "My name came from a white master. I don't know what name my mother called me when I was a baby. I have no idea what names she might have given any brothers or sisters. I don't even know if I *had* brothers or sisters. When I was maybe five or six, I was sold to another master. You've told me about your Auntie." A lump formed in her throat, and tears welled in her eyes. "There's no picture in my head of any woman who could be family. My momma's face is a blur. I don't know if there was a father who held me, or who thought of me as more than property he could use up and toss away. William, I have no past. I came from no one, nowhere. There's no one out there who wants to find me."

"Then let's be the last generation of our race without a past," he held out his hands to her.

She sighed. "Freedom for our kind won't be like families reuniting in Heaven."

"I know," he whispered.

William took her in his arms, and they wept together.

Executive Mansion—July 1863

The Army of the Potomac had been the Union army's weakest link since early in the war, and Lincoln finally found the right man to lead it—General John F. Reynolds. In Lincoln's mind, Reynolds was the country's finest military officer. Reynolds agreed to take command, under one condition—that he would be free from all political interference. That required a promise Lincoln didn't believe he was in a position to keep, so he withdrew the offer.

Less than a month later, nearly 200,000 troops—like monster storm fronts churning toward each other—swarmed the countryside around the town of Gettysburg in Pennsylvania. Reynolds led the left wing of the Union forces. His command included the I, III, and XI Corps of the Army of the Potomac and a cavalry division.

On the first day of battle, Reynolds exhorted one of his units that stalled at the edge of a wood. "Forward! Forward, for God's sake!" he shouted. "Drive those fellows out of those woods!" No sooner than the words left his mouth, a bullet struck him at the base of his skull.

Lincoln was in the telegraph room of the War Department when news of Reynold's death arrived. An explosion of pain erupted in his head. He collapsed in a chair, clutching the telegram. If only he had conceded to Reynold's conditions and given him command of the entire Army of the Potomac, the general would have been in his headquarters tent, not in the field. He still would be alive.

A day after the rebel invasion of the north had been turned back at Gettysburg, Lincoln stood at the long table, staring at a dispatch from General Grant, Commander of the Army of Tennessee—the rebels would surrender the Mississippi River port city of Vicksburg in a matter of hours. He brushed it aside. The burden of 60,000 men lost between both sides during those two battles crashed down on him.

A soldier barreled through the crowd of visitors waiting to call on Lincoln. Nicolay leapt in front of him. "Whoa," he shouted. "You can't go in there. State your business."

"Mrs. Lincoln was in an accident," the soldier blurted.

Lincoln rushed out of his office. "Where? How is she?"

"She was coming into the city from the Soldiers' Home. The horses took fright and bolted. She either jumped or was thrown from the carriage."

"Is she hurt?" Lincoln demanded.

"Only stunned, I think," the soldier replied. "Maybe some bruises, but the doctors say nothing seems to be broken."

"I need to get to her at once," Lincoln insisted.

"The surgeons at Mt. Pleasant are attending her," the soldier explained. "I was told she'll be brought straight here when they finish examining her."

"Where is William?" Lincoln asked.

"At Treasury, I believe," Nicolay replied.

"Go over and tell him to bring Nurse Pomroy."

Soldiers' Home—July 1863

Lincoln learned his wife's mishap may not have been an accident. The tongue became suspiciously separated from the carriage, causing the horses to bolt. She gashed her head on a sharp rock when she leapt from the runaway rig. To make matters worse, intense headaches had kept Mrs. Lincoln bedridden, and the ugly gash became infected. Doctors feared the city's brutal heat and unsanitary conditions were thwarting her recovery, so they ordered her moved to the cottage under Nurse Pomroy's care.

Lincoln paced the anteroom outside his cottage office one evening, pausing occasionally to stare toward the cemetery. He could not shake the trauma of 60,000 dead, wounded, captured, and missing in less than a week. He replayed in his mind something Emerson said to him months earlier—*fires, plagues, revolutions, and calamities of all sorts serve to break up entrenched routines, clear the arena of corrupt contests, and open a fair field to all men.*

When Nurse Pomroy appeared in the doorway to report on Mrs. Lincoln's progress, Lincoln stood at the window, weeping. As she approached, he murmured, "Lord have mercy on those poor fellows."

"Yes, He will," she whispered.

"This is a righteous war," he insisted. "And God will protect the right, though with many lives sacrificed. I have done the best I could, trusting in God, but if the rebels keep Port Hudson, we are all but lost. If we could only take it from them, I think we shall have a great deal to thank God for."

"Prayer will do what nothing else can. Will you not pray?"

"Yes, I will." He pressed his forehead against the window. "And you should pray for me."

Around midnight, one of the cottage guards delivered a telegram to Lincoln. After reading it, Lincoln ran down the hall and burst into the room where Nurse Pomroy sat with his wife. "Good news!" he shouted. "Good news! Port Hudson is ours!

The victory is ours! God is good. The rebellion is split in two, and the Father of Waters again flows unvexed to the sea."

Mrs. Lincoln smiled for the first time since the carriage mishap. "Yes, God be praised. It is wonderful at long last to see such relief on my husband's face."

CHAPTER EIGHTEEN

Contraband Camp—July 1863

Every new resident at Contraband Camp came with a story. Some wore theirs like a new shirt they couldn't wait to show off. Others harbored dark secrets within the catacombs of their minds. The newcomer William was shaving tried to keep his horrors locked away, but according to camp gossip, his ran amok most nights while he slept.

"What do you think of the 54th Massachusetts?" William asked. "Those boys sure have folks talking."

The newcomer mumbled something unintelligible.

William continued, "That Sergeant Carney showed what our people are made of. I wish I had been there to see him save those regimental colors."

The man tore off the barber's cape and threw it at William.

William fired back. "It's high time we stood up and stood out. Fight for what we deserve."

"What do you know about fighting, boy?" He grabbed William's hands and glared at them. "Just what I thought. You know nothing about fighting."

"It doesn't take knowing." William yanked his hands back. "It's takes having something worth fighting for."

"Let me tell you what war is." He grabbed William's vest and jerked him so close spittle sprayed William's face. "It's a swirling inferno swallowing everything around you. Moses's pillar of fire would flicker like a dying candle next to it. War is burnt sulfur choking your lungs, twelve-pound iron balls ripping away arms, legs, shoulders, spleens, leaving oozing craters in human flesh. It's the glint of steel plunging into the beating heart of a man next to you, his life's blood spurting into your mouth, its coppery tang drawing bile into your throat. War is coming home ashamed you made it out alive."

William peered into the man's eyes. Hell glowered back.

"I was there. I watched Sergeant Carney save those colors." The man hobbled away.

William's gaze remained fixed on the man's path, even after he was out of sight. The man's gimp hadn't drawn William's attention when he came to be shaved.

Moments later, Mariah brought William some freshly laundered towels.

William blinked.

"Is something wrong?" Mariah took his hand.

"No." He shook his head to unscramble his thoughts. He repeated, "No. I'm fine."

"You look like you've seen a ghost."

Executive Mansion—July 1863

William lay wide-eyed in his bunk and unfolded a copy of the order Lincoln had issued from the mansion that afternoon. Lincoln wanted him to have a copy as a keepsake, told him it was evidence things were changing. The order sprang from Professor Lieber's months-long work to establish a new code for humane and equal treatment of all battlefield combatants.

> *Executive Mansion,*
>
> *Washington D.C.,*
>
> *July 30, 1863*
>
> *It is the duty of every government to give protection to its citizens, of whatever class, color, or condition, and especially to those who are duly organized as soldiers in the public service. The law of nations and the usages and customs of war as carried on by civilized powers, permit no distinction as to color in the treatment of prisoners of war as public enemies. To sell or enslave any captured person, on account of his color, and for no offence against the laws of war, is a relapse into barbarism and a crime against the civilization of the age.*
>
> *The Government of the United States will give the same protection to all its soldiers, and if the enemy shall sell or enslave anyone because of his color, the offense shall be punished by retaliation upon the enemy's prisoners in our possession.*
>
> *It is therefore ordered that for every soldier of the United States killed in violation of the laws of war, a rebel soldier shall be executed; and for every one enslaved by*

the enemy or sold into slavery, a rebel soldier shall be placed at hard labor on the public works and continued at such labor until the other shall be released and receive the treatment due to a prisoner of war.

ABRAHAM LINCOLN

A premonition looped through William's mind. He knelt on a battlefield without his rifle, surrendering to rebels, to be killed or sold into slavery, never to see Mariah again. Never to find Grace or Maddie. Mariah stood above him, a child clinging to her leg, the demoniac from the 54th Massachusetts lurked behind her. Eerie laughter filled his ears. Voices chanted, "no freedom."

William sat up and pulled on his slippers. He guessed Lincoln wasn't sleeping either—Lincoln rarely slept more than three of four hours on the nights he stayed in the city. William went to the kitchen, made a pot of tea, carried it upstairs, and set it on the long table. Lincoln continued pacing, dressed in his threadbare nightshirt, the backs of his slippers stomped down to accommodate his large feet. He paused at the window and stared into the dark night. "You cannot sleep either?"

"I have a lot on my mind, sir."

"If I had anything of value, I would gladly exchange it for the ability to turn off my thoughts." Lincoln gestured to one of the gas lamps. "The same way we turn off these infernal things."

William replied, "They don't make as big a mess as lanterns."

"So, what's on your mind, son?"

"Nothing as great as what's weighing on you, sir. That's for sure."

"How can ever wash all the blood off these hands?" Lincoln turned his palms up. "How did it ever come to this?"

"You only wanted to do what's right."

"Is that so? What if I told you I am not certain what right is, anymore?"

"Liberty for everyone is what's right," William insisted.

"At what cost? What of mercy? What of morality? How can we hold our heads up if we behave no better than our enemies? If we take our own vengeance?"

"Here's what I know about mercy and morality." William drew his shoulders back. "Mariah knew some of General Lee's slaves at Duff Green's Row—ones who escaped when the general and his family fled their plantation. You admire him. Say we should forgive his treason. What should we do about his cruelty? He refused to set his wife's slaves free, even though her father's will required him to do it. Mrs. Lee complained when he whipped those poor souls until they bled, just to make examples of them, just to show them their place. What kind of mercy, what kind of morality was that?"

"But are not my hands also unclean?" Lincoln asked. "Have we not prolonged this conflict by pursuing righteousness with unrighteousness?"

"I don't know," William replied. "But it seems to me the Almighty himself suffered greatly for a good cause. Today you have staked a claim that the life of a colored private is equal that of a white officer. As Mr. Victor Hugo claimed in his story *Les Misérables*, 'if liberty is the summit, equality is its base.' Is equality not a good cause, sir?"

"Such policies won't be good enough if the general populace rejects them, as they did just days ago. Men, women, and children rioted in New York," Lincoln argued. "The scenes which have been described in the newspapers are deplorable—200 colored orphans burned out of their shelter, dozens of colored men lynched on lampposts. The mayhem was ostensibly over the draft, but the grievances that drove a large mob to violence had been festering long before this war. At the heart of their agitation is the principle you doggedly pursue, that whites should accept equality with the Black race—a principle far more easily understood than put into practice."

"It's only hard for those who make it so," William said.

Soldiers' Home—August 1863

By mid-August, Mrs. Lincoln recovered enough from her carriage accident to travel north to New York for an extended vacation. She encouraged William to take Mariah, during her absence, to the cottage grounds for a romantic picnic. Mrs. Keckly had agreed to chaperone.

The Sunday morning of the picnic, Mariah ached all over. What little energy she hadn't spent the previous day had dissipated during a fitful night. As she sat in the church pew, stealing glances at William, her back ached. She wasn't about to complain, though. It had almost taken an act of Congress to extract Mrs. Cosgrove's consent for the picnic.

When William brought the carriage around to pick her up, she welcomed his insistence that she ride in the back like Cleopatra while he drove. Mrs. Keckly, who sat next to her in the carriage, wouldn't have allowed him to treat her like anything less than a queen.

A few minutes after William nudged the horse forward, Mrs. Keckly leaned over and whispered to Mariah. "You look a little peaked."

"Just tired," she replied. "Didn't sleep well last night."

"Please tell me you're not—"

"Of course not!" Mariah jerked back.

"I'm sorry," Mrs. Keckly said in a low voice. "You're tired. Your face is flushed. When you boarded the carriage, you winced from some sort of ache or pain. My mind just went there."

"I'm fine," Mariah whispered. "Just don't say anything to William. I don't want to ruin our outing."

Mrs. Keckly pinched her lips tight.

William glanced at them. "What are you two up to back there?"

"None of your business," Mariah barked.

William shrugged.

"And to make it clear," Mariah added. "We ain't been misbehaving."

"Have not been. We need to keep working on your diction if you're going to get anywhere in this world."

"Yes, ma'am. Have not been. William reminds me of the same things. He says a Mormon mistress schooled him and his brother after she agreed to let them buy their freedom."

Later that afternoon Mariah cuddled next to William on the cottage lawn as he read to her from *Les Misérables*. He cradled her head against his chest. "Are you feeling all right?"

"I'm fine." She pulled away. "Why?"

He put his hand on her forehead and cupped her cheek. "You're burning up."

"I don't feel well." She leaned into him.

William called to Mrs. Keckly, who had been reading on the back porch. She hurried over, collected the picnic fixings, and followed as William carried Mariah to the carriage.

"Take her to Mrs. Cosgrove's," Mrs. Keckly directed.

"What about the camp hospital?" William asked.

"Mrs. Cosgrove's home is cleaner, and she can arrange for better care."

When they arrived at Mrs. Cosgrove's back door, William helped Mariah down from the carriage and draped her arm over his shoulders. Mrs. Keckly followed as he helped Mariah walk to the house.

The matron met them at the door. "What happened?"

"She's burning with fever," William replied.

"Not in here." The matron blocked the doorway.

"What's wrong?" William glared at the matron.

"I told Mrs. Cosgrove that girl shouldn't be spending all her time over at that camp with those monkeys and their sickness."

Mrs. Keckly angled between William and the matron. "Wait just one minute."

The matron crossed her arms. "When I saw her this morning, I knew something was off. Mrs. Cosgrove told me if she came back ailing with fever, to send her over to that hospital of theirs."

"We shall see about that." Mrs. Keckly tried to press past the matron.

Mrs. Cosgrove appeared behind the matron. "She is exactly right. I will not have that sickness coming into my house."

William whispered to Mariah, "Come on. Let's go."

"I'm going to be sick." Mariah's stomach churned.

"Well, I'll be," Mrs. Keckly shouted. "I hope you can find a good seamstress, Mrs. Cosgrove."

William led Mariah back to the carriage and helped her in. Mrs. Keckly followed, muttering under her breath.

Mariah languished with fever in the women's ward at Contraband Hospital, and William kept vigil at her bedside. Mrs. Keckly had angled for an exception to the rule that banned men from the women's wards. The surgeon-in-charge dared not deny her request. Mrs. Keckly was one of the Contraband Relief Society's principal fundraisers and Mr. and Mrs. Lincoln were among her benefactors.

Near the end of a couple of weeks, the fever was replaced by small reddish spots inside Mariah's mouth and on her tongue. Surgeons immediately quarantined her in the smallpox ward.

William returned to the city and collapsed on his basement bunk, weak from lack of eating and sleeping. His throat ached, not from sickness, but from grief. Images of burn piles engulfing blankets and clothes from the smallpox ward were embedded in his memory, as were descriptions of the worst cases—bodies caked with black lesions, violent fevers, hemorrhaging, the whites of patients' eyes turned blood red. After that, they died. William wept.

A knock came at the door. "Go away," he murmured.

The door opened. Lincoln stood at the threshold. "What can I do to help?"

"She has the pox," William muttered.

"If there's anything I can do, just ask."

"Thank you, but you have enough worries." William buried his head in his hands. "I'm not supposed to be a burden."

"You're not a burden. You're like a son."

William shook his head. "I don't think Mrs. Lincoln would like to hear you have a Negro son."

"Why not?" Lincoln laughed. "She's fine with being married to a Black Republican president."

William smiled weakly.

He returned to the camp each afternoon for the next several days, asking nurses for updates on Mariah's progress. Whenever he learned something new, he reported back to Lincoln and Mrs. Keckly. After doctors determined she was clear of smallpox, they moved her to a tented women's ward while she regained her strength.

One night after she moved to the tented ward, a storm struck with violent winds pushing torrential rains. The deluge was so intense William worried the city's sewage canal would overrun its banks, swamping the camp. He imagined effluence seeping from under the floorboards of the sick bays and festering—pestilence invading Mariah's straw mattress and bedclothes. She was in mortal danger. If some other disease didn't strike, pneumonia might overtake her weakened lungs as she breathed squalid air.

William bolted from his bed, scurried to the stable, and drove off in Lincoln's carriage. A steady downpour persisted as he arrived and found nurses at work in Mariah's ward, struggling to patch leaks in the tent's walls and roof. Mariah was not on her cot but huddled with other patients in a corner on the rain-drenched wood floor. Torn canvas flapped overhead. William pulled her up, slung his coat over her shoulders, and ushered her out to the carriage.

An hour later, he parked in front of Slade's boarding house. Mr. Slade had likely gone to the mansion already, but William figured Mrs. Slade would be preparing breakfast for her boarders. He ushered Mariah up the steps to the front door and knocked.

Mrs. Slade didn't need to hear why they were at her door. She turned the morning chores over to her oldest daughter,

Josephine, and heated water for a bath. After the bath, she dressed Mariah in dry clothes and put her to bed with a clean quilt. The Slades had only one spare room, and it had to be turned over at the end of the month to a new boarder. William would have to make other arrangements for Mariah after that.

Executive Mansion—September 1863

William dropped off a message from Secretary Chase late one afternoon at the new First National Bank of Washington. As William left, the bank's cashier gave him a pouch to deliver to Lincoln.

When William handed over the pouch, Lincoln pointed to the chairs by the window. "Come over here and sit with me. I think this concerns you."

"What business does the bank have with me?" William asked.

Lincoln opened the pouch and shuffled through the documents. "Yes. As I expected." Lincoln peered over his steel-rimmed glasses. "I understand you and Miss Mariah are wrestling with a knotty problem."

"Where did you hear that?" William asked.

"Mr. Slade."

William stared down at the floor. "You see, Mariah has been staying with Mr. and Mrs. Slade since the storm tore up the hospital tents."

"Yes. He told me about that. I understand Mariah has to give up her room on account of a new renter."

William nodded.

"Is there a reason you did not ask if she could have a room in the basement?"

"I didn't think Mrs. Lincoln would approve," William replied.

"You might have been right, but I could have pressed her. I did check, however, and we're all full up it seems."

"I knew that, too. I thought about begging Mrs. Lincoln to let Mariah stay in my room—"

Lincoln held up his hand. "Mrs. Lincoln would not have budged on that."

"That's why I didn't ask."

"Forgive me if I'm sticking my nose where it does not belong, but—"

"Yes?" William asked.

"Do you love her?"

"Very much, sir."

"Does she love you?" Lincoln asked.

"I suppose so."

"Has she told you she does?" Lincoln pressed.

William squirmed in his chair. "Well, yes."

"Do you intend to marry?" Lincoln removed his spectacles.

"When she had smallpox, I had nightmares. I was hunkered down in a trench, clutching my rifle, waiting for the sergeant to sound the charge. Mariah would be standing above me on the edge, begging me to come home. A baby sat at her feet, clinging to her leg, crying. All I wanted to do was throw down my weapon and hold her in my arms."

Lincoln laid the documents on the table between them. "The bank has agreed to lend you $150 for buying property of your own. If you want, Mariah can have a place to live until you are married then you can move in with her."

"The bank wants to lend me money?" William's eyes widened. "They would lend money to a Negro?"

"There's a thing called an endorsement," Lincoln replied. "When the President of the United States gives one and when he agrees to issue to the bank the first $5 National Bank Notes that come off the government's printing press, he can get them to do almost anything he wants."

"You did that?"

"Of course." Lincoln pushed the documents closer to William. "You have to sign the loan as borrower and accept full responsibility to repay every last cent, including interest."

"But who's going to sell me a house? I know Mr. Slade owns property, but he says it's a big risk. A white man could swoop in and steal the title with phony documents. No court is going to stand up for any Negro over a white man."

Lincoln nodded. "I understand the risk. I used to handle all of Billy Florville's properties back in Illinois. Now, Herndon takes care of them. If you run into trouble of that sort, I shall stand behind you."

"The only problem is, I don't know what Mariah wants."

"I cannot help you with that." Lincoln returned his spectacles to his pocket.

William spent the next week scouring Washington's first and second wards. A block of row houses on R Street near Contraband Camp caught his eye. A sign in the window of one of the houses read *For Sale*. William scribbled a note and went to find Slade. He figured Slade knew the ins and outs of buying property in the city—especially pertaining to Negroes.

Slade caught the glint in William's eyes when they met in the hallway outside Lincoln's office.

"I found a house," William blurted.

Slade was trapped between celebration and confusion.

"Did you hear me? Mariah and I can get married."

"Whoa," Slade said. "You have not talked with Mariah?"

"What do you mean?" William asked.

"She's packing to move back to the camp."

William spun around and raced to the stables to saddle one of the horses.

Slade Boarding House—September 1863

When William arrived at Slade's boarding house, he bounded upstairs and burst into Mariah's room.

She turned to greet him.

"What are you doing?" he asked.

"I'm packing—going back to the hospital. I'm going to be a nurse."

William threw up his hands. "Am I the last person you were going to tell?"

"I just came from there," Mariah replied. "The surgeon offered me the job in the smallpox ward this morning."

"I didn't know you were looking for work."

"I can't stay here forever. I need a place to stay and a way to support myself."

"Why?"

"What do you mean, 'why'?" Mariah crossed her arms.

"I'm going to support us."

Mariah froze.

William swallowed hard. "I want to marry you."

"You want to marry me or own me?"

"Marry," he repeated.

"So, I can still be a nurse?" she asked.

He paused.

"I thought so." She turned and continued packing.

"No. I mean, yes," he stammered. "You can still be a nurse."

She stopped packing. "What about going to war?"

"I promise. I'll never leave you. Not for war or anything."

"What if I go to war?" she asked. "As a nurse."

"I'll go with you. I'll be a nurse, too."

"Fine."

William tilted his head. "Does that mean yes?"

She threw her arms around him.

He leaned back. "But what if I'm drafted?"

She gazed into his eyes. "Then I'll go with you."

"I'm going to buy a house," he whispered.

"How?"

"That's what I came to tell you. Mr. Lincoln helped me get a loan."

"You want me to marry a man who's deep in debt?"

"I have two jobs," he replied. "With your wages, we'll have more than enough."

"You want to marry me for my money?" Mariah punched him gently.

"No. I want to marry you because I love you."

"Well, I guess that's a good enough start."

CHAPTER NINETEEN

Gettysburg, Pennsylvania—November 1863

Lincoln's sallow, sunken-eyed visage raised William's alarm the morning they were to leave for Gettysburg. William suggested they stay home. Lincoln insisted the trip would not be taxing. He would rest on the train and get a good night's sleep after they arrived. He would not be giving the main address at the cemetery the next day. He would listen to Senator Everett's certain-to-be-lengthy, dramatic speech. Lincoln's speech would be only twenty-nine lines. Then he'd pay his respects and board the train back to Washington.

The five-car *Northern Central Special* passed through Hanover Station about six o'clock in the evening—they were just under an hour from Gettysburg. A few minutes earlier,

Lincoln began complaining of dizziness and achy joints. William reached into his sack and offered an apple. Lincoln took a bite and rested his head against the window. He held the apple limply. William retrieved the apple to prevent it from slipping out of Lincoln's hand and tumbling to the floor.

Cabinet members Seward, Blair, and Usher rode in the same railcar, along with other dignitaries, a few journalists, and Nicolay and Hay. Mrs. Lincoln remained in the city, tending to Tad who had been ill with fever for two weeks.

On their arrival in the town of Gettysburg, Lincoln braved a crowd that descended on the depot and rode horseback directly to the cemetery to assess the area and review plans for the next day's ceremony. Afterwards, he settled in at the home of David Wills, a lawyer who originated the idea of a national burial ground on the battlefield where more men died than at any other place in the war. Mr. Wills had prepared a second-story guestroom that overlooked the town square for Lincoln's stay.

After bidding his host good night, Lincoln and William retired to the guestroom where Lincoln sat at a small desk, pain wracking his body. He battled exhaustion but had been inspired by the day's sights and wanted to make changes to his speech. He read aloud revised passages and asked William, "What do you think?"

On one occasion, William pointed to a place in the speech, saying, "Mister Longfellow wrote some verse that might fit here. *Lives of great men all remind us we can make our lives sublime, and, departing, leave behind us footprints on the sands of time.*"

"By Jove, I think you're right," Lincoln replied. Then he inserted the words: *The world will little note, nor long remember what we say here, but it can never forget what they did here.*

When Lincoln was satisfied with all of the changes, he went to Seward's hotel room for final suggestions.

When Lincoln returned to the guestroom, William insisted on staying the night with him, in case his condition worsened. Lincoln was too fatigued to argue.

Lincoln rose early the next morning, feverish and achy. Nonetheless, he rousted Seward from bed to join him and an army scout on a horseback ride. William rode along, as well. They headed west from Gettysburg and up the steep climb to Lutheran Theological Seminary. The institution sat atop a ridge overlooking a broad valley. Rebel units had descended from the seminary to the valley floor, winding through woods. The scout led them along the route the rebels had followed on their surprise attack against General Reynolds' left wing. After crossing a field, they came to the wood where Reynolds suffered his fatal wound. Lincoln took off his hat and bowed his head. Tears welled in his eyes.

After returning for breakfast at the Wills's home, Lincoln made additional changes to his short speech, which had grown to thirty-eight-and-a-half lines.

At the ceremony that afternoon, Lincoln took his place with other dignitaries on a wooden platform. Rows of white grave markers—thousands of them—covered a slope below. Near the platform from behind a large oak, William kept his eye on Lincoln's every move. Lincoln sat like a rag doll propped in a chair. Sweat glistened on his sallow forehead. To William, he looked forlorn, uninspired by the news he had just received that Tads' fever had broken.

While Former Senator Edward Everett of Massachusetts, the principal speaker, spellbound the audience for more than two hours, Lincoln's headache grew more intense. His throat was raw. William spotted him wincing from time to time and shifting in the chair to ease aches and pains or to hold back bile that was worming up his throat. William imagined the memory of Willie's futile war with fever must have been preying on Lincoln's mind.

When Lincoln rose to speak, he unfolded his lanky frame—more awkwardly than usual—and took two pages from his pocket. Before he put on his spectacles, he squinted into the distance, straining to bring into focus the woods where General John Reynolds met his end.

He began.

> *Four score and seven years ago our fathers brought forth on this continent, a new Nation, conceived in Liberty, and dedicated to the proposition that all men are created equal.*
>
> *Now we are engaged in a great civil war, testing whether that Nation, or any Nation so conceived and dedicated, can long endure. We are met on a great battlefield of that war. We have come to dedicate a portion of that field, as a final resting place for those who here gave their lives that that Nation might live. It is altogether fitting and proper that we should do this.*
>
> *But, in a larger sense, we cannot dedicate — we cannot consecrate — we cannot hallow — this ground. The brave men, living and dead, who struggled here, have consecrated it, far above our poor power to add or detract. The world will little note, nor long remember what we say here, but it can never forget what they did here. It is for us the living, rather, to be dedicated here to the unfinished work which they who fought here have*

> *thus far so nobly advanced. It is rather for us to be here dedicated to the great task remaining before us — that from these honored dead we take increased devotion to that cause for which they gave the last full measure of devotion — that we here highly resolve that these dead shall not have died in vain — that this Nation, under God, shall have a new birth of freedom — and that Government of the people, by the people, for the people, shall not perish from the earth.*

Lincoln walked off the platform at four o'clock in the afternoon and returned to the Wills's home for a late lunch and informal reception. William kept close watch on Lincoln, whose typically light appetite was less than scant. Lincoln braced himself against a wall while in the hallway shaking hands with visitors. Among them was 69-year-old John L. Burns, a former Gettysburg police constable and veteran of the War of 1812. When Lincoln learned, even before leaving Washington, that Burns had been wounded three times during the massive early July battle, he insisted they meet. Burns received his wounds while aiding General Meredith's Iron Brigade on the first day of fighting.

William wasted no time in getting Lincoln aboard the Washington-bound train after the reception. Lincoln's malaise deepened, his head wobbled, and he stared blankly as the railcar passed a stack of white caskets—bodies of battle casualties who had died in recent days at Gettysburg hospitals. Lincoln stretched out on a bench and laid his head on William's lap as the train steamed out of Gettysburg.

William called for cold water and towels to bathe Lincoln's head and chest as the fever raged. Reddish eruptions on Lincoln's skin were tell-tale signs of a smallpox infection. That was one of many things William learned from listening to Mariah describe her work at Contraband Camp.

William was not unaware of the risk he was taking, exposing himself to such a contagious, often-fatal disease, while continuing to bathe Lincoln with the cool, wet towels. But paramount on his mind was the truth that the nation could not survive without President Lincoln—anymore that he could not envision going on living without Mariah.

Mariah ... what if he ... what would she do? A new thought crossed his mind. If someone had reacted sooner when his brother, Thomas, was stricken with fever, he might have survived. William laid another cool towel over Lincoln's brow.

Executive Mansion—November-December 1863

Lincoln returned to the mansion so weak and debilitated by pain that William and Nicolay carried him upstairs to his bed.

When Dr. Stone examined Lincoln a short time later, he reported, "Mr. President, it appears you suffer from a severe cold."

William shook his head. "But what about the rash?"

Dr. Stone sneered. "I was unaware your man, here, is a trained doctor. Maybe my services are unnecessary."

"He's worried my malady is more serious," Lincoln answered, his voice shaky. "I am sure he meant no disrespect."

William pursed his lips.

"Well, I suppose it wouldn't do much harm to quarantine you for a few days here in your chamber." The doctor glared at William. "A good rest is sometimes the best medicine for the common cold. I am certain your man can fetch whatever materials you need to keep up on the nation's business."

During Lincoln's illness, William served as his principal contact with the outside world and as enforcer of the quarantine. Even Mrs. Lincoln was kept away from her ailing husband. Mariah joined William for night-long vigils when she was able to get away from the smallpox ward at Contraband Camp, never burdening William or Lincoln with reports of the camp's fast-deteriorating conditions.

William ran regular errands to the War Department for reports from the front that he relayed to Lincoln. In Tennessee, rebels continued their assault on Union troops in Chattanooga until Grant finally defeated Braxton Braggs's forces. In Virginia, General Meade bombarded Lee's army, but inexplicably withdrew. In Georgia, Union General Hooker was defeated. Later in Tennessee, rebel General Longstreet failed to take a Union fort due to poor quality gunpowder. Lincoln meekly regarded Longstreet's misfortune as a victory.

As smallpox continued its siege on Lincoln, William resolved to provide comfort in any way he could, knowing there was little else that could be done. When the red rash developed into scattered blisters, Dr. Stone changed his diagnosis to bilious fever. A couple of days later, Dr. Stone changed his diagnosis again. Scarlentina. Then fluid-filled sacs developed on Lincoln's skin, and William convinced Nicolay it was time to call in a second doctor.

Dr. Washington Chew Van Bibber examined Lincoln and told him, "If I were to give a name to your malady, I should say that you have a touch of varioloid."

"Then am I to understand I have the smallpox?"

Doctor Van Bibber nodded.

"How interesting." Lincoln sighed. "I find that every now and then, unpleasant situations in life may have certain compensation. As you came in just now, did you pass through the waiting room?"

"I passed through a room full of people, yes," the doctor replied.

"That's the waiting room, and it's always full of people. Many of them have been here for days, even sleeping in their seats so they do not lose their places in line. Do you have any idea what they are there for?"

"Perhaps I could guess," the doctor replied.

"They are there, every mother's son of them, for one purpose only—they wait for me to get well so they can get something from me. For once in my life as president, I find myself in a position to give everybody something."

By the tenth day of Lincoln's illness, his fever subsided, and the blisters dried. He began contending with itchy, peeling skin. William breathed a sigh of relief. This had been the turning point in Mariah's recovery. If the blisters had spread and ballooned, one on top of the other, Lincoln wouldn't have survived. Once, while alone with Lincoln, William confessed, "If you had come to the point of death, I would have begged God to take me in your place."

"I reckon God didn't know that were so," Lincoln replied. "For he would have gotten the better end of the bargain and would have taken your offer without argument."

In early December, Lincoln got out of bed to walk briefly. The itching subsided, replaced by pock marks. Weakness held him back from resuming a full work schedule for a few more days, and the public remained nervous. To allay their fears, Lincoln attended a performance of *Henry IV* at Ford's Theater.

Soon after Lincoln returned to work, he sent a ship to Hayti to bring back 453 former slaves who had survived his failed colonization experiment. Lincoln decided the government's energy and investment was better spent on building and maintaining freedman villages at home.

He also approved an order to close Contraband Camp and move the residents to a new freedman's village on the grounds of General Lee's former plantation at Arlington. Polluted drinking water, inadequate sewage, lack of supplies, and a shortage of stoves for heating had turned the camp into a breeding ground for disease. Contraband Hospital would remain open even though the Camp's military commander complained the hospital had become a house of death and decay, rather than healing.

Contraband Camp—December 1863

William was helping Mariah in the smallpox ward when the order came for camp residents to report to the Army Quartermaster for relocation. Mariah threw up her hands, "They're not solving anything. All they're doing is packing up a disease and giving it a new address."

William reached out to her, offering consolation.

She recoiled.

"I'll talk to Mr. Lincoln," he said.

"What makes you think he'll do anything?" she shouted. "At least Major Augusta cared, but things have fallen apart these last two months since they transferred him out. With the new white commander, we've gotten no blankets, no stoves. The best we have is clothes that barely preserve decency, let alone keep folks warm—and it's already winter, for God's sake. But Mr. Lincoln is cozy in that fancy mansion. If he is so concerned, why doesn't he come and see for himself how he can help? I'll tell you why—all the white folks building their fancy new homes nearby don't like knowing we exist. Something becomes a problem, just move it somewhere it can be ignored."

"No. He's been good to us," William pleaded. "It might have taken him a while, but he freed thousands of our people and let them go into the army. He gave us a chance to fight our own fight."

"*Pfft*. The freedom he gave us was ours to begin with. And he still pays colored soldiers half what whites get. Those of us braving diseases at the camp make far less. He thinks we're not good enough to share the load equally."

"But he is making a difference," William insisted. "Remember the loan? That house we're going to buy up on R Street? What other white man would do that for us? Maybe he'll make all this right if I ask him."

"You can try if you want," she conceded. "But it's time people—our people—stood up for ourselves."

"Fine. Just don't do anything to stir the pot. Not until I talk to him."

Executive Mansion—December 1863

William hurried back to the mansion where he found Lincoln finishing a letter before attending theater that evening. Lincoln continued writing as William lodged his complaint.

When William begged him to delay the move until winter's brutal weather passed, Lincoln replied, "I understand your passion over the problems at the Camp, but Quartermaster Greene assures me the move is in everyone's best interest. The residents are living in unsanitary, squalid conditions. The smallpox crisis at the Camp is out of hand. Poor souls are dying every day."

"That's not so," William objected. "The illness has been contained. There's sufficient housing and bedding. We only lack enough warm clothes and heating stoves for everyone."

"At the new village, things will be better," Lincoln insisted.

"Folks at Contraband Camp are afraid of the new village."

Lincoln asked, "On what basis?"

"Crossing the river in the bitter cold. Rumors of raids by rebel guerillas. Many of the older residents remember the superintendent at the new village. He was cruel when he was director at Contraband Camp—worse than many slave owners. They don't want to be under his thumb again, especially at General Lee's old plantation—that place provokes horrible memories for many."

Lincoln rubbed his brow. "What can I do to make this pill easier for the folks to swallow?"

"Wait until spring. In the meantime, end the segregation of men and women in the barracks. Families want to live together. Being separated is something they thought would end with freedom." William paused then straightened, his voice strong. "If you truly want to do good by them, give them what they need to live humanely right where they are, among their friends here in the city. Come and see for yourself."

Lincoln patted William on the shoulder. "I'll see about it."

Contraband Camp—December 1863

William returned to Contraband Camp and reported Lincoln's reaction, but Mariah dug in her heels. The residents were staying put, and the government better provide the leadership and services they needed. She began organizing a movement to resist the removal order.

When the deadline passed for Contraband Camp's residents to report to the Army Quartermaster, only a fourth of the folks had complied. More than a hundred had already fled to temporary shelter in the surrounding area. Mariah's resentment over the government's neglect deepened, even as William held out hope the bond he had forged with Lincoln would pay off. It wasn't as if he was crying for the moon. He only asked to delay the move until spring and make folks as comfortable as possible in the meantime. If only Lincoln could come and see for himself what was needed, he would be able to make a way for people to stay in the city where they had begun to put down roots.

Three days before Christmas, Lincoln had not given William an answer. Instead, army wagons rolled into the Camp, one of them carrying a detail of soldiers. As soon as the blue-clad infantrymen jumped out of the wagon, they began rounding up the remaining residents—pushing and shoving with their weapons, only giving them time to gather a few of their sparse belongings.

An old man sat on his straw mattress in the barracks, shouting, "I's been sent off to one plantation after 'nother since I was a boy ... carried off to that Duff Green's Row by my sister's boy ... whisked off here ... never asked what I cares for. Now that the government says I's free, I's stayin' put."

Several soldiers approached. More than a dozen residents gathered around the man, locking arms to form a human barricade, and yelling at the soldiers to go away. The soldiers charged the resisters, grabbing wherever they could gain a solid hold and wrenching several to the ground. With the wall of defenders breached, two soldiers broke through and yanked the old man from his bunk. He dropped to the ground and insisted on being dragged.

William stood, his mouth agape, while Mariah cajoled the residents to keep resisting. William pleaded with Mariah. He could turn Lincoln to her side if he gave it one more try.

“Talk all you want,” she sputtered. “But I’m not waiting on him. Besides, why are we always worried about pleasing white folks. It’s about time they understood we are equal to them in the eyes of God.”

William rode hard toward the mansion. Surely, Lincoln would order the army to stop the removal. He probably had been preoccupied with more urgent business and didn’t know what was happening.

William bounded up the stairs to Lincoln’s office and found him at his desk, grinning broadly. “Sir, may I have a minute?”

“Of course.” Lincoln held up a letter he had been reading. “And you might be interested in this. Billy Florville wrote me. He says our dog, Fido, is healthy and happy.”

“That’s good,” William replied, fingering the brim of his hat as he held it at his waist.

“He also says he is sorry to hear about my illness and hopes I am getting well. I must write him and tell him his wishes are realized and we all have you to thank for that.”

“It was the Almighty’s pleasure that I could help, sir.”

“So, what is it you need?” Lincoln asked.

Lincoln exploded when William explained that Mariah was leading the Contraband Camp residents in a rebellion against the government’s plans. He demanded that William reel her in.

William turned and started for the door but stopped. Lincoln’s words “reel her in” reverberated in his ears. No. That wasn't the way it would be. Speaking truth was the highest form of loyalty, and he could be loyal to both Mariah and Lincoln by doing exactly that.

William walked back and stood toe to toe with Lincoln. "You are the one who's wrong. We have flesh and bones and we bleed the same as you and every other white man. All we ask for is our God-given humanity. Instead, you treat us like livestock. You think you have freed us, but you have not. Not until you recognize our equality. Not until you pay Negro soldiers the same as whites. Not until you promote Negroes to be officers in your army. Not until you come to our aid, just as you would for any suffering white man, woman, or child. Just as you should have done for those Sioux Indians in Minnesota."

William stormed out of Lincoln's office, his jaw tight and fists clenched. The Missouri farmer's old Negro had been right—*only a fool Negro trusts a white man. No matter how nice they seems, they always use you up and casts you aside when they's done.* Just like Captain Brown wanted to impose his North Star on William, Lincoln would sacrifice the humanity of 4 million Black *stumbling blocks* in order to save the Union.

Contraband Hospital—New Year's Eve 1863

Mariah dabbed the forehead of a Negro patient in his teens.

William pulled a chair from another patient's bedside and sat next to her. "How bad is he?"

"Too early to tell. Doctor says we'll have to wait to see if there's going to be blisters."

"I worry about you working day and night around all this sickness." William bowed his head.

"It's no different than it's ever been."

William handed her a fresh, wet towel. "We should start planning our wedding."

"I thought we were going to wait until ..." She faced him and searched his eyes.

He grinned.

"No?" Her lips curled into a smile.

"Yes," he answered. "I was just at the bank. I bought the house on R Street."

She dropped the towel and threw her arms around him. "I can't believe it," she shrieked. "We're going to own a house."

William pulled back, his jaw tightened. "As long as Mr. Lincoln lets it go through."

"You'll have to patch things up."

"Not until he apologizes. Besides, I still have my Treasury Department job."

Mariah's eyes widened. "That won't be enough to cover the loan. What if—"

"I suppose we'll see."

"You're going to gamble our future just to prove you're the bigger man? Have you stopped to think about the kind of home you want to raise children in?" She folded her arms across her chest.

He straightened in his chair. "And working around all this sickness isn't a bigger gamble?"

CHAPTER TWENTY

Executive Mansion—January 1864

Lincoln received a message from the bank on Monday after the new year. William had requested to draw on his loan to purchase property on R Street. He endorsed the bank's memorandum and put it in a messenger pouch along with William's December payroll draft. Slade passed the pouch to William a couple of days later.

Lincoln still refused to have his hair and beard trimmed by anyone other than William. At last, Mrs. Lincoln strode into his office with Slade in her wake. She stamped her foot. "Enough is enough."

Lincoln sat down hard in the barber's chair, and when Slade began clipping, Mrs. Lincoln left the room.

"By now," Lincoln said, "he must have heard about the four Africans who joined the receiving line at our New Year's reception. Have you seen anything of him lately?"

Slade hesitated.

"Is there a problem?" Lincoln asked.

"I was hoping William would tell you himself."

Lincoln scowled. "I was hoping Jeff Davis would give up this infernal war."

"William paid me a visit a couple of weeks ago. He and Mariah plan to marry in the spring."

"I reckon I shall have to send him my congratulations. Maybe I can get his address from the bank."

"He spends all of his time at Contraband Hospital, helping Mariah. I suppose that's where he sleeps."

"Thank you. If he does not show himself in a couple more days, I shall go there personally and drag him back."

Slade shook off the barber's cape and offered Lincoln a mirror.

Lincoln waved him off.

Contraband Camp—January 1864

Mariah sat at William's bedside, her head bowed, hope fleeting.

"Mariah," William wheezed.

"*Shh* ... save your strength."

"It's no use." He coughed. "I know what happens in cases like mine."

Mariah's tired, swollen eyes ached. He was right. He'd watched her comfort too many on the throes of death in the camp's smallpox ward. The disease had taken his sight. It was only a matter of time before it claimed his last breath.

"I only wish—" he murmured.

"No regrets," she whispered.

"I can't see your tears—but I know they are there."

Her throat seized up. "Hold my love in your heart."

"I never wanted to cause you pain."

"You've brought me more joy than I could have imagined."

"I wish I could have found Grace and Maddie. You would have loved them both."

"I'm sure your brother is watching over them."

He coughed. "I suppose I'll be seeing Thomas soon."

"When you get there, don't go wasting your time watching after me." Her voice cracked. "I'll be just fine."

"I'll always watch over you."

She leaned forward and kissed his head. "Close your eyes now and get some sleep."

* * *

That evening Lincoln saddled his horse and slogged through muddy streets to what remained of the Camp. The tents were gone. Everyone had moved out, except the medical staff and patients who were relocated to the old barracks.

A wisp of smoke rose from the kitchen chimney. The warm glow of a lantern filled the window.

Lincoln hitched his horse to a post and tried the latch on the kitchen door. It clicked. He eased the door open.

Mariah sat alone at a table, her head in her hands.

"Excuse me," he said.

She didn't look up.

"I am looking for William. Is he around?" Lincoln asked.

"You can't see him."

"Miss Mariah?"

She glanced at him.

"I am—"

"I know who you are."

"I imagine you're angry," he said.

"I'm tired."

"If I could just talk with him," Lincoln pleaded.

She shook her head. "You can't."

"I need him," he begged.

"Me, too." She peered at Lincoln, her eyes red and swollen.

"Mr. Slade told me you're getting married. That's wonderful."

She burst into tears.

"Tell me. What's wrong?" Lincoln laid his hand on her shoulder.

"Smallpox," she muttered through her sobs. "He's going to die."

"Where is he?" Lincoln asked.

"The barracks across the way." She wiped her tears.

Lincoln bolted out the door and crossed the path to the old barracks. When he barged in, he almost collided with a surgeon. Lincoln demanded, "Smallpox ward."

"It's under quarantine," the surgeon answered. "You cannot go in."

"I am the president and I have been inoculated."

"If you insist. Follow me."

As they walked briskly down a hallway, Lincoln explained, "I am here to see a smallpox patient, William Johnson. Do you know which bed he's in?"

The surgeon led him to a far corner of a crowded bay. William's bed was isolated from the others.

Lincoln gazed at William's face, damp with sweat. William's mouth hung open, lips swollen, tongue covered with black ridges. More shallow dark ridges formed over his face and arms as if an infestation of leeches had burrowed under his skin and died there.

The surgeon fetched a chair. "Take as long as you need, but I don't believe he'll know you're here. He does not have much time left."

"There must be something you can do," Lincoln pleaded.

"All we can do is keep him as comfortable as possible." The surgeon started to walk away but turned back. "In this place, any amount of comfort is a luxury."

Lincoln's eyes misted. "There is so much need, but so little ability to act."

Mariah joined Lincoln at William's bedside. She held William's courier pouch in her lap. "The surgeon gives him medicine to help him sleep."

"Sleep is good." Lincoln's voice had grown hoarse.

"He asked me to give this to you." She handed the pouch to Lincoln. "It's his payroll check and some other personal papers. He thought Mr. Hay could take care of them." Tears streamed down her cheeks.

"I will tend to them." Lincoln clutched the pouch.

She sniffled. Lincoln offered his kerchief. She thanked him and blew her nose.

"If there is anything I can do," Lincoln whispered.

"That's kind of you, sir, but I like being free, standing on my own. William and I came to an understanding about that. I could be me. He could be who he—"

She wept.

Lincoln bowed his head. "Freedom is a precious thing."

"Liberty is the summit," she murmured. "Equality is its base."

First National Bank of Washington—January 1864

Lincoln stopped at the bank across the street from the mansion and gave the cashier William's payroll draft to exchange for greenbacks. The cashier smiled. "Do you run errands for everyone you employ?"

"This, sir, is something out of my usual line, but the president has a multiplicity of duties not specified in the Constitution or acts of Congress. This is one of them."

The cashier counted out fifty dollars in greenbacks. Lincoln thanked him and took the money to a desk where he sorted it into envelopes according to William's instructions.

Executive Mansion—January 1864

The mansion doors opened to the public for one of Mrs. Lincoln's regular formal receptions at eight o'clock on the last Tuesday evening of January. Eight thousand crammed into the lobby and parlors. Many had waited hours in the bitter cold before they entered.

Among those in attendance, an English doctor named Thompson walked in with a beautiful 18-year-old woman on his arm. Her skin was fair, and her eyes deep emerald. Only three people noticed the whites-only rule had been violated—for a second time in less than a month. One of the three who noticed was Mrs. Lincoln. After four Negro gentlemen joined her white guests at the New Year reception, she put her foot down and reminded everyone that the rule remained in force.

The second person who recognized young Josephine Slade was her father. While Slade beamed with pride at his daughter's act of rebellion, he knew there would be hell to pay in the morning. Mrs. Lincoln might have overlooked the incident in front of her guests, but in the privacy of her chamber, she would give Slade a piece of her mind. Josephine often chaperoned Tad when he played with her brothers and sister in the Slades' 1st Ward home. She also worked as a seamstress in Mrs. Keckly's thriving business, sometimes assisting at the mansion with Mrs. Lincoln's wardrobe.

Lincoln was the third to recognize Josephine. He welcomed her and the doctor with hardy handshakes, a smile, and a wink. Josephine winked back. She admired him for his evolving opinions on Negro equality and women's suffrage. His thinking had come a long way since the war began. She had noted his progress as he shared private thoughts, out of the public eye, at her father's home. However, Josephine's friend, Lucy Colman, who dared her to attend the reception on Dr. Thompson's arm, doubted Lincoln wanted anything more than to end the war and save the Union. Ending slavery, Lucy Colman insisted, was a secondary concern and Negro equality had never been so much as a visitor in his mind.

The next morning a message arrived at the mansion from Contraband Hospital. Lincoln dropped into a chair at his desk and wept. After composing himself, he passed through the basement on his way to the stables, pausing at the door to William's old room. It had remained vacant since the day they argued. At some point, William's sparse belongings had been removed. Nothing remained for Lincoln to keep as a memorial of their friendship.

Contraband Camp—January 1864

An icy wind stung Lincoln's eyes as he galloped toward Contraband Hospital. At that moment, the only war on his mind was the one waged on him by Providence. When he reached the hospital, he tied his horse and raced to the barracks, down the hallway, and into the bay where he had last seen William.

Lincoln spun around, searching for someone to help him. He approached a nurse. "I am looking for William Johnson."

"I'm sorry, sir. He's gone."

"I know. Where did they take him?"

"To the dead house, sir."

"Where is that?" Lincoln asked, his eyes misting.

"Up beyond the stables."

Lincoln bolted out of the barracks and raced past the stables. At the door to the dead house, he paused and calmed himself.

Inside, he found Mariah preparing William's disfigured body for burial. He approached and put his hand on her shoulder.

She turned and Lincoln pulled her to his chest. They wept in each other's arms.

"I left a note for Nicolay," Lincoln whispered. "He's arranging a coffin for the burial."

"We have coffins."

"No. That will not do," Lincoln murmured. "Let me tend to it."

"Thank you." She bit her lip.

"The last words we exchanged were in anger. He deserved much better than I ever gave him."

She wiped her tears. "I'm guilty of that, too."

"Is there anything I can do for you?"

"Honor William. What he wanted most in this life was for his manhood and his God-given equality to be respected. He and his older brother, Thomas, bought their freedom with hard work. Thomas died of fever, and William promised to protect his family—his wife and daughter. But they were separated when Border Ruffians attacked the village. They were made slaves again. William escaped with the help of some abolitionists. He was looking for Grace and Maddie when he met you."

"He never told me any of this."

"You were his last hope. He thought if all the slaves were freed, families could find each other. But he stopped trusting you. He complained you saw emancipation as a stumbling block to peace, that you valued peace above liberty. With peace bought so cheaply, Negro freedom would be nothing more than an exchange of one master for another. Wounds would continue to fester. Rebellion would be inevitable."

Lincoln furrowed his brow. "What more could I do?"

"William believed 'liberty is the summit and equality is its base.' He read that in a book. He thought if white people could see Negroes as equals, much of life's miseries would disappear. The Good Book has a rule—do to others what you would have them do to you."

"How can I do that? I am bound by so many constraints."

"Break loose from your shackles. Free yourself first, so you can free others."

"What will you do, now?" Lincoln asked.

"Keep nursing, I guess. Maybe I'll take up William's search for Grace and Maddie."

Executive Mansion—January 1864

Lincoln sat at his desk and shuffled through papers, searching for the manifesto he had written in the weeks before leaving Springfield. He had reread it many times since taking on the mantle of the presidency. He read it again, focusing on its essence.

> *No oppressed people will fight and endure as our fathers did, without the promise of something better than a mere change of masters ... something entwined more closely about the human heart ... the principle of "Liberty to all" ... the principle that clears the path for all, gives hope to all, and, by consequence, enterprise and industry to all.*

Each morning thereafter, Lincoln read the manifesto before he did anything else, and William's words echoed in his mind: *If liberty is the summit, equality is its base.*

Equality would become his true north.

First National Bank of Washington—February 1864

Lincoln crossed the street to the bank several days after William died. No sooner than he stepped through the door, the cashier approached. "Mr. President, I hear the barber who used to groom you is dead."

Lincoln's voice trembled. "I bought a coffin for the poor fellow and gave him a proper burial."

"I do not want to seem indelicate," the cashier replied. "But I've been thinking about the loans we made."

"No apology is required," Lincoln said. "I was intending to take care of them."

"There is no need. The bank is prepared to forgive his loans."

"No, you don't." Lincoln argued. "I endorsed the notes and am bound to pay them. It is your duty to see that I do."

"Yes, sir, but it has been our custom to devote a portion of the bank's profits to charitable objects, and this seems to be a most deserving one."

"I appreciate the sentiment, but I must fulfill my obligation. It's the least I owe William."

"I will tell you how we can arrange this," the cashier said. "The loans to William were joint ones between you and the bank. You stand half of the loss, and I will cancel the other."

"That sounds fair, but it's insidious. You are going to get ahead of me. You are going to give me the smallest note to pay. There must be a fair divide over poor William. Reckon up the interest on both notes, and chop the whole straight through the middle, so that my half shall be as big as yours. That's the way we will fix it."

The cashier offered a handshake.

Lincoln took his hand and shook it heartily.

"After this, Mr. President," the cashier said, "you can never deny that you endorse the Negro."

Lincoln smiled. "That's a fact that I do not intend to deny."

Executive Mansion—April 1864

Slade brought Lincoln his newspapers, having made sure an article concerning Major Alexander Augusta would be the first item to catch Lincoln's eye. A public furor erupted when the major, one of the army's highest-ranking colored officers, was put off a streetcar and made to stand in the driving rain.

Lincoln had met Augusta months earlier at Contraband Hospital while the major was posted there as surgeon-in-charge.

"This needs to be made right," Lincoln demanded. He called for Nicolay and instructed him to invite Augusta to the next public reception at the mansion.

A couple of weeks later, Major Augusta and his aide, Dr. Anderson Abbott, wore military dress uniforms when they arrived for the last formal reception of the season. Benjamin French, Commissioner of Public Buildings, greeted them on the mansion steps and ushered them to the head of the long line of white guests.

"Mr. President," French said. "I am privileged to introduce Drs. Augusta and Abbott."

Lincoln extended his hand to Major Augusta. "You have my sincere apology for the way you were treated recently on our city's streetcar."

"Thank you, sir," Major Augusta replied.

Bob, who had been at his mother's side, walked over to his father and muttered, "Are you going to allow this invasion?"

Lincoln recoiled. "Why not? They are my guests."

Bob shrunk back and returned to his mother's side.

Drs. Augusta and Abbott strode off and mingled with the others. Some greeted them warmly, others exchanged tentative handshakes, and a few turned away.

* * *

In the weeks after Major Augusta's so-called invasion of the mansion festivities, Lincoln and his Cabinet debated their response to the massacre of colored soldiers by rebel forces following a battle at Fort Pillow. More than three hundred colored troops who surrendered on the field of battle were executed after laying down their arms. The previous July, Lincoln threatened to retaliate in such incidents by executing an equal number of rebel officers held in Union prisons. Jeff Davis had thrown down the gauntlet.

Lincoln could not erase from his memory his arguments with William over the principle that equality is the base on which liberty stands. Alongside William's words, Mariah's admonition rang in his ears—"Break loose from your shackles. Free yourself first, so you can truly free others."

He drew up instructions for field commanders around Richmond, Virginia, and Charleston, South Carolina, ordering them to execute any rebels they captured who were directly responsible for the massacre at Fort Pillow. He also directed the War Department to identify by name three hundred rebel officers in Union prisons to be held as hostages. If there were further violations of the laws of war regarding white and colored Union soldiers, the hostages would be executed.

Lincoln added a second order suspending all exchanges of prisoners between the two armies until the rebels agreed to exchange colored soldiers on the same terms as whites.

After signing the orders, he placed them in William's courier pouch that Mariah had given him. He called for Nicolay and said, "Here. Take this to the War Department and deliver it to Mars."

Nicolay reached for the pouch, but Lincoln held it back.

"Sir?"

"Make sure you bring back my pouch," Lincoln replied.

EPILOGUE

Executive Mansion—June 1864

Lincoln signed *An Act making Appropriations for the Support of the Army for the Year ending the thirtieth June, eighteen hundred and sixty-five, and for other Purposes*, which established equal pay for colored soldiers in the Union army. The bill also authorized back pay to compensate for unequal pay received by certain soldiers prior to passage of the act.

Executive Mansion—April 11, 1865

Lincoln delivered a speech from a second story window of the mansion three nights before an assassin's bullet tore into his brain. For the first time, he advocated extending the citizens' right of suffrage to freed slaves. He did so, cautiously, as if probing the ocean of equality with a bare toe. On the lawn below, the renowned actor John Wilkes Booth seethed.

AUTHOR'S NOTE

The Turn does not pretend to offer answers as much as it raises the question: why does history record what it does?

Abraham Lincoln's world was populated by a diverse collection of people, from salt-of-the-earth farmers, runaway slaves, and the powerful elite, to neighbors, friends, family, and cronies. *The Turn* is a story that brings overlooked characters, particularly William Henry Johnson, into the spotlight. The usual cast of characters who dominate accounts of Lincoln's life take a backseat, but the events are real, or at least realistic, according to historical records. It is important to keep in mind, though, that I am a novelist and avocational historian. I write to explore themes and convey messages through drama. *The Turn* is a biographical novel in the style of Irving Stone, not an academic treatise.

William Henry Johnson was a real person whose life intersected with Abraham Lincoln's life between late 1859 or early 1860 and January 1864. Only a handful of facts about William were ever recorded. Among them, historians estimate he was 25 years old when he met Lincoln. In late 1861 Lincoln wrote that he had known William for less than two years. William worked for Lincoln in Springfield as a laborer. At least one anecdote places William on the train with Lincoln as they traveled to Washington for the inauguration. A note in Lincoln's handwriting indicates William was to have served as his valet but was spurned by other domestic staff at the White House because his skin was too dark. Elizabeth Keckly's memoir corroborates this understanding as does an account by John Washington in an anthology of recollections, *They Knew Lincoln.* Records exist of two bank drafts by Lincoln for $5 each made to William Johnson.

William's presence with Lincoln at Gettysburg, including the train ride from and back to Washington, was recorded by a journalist who traveled with the presidential entourage. During that trip, the journalist reported that William was the most valuable member of Lincoln's party, which included Secretary of State William Seward and two other Cabinet members. David Wills, the man who hosted Lincoln in his home during the Gettysburg visit, witnessed William in Lincoln's room, assisting the president with changes he was making to the Gettysburg Address. Historians acknowledge that Lincoln suffered from smallpox on his return from Gettysburg to Washington and that William attended him.

A bank cashier in Washington recalled Lincoln cashing William's payroll check in January 1864. Lincoln explained that his "barber" was sick with smallpox as he placed the greenbacks into envelopes per William's instructions. Days later, a journalist recorded a conversation between Lincoln and the same banker about two loans the bank had made to William with Lincoln as co-signer. The banker offered to forgive them in full, but Lincoln insisted on paying them. After some discussion, Lincoln and the banker compromised. They split the debt in half. In the same conversation, Lincoln said he paid for William's burial.

History has sparse records of William Johnson's life. He does not appear in census records. There is no record of his birth nor of any family relations. It is unknown whether he was a slave or freeman. Even his burial site is open to debate.

So, what makes William Johnson's life compelling? That question prompted me to examine his life events in relation to the timeline of Lincoln's dramatic shifts in policy regarding racial equality, particularly with respect to African Americans of his day. I began by noting that William Johnson appears to have been the first Black person to work closely with Lincoln on a day-to-day basis. While it is true that Lincoln had contact with African neighbors and businessmen in Springfield and he provided legal representation for some of them, his interactions seemed to have been governed by the customs of segregated society. William appears the first to have had regular conversations with Lincoln in the privacy of his office and bedroom.

The extraordinary personal investment Lincoln appears to have made in William implies they shared a deep bond. The proximity of William's death to dramatic shifts in Lincoln's racial policies suggests their relationship played a key role in turning Lincoln's thinking on racial equality.

Note that italicized block quotes are directly from public domain documents. Non-italicized block quotes are fictional.

DL Fowler

SUGGESTED DISCUSSION QUESTIONS

1. Much of the novel's characterization of William Johnson is speculative. What issues does this presentation prompt you to consider?

2. Historians know many of the details of Elizabeth Keckly and William Slade's lives, but William Johnson is largely an enigma. Why do you think this is the case?

3. What do you think was the basis for the bond between Lincoln and William Johnson?

4. Are there places in the book where you notice William's absence or thought he was overlooked? If so, what was your response?

5. Nurse Rebecca Pomroy seems to have had a profound effect on Lincoln's emotional and spiritual journeys. Why do you think she was able to have such an impact?

6. Native Americans fought alongside white Union soldiers from the early days of the Civil War, but that was not the case with people of African descent. How did Lincoln distinguish between the two groups?

7. What factors led Lincoln to change his mind about enlisting Black soldiers in the Union army as combatants?

8. What are some other examples of Lincoln's race-based policies?

9. How were Lincoln's views on race similar to or different from the prevailing racial views of southern leaders?

10. Did reading the novel change your thinking about Lincoln in any way?

11. Were William and Lincoln martyrs?

12. William Johnson used the phrase "if freedom is the summit, equality is the base," and Elizabeth Keckly used the phrase "equality is the bedrock of freedom." What do those phrases mean to you?

13. The novel focuses on a small cast of characters with whom Lincoln interacted daily and at close quarters. There were many other people who influenced Lincoln: politicians, journalists, friends, family, and clergymen. Who do you think likely influenced him the most during his presidency?

14. Why do you believe history records the people and events that it does?

15. In what ways can the story of *The Turn* be applied to contemporary American culture?

ACKNOWLEDGEMENTS

The Turn would not have come to life except for the insights, encouragement, and support from many special people. Among many others, I am especially indebted to my editor, Cheryl Ferguson Feeney, who holds my feet to the fire and pushes me to get the most out of every word I put on the page; my wife and proofreader, Judi Fowler, who patiently and lovingly gives me the space I need to follow my passions; my beta readers, Robert Dugoni, Jerry Pugnetti, Andy Becker, Richard Heller, and Alisa Weis for their valuable perspectives and cheerleading; Adam Jackman, my hometown librarian, for his support, and Dr. James Cornelius, former curator of the Lincoln Collection at the Abraham Lincoln Presidential Library for his insights and inspiration; Leonard Pitts, Jr. whose *Miami Herald* columns and tweets remind me daily why William Johnson's story deserves to be told; my friends, Sean Brown, April Emerson, Diptiman Chakravarti, Christina Butcher, Joe Kempston, Harold and Cecelia Kafer, Kit Wilson, and EC Murray for their persistent encouragement; and the Pacific Northwest Writers Association for opportunities to hone my craft, not the least of which are the annual writers contests and conferences.

I am particularly grateful to Jackie Casella for her leadership and devotion to advancing our local community of wordsmiths and artists, and to KM Weiland for her remarkable books and blog posts on the craft of storytelling.

ABOUT THE AUTHOR

Award-winning author DL Fowler (the Lincoln Guy) transports readers into his characters' inner worlds. His bestselling work, *Lincoln Raw—a biographical novel,* imagines Lincoln perception of the world in which he came of age. *Lincoln Raw* is curated in the Lincoln Collection of the Abraham Lincoln Presidential Library.

When not crafting his own stories, Fowler shares techniques for leveraging psychology and language to embed readers in vicarious, visceral experiences. After graduating from University of Southern California with a BA in Humanities, he served as a linguist in the US Air Force. Later he pursued a career in finance and now lives with his wife in Gig Harbor, Washington.

Made in the USA
Middletown, DE
15 February 2021